Sunrise on Cedar Key

Also by Terri DuLong

Casting About

Spinning Forward

"A Cedar Key Christmas" in *Holiday Magic*

Published by Kensington Publishing Corporation

Sunrise on Cedar Key

TERRI DuLONG

KENSINGTON BOOKS
www.kensingtonbooks.com

KENSINGTON BOOKS are published by

Kensington Publishing Corp.
119 West 40th Street
New York, NY 10018

All Kensington titles, imprints, and distributed lines are available at special quantity discounts for bulk purchases for sales promotion, premiums, fund-raising, educational, or institutional use.

Special book excerpts or customized printings can also be created to fit specific needs. For details, write or phone the office of the Kensington Special Sales Manager: Kensington Publishing Corp., 119 West 40th Street, New York, NY 10018. Attn. Special Sales Department. Phone: 1-800-221-2647.

Kensington and the K logo Reg. U.S. Pat. & TM Off.

ISBN-13: 978-0-7582-6865-5
ISBN-10: 0-7582-6865-3

First Kensington Trade Paperback Printing: November 2011
10 9 8 7 6 5 4 3 2 1

Printed in the United States of America

With love for my newfound British cousins—
Julia, Sarah, and Stephen Bradbury.
I'm so glad you found me after over sixty years

1

I was awakened to the insistent ringing of my cell phone on the bedside table. My glance at the digital clock told me it was five-thirty. Who on earth would be calling me so early?

I answered to hear the voice of Jim Jacobs, Cedar Key's fire chief.

"Miss Gracie . . . I'm afraid I have some bad news for you. We had a humdinger of a thunderstorm here on the island during the night. I hate to have to tell you this . . . but lightning struck the coffee shop, setting it on fire. The volunteer fire department got the call about three, and when we arrived, the building was fully engulfed. At three in the morning, with nobody out and about, it got a pretty good head start. That wind was blowing about twenty-five to thirty miles an hour, and that sure didn't help. I'm so sorry to have to call and tell you this."

Lightning? Fire? Coffee shop? What the hell was he talking about? Shaking my head in an attempt to clear it from sleep, I said, "Oh, my God! Was anybody hurt? Are you telling me my place is . . . gone?"

"No, nobody was hurt. But yeah . . . I'm afraid there isn't much left of the structure. I know you're in Brunswick helping your aunt with her move. When were you planning to return to Cedar Key?"

"Later today. After the movers load up the furniture. They came for the boxes yesterday, so we were planning to leave here this afternoon, but we could get on the road sooner. Oh, God, I can't believe my place is gone!"

"No, no, you take your time. There's no rush for you to get back here, but do me a favor and call me when you come off Three forty-five and hit SR Twenty-four. I want to meet you at the scene. And Miss Gracie . . . I can't tell you how sorry I am, and I know sometimes words don't help, but I'm sure glad you weren't in your apartment when the fire started."

I knew he was right—but at the moment my only thoughts were focusing on all that I'd lost. Sitting on the edge of the bed I tried to visualize what my former residence and business must look like now—ten years' worth of my life, literally gone up in smoke.

A wet nose nudged my elbow, and I looked down to see Annie gazing up at me with soulful brown eyes. Looking more like a stuffed toy than a fifteen-pound cream-colored canine of questionable ancestry, she always brought a smile to my face. My vet placed her heritage somewhere between a schnauzer and a poodle, with maybe a tad of spaniel. An orphan, she'd found her way to the door of my coffee shop during a downpour a few months before, and her exact combination of breed would remain a mystery. Which was fine with me. I attempted to find her owner, but it was apparent the poor mutt was indeed an orphan. Hence, the name *Annie.* I took her to the vet and was informed she was about nine months old and needed to be spayed, have her shots and a flea treatment, and get started on heartworm protection. All of which I did, and when I went to bring her home, the look in her eyes and exuberant wag of her tail convinced me we were meant to be together. Especially since I'd lost my precious Mr. Whiskers only a few weeks before Annie's arrival. A sudden heart attack took him to the Rainbow Bridge at age fifteen.

I patted her curly head as I felt moisture filling my eyes. "And now we're both orphans, Annie."

A soft knock on the door caused me to swipe at my tears.

"Gracie, are you awake?" I heard Aunt Maude say.

I got up and opened the door to find my aunt tying the sash on her cotton robe.

"I thought I heard a phone. Is everything okay?"

"You did; it was my cell phone. I'm sorry it woke you."

"No, no. I was awake. What's wrong?"

Her love and concern brought forth the flood of tears I'd been trying to hold back and propelled me into her waiting arms.

"Oh, Grace, sweetie," she murmured into my ear. "What's going on? Who called you?"

She then led me to my bed, where she sat beside me, one arm around my shoulder.

"It was Jim Jacobs, the fire chief from Cedar Key," I relayed, and went on to explain what had occurred a few hours before.

"Oh! Lord! What a terrible thing to happen. Was anybody hurt?"

I shook my head, sniffled, and reached for a tissue from the bedside table. "No, thank goodness. But everything is gone, Aunt Maude. *Gone!* My apartment, my business . . . everything."

I felt her soothing hand brushing back the curls that framed my face.

"I know. This is a terrible shock for you, but we'll get through it. Like we've gotten through other crises. Together. Did Jim think you should leave now to go back?"

"No, there's not much I can do at this point. From the sound of it, there's nothing for me to salvage. I told him the movers were coming this morning and that we'd be there by early evening."

Aunt Maude stood up, her full five feet seven inches hovering over me. "Okay. Then why don't you take your shower and I'll go downstairs to get coffee and breakfast started. Then we'll figure out what you're doing."

Leave it to my aunt. She'd always had a wonderful way of taking charge, and even during some difficult events of my life she made me feel there was always hope.

I watched Annie follow her into the hallway and downstairs before I headed to the bathroom.

After stepping out of the shower, I applied my favorite L'Occitane body lotion. The scent of verbena filled the room and lifted my sprits momentarily. Looking into the mirror, an oval face, dark green eyes, and a cloud of shoulder-length auburn curls stared back at me. I didn't look like a thirty-six-year-old homeless person—my entire life had changed, but I still looked like me.

After applying minimal makeup and throwing on jeans and a T-shirt, I followed the wonderful aroma of coffee down to the kitchen, where I also now caught the additional aroma of Aunt Maude's croissants baking in the oven. That smell never failed to remind me of the days I had spent in France with my aunt, soaking up the Parisian way of life at a terrace café, sipping strong coffee with the fragrance of baked goods from the local patisserie in the air.

Maude stood at the counter, her back to me, placing various cheeses and meats onto a platter. She showed no signs of osteoporosis with her straight posture. Snow white hair was pulled back into a classic French twist, and she looked a good five years younger than her seventy-two years. My heart swelled with love for her. She had always been more of a mother to me than an aunt, especially when both of my parents were killed in an automobile accident in France. Due to my parents' antique business and travel, I had spent the majority of time here in my aunt's house. A house that also became mine after my parents' death. Aunt Maude raised me from the age of twelve, always giving me a sense of love and security.

She turned around to the sound of Annie running up to me.

"You look better after your shower. Coffee's ready, and it won't be too much longer for the croissants. I'm just reheating them."

"Thanks," I said, leaning down to give Annie a pat. Then I poured the rich, strong liquid into a mug and took a sip, savoring the flavor. "The movers arrive at eight, right?"

My aunt nodded and joined me at the table. "Yes, and I don't know what I would have done without you here this past week to help me get all those boxes packed."

I smiled. "Are you kidding? To have you move to the island permanently, I would have done anything."

My trip back to Brunswick, Georgia, the previous week had been my first in ten years. When Aunt Maude had supported my decision to relocate, she understood my reluctance to return to Brunswick. It had been agreed that she would be the one to make the trip to Cedar Key a few times a year so we could visit in person, rather than just having our daily phone calls. So Aunt Maude faithfully crawled along I-95 in her oversized blue Cadillac to visit the niece that she'd raised. Not once did she make me feel selfish or foolish for not wanting to return to my hometown—and risk the chance that I might bump into Beau Hamilton.

But the previous year she'd been diagnosed with macular degeneration, and we both knew that her driving days to Cedar Key were over.

My aunt laughed. "Well, I'm not sure if I should call it luck, divine intervention, or serendipity, but when you told me about the Coachman House going up for sale a few months ago, I knew it was time for me to begin a new adventure, and if that adventure brought me to where you were, all the better."

The thought of what I'd lost came rushing back to me. "And now I'm homeless," I said, hating the whine in my tone.

"Grace Ann Stone, you are not homeless. You will stay with me tonight at the Faraway Inn. Tomorrow we'll get my new place in shape, and don't forget, Coachman House has another apartment on the second floor. Even though I knew you had your own place above the coffee shop, I thought that apartment upstairs from me would be ideal for you, and now . . ."

"Really?" I hadn't given that a thought since I'd received Jim's phone call. "Weren't you going to rent that apartment?"

"Well, since I have nobody lined up yet, of course *you* can have it. As I said, when I thought about buying the place, I knew it would be perfect for the two of us, but I certainly didn't expect you to give up your own place, so I knew I could find somebody to rent it."

Things were suddenly beginning to look a tad brighter. Jumping up from the table, I leaned over to kiss my aunt's cheek. "Consider me your new tenant, and of course I'll pay you rent."

Maude pulled me into a tight embrace. "There's plenty of time to discuss that," she said.

A low growling sound drew our attention to the hallway off the kitchen.

Annie was curled up at one end of the hall having a staring

match with Aunt Maude's cat. I think it could be safely said that Lafitte probably tipped the scales a good five pounds higher than my little pooch did. Lafitte was a robust (being kind here) gray and white Maine Coon cat. This breed was known for their increased size, and Lafitte had an increased amount of attitude to match. Not in a mean way, but more in a patriarch sort-of way. He was in charge, and from the moment Annie arrived, he'd made sure she knew it. Poor little Annie was still trying to decide if this humongous amount of feline fur was friend or foe.

When she saw me enter the room, her tail started wagging, but she didn't give up her post.

Wiggling her leash in my hand, I said, "Hey, girl. Are you up for a short walk around the square?" Certain things in life caused Annie extreme joy—her leash and the anticipation of a walk was one of them. She came racing over, temporarily forgetting the staring match. She jumped in circles and whimpered, which I took to be an emphatic *yes.*

"I'm just going to take her out for a quick walk," I told my aunt. "I'll be back shortly to have one of your delicious croissants."

2

Following Annie's walk and breakfast, I headed upstairs to my bedroom. After stripping the bed of linens, I placed them into a plastic bag to be laundered once we arrived on Cedar Key. Looking around, I let out a deep sigh.

This house held so many memories for me. Not all of them good ones. I had always loved this bedroom. The Victorian style boasted a mansard roof, creating my private domain from age twelve until fourteen years later—the day I got a phone call making me realize it was time to leave Brunswick for good. The events of that day and the ones that followed had turned my life upside down. But I had survived, and I would survive the recent upheaval in my life—once again, with Aunt Maude's love and support.

"How're you doing up there?" I heard her holler up the stairs. "The movers will be here in about twenty minutes."

"Good," I hollered back. "Be right down."

Standing at the window, I took a final look outside, across the square to the house my parents had once owned. Staring at the two-story Victorian left me devoid of emotion. No warm and fuzzy feelings for the house I'd been brought to as a newborn. No childhood remembrances of Christmas, Thanksgiving, or birthday parties. If my parents had even been home for these events, they were exhausted from the travel their business required. Therefore, all of these events, along with most of my childhood memories, had been experienced here, at Aunt Maude's house.

Going downstairs, I heard the phone ringing and walked into the kitchen to hear my aunt say, "Good morning, Suellen. Yes, she's right here. Hold on."

I felt a smile cross my face as I took the phone. There's a lot to be said for a childhood friend you've known since the first grade.

"Hey, what's up?"

"Well, you sure don't sound as perky as I thought you'd be this morning. You're heading back to your beloved Cedar Key and taking your aunt with you."

I let out a deep sigh. "I'm afraid I got some really bad news a couple hours ago," I said, and went on to explain about Jim Jacobs's phone call.

Suellen's audible gasp came across the phone line. "Oh! My God! I can't believe this! Are you saying your coffee shop *and* your apartment are . . . gone?"

"That's exactly what I'm saying. Totally gone."

"Oh, Gracie, I'm so sorry to hear this. What are you going to do? Where will you live? Where will you work? Is there anything at all you might be able to save from the fire? What can I do to help you? Just tell me. I'll do anything to help you. . . ."

Suellen hadn't changed since the first time I met her. She was easily excitable, and sometimes her speech raced along faster than the Daytona 500, causing me to lose half her words. For a Southern girl, her pace in speaking was more like a Yankee.

I laughed. "Take a breath, slow down," I told her. "I honestly don't know what I'm doing, except that tonight I'll stay with Aunt Maude at the Faraway. She had booked there for two nights because the movers won't have everything unloaded from the truck till sometime tomorrow afternoon. I won't be on the street homeless—my aunt has already said that she wants me to take the apartment upstairs from her. Beyond that . . . I honestly don't know."

"Well, I was planning to go down there in a couple weeks, but I could come now if you need me. Really, it wouldn't be a problem. I'll just call Miss Dixie at the Inn and tell her I need a few days off."

"Suellen, you're too sweet. Really. But no, let's stick with the original plan. Come and visit me in a couple weeks. I should be pretty well settled in my new place by then."

"Okay, if you're sure. But if you need me, you know I'm just a phone call away." She paused for a moment and then asked, "And you still haven't seen Beau since you've been here?"

"No, and we'll be leaving this afternoon so I managed to avoid that." Damn. Why did just the mention of his name still have the ability to speed up my heart rate? Not wanting to discuss Beau Hamilton, I said, "Thanks for your help, Suellen. I'll call you later to give you an update on the fire."

With Aunt Maude beside me, Lafitte in his cat carrier, and Annie curled up on the backseat, I made the drive from Brunswick to Cedar Key. Minimal conversation between my aunt and me allowed my mind to race and try to sort out what had happened, but when I stood on Dock Street and stared at the remains of my business and home, I still couldn't comprehend the impact of my loss.

I heard Jim and Aunt Maude talking as if from a distance while my eyes took in the charred structure that no longer resembled my pride and joy. My second-story apartment had pretty much ended up in the ground floor coffee shop. Three walls of what had been my living space had disappeared. Only black rubble was left for the entire world to see. My beautiful sign, COFFEE, TEA AND THEE, now hung at a grotesque angle with the wood buckled and the words barely legible. How could this happen? How could all that I loved and valued be taken from me in a heartbeat?

Before I even realized what was happening I felt tears streaming down my face as my legs turned to jelly. The scene before me blurred, and I felt strong arms go around my shoulders to support me.

"Miss Gracie? Miss Gracie, are you okay?" I heard Jim Jacobs say with concern.

Okay? I'll probably never be okay again, I thought, and only continued to sob harder.

Then I heard another male voice. "Maybe we should get her away from here for now. I have the golf cart. Why don't we go over to the bookshop for some coffee?"

Swiping at my tears I looked up to see Lucas Trudeau speaking to Aunt Maude.

"Brilliant idea," she said, grabbing my elbow and steering me to the vehicle at the curb.

"Call me when you feel ready," I heard Jim say as Aunt Maude settled herself on the backseat and Lucas got in beside me.

It wasn't until I was comfortably seated in a deep cushy chair following a few sips of rich, dark coffee that my brain seemed to resume working.

I glanced at Lucas and Aunt Maude sitting across from me. "Great coffee. I better watch out or you'll put me out of business." I let out an exaggerated chuckle. "Oh, wait! I *am* out of business." I could feel moisture filling my eyes again.

"I was so terribly sorry to hear about the fire," Lucas said. "If there's anything at all I can do to help you, please let me know."

I saw the concern on his handsome face. "Thanks, but I'm not even sure what day it is, let alone what *I'm* going to do."

"Well, today is Friday," Aunt Maude said with a note of determination in her tone. "And what you're going to do is first things first. We're both booked for tonight and tomorrow night at the Faraway Inn, so we have a roof over our heads. When you feel up to it, Jim said that they'll assist you with trying to salvage what you can from your apartment. And then . . . well, we'll take it all one step at a time."

Leave it to Aunt Maude to be sensible, but I failed to find any comfort in her words. The knowledge that I'd lost both my livelihood and my home was all that I could focus on.

"I'm serious about my offer of help. This isn't an easy time for you."

Although he spoke fluent English, I still heard the French accent in his speech and recalled the day six months before when

Lucas had walked into my coffee shop for the first time. With those dark curls in a longer-than-conventional length, the olive skin, mahogany eyes, and knitted scarf circling his neck in a way that only the French can master, he had oozed a certain *je ne sais quoi* that I rarely observed in American men.

"Thank you," I told him, and it was then that I noticed my surroundings. Lucas had done a wonderful job of having the bookshop restored. The walls had been painted a buttery yellow, adding a warm glow to the rectangular room. Just below the ceiling a border print of large, vivid sunflowers looked down on me, with oak wainscoting circling the middle half of the walls. The cushy chair I sat in matched the other three, and all of them formed a cozy circle around a coffee table displaying some nonfiction books. But the major change was the archway that had been added when the wall had been broken to allow more space.

I rose and walked toward the archway, exclaiming, "Oh! Lucas, you've done a magnificent job with the restoration." I peeked into the new room. This space was a large, empty square, and I saw lots of potential.

"I'm glad you like it. I still have a lot of work with this extra room, but at least I can be open for business."

Aunt Maude came to look and said, "What are you planning to do with it?"

Lucas shook his head. "I'm not quite sure yet. I have a few ideas, so we'll see."

I swept my arm out toward the bookshop. "Your decorating is perfect, Lucas. I really love it. The ambience you created is ideal for book browsing."

"That's what I was hoping for, so thank you."

I took the final sip of my coffee and let out a deep sigh. "Well, I think we should be going. I know there have to be a million things for me to tend to."

Aunt Maude put her arm around my shoulder. "And that's why you have me," she said with affection.

"Thank you," I told Lucas. "Thanks for rescuing me from my meltdown on Dock Street."

He laughed, and once again I realized what a killer smile he had.

Just as we reached the door, he said, "I was wondering . . . I mean . . . I know you'll both be busy getting settled in, so . . . would you like to come to my place some evening for a home-cooked meal?"

Before I even had the chance to consider, I heard Aunt Maude say, "Why, *Monsieur* Trudeau, that would be wonderful. I never turn down a meal prepared by a Frenchman. *Merci beaucoup.*"

Lucas laughed again. "How about Monday evening? Would that be convenient for you?" he asked, looking directly at me.

"Ah, yes, I think so," I said, waiting for Aunt Maude to say something. Which she didn't. She simply stood there with a devilish grin on her face. "Yes, I'm sure our social calendar is free."

"Great. Is eight o'clock okay?"

"Perfect European time for dinner," Aunt Maude said. "Now, will you be so kind as to give us a lift back to the Faraway? We dropped off Lafitte and Annie at our cottage and walked over to Dock Street."

"Absolutely. My chariot awaits," Lucas said, as we followed him to the golf cart.

Annie lay curled up on the bed as I unpacked my piece of luggage. It hit me that the clothes I'd had with me in Brunswick were the only clothes I owned at the moment. It was obvious from what I'd seen that all of my other ones had burned to a crisp. This brought on a fresh flood of tears just as my cell phone rang. Blowing my nose I saw Suellen's name on the LED.

"Hey, girlfriend," I said.

"I know this is a really stupid question, but . . . how're you doing? I wanted to make sure you arrived there safely. Have you gone to assess the damage yet? I'm so worried about you, Grace. *Are* you okay? I mean, is there anything I can do? Do you want me to come there and help you?"

Just hearing Suellen's voice made me feel a little better. "No, no, you don't need to come. And . . . I'm okay. The building is pretty much a total loss. We just got back from there."

"Well, you don't sound okay, and who would be? What a terrible thing to happen. I still can hardly believe it."

"You and me both. But really, I have Aunt Maude, and somehow I'll get through this." I let out a deep sigh.

"Well, sugar, if you need anything, anything at all, you be sure to call me. You know I can be on that little island in four hours. Okay, I have a busy weekend at work, but I'll call you Monday evening."

"Oh, Aunt Maude and I have been invited to dinner Monday evening."

"That's great. Somebody being neighborly?"

Knowing full well what Suellen's reaction would be, I still decided to be honest. "Well, I guess you could say that. It's Lucas Trudeau who invited us."

I heard an intake of breath on the line, and then Suellen said, "Well, girlfriend, you don't waste any time, do you? Good for you! Getting hooked up with a good-looking guy like that will do wonders to help you through this crisis."

I shook my head and laughed. "Suellen, it's not like that at all. He knows the situation with the fire and Aunt Maude moving here and, well, he's just being nice. That's all it is."

"Right. A drop-dead handsome Frenchman invites you to his home for dinner and . . . he's just being *nice*. Okay, sugar, if that's what you want to believe."

To be honest, I wasn't sure *what* I wanted to believe, but I knew the days ahead weren't going to be easy, and if Lucas offered to cook a meal for my aunt and me—well, who was I to decline?

"Suellen, you really need to stop reading so many romance novels."

"My point exactly. So when a really nice fellow comes along, who just happens to be exceptionally good looking *and* has a sexy French accent, then, Grace Stone, you need to sit up and pay attention."

I laughed again. "Give it up. It's just a dinner. *With* a chaperone."

"Right, sweetie. Whatever you say. I'll call you next week. Love ya."

Shaking my head, I clicked the disconnect button on my cell.

"She's a hopeless romantic," I said out loud, causing Annie to pop her head up and look at me curiously. Sitting on the bed I began stroking her head. "Well, girl, we're in quite a predicament, aren't we? Here we are—our home is gone, I have no job, no clue where I'm going from here, but we have each other. And for right now, that'll have to be enough."

Annie edged closer to me, whined, and licked my hand.

$\mathscr{E}$ 3 $\mathscr{E}$

When I opened my eyes Monday morning, it took me a minute to orient myself. Although it wasn't what I'd woken to for the past ten years, the room still had a comforting and homey feel to it. The furniture that had sat in my bedroom in Brunswick was now arranged in the second-floor apartment of Coachman House.

A new box spring and mattress had been added when I'd returned after graduating college, but the same thick, scrolled, mahogany headboard was behind me. My glance scanned to take in the large matching bureau, vanity, desk, and bookcases.

My plan for the day was to get the drapes hung and the rest of the apartment in a livable condition. Right now boxes consumed a lot of the space. The digital clock that I'd unpacked the day before read 6:42. As I stretched and yawned, Annie jumped on the bed to greet me.

"Good morning, girl. See, I told you we wouldn't be homeless. Come on, let me get the coffee going and I'll bring you outside."

The bedroom I'd chosen was the larger one with attached bathroom at the back of the house. The hallway led to the second bedroom and bath, which looked out onto F Street. I peeked in to see the futon and bureau the movers had placed there yesterday. A bit skimpy right now, but it would be the perfect guest room for Suellen's visits.

Turning right off the hall, I stood and stared at the large, open great room that flowed back to the kitchen and dining area. Sunlight streamed through the picture window that dominated the far wall of the kitchen, giving a view of the deck and garden below.

Like the guest room, these rooms also looked empty. A black leather sofa and matching chair were all that occupied the great room, but the focal point was the intricately carved fireplace on the outside wall. I walked over to run my finger along the beautiful oak mantel, feeling the indentations of scrollwork done by a carpenter many years ago. I was immediately transported to the fireplace in my aunt's parlor. As a child, I loved to touch the wood surrounding it, feel the solidness and stability. A sense of serenity enveloped me, but I swung around quickly because I could have sworn I wasn't alone in the room.

Only Annie sat there patiently waiting to be taken outside. *Get a grip, Grace,* I thought. *You haven't had those types of feelings since you were twelve.*

Walking into the kitchen, I pushed the button on the coffeemaker that I'd prepared the night before.

I opened the door that led out to the deck and inhaled the clean, refreshing smell of the Gulf. "Come on, Annie. You don't need a leash, because you now have a fenced yard."

She followed me down the steps and promptly began sniffing around. I stood there taking in the overgrown garden, knowing how much Aunt Maude would enjoy bringing it back to life. Situated in the center was the old carriage house. Both Coachman House, which had been named for Ben Coachman, a previous owner, and the carriage house had been built between 1870 and 1884. Although the house had been totally renovated seven years before, it had been vacant for the past few years. The structure of the carriage house was sound, but the inside would need an overhaul if my aunt planned to do anything with it.

I turned around to the sound of her voice.

"Good morning. Did you sleep well?"

"I did," I said, smiling as my aunt passed me a mug of coffee. "And what time did you get up? Four o'clock?"

My aunt laughed. "Not quite. Five. I've been busy unpacking and trying to get organized. I hope I didn't wake you with any noise."

Now it was my turn to laugh. "Are you kidding? The walls in that place must be three feet thick."

"Actually, the exterior and interior walls are fourteen inches thick. That's the beauty of old houses. They were built for quiet and privacy."

I nodded, looking at the back of the house. My aunt had an identical deck below mine, and the large windows not only gave a feeling of welcome but allowed the house to be bright and airy inside.

"I still can't believe you bought this place. I've loved it from the first time I ever came to Cedar Key. There was just something about it—maybe a pull to the past. I don't know, but I'm thrilled that you now own it, and I feel pretty fortunate to be living here with you."

"I always loved this house too. When I'd come to visit you and stay at the B and B, I'd walk over here and just stand on the sidewalk staring at it. I think I always knew I wanted to be the owner. I had even gone downtown to the library to find out the history on it. It's a fine example of Greek Revival townhouse form, and of course it's only one of the two surviving tabby houses on the island. I was always impressed with the fact that this house was built with burned oyster shells, sand, lime, and water. You're just like I am, Grace. You're drawn to the mystique of old houses. Ah, if only these walls could talk."

This reminded me of the feeling I'd had in the great room. "Hmm, I wonder if it comes with a resident ghost," I joked.

My aunt's expression turned serious. "I wouldn't be at all surprised," she said. "Now, how about a nice hearty breakfast to start your day?"

"Oh, no. Just because I'm living upstairs from you, I don't want you catering to me. I'm a big girl now. There's no need for you to be cooking my meals."

Maude smiled. "I understand, but you have to indulge me on our first morning here. I was going to whip up some omelets, sausage, and grits."

I laughed. "Guess I can't refuse that," I said, following her into her apartment with Annie close at my heels.

"Oh, your kitchen looks great. Gee, it looks like you've always lived here. You've been working hard."

I looked around and saw an oak table with four chairs placed against the half wall separating the kitchen and a proper dining room, which was the only difference between the apartments.

"Are you just going to leave the carriage house empty?" I asked, sitting at the table while my aunt began preparing breakfast.

"Well, I'm not sure. I've given some thought to maybe opening a small business."

"A business? Another antique business like you had with my parents in Brunswick?"

"No. As much as I always enjoyed that, I knew when I closed my shop five years ago that was the end of my antique business days." She paused for a moment while pouring the omelet batter into the fry pan. "I was thinking along the lines of knitting."

"Knitting? But Monica owns the yarn shop in town, and you must realize this small town doesn't warrant two of them."

My aunt laughed as she turned from the stove. "Yes, I realize that. But I was thinking about offering weekend knitting retreats for women."

She definitely had my interest. When it came to this craft, my aunt and I were avid, addicted knitters. I couldn't remember a time that Aunt Maude wasn't working on one project or another, and I still recalled my excitement when she'd given me my first pair of needles and a skein of yarn when I was eight years old. She had patiently taught me the basics, which then enabled me to also become a proficient knitter.

"That sounds great," I told her. "What do you have in mind?"

"I'm not quite sure," she said, stirring the grits. "My plan is still in the early stages, but I was thinking about doing some major advertising, especially on the Internet. There's been such a renewal for knitting lately and there's a lot of knitting websites and blogs. We now have large knitting conventions across the country, all kinds of knitting groups at yarn shops, and as much as I love the act of knitting, I think part of the renewed interest is because it's something that brings women together. An activity that allows them to relax, talk, get to know each other, probably even share secrets. So why not have a place for them to gather for an entire weekend, on a beautiful island, surrounded by quiet and Mother Nature? A place that will offer them a getaway to just come together as women, friends, sisters, whatever."

"Oh, I love it!" I said, feeling the sadness of the past few days being replaced with excitement. "That's a fantastic idea. So you're thinking of using the carriage house as a knitting workshop or studio for the women?"

My aunt nodded as she placed our plates on the table and sat down. "Exactly. It will need some refurbishing but not any major work. We have a lot of various lodging on the island, so they would do their own bookings for accommodations. But the carriage house has a bathroom and even a galley kitchen. So we could offer a luncheon, which would be included in the price for the weekend. I was thinking about getting with Monica and Dora. If the women don't bring their own yarn, perhaps Monica could give them a bit of a discount if they purchased it there at Yarning Together. And maybe we could get Dora to help us if we offered advanced classes on knitting. But most of all, it would be two full days for women to bond and connect."

"I'd say you've already given this quite a lot of thought, and I have a feeling it would be wildly successful." I took a bite of my aunt's delicious grits. "I'd be more than happy to help you in any way I could."

"I was hoping you'd say that. I'm not very computer literate, I'm afraid, but I know enough to realize how important an online presence can be. I could really use your help in setting up a website, maybe even a blog, and getting the word out with some advertising."

"Absolutely," I said, my excitement notching up another level. "Oh, and Facebook. I'll set up a page on there, which will help in getting the word out." I took a sip of coffee as another thought occurred to me. "How about if you also include a Blue Moon ceremony on the final evening? You know, like Dora and Sybile started years ago."

My aunt nodded. "I remember Sydney and Monica telling me all about that during one of my visits here. They had the final one just before Sybile passed away, and from what they said, it certainly was a means to bring Sydney closer to her mother and daughter."

"Right. We could get all the details from Dora. But I'm sure women would love that. An actual ceremony to validate being a woman and the relationships that we share."

"I think that ceremony would be a wonderful addition to the knitting retreat weekend. So can I count on your help with that as well?"

"Definitely. I'm sure Monica will give me any information I need, but with her being pregnant she's pretty busy getting ready for her new arrival in March. When Suellen gets here, she can help. She'll enjoy being involved in something like this."

"Okay, then it's settled. You and I are going to begin a knitting retreat weekend on Cedar Key. But—and I don't want any arguing from you—if you'd like to do this with me, and God knows I could really use your help in a million different ways, I want to make you a partner in this. An official partner."

I had an idea where my aunt was heading. "I'd love to do this with you, but I'm doing it because of exactly that. Because I *want* to."

"And you're going to be on a payroll. We're going to see an attorney and an accountant, because I want to set this up as a small business and have it as a limited liability corporation. This way if, God forbid, somebody wanted to sue us for injuries on the premises or anything like that, our primary assets would be safe."

I shook my head and smiled. "Leave it to you. Sounds like you've got all the bases covered."

"Not quite. We have to come up with a name for the retreats and business, so you can be thinking about that."

That old saying popped into my head, "When one door closes, another one opens," and although my heart still ached with my recent loss, hearing Aunt Maude's exciting new plans for both of us lifted my spirits.

Little did I know then that my aunt's relocation would also produce a fly in the ointment—in the form of my sister, Chloe.

❦ 4 ❧

When I left my aunt's apartment following breakfast I noticed her tarot cards sitting in a stack on the kitchen counter, which made me realize I'd neglected to read my own cards for the past three days. Almost all of our French ancestors had been brought up reading the cards, and by the time I was ten years old, I was following generations of LaVassier women.

Reaching inside my bureau drawer I removed the black velvet pouch that held my cards and brought them to the kitchen. Pulling up a stool, I let out a deep sigh. Just holding the cards transferred a sense of positive energy for me. Normally I also lit some incense and had my crystals nearby, but since I hadn't completed unpacking yet, I'd have to make do.

While I was at my aunt's house the previous week I was more than a little surprised to see the Rebel card appear each morning in my spread—a card that had not shown up for ten years, a card that had always represented Beau.

I shuffled three times and let my mind wander before reaching for the top card. Damn. There it was again, and despite the passage of time, the thought of Beau Hamilton still had the ability to bring back long-forgotten memories.

The Rebel card depicted the image of a man with authority.

With the sun on his shoulder, he's holding a torch and uses this inner light to guide himself to the beat of his own drummer. The card represents an individual who possesses a lot of magnetism and charisma.

That was certainly Beau Hamilton. My mind began to drift back to the pull that he'd had on me from the moment I'd met him, the laughter, the fun we'd shared, the incredible lovemaking—followed by the tears, the disappointment, and the guilt for allowing myself to be in a situation I had no business being in.

Why the hell was his card showing up now? After all this time. I put it aside, closed my eyes, and took in a few more cleansing breaths before removing another card.

This one was the Number XI Major Arcana and represented *breakthrough*. The card signified facing one's inner demons and coming to terms with the pain of the past.

What the hell was this supposed to mean? I had come to terms with my past after leaving Brunswick ten years ago.

Blowing out a whoosh of air I reached inside the deck for another card, which was a minor arcana and represented *stress*. Gee, big surprise here.

The final card I removed was the one that always represented my sister. The Thunderbolt card, which signified holding on tightly to any security. Yup, that was Chloe. Queen of control freaks.

Chloe was twelve years older than me and we'd never been close. Over the years I came to understand that our age difference had nothing to do with this fact. Our lack of a sisterly relationship had more to do with Chloe's self-centered personality and her choice to isolate herself from Aunt Maude and me.

I replaced the cards inside the pouch, got up, and stretched. As I was about to tackle unpacking some boxes I heard a knock on the kitchen door.

"Monica," I exclaimed, when I saw my friend standing on the deck. "Come on in, but don't mind the mess."

She pulled me into a tight embrace. "Gracie, I'm so sorry about the fire. I would have come by sooner, but Adam and I just got back last night. We took Clarissa to Disney for the weekend. How're you doing?"

I indicated a stool for her to sit on as I joined her at the breakfast bar. "Actually, better today than Friday. I think the shock of it is wearing off, and Jim Jacobs was right—at least I wasn't there when the fire occurred."

"Isn't that the truth. I drove past there this morning, and it looks like you lost just about everything?"

I nodded. "Yup. But I'm pretty fortunate to have this apartment."

Monica's glance took in the kitchen and scanned to the great room. "I've always loved this house, and I know you did too. Do you think you'll be rebuilding the coffee shop?"

"I seriously doubt that. With the FEMA laws, if I did rebuild, it would have to be a stilt structure, and I just can't see some of the older folks climbing so many stairs for a cup of coffee."

"Hmm, I see what you're saying. But maybe you could lease another piece of property."

"No, I think my coffee barista days are over. However...I think I'll be going into the yarn business."

I saw the expression of surprise that covered Monica's face and laughed. "No, no. I won't be your competition in town," I assured her, and went on to explain Aunt Maude's plan.

"Oh, Gracie, I think that's a great idea. What a perfect thing to do with the carriage house, and be sure to tell Maude I'd be more than happy to give discounts to the women attending the retreats."

"She was hoping you'd consider that, and also that maybe Dora would help us with some advanced knitting classes."

"I have no doubt she'd love that." She reached over to pat my hand. "And Grace, I'm not saying the fire was a good thing, but who knows. This new path could take you in a wonderful direction."

"Could be," I said, and shrugged. "So how are *you* doing? I have to say, pregnancy seems to agree with you. You look great."

I still had no idea where my life was headed, but here was a woman who a year ago had no clue what she wanted when it came to motherhood. She'd almost convinced herself she never wanted children—and then her stepdaughter, Clarissa Jo, came into her life and proved her totally wrong.

"I'm doing wonderful. Barely any morning sickness. Just a little tired, but that's to be expected in the first few months. My main problem is keeping Adam and Clarissa from waiting on me hand and foot."

I laughed. "Hey, enjoy it while you can."

Monica glanced at her watch. "I need to open the yarn shop. It's almost ten. I hope you won't be offended, but . . . I brought you some clothes. I know you lost pretty much everything in the fire." She patted her tummy. "And even though I'm only nine weeks along, it won't be much longer till I'm in maternity clothes. So I brought you a few bags of things I thought you could use. We're the same size—right now, anyway—so I want you to have them. They're downstairs on the golf cart."

Monica's kindness brought moisture to my eyes. "Oh, gosh, are you sure? That's so nice of you." I stood to give her a hug before following her down the stairs.

Three large shopping bags sat on the golf cart seat.

"Now, it's nothing fancy," she said. "Well, except for a few dresses and skirts—absolute musts in a single girl's wardrobe. But mostly shorts, jeans, and tops. That sort of thing. Oh, I threw in a few pairs of heels, too—another mandatory item."

"Thank you so much, and I'll return them as soon as I get around to doing some shopping. But I'll probably kill myself in these four-inch stilettos," I said, removing a gorgeous pair of black, strappy designer heels.

"Oh, you will not, and don't worry about returning them any time soon. I have a feeling it'll be next summer before these might fit me again."

I stood on the curb with the bags at my feet watching her drive away as I waved and blew her a kiss. Monica did look great. Maybe it was that glow that pregnant women seemed to have. I momentarily felt a sliver of jealousy go through me. We might be extremely good friends but not close enough that she was aware of the longing I'd managed to suppress for so many years.

I had spent the morning and early afternoon getting my new place in shape. Boxes of essentials had been unpacked. Aunt

Maude claimed to have an overflow of dishes, cooking items, glassware, towels, and linens, and I was the recipient. Many of the items had been things from the antique shop, packed away for years, that she couldn't bear to part with, and now I was able to put them to use.

Glancing at my watch, I saw it was two o'clock and realized that I'd worked through lunch. Definitely time for my afternoon coffee break.

Hollering to Annie, I headed for the back stairs. "Let's go see if Aunt Maude would like to join me for coffee."

"Come in," she called at my knock. "I'm in the front room."

I found my aunt sitting in her favorite cushy chair, feet elevated on a hassock, knitting away with one eye on her favorite soap opera.

"Am I interrupting?" I asked.

"Don't be silly," she said, placing the beautiful beige cable sweater on the end table and getting up. "I was hoping you'd come down for a visit. Getting settled in?"

I followed her to the kitchen. "I'm making a dent. So I'm getting there."

Watching her scoop coffee into the filter and fill the carafe with water, I smiled. "I could use some of that."

"And I bet you didn't stop for lunch," she said, uncovering tin foil from a perfectly shaped banana bread. "So we'll have some of this to go with it. Dinner's not till eight at Lucas's, but we don't want to ruin our appetite for that French dinner, so this should tide you over."

After my aunt placed the coffee and dessert plates on the table she joined me, and I noticed her expression had grown serious.

"Anything wrong?" I asked, taking a bite of the delicious banana bread I knew she'd baked earlier that morning.

My aunt took a sip of coffee before speaking, and I knew she was formulating her thoughts. Living with somebody almost all of your life enables you to know them pretty well. But I wasn't prepared for what she was about to tell me.

"I wouldn't say exactly *wrong,* but I got some disturbing news earlier. Your sister called me."

Disturbing news coming from Chloe had been a pattern over the years. Since she seldom called me at all, the news I got always came secondhand from my aunt. Like when my oldest nephew, whom I also barely knew, graduated college and chose to move to New York for a job. Chloe had had a hard time letting go. Or when Parker was bogged down at work and had to cancel their European vacation. Or the designer she'd hired to remodel their large and elegant home on St. Simons Island up and quit on her, accusing her of being much too difficult to work with.

I let out a sigh. "Now what?" I asked, although I wasn't the least bit interested.

"Well, ah ... it seems that she and Parker have separated. He moved out of their house."

"What? He left her? Miss High and Mighty of the Snobby Wives Club? No! Did he finally, after all these years, get tired of living with a control freak?"

Aunt Maude took another sip of coffee. "I'm afraid it's a bit more involved than that. He left her for another woman."

Oh! God! "Are you serious?"

My aunt nodded. "And making it even worse, the woman works for him at his real estate agency, and ... she's twenty-two years younger than Parker."

Holy shit! That would make her, what? Twenty-eight years old. Not even my bitchy sister deserved a slap in the face like that. I couldn't imagine what that must do to a woman's self-esteem. "Maybe he's just going through a midlife crisis? I mean, he just turned fifty. Sometimes this happens, but it never amounts to anything."

My aunt shook her head. "I wish it were that simple, but I'm afraid there's a bit more to it. Apparently this girl ... woman ... is pregnant with Parker's child. He's pushing for an instant divorce so that he can marry her."

"Oh. My. God," was all I could think of to say.

Aunt Maude let out a deep sigh. "Exactly. Needless to say, it's a terrible situation. The good thing is that Chloe will be okay financially. She got herself an excellent attorney, and the papers have been filed for the divorce. Which means it will be final and he'll be free to remarry before she has the baby in December."

My sister's life was beginning to sound like an episode from one of my aunt's soap operas. "Well, when did this all come about? How long has Chloe known? When did Parker move out?" I had a million questions.

"It seems it all came to a head this past June when he confronted her about the woman and he moved out."

"June! You mean to tell me her marriage broke up three months ago and she's just *now* getting around to telling you about it?"

My aunt fingered the edge of the tablecloth. "Well, you know Chloe. Never one to let anybody think something was amiss in her life. She's never been like you, Grace. Wanting to confide and really be a part of the family."

"Right. She'd rather be a phony and live her little fairy-tale life, making everyone think her marriage and lifestyle was the ultimate dream of all women. So, why now? Why the heck did she suddenly decide to share the truth with you?"

Aunt Maude got up, poured more coffee into our mugs, and sat back down. "That's what you and I need to discuss," she said.

Uh! Oh! I didn't like the sound of this at all. "What do you mean?"

"You have to know how humiliated Chloe is. They've lived in St. Simons their entire married life, raised the boys there, made a huge circle of friends." Aunt Maude paused to take a sip of coffee. "She's mortified. Can barely bring herself to go out once a week grocery shopping for fear of bumping into a friend asking a million questions."

I could understand that. Wasn't that part of the reason I wanted to leave Brunswick ten years before? But I sure didn't expect what Aunt Maude said next.

"The reason she called me and told me everything now is because she knew I was here. She knew I relocated to Cedar Key."

"And so?" I asked, not really wanting to hear the answer.

"She needs to get away from that area where Parker and his new wife will be living. From the sounds of it, Chloe has pretty much turned herself into a recluse these past few months. Obviously, she no longer feels comfortable attending any of the social functions in the area. It's a very awkward situation for a woman. And so . . . I honestly didn't see that I had any other choice, Grace, and I hope you won't hate me . . . but when she asked if she could come here and stay with us, I just couldn't say no."

I jumped up and began pacing the kitchen floor. "You've *got* to be kidding me!" I yelled. Leave it to Aunt Maude—always trying to make things right. But this time it was far from right for *me*. Here I was, trying to get my own life back in order after losing so much, and the sister whom I barely knew and couldn't stand was being tossed right smack in the middle of it. "When is she coming?"

"She's driving down this week and will be here on Friday."

I let out a loud groan, grabbed my coffee mug, and headed to my apartment to calm down. It certainly became clear to me now why Chloe's card was showing up in my read. *I ought to burn that damn deck of tarot,* I thought, stomping up the stairs.

$$\backsim 5 \backsim$$

With the help of herbal tea, lavender incense, and Enya's music coming from my CD player, I did manage to cool down by the time I had to get ready for dinner at Lucas's.

I even managed to feel a bit selfish. Yeah, my own life had been turned upside down ten years before, but I was only twenty-six, re-silient and determined to start over and find happiness. How much harder it must be for a woman pushing fifty. Not impossible, by any means. Just more difficult. Besides which, I had always been fairly independent and I liked it that way. Whereas Chloe had gone from college straight to the role of wife and mother. She'd always had Parker as her partner in life. I'd bet anything she'd never attended an evening social gathering alone.

And now that I'd calmed down, I had to agree with Aunt Maude. What else could she do? Turn Chloe away to get through this life crisis on her own? Of course not. I guess it didn't matter what Chloe's behavior and attitude had been in the past. I was a firm believer in focusing on the present. So it looked like I was going to have to suck it up and make some attempt toward a rela-tionship with my sister. If nothing else, I had to do it for Aunt Maude. And now I owed her an apology for storming out the way I had.

* * *

"So you forgive me?" I asked.

My aunt leaned over to give me a tight embrace. "Oh, Grace," she said, laughing. "Of course I forgive you. Besides, don't you think I know you well enough by now? You have a bit of that quick French temper we both share, but if you're left alone to think, you also never stay angry or hold a grudge. That's a very good trait to have."

"Yeah, probably. Well, I got to thinking about it, and even though Chloe and I have never been close, what Parker did is unforgivable. No woman deserves this. I mean, geez, if he wanted out of the marriage he should have just been honest and told her, not wait until it reached the level that it did."

"Well, in my experiences with people, I've found that honesty is a very elusive trait. Maybe that's why I value it so much and admire people who have no problem exhibiting it. It's not always easy being honest. Many times it's downright difficult, but it's still the best thing to do."

I had to agree.

"Well, I'll be honest right now," I told her. "I truly cannot see my uppity sister living on this island. She's never even *visited* here. Does she know we have no pharmacy, no doctors, no movie theater? Not to mention that the closest upscale shopping is an hour away in Gainesville?"

"I told her all of that. It didn't seem to matter. I think she's feeling so alone in her life right now that all of those amenities are secondary."

Another thought occurred to me. "Where will she be staying? Oh, please do *not* tell me I have to share my apartment with her." I loved Aunt Maude dearly, but living with my sister would be stretching that love to the breaking point.

"No, no, of course not. I wouldn't subject you to that," she said, laughing. "Chloe's going to stay here with me. I have the extra bedroom, but she also mentioned looking for her own place—a small cottage that she could rent."

I let out a sigh of relief. "Oh, good. Did she say what she plans to do here? To keep busy? She's never worked outside the home."

"We did talk about that briefly. Her college degree was in textile design, and although she never pursued that once she married, Chloe has continued with her knitting. She's won many awards for her projects, and some of her beautiful pieces brought in a good sum of money for all the fund-raisers she was in charge of."

"So you're going to have her help us with the knitting retreats?"

"If it's all right with you, yes."

"Of course it's okay. Chloe was always an expert knitter, plus she might enjoy something like that."

"That's what I was thinking. You're handling the advertising part of it, with the website and bookings when they start coming in, so maybe she could come up with some ideas for instruction and classes. I need to get ready to leave for Lucas's, but we'll give this some more thought."

"Sounds good," I said, leaning over to kiss my aunt's cheek. "I'll be back down within the hour."

Going through the bags that Monica had dropped off had brightened my mood. There's always something about new clothes, even borrowed ones from a friend, that has a way of perking up a woman. I'd planned to wear jeans and a T-shirt to Lucas's home for dinner, but after going through my care package, I changed my mind.

Instead I chose a black and white sundress. Twirling around in front of the mirror, I smiled. Not bad, and although I loved Monica's stilettos, the black mules with a one-inch heel were more appropriate.

"Okay," I said to Annie, patting the top of her head. "You be a good girl while I'm gone."

She looked up at me and then plopped her head back on the sofa to resume her nap.

I found Aunt Maude waiting for me on the porch. "All set for our *diner français?*"

"*Oui, mademoiselle,*" was her reply.

We walked the short distance to Lucas's house on Second Street, and the look on his face when he opened the door made me happy that I'd chosen the sundress over the jeans.

"Bonsoir," he greeted us. Opening the door wider he never took his eyes from my face. "Come on in. You ladies look exceptionally lovely this evening."

Yup, definitely glad I chose the sundress. "Thank you," I mumbled, following him and my aunt into the small living room.

"Have a seat," he said, gesturing toward a chocolate brown leather sofa and two matching chairs. "A glass of wine before dinner? I have a nice red I brought back from France."

"That would be nice, Lucas. Thank you," my aunt said, choosing a spot on the sofa.

I settled myself next to her and looked around the room. Even for a bachelor living alone I could see that Lucas had added some personal touches. A few large prints of museum exhibits in Paris adorned the walls. The coffee table held a centerpiece of fresh, brightly colored mixed flowers, and on the mantel above the small fireplace were framed photographs of locations that I recognized from the south of France.

"Here we go," he said, returning from the back of the house carrying a tray holding three glasses of wine.

After offering my aunt and me a glass, he removed his and held it up. "Here's to your new home, Maude, and good days ahead for you, Grace. *A votre santé!*"

"Thank you," my aunt said as I nodded.

I took a sip of the dark red liquid. "Oh, this is wonderful, Lucas. Makes me feel like I'm back in France."

"It *is* good," Aunt Maude agreed.

"I'm glad you like it. Dinner will be ready in about twenty minutes."

"Good. Then I'll have time to tell you all about my news." She went on to tell him about the knitting retreat weekends she was planning.

"Oh, that's very happy news, Maude. Knitting has become quite popular once again, so I have no doubt your new business will be a wonderful success. And how fortunate to have Grace as your partner." His gaze now swung to me. "So do I understand this to mean that you won't be rebuilding your coffee shop?"

"I'm afraid not. It would involve way too much because of the existing FEMA laws. It just wouldn't have the same feel to it as my other place did, and besides, it would be difficult for a lot of people to navigate the stairs required."

Lucas nodded. "Yes, I see what you're saying. Well, it's easy to see that you share a very close relationship, so I have no doubt that you'll enjoy beginning this new venture together."

"Are you all settled in at the bookshop?" I asked. I had been so upset when I was there on Friday morning I wasn't even sure if he'd officially opened yet.

"Just about. My grand opening is this coming Sunday, and I'd love it if you both could be there. Three o'clock, wine and cheese, and although you've already gotten a sneak peek, it will give the rest of the community a chance to see it."

"That would be very nice, Lucas," my aunt told him.

"Yes, we'll definitely be there. Are you planning to stay here permanently now?"

"Well, except for some trips back to Brunswick to check on the bookshop there, yes. Mrs. Beckett really has everything under control for me. I thought about selling the Brunswick shop but in all honesty, I feel like I'd be depriving Mrs. Beckett of something she really enjoys. Besides, I'm the only bookshop in Brunswick, so I think my customers would also be disappointed."

"I'd say it works out well all the way around." My aunt took a sip of her wine. "Kind of like Grace and me," she said with a smile.

I reached over to pat her hand. "You're absolutely right," I told her as my cell phone rang in my handbag beside me. "Oh, excuse me," I said, getting up and going outside to the porch to take the call.

As soon as I heard my sister's voice I wished I'd remembered to let the calls go to voice mail.

"Grace?" Chloe bellowed across the line. "I'm trying to reach Aunt Maude and there's no answer at her place. She was supposed to call me back." There was a pause, and then her tone became more subdued. "I imagine she told you about Parker and that I'm coming to Cedar Key?"

"Yes, yes, she did. I'm really sorry to . . ."

She instantly cut me off. "Well, she was supposed to get some information for me about storage units in the area. Do you know where she is?"

Offering my sympathy seemed like a waste of time. "Actually, she's here with me. We're at a . . . friend's house. For dinner. I came out on the porch to take the call."

"Well, could I speak to her?" Impatience laced her words.

"We were just about to begin dinner, Chloe. Can I have her call you back later tonight? Or would you prefer in the morning?" I was not going to let my sister, the drama queen, ruin a nice evening.

After a moment's pause, she said, "It's up to Aunt Maude. God knows I'm awake till all hours, so she can call me later. Bye."

With that, I heard the line disconnect and shook my head. Feeling bad for her situation was one thing, but I wasn't about to accept the crap that Chloe was famous for dishing out.

I took a deep breath of air, walked inside, gulped the rest of the wine in my glass, looked at my aunt, and said, "That was Chloe."

"Oh, my," was her response, knowing full well what a conversation with my sister was capable of doing to my mood. "Oh, no, I was supposed to call her back."

"Right. I explained you'd call her later when you got home. So it's not a problem."

Lucas sat there looking from my aunt to me, a confused expression on his face.

"Do you have any brothers or sisters?" I asked.

"I'm afraid not. I'm an only child."

"You're lucky," I said. "I'm sorry. That was my very difficult sister, and let's not ruin a nice evening by discussing her."

Lucas nodded as he stood up. "Just give me a few moments and dinner will be ready."

Following an exceptional dinner of roast lamb, au gratin potatoes, and fresh vegetables, we were enjoying coffee and dessert on the back deck.

"I do believe you missed your calling, Lucas," my aunt told him.

"With your exceptional abilities, I'm sure you could be a top chef. That dinner was simply out of this world—and this tarte tatin . . . I think it's the best I've ever had."

I had to agree on all counts. I took another bite of the luscious upside-down apple tart and savored the caramelized flavor. "Where on earth did you learn to cook like this?"

Lucas laughed as I saw a look of pride cross his face. "From both my mother and my grandmother. I think that unlike most American men, French boys are encouraged in the kitchen as much as little girls. I do enjoy cooking, but if I had to make a living at it, I'm not sure I'd enjoy it quite as much."

"Well, you certainly put me to shame," I told him. "Cooking has never been one of my best attributes."

"Ah, but I'm sure you have talents in other areas."

Why did the way he said that have a sexy connotation to my ears?

"You're very right," my aunt said. "Grace is an expert knitter. You should see some of the wonderful work she's done over the years."

"That's an admirable talent, and maybe someday you'll show me some of your work."

Hmm, did this constitute an almost-date?

"I'd love to," I said, feeling my cheeks grow warm. "By the way, your coffee is superb, and I'd bet anything you brought it back from Paris, didn't you?"

He nodded. "Oh, yes, on my most recent trip over there. I seem to be unable to return to the States without French coffee and chocolate."

I smiled. "Those are also the two items I always returned with." Well, we had something in common.

It was close to midnight by the time my aunt and I left Lucas's house. I had thoroughly enjoyed the entire evening and especially Lucas's company. I had also thought that perhaps the hint of a bona fide date—minus my aunt—might be forthcoming. But it was not.

❧ 6 ❧

After taking Annie for a walk through the downtown area, I had returned home and was enjoying my first cup of coffee on the front porch. The phone beside me rang, and I was happy to hear Suellen's voice.

"Okay," she said. "Tell me all about Lucas Trudeau. Don't leave anything out. You know me. I love details. I'd popped by his bookshop here in town and got to meet him, so believe me, I know that man is hot! Tell me all about the dinner last night."

I took a sip of coffee and then shook my head laughing. "Suellen, you're incorrigible." I often wondered if she was the avid romantic she was because of her mother and the reason she named her daughter Suellen. Suellen's mom had been named Careen. Both had been named for the sisters of Scarlett O'Hara. Suellen's grandmother and her mother were devoted *Gone with the Wind* fans, something that had been passed on to my friend. She in turn named her one and only daughter, Ashley, based on another character from that novel. I often wondered why she hadn't just named her Scarlett. "I told you. I really don't know Lucas that well. I mean, I'm not even sure I could say we're friends yet. *Acquaintance*—that's a better word to describe our relationship."

"Acquaintance? Oh, girlfriend, that is *so* boring. But not to worry, what with him relocating to Cedar Key, I'm sure you'll have plenty of opportunity to notch up a level or two from *acquaintance.*"

I smiled. She actually said that word like it was distasteful in her mouth.

"Tell me how that brilliant, beautiful, and wonderful goddaughter of mine is doing."

Suellen's voice morphed into a softness that the mere mention of her daughter always brought about.

"Oh, Gracie, she couldn't be doing better. I can hardly believe she's started her sophomore year at UGA. She loves the University of Georgia, and she's had a great summer working at a vet clinic in Athens."

I recalled all the years that Ashley had brought home stray dogs and cats, cried over wounded birds, and once even begged to adopt a raccoon that had been hanging around their yard. So I wasn't surprised at all when I learned she planned to major in veterinary medicine.

"She's one great girl, Suellen, and you should be very proud. It's not easy raising a daughter on your own."

"Oh, I don't know how much I had to do with the way she turned out. Sometimes parenthood is just a crap shoot. You do everything you can and still, the adult child can be a disappointment. And yet look at how many kids come from the most horrible childhoods . . . and they grow up to be admirable and outstanding human beings. Go figure, I say."

As Suellen's best friend, maybe I was a bit prejudiced, but I knew firsthand what she'd endured in her short marriage to Ashley's dad. Jack Daniels had always been his best friend, and it never failed to have a tendency to bring out the worst in him. Although it's probably the only thing she'd never confided in me, I have no doubt that Mason McSwain had been physically abusive to Suellen before she took her fifteen-month-old daughter and moved in with her mother. Mason had quickly left the area after that, and nobody had heard from him in almost twenty years. All for the better, I say.

I then went on to tell her about the new business and knitting retreats. "I'm really excited about all of it."

"Oh, you should be, and it sounds like a lot of fun. Imagine . . . women coming from all across the country to knit while they connect and bond. I love the idea, and I wish you both a huge success with this."

"Thanks. I'm really looking forward to all of it—except for one small surprise that Aunt Maude sprung on me."

"What's that?"

"Well, I'm afraid my sister is about to be divorced," I said, and then explained Chloe's situation.

"Good God! You've got to be kidding! Parker did that to her? I mean, really, we all know what a bitch Chloe can be, but geez . . ."

"My thoughts exactly. And so—looks like she'll be here this Friday to lick her wounds and try to recover her life."

"Wow. Imagine though, she gives him all those good years and now—she's left completely alone. Sometimes life's a bitch, huh?"

"Isn't that the truth? Well, I need to get moving here. I have to get downtown to go through the pitiful rubble that was my house and former business."

"Oh, sugar, I wish I could be there to help you. But I'll see you in two weeks. Call me soon."

"Will do," I said, hanging up and heading inside to the shower.

I spent a discouraging two hours sifting through what remained of my belongings. Following Jim back to the pavement, I mopped the sweat from my forehead and stared at the golf cart Ali had let me borrow. "It's pitiful that's all I have to show for ten years of my life," I said, gesturing toward a few items of clothes, two books that had managed to avoid being charred, and wind chimes that had hung in my coffee shop. Everything else that I had possessed was either burnt or ruined with the odor of smoke. Like all of my knitting—skeins of brand-new yarn that weren't destroyed now carried a sickening smell.

"I just want to say again how sorry I am, Miss Gracie."

"I know, and thank you. I'm really grateful that I left a lot of my personal belongings at my aunt's house when I moved here. Like photographs of my parents and things with memories. Well—I called the company you recommended, and they'll be here tomorrow morning to demolish what's left of the structure."

"Okay. There's no need for you to be here. The fellow gave me a call and I told him I'd meet him at nine."

"Thanks. I really appreciate it. This was bad enough, going through what little was left. I don't think I could stand here and watch it all come tumbling down."

"I understand, and if you need anything at all, just give me a ring."

"I will," I said, getting in the golf cart and heading to Second Street.

As I approached the bookshop I saw Lucas out front touching up some paint around the door. He looked up, saw me, and waved.

"How're you?" he asked.

I pulled the golf cart to the curb and got out. "Not bad, considering I just rescued what little was worth rescuing from the coffee shop and my apartment." I pointed to the few items.

"That was all you could get, huh? What a shame. None of the equipment in the coffee shop or any of your furniture?"

I ran a hand through my hair and shook my head. "Nope. That's it."

"I just made a fresh pot of coffee. Would you like to join me? I was going to take a break."

"Sounds good," I said, following him inside as the wonderful fragrance of lavender hit my nostrils. "Ah, lavender potpourri from Provence?"

Lucas nodded as he filled two mugs. "It has the ability of providing a relaxing atmosphere, don't you think?"

"I do. I always had bowls of it around my apartment, and I normally have lavender incense burning when I read my cards."

"Your cards?"

Damn. Why did I mention that? He'll probably think I'm a total fruitcake. "Ah . . . well . . . yeah, I read my tarot cards. Are you familiar with those?"

"Are those the things with quite vivid pictures on them and people use them to tell their future?"

I nodded. "Yeah, all the women in my family have used the

tarot, so guess I followed in their footsteps." He didn't seem surprised.

"My grandmother always used to read her cards and those of people in the village. So do you do it just as a hobby or are you quite good at it?"

I laughed. "I'd say it's more than a *hobby* and I think I'm usually pretty good reading them. Did your grandmother read yours?"

Lucas took a sip of coffee before answering. "No. As a small child and teenager I always wanted her to—but she said I didn't need to know my future. I should just live it."

I found this interesting, because many times if a reader senses something negative or disturbing from somebody's vibes or aura, rather than bring forth this information with the cards they might refrain from reading them. Is that why Lucas's grandmother had refused? I realized I knew very little about him.

"Well, I'd say you're doing just that—*living* it." I knew he wasn't presently married but wondered if he had been when he lived in France.

"Yes, I try. Life is very fragile. We have to make the most of the moments we're given, don't you think?"

"I absolutely do." His tone had become pensive, and I thought it best to change the subject. "Are you all set for your grand opening on Sunday?"

"Yes. I'm going into Gainesville Friday to pick up the wine and cheese."

"My aunt and I are looking forward to coming. Oh, I almost forgot . . . my sister, Chloe, is arriving on Friday. She'll be staying with my aunt. Unfortunately, her marriage has broken up and she's relocating here. Would it be okay if she comes with us on Sunday?"

Lucas's expression looked genuinely pained. "I'm very sorry to hear that, but how nice she can rely on you and your aunt to help her through this difficult time. And yes, by all means, bring her to the grand opening."

"Thanks. By the way, is it a secret or can you share what you're thinking of doing with the other room?" I asked, looking at the archway.

Lucas laughed. "Oh, it's not a secret. Well, my first idea was to simply add more bookshelves and seating areas for patrons. And then I thought it might be nice to have a coffee café—you know, like the large bookstore chains have. But I didn't want to take away business from you."

"That was really nice of you to consider that, but as you know—my coffee shop is now history. Actually, I think that's a great idea. I mean, gee, where will the locals go now to hang out and gossip?"

A killer smile crossed Lucas's face. "Really? You wouldn't mind?"

"Of course not. The island needs a place to gather. Besides, I've committed to being a partner with Aunt Maude in her new venture, so I'm sure that'll keep me busy."

"Well, then—I think that settles it. But could I impose upon you to give me some guidance? Maybe in the design and ordering whatever equipment you think might be best? I promise not to bother you too much, but maybe when you're free we could do some—what do they call it?—*brainstorming* together."

I couldn't remember the last time a suggestion had appealed to me quite as much. "I think it'll be fun, Lucas, and I'd love to."

I returned home to find Aunt Maude sitting on her back deck at the patio table surrounded by notebooks and assorted papers.

Annie ran to greet me, and I picked her up to cuddle. "Were you a good girl while I was gone?"

"She's delightful. Did you do okay getting your things?"

I put Annie down and joined my aunt at the table. "Yeah, what little there was. What are you up to here?"

"Well, I'm getting organized. Making notes on things we need to do to remodel the carriage house. I've already called a contractor, and he'll be out tomorrow morning to give me an estimate. Something else I think we should consider is a cleaning girl. I always had one for my house in Brunswick and I'd like a girl here, and she could also do the carriage house for us. What do you think?"

"Great idea for your apartment and the carriage house, but I rather enjoy cleaning my own place. Gives me time to chill out and think."

My aunt laughed. "Okay. I popped by the Bed and Breakfast, and Ali suggested somebody. She's new to the island and Ali wasn't able to give her any work, but it sounds like the girl could use more money."

"Good. Hopefully she'll be interested. Have you contacted her?"

"Ali said she knew how to reach her. So I told her to find out if the girl—her name is Rachel Ellis, by the way—could stop by tomorrow morning so we could meet her."

"Sounds good to me."

"Okay," my aunt said, getting up. "Let's go take a look at the carriage house and see if we can come up with some ideas."

I followed my aunt to the tabby structure. French doors ran the entire length, creating a pastoral atmosphere in the middle of the garden.

"I can see a few bottles of Windex are going to be needed to make all that glass shine," I said, as my aunt unlocked the door.

We stepped inside to a large, bright, and airy room. The roof above me had two skylights, allowing the sun to stream in. Two large picture windows flanked each side of the room, and at the far end was a staircase leading upstairs to a loft overlooking the area where we stood.

"Wow, this is great," I said, walking toward a galley kitchen along one side of the room.

My aunt nodded. "I think so too," she replied, bending over to open the door of the small refrigerator under the counter. She turned the faucet on the stainless steel sink and nodded again. "Yes, I think this will be just perfect for our knitting retreats. Over there," she said, pointing toward a door on the opposite wall, "is the bathroom, and I think that loft upstairs will be just perfect for your office."

I smiled and had to agree with her. "The lighting in here is ideal for knitting, too. Of course we'll have lots of lamps, but it's always nice to have natural lighting. And how about furniture? Have you given any thought to the decorating?"

"I have. I thought maybe we'd get a fresh coat of white paint for the walls and a border print at the top with some butterflies and flowers, which is always soothing to the eye. Some sofas and a couple love seats, along with a few cushy chairs with ottomans. That should do it for seating. And then of course some tables and lamps. We'll need a dinette table with chairs over there near the galley kitchen for our luncheons. We have to decide how many women we'll have at each retreat. Oh, and have you come up with a name yet?"

"I think we should keep the retreats fairly small, like six women. This will allow it to be more intimate, and women who come alone without a friend or relative won't feel out of place."

"Good idea. And with you, Chloe and me, that'll be nine."

"As far as a name for the business, I'm afraid I haven't come up with anything more creative than Blue Moon Knitting Retreats."

"I like it," my aunt said. "Simple and to the point. Also very appropriate since each retreat will end with a Blue Moon ceremony. I was thinking about a logo also, something we could put on our website and letterheads. How about a simple outline sketch of the island with a ball of yarn and needles in the middle?"

I could visualize it in my mind's eye. "Oh, I like that a lot. Perfect. And since we're focusing on the blue moon, how about a small one hovering above the sketch of the island? We'll get a graphic designer to do something up for us and we'll have it put on all of our business cards also."

"Great idea. Well, we've accomplished quite a lot here and we're on our way. Once the workmen get started with the refurbishing, we can think about going into Gainesville to order the furniture. Now I think we've earned ourselves a nice glass of sweet tea."

7

Aunt Maude and I met with Rachel Ellis the following morning. I'm not sure what I expected, but this girl didn't look a day over seventeen. Very slim, almost to the point of looking gaunt, she was wearing a faded pair of shorts and a blouse. Thick, mahogany-colored hair was pulled back at the base of her neck and secured with a scrunchie. But when she walked in the kitchen and greeted us, a smile lit up her face, transforming her drabness into borderline pretty.

"Hi," she said, extending her hand. "I'm Rachel Ellis."

"It's nice to meet you," my aunt told her. "Have a seat. Would you like a cup of coffee or tea?"

"Oh, no, thank you."

I let my aunt begin the interview and heard her say, "So you just recently moved to Cedar Key, Ali told me. Where is it that you lived before?"

"Down by Miami."

"I see. This is such an obscure little island. Do you have family here?"

"Oh, no, actually I really don't know a soul here."

I could see it was going to be like pulling teeth to get much information from her. "Are you here alone? Or with a husband?"

It was then that I noticed she was beginning to squirm in her chair, avoiding eye contact with me.

"No, I'm, ah . . . divorced. But I have a six-year-old son. Max started first grade here last week."

"Oh, how nice," my aunt said. "Well, I hope you'll both like it here. Okay, so you have experience cleaning? I need somebody once a week to clean my apartment. I'm not fussy which day, so whatever will be more convenient for you. Then we'll need you to clean the carriage house in the garden every Monday after the weekend knitting retreats. Would that work out for you?"

"Oh, yes, that would be great, and I could do your apartment every Friday. I could drop Max at school and come directly here."

I noticed she didn't answer the question about experience. "Do you have references from previous cleaning jobs that you had?"

Her squirming now became more noticeable, and she fingered the edge of the tablecloth.

"Um . . . well . . . No, I'm afraid I don't. I need to be honest with you. I've never actually worked for somebody else doing cleaning. But I've taken care of my own house, and I'm an excellent house-keeper. I also learn very fast, and I really, really need this job."

My heart went out to her. In this economy many people were desperate for work. Any type of work that supplied some kind of paycheck. I looked at my aunt.

"Well," she said. "You certainly sound motivated, and that's an excellent trait to have. If it's okay with my niece here, I'd like to offer you the position. Why don't we say you'll be on a three-month trial basis? Maybe you could begin this Friday cleaning my apartment. We're going to be having workmen in the carriage house for a while, but then perhaps you could help us with getting everything arranged in there. We're thinking we'll be ready to begin the knitting retreats after the holidays in January."

Rachel was staring at me waiting for my answer. "I agree," I told her. "I think a three-month probation is fair."

"Oh, so do I. That's fine with me. I'll do a good job. I really will, and thank you ever so much."

Yeah, I'd lost everything in a fire, but I knew how fortunate I was to have Aunt Maude to help me through a bad time. It was obvious this poor girl had nobody. The gratitude she displayed for a simple cleaning job made me realize there's always somebody else that has it much worse.

"That's wonderful," Aunt Maude said, sliding a paper across the table. "If you'll just fill this out with your name and address and phone number, we'll be all set."

The excitement vanished from Rachel's face. She looked down at the paper and hesitantly picked up the pen to fill out the information. Not wanting to make her more nervous, I got up.

"I think I'll have another cup of coffee. Aunt Maude, how about you?"

"That sounds great, and I think I'll help myself to one of those delicious muffins I baked this morning. Are you sure we can't interest you, Rachel?"

Her head popped up from the paper. "Oh, no. Thank you, anyway."

My aunt followed me to the counter and we both remained silent.

I poured two mugs of coffee while my aunt got her muffin. Settling ourselves at the table, I told her about Lucas's plan to turn the extra room at the bookshop into a coffee café.

"What a marvelous idea."

"Yeah, and he asked if I'd help him with the design and ordering some of the equipment he'll need. You know, because I had my own coffee shop."

My aunt laughed. "Right, Gracie. I'm sure that's the only reason he asked for your help."

"What do you mean?"

"I mean I think he's attracted to you."

Before I could reply Rachel passed the paper to my aunt.

"Oh, you're staying at the RV park out on SR Twenty-four?"

"Yeah, for right now, anyway. Max and I drove here in our travel trailer, so it made sense staying at the park."

My aunt nodded. "Do you have a cell phone? You didn't list any phone number."

"No, I'm sorry. I don't."

She probably couldn't afford one. "Well, if we needed to reach you we could call the office at the RV park. Right, Aunt Maude?"

"Yes, of course. That won't be a problem."

"Oh, good. Then I'll see you at nine Friday morning?"

Maude nodded. "That will be great, and I look forward to seeing you then."

Rachel turned toward the door to leave and then stopped. Turning around, she said, "Thank you both so much. I really appreciate you giving me a chance. Bye."

I got up to watch her leave. She actually skipped her way along the walkway to the curb. It was then that I noticed the beat-up travel trailer. She opened the door on the driver's side, got in, and started the ignition. Yup, some people did have it pretty bad. The only means of transportation this poor girl had was also her place of residence.

"Hello," I hollered, walking into the bookshop later that afternoon.

Lucas appeared from the back—that killer smile of his causing my stomach to flip-flop. This guy sure had a way of nudging up my desire meter.

"Bonjour," he greeted me, and I almost expected the cosmopolitan kiss on both cheeks, which, of course, was not forthcoming.

"How are you this afternoon?" he inquired.

"Fine, and you?"

Was it my imagination or had his eyes scanned me from head to foot, thereby increasing his smile?

"I'm good, very good."

I had to stop myself from saying, *I'm very glad,* and I suppressed a giggle when I realized we seemed to be indulging in an overly polite greeting. "Well, if you're not busy, I thought maybe we could discuss the plans for your coffee café."

Clearing his throat, Lucas gestured toward the new room. "That sounds good. There's a table in here."

"Great," I said, following him and not missing the fact that this man really looked great in jeans.

I saw that he'd also set up another table, which held a coffee-maker and . . . were those croissants?

"Would you like some coffee and croissants while we talk?"

Oh, yeah, definitely a man after my own heart. When it came to France, there were four things I could never resist—wine, coffee, chocolate, and croissants.

"How nice," I said. Not possessing an ounce of shyness, I proceeded to place the buttery, delectable crescent on a plate before pouring myself a cup of coffee.

Lucas did the same and then joined me at the table.

I took a bite of the heavenly roll, closed my eyes for a second to allow my palate to experience the exquisite pleasure, and oh, God! I think I actually *moaned*.

Lucas laughed, and my eyes flew open as I felt my cheeks heating up. Cripe, I felt like I'd shared an intimate moment with him.

Covering my embarrassment, I joined his laughter. "My God, that is *so* good! And I know you brought those back from France."

"I did." His smile widened. "And I'm very pleased to see that you enjoy it so much."

He *was* referring to the croissants, right?

"Oh, I do," I said, and then took a sip of coffee. While I didn't exhibit the same reaction that the croissants had caused, I nodded. "And the coffee is delicious too."

"Good. Well, what do you suggest we do with this empty room?"

We? Silly me, but I really liked the sound of that.

"Hmm," I said, looking around. An instant vision came to me. "I think you want to create a cozy atmosphere. You know, a place that will not only beckon people to purchase coffee but cause them to want to stay awhile. Spend some time here socializing and feeling comfortable."

"Ah, much like your place was."

"Well, yes, I suppose so. But this is *your* place, so don't let me take away whatever vision you might have."

"That's just it. My area of expertise is running a bookshop. I can do that quite well, but a coffee café? I'm afraid this is where I'm relying on you."

Really? Well, be my guest to rely away.

I took another bite of croissant and refrained from any further outburst while I gave my vision some more thought.

"You have a great window and shelf over there," I said, pointing to the front of the room. "It might be nice to set up a coffee display. Some brightly colors mugs, maybe a French press. Oh, will you also be serving tea?"

"What do you think?"

I recalled the day that Lucas had first walked into my coffee shop. It wasn't coffee that he ordered—it was a cup of tea.

"Yes, I think offering tea is a good choice. So you could also display some teapots with an unusual design. On one of your trips back to France, you won't have any problem finding a few of those."

"That sounds good."

"I think maybe you should have a long wooden counter built back there," I said, pointing to the back of the room. "This is where your patrons will order the coffee. And you'll need to have some small tables with four chairs. I'd arrange those against the wall, because you also want to have some cushy seating in the middle. A few love seats, maybe some chairs like you have in the bookshop."

"I like it," Lucas said. "I can visualize it and, yes, I like it very much. What do you think about decorating? What décor should I use?"

"Well, since you're French, why not go with black and white for colors? On the walls, maybe you could hang some prints of French scenery or maps?"

"Yes, yes. I like that as well. And equipment? What, exactly, will I need to order?"

"Oh, darn," I said. "I have catalogs and I meant to bring them with me. I'll make a note so I don't forget."

I reached across the table for the pen and paper at the same time that Lucas did, and our hands touched. I swear I felt an electric jolt travel through my arm. I glanced up to see his dark eyes on my face, and neither one of us released our hands from each other.

Lucas smiled. "Sorry," he said, slowly pulling his hand away. "Here, you can use the paper and pen. Let me get another one."

He got up quickly and headed into the bookshop. God, what was that all about? I couldn't ever recall touching a man's hand and experiencing a reaction like that.

"Okay," he said, coming to sit back down. "I'll also make a few notes."

I looked at his curly head bent over the paper as he wrote, and this time I was certain we felt a mutual chemistry.

"Very good. I think we've accomplished a lot, but I'd really like to see that catalog so I can get the needed equipment ordered. Is there . . . is there any chance you might be free this evening for dinner? And you could bring the catalog so we could discuss it?"

Oh. My. God. Was he asking me out on a date? *Don't be foolish*, I thought, *it's simply a business meeting.*

"Ah, no. I mean, yes, I'm free. . . . I don't have any plans this evening."

"Great," he said, standing up, and I got the distinct impression that *this* meeting was over. "Is the Island Room okay? I can call there to reserve a table."

I also stood up and reached for my bag. "Yes, that would be fine. What time should I meet you there?"

He seemed to hesitate and then said, "How's seven o'clock sound?"

See, I told myself, *it's not a date. He isn't picking me up at my home.* "Great. Seven is great," I said, and headed to the door. "I'll see you then."

8

What few clothes I had left from the fire lay sprawled across my bed. I really *did* have to do some serious shopping. Here it was four-thirty and I still couldn't decide what to wear for dinner with Lucas. Damn. Then I remembered Monica's generous offer. Time to give her a call and see if she could help me out.

"Of course I can help you," she said. "Come on over to Monica's Boutique and choose whatever you'd like."

"You're a lifesaver," I told her. "Be right over."

I held the mint green sundress in front of me. "What do you think?"

"With that auburn hair of yours, I think that color goes way better on you than me. Try it on and let's see."

I came out of the bathroom and twirled around.

Monica nodded her head. "Absolutely! You look really hot in that dress."

Hot? Did I actually want to look *hot?* Why not? Hot can be a good thing for dinner with a handsome guy. Never mind that it was only for business.

"You think?" I questioned, looking in the full-length mirror. The cutout on the back was cute, the V-shaped neck in front was just low enough to be appropriate, the length came just to my knee, and Monica was right, the color did go well with my hair. My hair! How would I wear it?

"Love the dress, but what am I going to do with this?" I asked, running my hand through my curls.

"Up. You have to wear it up with that dress. It'll be cool off your neck, plus just a tad seductive."

I laughed. "Seductive? I told you, it's just a business meeting."

Now it was Monica's turn to laugh. "Yeah, right. You seem to forget I was there that day Lucas first came into your coffee shop. I saw the *way* he looked at you."

"Well, if that look meant anything, then he sure has a strange *way* of showing it. He's really made no attempt to get better acquainted on a personal basis."

"You might think tonight is about business. Trust me, I'd bet anything it's not."

I ignored Monica's comment. "White heels with the dress, do you think?"

"Yup, and I have just the pair," she said, going to her closet. "Here, try these."

I took one look at the four-inch heel and smiled. "Really?" Now these were hot. Open toe, open back, and all slim straps.

"Really," she said, as I slipped my feet into them. They were surprisingly more comfortable than they looked.

"Okay," I said, twirling around once more and pleased with the reflection I saw in the mirror. "Like I said, you're a lifesaver, Monica."

"Glad I could help. Only one thing . . . I want all the details tomorrow morning. Got it?"

"Got it," I promised.

Sitting across from Lucas at the Island Room, I did feel *hot.* By the look on his face when I walked in, he may have been thinking that exact word. Of course, I could be all wrong, but it seemed like I was able to read his mind from the expressions on his face. And the one he had when I walked in certainly made me feel like a woman. Maybe even a *desired* woman.

"Bonsoir," he said, standing up as I approached the table, formally extending his hand.

"Bonsoir," I repeated, taking his hand, and that electric jolt I'd felt this morning was even stronger. Feeling flustered, I let go of his hand as he pulled out my chair. With a European man, chivalry is never dead.

"You look very nice this evening," he told me.

I said a silent *thank you* to Monica before verbally thanking Lucas. I noticed he looked pretty dashing himself with pale blue blazer, open-collared shirt, and gray dress slacks.

The waitress came to take our drink order, and we both ordered a glass of Pinot Noir. When it arrived, he touched his glass to mine and said, "To a great coffee café."

"Yes, and much success," I said, before taking a sip. "Oh, I have the catalog." I reached in my tote bag and passed it across the table.

Lucas opened it and began turning pages. "Do you have any suggestions?" he asked.

"Well, you can never go wrong with a Bunn or Braun coffeemaker. Personally, I feel they're the best. And will you be serving espresso and cappuccino?"

"Oui," he said, reverting to his native language as he continued turning pages.

I smiled. "Toward the back of the catalog, you'll see the machines for those."

By the time dinner arrived, Lucas had made all of his selections. With my guidance, of course.

"Thank you very much for helping me," he said. "I'll be ordering everything on Monday, and I've already spoken to the workmen about coming in to build that counter and do a few other things."

"That's great. So I'm sure it won't be long before your coffee café is open and ready for business."

"Well, there's still the problem of furniture. Those tables and chairs you mentioned, along with the love seats. I got the ones for the bookshop in Gainesville."

I took a bite of my pork and nodded. "Right. You'll be able to find whatever you need there."

"Yes, well . . . the problem is . . . for the coffee café, I'm still not sure exactly what I should purchase."

"Oh," was all I could think of to say.

"So . . . is there any chance . . . I mean, I know how busy you are helping your aunt, but . . . do you think possibly you might be able to drive into Gainesville with me and help me make a selection?"

Yes, true, this appeared to be another business-related outing. But I enjoyed Lucas's company and the thought of spending much of the day with him certainly appealed to me. Besides, I was being *neighborly* by helping him out, right?

"Actually, I'm not that busy. I'm doing well getting the website set up, and I should have that finished by early next week. When were you thinking of going?"

"I thought perhaps this Friday?"

Damn. The day Chloe was arriving, and I didn't want to start off on a bad foot with her by not being around when she got here.

"Well, uh, that really wouldn't work for me," I said, and explained that it was Friday my sister would be arriving.

"Oh, that's right. You had mentioned she was moving here, and I can certainly understand why you should be home to greet her." He took a sip of wine. After a few moments he said, "Would Thursday be better for you? Do you think you could go with me then?"

I smiled at him across the table. "Yes, Thursday would be fine, and I'd love to."

"Wonderful. I will pick you up at your house about nine? How would that be?"

Pick me up? Okay, okay, I know it's only to go furniture shopping, but still . . .

"Yes, nine would be great," I said, and shot him another smile.

Following dinner, Lucas suggested we have coffee on the outside porch overlooking the water.

I decided to take a chance and ask more about him.

"So," I questioned. "Do you still have relatives in France?"

"Well, my parents are both gone, but yes, I do have aunts, uncles, and cousins in the south of France. I don't see them very often, but we do still stay in touch. Computers and e-mails are a wonderful invention, are they not?"

"Yes, they certainly are." I decided to get a bit more inquisitive. "Have you ever been married?" I asked, jumping right in.

Lucas put his head down and began fingering the spoon. For a minute I didn't think he was going to answer. I should have known better. The French are not like Americans—telling personal things, like the tabloids in our country were famous for.

"I was," he said quietly. He looked up and his eyes met mine.

Not only could I read his expressions, I discovered in that moment the pain that was revealed in those eyes, and for one of the few times in my life, I didn't know what to say.

"Danielle passed away eight years ago."

Without even thinking, I reached out and touched his hand. "I'm so sorry. She was so young. Was she ill?" I asked, never thinking he could have lost his wife in death.

"No, she was not ill. It was an automobile accident, and Danielle was thirty-five when it happened."

"I'm sorry," I said again, and now felt bad for bringing up the subject. I also wondered if possibly Lucas had been driving the car and that accounted for some of the pain I saw in his eyes. That and grief, of course.

"How about you?" he now questioned. "Have you been married?"

I shook my head. "No." I then surprised myself by mentioning a little about Beau. "But I did have a long-term relationship years ago. I had just graduated college. I was working in our family antique shop in Brunswick. That's where I met him. He came in to make a purchase. We were together a little over four years."

"I see. So it was not to be, this relationship?"

"No, I suppose it wasn't." I reached up to push a strand of hair away from my face and shrugged. "I was young when we met, only twenty-two. And much younger than he was. Beau was twelve years older than me."

"This age difference? Do you think that accounted for the problem?"

"Oh, no. Not at all. It was many other things. By the way," I asked, now wanting to change the subject, "can I ask your age?"

Lucas laughed. "I am forty-six. Am I an *older* man to you?"

I smiled. "Not by my standards. I'm thirty-six, and I've always felt that age is simply a number. I think Aunt Maude is a good example of that."

"Indeed she is," he said, looking out toward the water. "We have a beautiful sunset tonight."

I followed his glance to the west. "We're fortunate to have them most nights on the island."

"I like this island," he said. "I'm glad I discovered it and will be staying here." He turned to face me. "And thank you for having dinner with me this evening."

"I enjoyed it very much." I glanced at my watch and saw it was a little after nine. Where had two hours gone? I couldn't believe how the time had flown by.

"Do you need to leave?" Lucas asked.

"I really should get home to let Annie out. I told her to be a good girl while I was gone."

Lucas stood up and laughed. "I'm driving up to Brunswick on Saturday to bring Duncan to his new home here. Mrs. Beckett has kept him for me while I get settled in, but it'll be great to have my companion with me again."

"That's right. I remember you mentioning that you had a Scottish terrier when we first met."

"Yes, Duncan is my little companion and a good boy."

We walked out to the parking lot together.

"May I give you a ride home?" he asked.

"I have my car, but thank you."

We stood there staring at each other for a brief moment. Lucas seemed reluctant to leave, and suddenly he leaned over, kissing both of my cheeks twice, and said, "Well, I will follow you in my car, just to be sure you arrive safely."

I smiled. "That would be nice," I said.

Driving up Second Street, I glanced in my rearview mirror and felt a warm feeling go through me. After so many years of not having a man in my life, it felt reassuring to know that the one following behind was doing so because he was concerned for me. Yes, that was a good feeling.

When I pulled up in front of the house, I got out, hollered thank you, and waved.

Lucas called back, "See you Thursday morning at nine."

Falling asleep that night, I replayed the entire evening again in my head. All of it was wonderful, but the thing that surprised me the most was the fact that I had shared something about Beau with him. Except for Aunt Maude and Suellen, I had never done that with one other person.

❧ 9 ❧

Friday morning, based on the events of the past week, I felt com-
pelled to do a tarot reading. Annie and I had taken our walk,
and I was enjoying my second cup of coffee. Before shuffling the
cards, I decided to burn some sage and cedar in the kitchen.

Sitting down at the table, I reached for the deck and allowed my
mind to wander.

The revelation from Lucas about the death of his wife dominated my thoughts. I recalled the phone conversation with Suellen.

"So the poor man is probably still grieving over his loss, do you
think? Maybe that's why he's not actively pursuing a relationship
with you?"

"That's what I'm thinking," I'd told her.

"Wow, imagine loving so deeply that even eight years later he
can't bring himself to think about loving another woman."

I had felt a stab of jealousy go through me. "Well, I'm not saying
that's the way it is," I'd told Suellen. "I'm just thinking it might
possibly account for the reason Lucas is keeping what we share on
a strictly platonic level. I mean, dinner with him the other night
was great, and our shopping spree yesterday was fun, and although
I do think we have chemistry together, it's just a friendship."

I let out a deep sigh as I continued shuffling the cards.

Was that the reason? Was Lucas holding back with any romantic overtures because of the wife he'd lost? Could be, and yet I got the distinct feeling he was attracted to me, and there was no doubt that I was attracted to him. And how about our shopping spree? We had talked nonstop on the drive to Gainesville and back. No, not about anything profound, just enjoyable conversation. And over lunch—at that intimate French restaurant he suggested—he had reached out and squeezed my hand, thanking me for accompanying him to make furniture selections. The look in his eyes had been genuine, which led me to think that he *cared* about me.

I blew out a deep breath. *That's just it,* I thought, *maybe even though he feels the attraction that I do, he's not willing to follow through on it. Maybe that deep love he has for his wife won't allow him to.*

"And how do you feel about that, Gracie?" I asked myself out loud.

I'm not sure, I thought, *but possibly it's better to have only a friendship with Lucas than no contact at all?*

I had no answers, but maybe the cards did. I stopped shuffling and removed the first one—the Page of Fire / Mastery of action card indicating *playfulness.* This card could definitely represent me, because the meaning for it was to start seeing the lighter side of life, the playfulness. When this card appears in a reading, something fresh and new is going to enter your life and you are ready for it.

Hmm, well, this certainly made sense. Especially in relation to Lucas.

I removed the next card and was surprised to see the Knight of Clouds. This one shows a knight completely covered in armor. The armor has buttons all over it, and they could detonate if touched.

This card seldom showed up in my spread. Could it represent Lucas? The figure in the card is angry and his face is full of pure rage. This person shows so much anger because beneath this anger is profound pain from something in his past.

Immediately, I recalled the pain I saw in his eyes Tuesday night when he told me about his wife's death.

The definition of this card also states that his anger is his armor to avoid further pain. This individual can change, but it will take time and a lot of understanding from those around him.

Well, I certainly had never seen Lucas display any anger, so I now doubted that this card represented *him.* I laid it aside and reached for the third one. The Thunderbolt card again, which represented Chloe. Not surprising, since she was due to arrive on the island within a few hours.

I returned the cards to their velvet pouch, got up, stretched, and blew out a deep breath.

Annie had been napping on the kitchen floor. She looked up at me expectantly.

"Yeah, come on," I said. "You can have a romp in the garden before I get to work on the computer."

I was sitting on the porch, sipping an iced tea and working on a gorgeous lacy scarf pattern, when the Lexus pulled up. A woman got out, stretched, and stood looking toward the end of the street at the water.

Chloe? True, I hadn't seen my sister in ten years, but still... Had I bumped into her out in public, I'm not sure I'd have recognized her right away. Gone was the slim and trim Chloe I'd always remembered and in her place was a middle-aged woman looking... well, there was no kind way to put it—frumpy. It was easy to see that she'd packed on about thirty pounds, and although the yellow pantsuit she wore was obviously pricey, the style would have been more suited to Aunt Maude. Her hair, which I'd always envied, had morphed from chestnut brown to a distinct salt and pepper, adding a few more years to her overall appearance. And the shine and sleekness was now missing. But there was no doubt that, yes, this was my sister.

I got up and walked down the stairs with Annie trailing behind me.

"Chloe," I hollered. "Welcome. Did you have a good drive?"

She turned to face me, and I now saw that lines had appeared around her eyes that weren't there ten years before.

"Grace," she said, and her gaze swept over me. "You're looking great, as usual."

Was that surprise I detected in her tone? Or sarcasm?

"You too," I lied, and attempted to give her a hug.

But I wasn't quick enough, because she moved away and was already unlocking the trunk of her car.

"Can I give you a hand with some of your luggage?" I asked.

"Yeah, that would be good." She reached in and gave me two Louis Vuitton bags. "I'll get the rest later."

As I schlepped through the gate toward the back door, I didn't miss the fact that she was only carrying her handbag and a small tote.

"Chloe," Aunt Maude called from the porch. "I'm so glad you arrived safely. Welcome to Cedar Key."

"I'll just take these into your room," I said, heading inside and feeling very much like a lowly porter at a hotel.

I deposited the heavy bags on the floor and blew out a deep breath. *Where are ya, Suellen, when I really need you?* I realized having Chloe around might be even more difficult than I'd anticipated.

When I walked into the kitchen I found Aunt Maude and Chloe at the table sipping iced tea.

"Grace, honey," my aunt said. "Come join us."

I accepted the glass she poured for me and sat down. Talk about feeling uncomfortable. She may have been my sister, but I had no clue what to say to her.

"After we finish the tea, I'll show you around," my aunt told her. "The contractors started working on the carriage house this morning—that's where we'll be holding the knitting retreats—so I'm afraid it'll be a bit busy around here for a few weeks."

Chloe nodded and looked around the kitchen. "It looks like a nice place. And your apartment is upstairs?" she asked, turning her head in my direction.

"Yeah, I'll take you up there later."

"I still can't get over the fact that you're going to be starting another business," she said, directing her attention back to my aunt. "I mean, you know . . ."

Maude shifted in her chair.

"No, I'm not sure I do, Chloe. If you mean because of my age, it's never too late in life to change course and begin a new adventure. Besides, I think Grace and I are doing quite well so far. We've managed to plan the knitting retreats, I've hired the contractors, so we're in the process of converting the carriage house and decorating. And don't forget, with me moving here it's also given *you* the opportunity to get away and start over."

Yes! You give it to her, Aunt Maude. She never was one to put up with Chloe's antics.

Now it was my sister's turn to shift in her chair and clear her throat. "Yes, well . . . and I do appreciate you taking me in. And before we go any further, let's clear the air about Parker." She looked directly at me. "I assume Aunt Maude has brought you up to date on everything, but I'd rather not have it be a topic of conversation. My attorney has the divorce in progress and . . . once that becomes final in December—Parker Radcliffe will be as good as dead to me."

"Fine by me," I replied, grateful that I didn't have to offer sympathy to my sister.

"Okay, good," she said, effectively cutting me off. "So tell me what you have planned for these knitting retreats and how I'll be involved." Her attention shifted back to Aunt Maude.

I had a flashback to years ago—sitting at the dinner table with my parents and Chloe. I was probably about five and she was a senior in high school. I'd been so excited about my upcoming dance recital and was trying to explain to my parents how my lesson had gone that day, but Chloe had effectively cut me off, telling them about what kind of gown she intended to get for her prom. Had it always been that way, I wondered? With her dismissing me like I didn't even exist? Or maybe more important, with her *wishing* I didn't exist?

"That sounds like it has a lot of potential," I heard her say. "Knitting has become quite the rage, even though it's been around for centuries. So I have no doubt you'll be fully booked for those weekends. And yes, I think I'd like to do a class on the Fair Isle sweaters. That's one of my specialties." As if remembering I was seated at the table, she turned to me and said, "You don't knit, do you, Grace?"

I smiled. That showed you how little she knew about me, not to mention the fact she'd paid no attention that I was knitting on the porch when she arrived. "Actually, yes, I do. Aunt Maude taught me many years ago."

"She also taught me. What would we have done without you?" she said, reaching out to touch my aunt's hand. "We certainly had no mother to speak of."

With that, she stood up, put her glass in the sink, and said, "Okay, well, I'm ready for the tour."

My aunt and I exchanged a glance. Was it my imagination or was there definite animosity in Chloe's voice when she mentioned our mother?

The three of us turned as Rachel came into the kitchen. "I'm all finished, Miss Maude," she said, sending a smile toward my aunt and me.

"Hey, Rachel. How're you?"

"I'm good, thanks," she answered, and looked toward Chloe.

"Rachel, this is my niece, Chloe. Grace's sister. She's just arrived from St. Simons Island and will be living with me. Rachel is my new housekeeper," she explained to Chloe.

My sister nodded. "I'm glad to see you'll be getting some help," was all she said.

As Rachel walked out the back door, the phone rang. "Hello, Ali. How are you?" I heard my aunt say.

"Alison owns the Bed and Breakfast on the island," I told my sister. "It's such a small town it won't take you long to get to know everybody."

"Oh, no," I now heard Aunt Maude say. "Well, that's certainly good news for Twila Faye, but I can see where that leaves you in a bit of a bind. But yes, I'll keep my ears open for you."

"Everything okay?" I asked as she hung up.

"Not really. I'm afraid Ali got some disturbing news this morning. Well, disturbing for her. It seems Twila Faye is going to be leaving the island and the Bed and Breakfast."

"What?" I could hardly believe my ears. She'd worked at the B & B forever. "What's going on?"

"Well, Twila Faye feels bad about leaving, but she's also quite happy. Her son, his wife, and her granddaughter are moving to Clearwater. He has a new job position down there and he wants Twila Faye to come with them. They've purchased a new home, and it has an in-law apartment attached, which will be perfect for Twila Faye."

"Oh, wow. Yeah, I can see how she'd be torn. She's so close to her son and his family. But leave Cedar Key? Gosh, she's been here all her life."

"Right, and believe me, I'm really happy for her. I think it's wonderful that her son wants to include her in the move, but . . . I'm afraid poor Ali will be lost without her. Twila Faye was her main housekeeper and her only full-time employee."

My aunt was right. "That's certainly bittersweet news."

"Yeah, it is. I guess Ali will be advertising for a new house-keeping manager. So if you hear of anybody, let her know. Come on, Chloe," my aunt said. "I'll show you around the apartment and then we'll go take a peek at the carriage house."

10

Chloe's first weekend with us passed with relative calm. Aunt Maude and I took turns taking her around the island, showing her various things. To her credit, although Chloe didn't rave about the scenery or anything else, she didn't display any negativity.

But on Sunday afternoon when we were driving along Second Street to the grand opening at the bookshop, I dreaded having to introduce her to Lucas. Mostly I worried that she might catch on that I was attracted to him, which had the potential of bringing out her snarky side.

To my relief, that didn't happen. Actually, she was very pleasant to him, and she even used her knowledge of French to speak a few sentences.

Lucas laughed. *"Très bien,"* he told her.

Was that a smile that crossed her face?

She waved her hand in the air. "No, not very good at all, I'm afraid, but thank you. I've gotten rusty not using my French in so long."

"Ah, but it does come back to you, no?"

Now it was bona fide laughter coming from my sister. "Yes, I suppose it does. So . . . I'm looking for suspense or mystery novels. Where might I find those?"

Lucas directed her to the shelf. "And please help yourself to wine and cheese," I heard him say before he joined me at the front of the shop.

"Your sister is very nice," he said. "Where is Maude? Is she not coming?"

"Thank you." I wanted to say, *It's your wonderful French charm that won her over.* "Yes, she'll be along shortly. The contractor stopped by to discuss something with her."

"The workmen have finished the counter. Would you like to see it?"

I followed Lucas into the adjoining room.

"Oh, it looks great. They did a very nice job."

"Yes, I think so too. The furniture will be delivered the end of this week, so it won't be much longer until the island will have a coffee café once again."

We both turned around to the sound of Chloe's voice.

"Oh, what's this?" she asked.

"Welcome to the coffee café," Lucas said, gesturing with his arm.

"What a great idea." Chloe walked around the room nodding her head. Running her hand across the wood of the counter, she looked at me. "So I take it you won't be rebuilding your place? Or will the two of you be in competition?"

"No, I'm afraid my days of serving coffee are over, but Lucas was kind enough to question me about that before deciding to open his own coffee shop."

Chloe's glance went from Lucas to me. "That *was* considerate."

Did I detect a tad of snarkiness in her tone?

"Actually," Lucas said, "I wanted to speak to you about that. I know you're busy helping your aunt and I hate to ask you for another favor, but I thought perhaps you might be able to give me a bit of assistance when I first open—teaching me how to operate the machines and make some of those fancy coffee drinks? I promise not to take too much of your time, and you certainly don't have to decide right now."

I felt a smile spreading across my face. "I'd be happy to help you out, Lucas. Thanks for asking. Just let me know when you need me."

Putting an end to any further discussion on the subject, Chloe held up three books in her hand. "Well, I think I'm all set for reading material. Will you ring me up?"

"Certainly, *madame*," Lucas said, heading into the bookshop.

I waited while Chloe's purchase was completed.

"It was very nice meeting you, Lucas," she said, extending her hand.

"*Enchanté,*" he told her, returning the handshake. "Grace, I will call you during the week? Perhaps when the furniture arrives, you could help me decide how to arrange it?"

"Sure. I'd like that," I said, but not before catching the intense expression on my sister's face.

After Aunt Maude returned from the bookstore, she joined Chloe and me in the garden.

"I do believe Lucas will have a success with that bookshop," she said, settling into a chair with her knitting. "The place was packed when I left."

I reached into my bag and removed the pale yellow sweater I was knitting for Monica's new baby. "I'm not surprised. His bookstore in Brunswick does very well."

"Oh, how pretty," Chloe said, leaning across from her lounge to get a better look. "Who's that for?"

"My friend Monica's new baby. She's due in March. We're not sure yet if it's a boy or girl, so I thought yellow would be a safe color."

"Is this her first?"

"Well, yeah, technically. But she has a ten-year-old stepdaughter, Clarissa Jo—Adam's daughter from a previous marriage, and he has full custody."

"Really?"

I heard the surprise in the question. "Yup, it's a bit of a long story, but the short version is that the ex was an unfit mother."

"Well, then no doubt the child is much better off where she's at," Chloe said matter of factly. "Speaking of children, don't you ever intend to settle down and have some of your own?"

Touchy subject and certainly one I didn't want to discuss with my sister.

"Oh, who knows. . . . I'm only thirty-six, and today that's still young enough to have a child. Many women aren't having their first until they're forty."

"I suppose so," she said, and continued knitting the socks she was working on. "And what about this Lucas? I take it you're romantically involved?"

Damn. Another touchy subject.

"Gosh, no, we're just friends. Why would you think that?"

"Well, first of all, you've never had a problem attracting the men, and second, from what I saw in the bookshop, I got the feeling you shared more than friendship."

Never had a problem attracting the men? Since she left home at seventeen, how would she even know this? I could feel my annoyance notching up, but not wanting to start an argument, I said, "Nope. We're just friends. Aunt Maude knew him in Brunswick."

"That's right. He owned the bookshop there. I always frequented Barnes and Noble, so I'm afraid I never did get over there."

Figures, I thought. *More chance of bumping into your snobby friends at the large chain.*

Then out of the blue, my sister really surprised me by saying, "You know, Grace, you were the fortunate one. You had those early years with our parents and then had Aunt Maude to raise you. Maybe that accounts for the way you are now."

Where the hell did this come from? And what did she mean by *the way you are now?*

I turned around in the lounge to face her better. "Well, yeah, it was great that I had Aunt Maude, especially after Mom and Dad died, but you have many more memories of our parents than I do, Chloe. God, you were already twelve by the time I came along."

"Exactly, so you really got the best of both worlds. When you were born our parents had more time to devote to parenthood, and when they died, Aunt Maude finished raising you."

Was she serious?

"You've got to be kidding! They barely ever had time for me. They were constantly traveling for the business, and when they *were* home, they were so wrapped up in each other it was like I was invisible." I neglected to add, *and if you had stuck around you would have known this.*

"It didn't seem that way to me. I went off to college and I assumed you went with them on those buying trips to Europe, and being the only child left at home gave them all the time in the world to spend with you."

Funny how we all perceive things differently. "Except that wasn't the case, Chloe. I got shipped across the street to Aunt Maude's house. Oh, don't get me wrong, I loved staying with her, but don't you think I knew I was far from the priority in their life?"

She remained silent, and I realized it might provoke anger on my sister's part, but I said, "Once you left home for college, you never looked back. God, you hardly even came home during summer vacation or holidays. You always had invitations from friends and you chose their company above ours. So I can see where you wouldn't know what really went on when I was growing up. And after you married Parker . . . it was the same. You basically excluded us from your life. Hell, I barely know my two nephews. So get over it, Chloe. My childhood didn't imitate those fifties television shows either."

"Well, I just thought . . . then how come none of it seemed to bother you? Look at you, going through life, always getting what you want, always achieving whatever it is you set out to do, always being happy . . ."

I glanced over at Aunt Maude, who had remained silent, head bowed over her knitting.

I shook my head. "Chloe," I said, "you don't know me at all. Not at *all.*"

And to be honest, I wasn't sure that she wanted to.

Later that night, trying to drift off to sleep, I thought about the conversation with Chloe. I had managed to avert an argument because we brought an end to the discussion about our parents. But I hadn't stopped thinking about it.

I found it amazing that she saw my life so differently than the way it actually had been. She knew nothing about my relationship with Beau. Nothing about the guilt and the heartache I experienced falling in love with a married man. She had no way of knowing about the child I'd lost and how much I'd still love a child of my own. No, Chloe didn't know about other failed relationships with men or that all my life I only wanted to find that special person—that one person who would love me above all else. Somebody I could be completely open with and know it wouldn't change his love at all.

My sister knew none of this, and yet . . . it seemed she resented me. I had the feeling that in her own misery and disappointment with herself and her life, she had come to see *my* life in a fictional way. The way she wished it could have been for her—the way it truly had not been for me.

Before I fell off to sleep I had the realization that that discussion with my sister had opened a door on our relationship. A door that led me to understand two things—I was now beginning to grasp the meaning of Chloe's behavior over the years, and the uncomfortable feeling that my sister had always wanted what *I* had.

❧ 11 ❧

By the time mid-October arrived, my aunt, Chloe, and I had managed to carve out an amicable routine of living together. The discussion concerning our parents had not been brought up again, and although I can't say my sister and I had grown any closer, we had managed to avoid confrontations.

Annie's whining caused me to turn over in bed and find her sitting on the floor staring up at me. Glancing at the digital clock, I saw that it was 5:48. A bluish light was filtering into my room telling me, along with Annie, it was time to begin my day.

"Good morning, girl," I said, swinging my legs to the floor.

Walking over to press the button on the coffeemaker, I continued talking to her. "Let me hit the bathroom, throw on some clothes, and you and I are heading to City Park to watch the sun rise."

Within ten minutes, fortified with a mug of coffee and Annie trotting along beside me, I headed down Second Street. Autumn had finally arrived, bringing the long-awaited cooler mornings, and I decided to spend a bit of time on the beach.

Walking toward the shore, I said a silent *thank you* that the beach area was totally deserted. Unclipping Annie's leash, I let her do her thing while I settled myself on the edge of the sand. I loved this time of day, when I could let my mind wander and sometimes even come up with all kinds of brilliant thoughts. I enjoyed planning my day, going over my to-do list and getting myself ready for the surprises that each new day usually brought.

Taking a sip of coffee, I recalled the delivery of furniture to the carriage house the day before. My plan for the morning was to get on the computer and do some research on those forums that my aunt had mentioned and then continue with the website design to advertise our knitting retreats, and then maybe I could . . .

My thoughts were interrupted by Annie and another dog barking loudly. Damn. Somebody had arrived to intrude on my solitude.

I turned around to see Annie happily scampering with an adorable wheaten color Scottish terrier. And Lucas Trudeau laughing as he watched them.

"Good morning," he hollered, and waved.

My first thought was, *Oh crap, here I am in grungy shorts, a stained T-shirt, no makeup on and barely awake.* But my second thought was, *Damn, he sure looks good first thing in the morning and an intrusion he's not.*

"Hey," I hollered back, noticing again how well this man wore a pair of jeans and how the bronze of his tan accentuated his good looks.

"Hope I'm not intruding," he said, walking toward me and then settling himself on the sand. "Duncan and I try to come down here every morning to begin our day. Isn't it great? With the water and the sky and the sun?"

Wishing again that I was a bit more presentable, I ran a hand through my hair and was grateful that maybe my curls gave a casual rather than messy appearance. "It is. It's gorgeous here."

"Did your furniture arrive yet for the carriage house?"

"Yes, yesterday, and it really looks great. Now I'll be busy setting up my office in the loft and finishing up the website design. How about you? Still on target to open the coffee shop this Friday?"

"Everything's on track, but it sounds like you'll be kept busy, and hey, if you don't have the time to stop by to help me with the machines, I'll certainly understand."

"Oh, no, I love being busy, and besides, I'd really like to help you. I think it'll be fun."

That killer smile crossed his face. "Good. Well, if you're free tomorrow morning maybe you could stop by and give me a quick course in coffee making."

"Sounds like a . . . plan." I had to catch myself to not say *date*.

Annie came bouncing over to me, tail wagging. Duncan was right behind her and I smiled. "Hey, girl, got your new friend with you?"

Lucas laughed. "She's a cutie."

I put out my hand to let him sniff it. "You're such a handsome guy, Duncan." Cuddling Annie to my chest, I said, "Yes, Mom approves."

Lucas laughed. "It looks like these two really hit it off, doesn't it?"

"Annie's very dog friendly, and it seems your Duncan is too. How old is he?"

"Just turned four. And Annie?"

"Well, we're not real sure. She was a stray and showed up at the coffee shop a few months ago, but the vet thinks she's about a year old."

"And you rescued her? That was a nice thing to do."

I ruffled the top of her head and smiled. "Yeah, I couldn't not take her in. I think we were meant for each other."

A look of wistfulness seemed to cross Lucas's face. "That's a wonderful thing when that happens." He jumped up and glanced at his watch. "Well, we need to get going. It's almost seven."

"Oh, us too," I said, clipping on Annie's leash. And then I had a thought. "Would you like to come by later today and take a look at the carriage house? We're still in the process of arranging things, but it's really beginning to shape up."

"Oh, I'd like that. Would after lunch be okay? Say around two? I'll close the bookshop for an hour."

"Perfect," I said.

"Duncan and I like walking downtown, so we'll head over to Dock Street now before heading home."

"And I'll see you later today," I said, before walking away.

After preparing myself a cup of tea I went outside to the carriage house. Standing on the flagstone walkway, I looked at the tabby structure and smiled. Sunlight glinted off the glass front. Our sign, done by a local artist, was suspended from a wrought iron bracket and hung to the side of the doorway. BLUE MOON KNITTING RETREATS was etched into the wood, and below it was an outline of the island, with a ball of yarn and needles inside and a blue moon hovering above it. We had come up with the perfect logo for our new business.

Unlocking the door, I stepped inside. The workmen had done a great job with the paint and border print, the furniture my aunt and I had selected blended perfectly, and the huge posters hanging on the walls showing scrumptious colors and fibers of various yarns added a cozy feeling to the room.

"This is *très chic.*"

I turned around to the sound of Lucas's voice and smiled. "Do you like it?"

Walking inside, he nodded. "I do. Very much," he said, as I saw his glance taking in the furniture and posters. "It will be ideal for a group of knitters. And that, up there?" he asked, pointing to the loft. "Will that be your office?"

"Yes. My computer and desk were also delivered yesterday. Come on, I'll show you," I said, leading the way up the staircase.

We stood in the large room that overlooked the main room below. Lucas walked over to the oak railing and looked down.

"You have a wonderful space for your office. I'm sure you'll be very happy here."

I walked over to the computer and booted it up. "I'll show you what I have done so far on our website," I said, sitting in the professional-looking leather office chair my aunt insisted that I get. I pulled up the website and could feel Lucas leaning over my shoulder as I caught a whiff of sensual, spicy aftershave.

Fumbling with the keys, I said, "Here it is. I only have a bit more to complete and I'll be up and running live, which means hopefully the phone will start ringing with bookings."

"I like it very much," Lucas said, as the spicy scent seemed to get stronger and sent my thoughts racing to things not at all connected to websites.

"Thanks," I said, pushing a bit on the chair to indicate I was standing up.

Lucas nodded his head. "Yes, your site has a very professional look to it. I have no doubt the business will be a huge success."

"We're hoping it will be," I said, heading to the staircase with Lucas right behind me. "Knitting is a very big . . ." My words were cut off because about halfway down, I tripped and could feel myself being flung down the rest of the steps where I ended up in a heap on the floor.

"*Mon Dieu!*" I heard Lucas exclaim as he raced down the remaining steps and knelt on the floor beside me, an arm around my shoulder. "Are you okay, Grace?"

I wasn't sure what had created the tears that blurred my vision—the pain in my right ankle or the genuine concern in his voice.

Embarrassment canceled out the pain. *Talk about a klutz!* "Ah, I think I'm okay," I managed to say. "How incredibly stupid of me."

Before I knew what was happening, Lucas was removing my sneaker from my swollen foot. "Stay here," he commanded. "I'll run inside and get some ice from Maude. Do you think we need to call nine one one?"

Oh, Lord, just what I need—an ambulance telling the entire island how klutzy I was. "No, no ambulance. Really, I'm fine," I said, making an attempt to stand up.

"Here, let me help you over to the sofa."

Lucas reached under my arm and gently brought me to a standing position. "Are you able to put any pressure on that foot?"

I turned to say *I think so* and realized his face was inches from mine. The spicy scent seemed to invade all of my senses and for a brief moment pressure on my foot was the last thing I was thinking of.

I quickly regained my equilibrium and did as I was told. "Yes," I told him. "I can put enough pressure to make it to the sofa."

With Lucas's arm around me—and I won't lie, it felt mighty good—I limped my way to the middle of the room.

"Okay," he said, taking charge again. "Sit right there and I'll go get that ice."

I watched him jog out the door and over to Aunt Maude's apartment. This wasn't good. And I'm not referring to the fall. I was beginning to feel way too attracted to Lucas Trudeau, and for the first time in ten years, the same type of feelings I'd had for Beau Hamilton were returning—and based on how that had ended, these feelings for Lucas had me concerned.

"Oh, my goodness," I heard my aunt say, and looked up to see her scurrying inside the carriage house, ice pack in hand. "Oh, Gracie, dear. You poor thing." She proceeded to kneel on the floor beside my swollen foot and apply the ice pack. "Are you sure we shouldn't call an ambulance? Are you in much pain?"

Actually, the pain was beginning to subside with the coldness of the ice. "No ambulance. I think I just twisted my ankle. I can't believe I fell down those stairs."

"Well, most accidents happen at home," my aunt said.

"What happened?"

The three of us turned to the sound of Chloe's voice.

"I'm afraid poor Gracie had a tumble down the stairs, but it seems to be just a twisted ankle, thank goodness."

I didn't miss my sister's glance going from me to Lucas.

"Yeah," I mumbled. "We were upstairs and I was showing Lucas my office and coming down . . . well, I guess I missed a step or something."

Lucas sat beside me on the sofa. "I'm just glad it wasn't anything more serious."

"Well, the ice should help," Chloe said, and then, as if dismissing the entire episode, she said, "It really looks great in here, doesn't it? I think it'll be the perfect place to gather those knitters. Speaking of which, did you finish up the website yet, Grace?"

So much for sisterly compassion. "Not quite. I planned to work on it this afternoon."

"You'll do no such thing," my aunt said. "You're not climbing those stairs again today. Lucas, maybe you'll be a dear and assist Gracie into my sitting room. We'll get you situated on the sofa in there."

"Of course," he said, standing up and once again putting an arm around me he managed to help me wobble my way out of the carriage house.

After I was situated on Aunt Maude's sofa, a cup of tea beside me, I realized that Lucas had closed the bookshop. "Oh, Lucas. You need to get back downtown to reopen your shop. I'm sorry I've kept you here so long."

"No, no. It's not a problem. That's one of the benefits of owning your own business." A smile crossed his face. "But it does look like you're in very capable hands now with Maude. Oh, and by the way, I'll certainly understand if you can't make it down there tomorrow to help me."

As if, I thought. "I'm sure my ankle will be fine by tomorrow. I'll be down after lunch, and thanks for all your help."

"You take care of yourself, and just let me know if you can't make it."

12

My foot was better the next morning—at least enough to allow me to meet Lucas as planned. I walked, with only a tad of a limp, into his bookshop and was greeted with that killer smile I was coming to love.

"Ah, the patient is better, I see," he said, coming to give me a kiss on each cheek.

"Much. Thank you. Aunt Maude insisted I barely move until this morning, so it had a good chance to heal."

"Very good. Then we can get started on you teaching me to become a coffee maker."

I followed him into the coffee café and let out a gasp. "Oh, Lucas, it looks wonderful," I said, as I realized he'd followed my suggestions to a tee. Wrought iron bistro tables and chairs lined the entire wall, and two love seats and a few cushy chairs filled the middle space. "It's certainly more upscale than Coffee, Tea and Thee was. I love it. I just love it."

"Then I'm glad," he said, a warm smile covering his face. "I hoped that you would."

My glance went to the coffee machines behind the counter. "Okay, let's get to work. But I have a feeling you're going to be a good student and learn quickly." I now saw the large sign hanging on the wall behind the counter listing the prices of various coffees and teas. "We'll go through your list one item at a time. You might want to take notes," I said, and smiled when he held up a notebook and pen. I loved an organized man!

I had been right. By the end of the afternoon, Lucas displayed the ability to operate the coffee machines and had an understanding of the various terms.

"I think we both earned a double espresso," he said, preparing the machine before setting two demitasse cups on the counter.

A soft whooshing sound filled the room, along with the aroma of great coffee.

I pulled up a stool to sit across the counter from him. That had been fun. A few hours of something so simple, yet I had enjoyed it tremendously.

As if reading my mind, he said, "That was fun, and thank you for being such a patient teacher."

"My pleasure," I said, lifting my cup to touch his. "And here's to great success. You officially open tomorrow, right?"

He nodded. "Yes. If you get a chance, perhaps you could stop by."

"Absolutely. I'll have to come and check on my star pupil."

"How's your sister doing? Do you think she likes it here on the island?"

"It's always hard to tell with Chloe. She's such a private person. Most of our conversations have been very generic, but I think she wants to like it here and settle in. My aunt and I are taking her to the yarn shop this evening. Monica has resumed the Thursday knitting nights for the winter, so we'll introduce my sister to the other women."

"That'll be good for her," he said, as I got up to place my cup in the sink behind the counter.

As I did, I dropped the napkin I'd been holding. Both of us bent down at the same time to retrieve it, and like the day before, our faces were inches apart. Neither of us moved for a second, staring into each other's eyes. But this time before I had a chance to pull away, Lucas leaned forward and placed his lips on mine with a soft, gentle kiss. I stood up slowly as he did the same, and now I was looking up into those gorgeous deep brown eyes, unsure what to do next. I felt his hands go around my waist as we continued standing there.

"That was nice," he said, before bending his head and allowing his lips to connect with mine again.

I slid my arms around his neck while savoring the intensity of his passion, which matched my own. His tongue slid inside my mouth, allowing me to remember what it felt like to experience desire and feel desired. As my libido began to notch up, I heard bells ringing in the distance. It was Lucas who broke our embrace, and I realized the *bells* I heard were the wind chimes on the bookshop door indicating he had a customer.

Lucas ran a hand through his curls and gave me a slow, sexy smile. "I'm sorry," he said. "That we got interrupted."

I returned his smile and let out a deep sigh. "Me too."

"Thank you again for your help."

I nodded. "I'll drop by tomorrow," I told him. "You know, just to make sure the coffee business is going okay."

I headed home along Second Street in a daze. What was that all about? Yes, I had suspected that Lucas liked me, but his kiss indicated a definite attraction. I think I could now tell Suellen that *acquaintance* no longer defined our relationship, but I wouldn't tell her what a great kisser this man was. I was still reeling from the emotions his kiss had stirred up. My mind wandered to the few guys whom I'd dated over these past ten years. None of them had had the impact on me that Beau Hamilton had created—none of them, until Lucas Trudeau. It seemed that up until now an invisible line had been drawn and Lucas hadn't been willing to step over it, despite the fact that from the first time I'd met him I felt a chemistry pulling us together. I didn't have the best track record with men, so prior to his kiss I felt maybe that chemistry was wishful thinking on my part—which I knew now it wasn't. One thing I did know for sure—I was becoming more and more attracted to Lucas Trudeau.

And did I want to risk possible heartache again?

* * *

I walked into the garden to find Chloe reclined on a lounge working on a gorgeous Aran sweater.

"That's beautiful," I said, sitting beside her and leaning over for a better look. "For you?"

"Thanks. No, it's for Mathis. He's working in Paris now, you know."

My nephew was working in Paris? "No, I didn't know. Actually, I don't know him or Eli very well at all."

Chloe nodded and continued knitting. "I know that—and it's my fault for not staying in touch with you and Aunt Maude. But yes—Mathis is working for a company that transferred him to France. He speaks fluent French—must be in our genes—and he loves it there. Although I don't hear from him much."

Amazing. My sister actually admitted that it was her fault for the lack of relationship I had with her sons, but I also noticed she had stopped short of saying *I'm sorry*. "And Eli?" I asked. "Where is he?"

"Living and working in Manhattan. He's with an accounting firm and seems to enjoy his work, but I don't hear from him very often either."

I wasn't sure what to say, so I remained silent.

"Years ago I thought I was doing it all the right way. The perfect wife for Parker—learning how to properly entertain for his clients, joining so many organizations and committees that would make him proud, being the perfect mother to Mathis and Eli. But I can see now that I didn't do any of it right."

The emptiness my sister felt came through in her words. I remembered what that deep void could feel like. "Nobody's perfect," I told her. "You were a good wife and a good mother." I refrained from saying *it's the sister relationship you never got right*. "People change. Kids grow up and become their own person. Life changes and . . . we have to change with it. For what it's worth, I think you're doing well. Because it's not easy starting over."

Chloe laid her knitting in her lap and looked at me. "You'd know that, wouldn't you? Coming here, alone, ten years ago. I'm not sure I could have done that all by myself."

Was my sister paying me a compliment? "Can I ask you something, Chloe?"

"Yeah."

"Why didn't you stay in touch with me and Aunt Maude? Why was it always Parker's side of the family for holidays and get-togethers? Why did you never allow me to get to know you or my nephews? Why were Parker and his family always more important to you than we were?" All the questions of my growing-up years tumbled out of me.

Chloe bent her head and remained silent for a few moments. "I don't know. I honestly don't know," she said, reaching over to give my hand a squeeze before standing up to walk into the house.

I looked around the group seated at Yarning Together and smiled. All the women I loved, sitting companionably, talking and knitting. It seemed odd to see my sister in this group, but there she was chatting away with Eudora Foster about some knitting patterns. Our conversation from the afternoon seemed to have been a slight opening for us as sisters. I knew we still had a long way to go, but everything begins with one small step.

"Okay, ladies," Monica said, clapping her hands together. "I have an announcement to make."

"Oh, that's right." Twila Faye leaned forward in her chair. "You had that ultrasound yesterday, didn't you? So what is it? Boy or girl?"

"Yes," Monica said, as we sat there waiting for her answer.

When she remained silent, Sydney looked at her daughter. "Well, don't keep us waiting. Am I getting a granddaughter or a grandson?"

"Yes," Monica replied again.

What the heck? And then it hit me. "Oh. My. God. You're having both, aren't you?" I exclaimed.

Monica burst out laughing. "Gracie, you're so perceptive, but not perceptive enough."

"You're having twins?" Eudora said with excitement.

"Twins! Girls, boys, or both?" Polly asked.

Monica continued laughing.

"Oh. My. God," I said again, as I finally caught on. "She's having triplets. You're having *triplets,* aren't you, Monica?"

Pure joy covered my friend's face as she got her laughter under control. "Jackpot, Grace. Yes—I'm having triplets! Two boys and one girl."

Sydney jumped up to hug her daughter as the room filled with laughter and exclamations.

I shook my head in disbelief. "Wow," I said. "Wow. When you do it, you do it well."

"I'm still as shocked as you are," Monica said. "I thought poor Adam was going to pass out when the doctor told us, but I swear his feet haven't touched the ground since he found out."

"Are you feeling okay?" Sydney asked, the mother and nurse coming forward.

"Wonderful. A little large," she said, and we all laughed.

"I thought you were kind of big for only four months along," I told her.

"You ain't seen nothing yet."

"What exciting news," Dora said. "How does Clarissa feel about this?"

Monica laughed. "Over the moon. We swore her to secrecy until I could tell all of you tonight, but tomorrow she gets to spread the news at school. She's so excited about all of it, and that just makes it even more wonderful."

"This certainly calls for a celebration," Chloe said, getting up. "I'll start passing out the lemon squares that Dora brought."

"I'll help . . ." Monica started to say.

I jumped up to give her a hug. "You'll do no such thing," I told her. "Between Adam, Clarissa, and all of *us,* you're going to really learn the meaning of the word *pampered* over the next five months."

After we finished the lemon squares and coffee, I saw Aunt Maude and Chloe coming from the back room, each carrying a large wicker basket overflowing with yarn and needles. They set them down in front of me.

"This is for you," my aunt said. "All of us felt so bad about you losing all of your yarn and supplies in the fire. So we all chipped in and bought you some replacements."

I looked down at the baskets of luscious colors and fibers and then around the room at the smiling faces. Moisture filled my eyes as I reached to fondle a soft skein of dusty rose cashmere. "I . . . don't know what to say. You guys did this for me? You're the best. The absolute best!"

Drifting off to sleep that night, I marveled at all the surprises the day had brought. My sister and I seemed to be turning a corner. My friend was pregnant with triplets. Friends and family had been very generous and kind to me. All of which were very good things. But what kept playing over and over in my head was the kiss I'd shared with Lucas, leaving a warm feeling in my heart as sleep overtook me.

❧ 13 ❧

I wandered into the bookshop and wondered if a bus had stopped out front. The shop was filled with customers. I could see Lucas at the counter ringing up sales as a few more patrons waited. Glancing into the coffee café, I saw most of the tables were filled and a few people were waiting in line with nobody behind the counter to fill their orders.

"Hey, Lucas," I said, walking up to the counter.

His head shot up from the cash register and a smile crossed his face. "Grace, good morning. As you can see, I've got an overflow of customers at the moment."

"Right. And some are waiting in there for their coffee," I said, tilting my head in the direction of the café. "How about if I go in and take care of them?"

Was that relief I saw cross his face? "Oh, that would be great. Thank you."

Walking behind the counter, I smiled at the line of patrons. "Thanks so much for waiting. Now what can I get for you?"

I proceeded to whip up cappuccinos, double lattes, espressos, and anything else the customers required. I had just finished filling the final order when Lucas walked in.

"You're a lifesaver," he said, joining me behind the counter. "I don't know what I was thinking—that I'd be able to handle both the bookshop and the coffee café at the same time."

"Well, it's a Friday. The weekends are the busiest times on the island. You might want to think about hiring somebody part-time for the coffee café."

"I think that might be a very good idea." He paused for a moment. "I don't suppose I could interest you in taking the job temporarily until I can find a replacement?"

He was offering me a chance to spend more time with him? "Well, I have the website up and running for the knitting retreats. I have the phone set to take messages on any bookings when I'm not there." I smiled at the expectant expression on his face. "Yes, I think I could do this for you until you find somebody."

"Really? Oh, Grace, I don't know how to thank you."

He pulled me into an embrace as I thought, *This is a very good start on thanking me.*

"I know how," he said, releasing me and stepping back. "Dinner. Dinner tonight at my place. I'll cook for us."

Just the two of us? With no Aunt Maude? This definitely qualified as a bona fide *date.* "Oh, Lucas, you don't have to do that," I said, hating myself for being so noble.

"No, I want to. Come over at eight. I look forward to it."

Dinner alone with a handsome Frenchman? This girl didn't need to be asked twice.

"So you spent the day working there with him?" Suellen asked later that afternoon on the phone.

I took a sip of sweet tea and stretched my legs along the sofa as Annie curled up next to me. "Yup. We were pretty busy, too, so he really did need my help."

"How convenient." I heard a giggle come across the line.

I joined her giggle. "You think? Well, the best is . . . he's cooking dinner for me tonight at his place as a thank-you."

"Oh, yeah, girl. You're movin' right along."

"I guess you'll be happy to know I've bumped up from *acquaintance.*"

Suellen laughed. "Very happy to hear that. Hey, one of us may as well have some romance in her life, because it sure isn't me. Seriously, I'm really happy for you, Gracie. Hell, it's time you get involved with somebody."

I chewed on my lower lip. "Hmm, maybe."

"What's with this *maybe?* I know you're attracted to him, and from the sound of it, he's just as attracted to you."

I reclined on the pillow behind my head. "Yeah, true on both counts, I think. But that's just it . . . do I want to get involved in a serious relationship again? It's a risk."

"You can't compare every man to Beau Hamilton. You went through a tough time—not only when you were seeing him, but after you left. But Gracie, you have to be open and willing to take another chance. Lucas seems like a really nice guy. And what? Do you want to end up like me—probably passing my days drooling away in a nursing home flirting with the young male doctors?"

I let out a burst of laughter. "Suellen, you're not going to end up that way. And besides, look who's talking. I don't see you making any attempt to meet Mr. Right."

"Yeah, well, this conversation isn't about me. Now, look, put on your sexiest dress, splash on some of that seductive French perfume you own, and go have a night to remember. Oh, and take notes if you have to, but I want all the details the next time we talk."

I hung up the phone still smiling. Suellen had a way of doing that. Setting me straight. Making me think. Giving me courage.

Later, I stood on Lucas's front porch and rang the bell. I heard Duncan barking, and a moment later Lucas opened the door.

His slow, appreciative glance made me happy that I'd listened to Suellen. I'd chosen a simple, sleeveless black dress and was grateful that my foot was completely healed, enabling me to wear a pair of sexy, black strappy heels. My choice of scent, Magie Noire, lingered in the autumn air.

"*Bonsoir,* Grace. Come in. Duncan, be a good boy and go lie down."

"*Bonsoir.* No, he's fine," I said, leaning over to pat his head.

"A glass of wine before dinner?" he asked, leading the way into the living room.

"That would be great," I said, situating myself on the sofa and then wondering if perhaps I should have chosen the chair.

He disappeared into the kitchen as I took a deep breath. Duncan sat looking at me expectantly, a red ball in his mouth. "I know I shouldn't be nervous," I told the dog, as I took the ball he offered and tossed it across the floor. "But I am."

"Here we go," Lucas said, returning with a glass of red wine in each hand. Passing one to me, he sat beside me. "Now, Duncan, no more playing." The dog obediently went to his bed in the corner, gave a snort, turned in a circle, and lay down.

Lucas touched the rim of my wineglass. "Thank you so much for all of the help you've given me. I truly don't know what I would have done without you today."

I smiled. "I enjoyed it. And you made a very good decision about opening that coffee café. I think you'll do very well."

"Again, that's all thanks to your valuable input and assistance."

"We can work out a temporary schedule for the weekends until you can find somebody."

"That would be great. Tell me how the knitting retreats are coming along. When do you think you'll be starting those?"

"I actually had a message waiting for me when I got home today, and I've booked our first customers. Two sisters from the state of Washington, and she had the nicest story. It seems they're both cancer survivors and they choose a spot to go together every year. To celebrate life. And this coming year, they'd like to come to Cedar Key for the knitting retreat."

"That's a wonderful story. Very inspiring."

"I know. We're going to have our first retreat the last weekend in January. That will give us time to take bookings and finish getting things organized."

"I hope you know that I wish you and your aunt a lot of success. I think dinner is about ready," he said, standing up. "If you'll excuse me for a minute."

"Can I help?" I asked, also standing up.

"No, no. Just take a seat at the table."

I walked over to the dining table, covered with a beautiful white lace cloth. Two place settings were already arranged. I sat down and took a sip of wine. Being here, in Lucas's home, sitting at his table, about to share a dinner he had prepared, had a warm and evocative feel. And I liked it.

"Some cognac?" Lucas asked, as he headed to the mahogany bar in the dining room.

"That would be nice. What a wonderful dinner that was. I think my aunt was right that you missed your calling as a French chef." The pork had been cooked to perfection, the roasted potatoes and vegetables were superb, and I'm sure I packed on twenty pounds with his delicious chocolate mousse.

Lucas laughed as he passed me a brandy snifter filled with amber liquid. "But then it wouldn't be enjoyable. It would be a job."

"Very true," I said. I took a sip of the wonderful French brandy.

He took a sip, placed it on the coffee table, and edged closer to me. Taking my hand, he said, "I think what we have here, with us, has become more than just friendship."

I knew he was right. We had enjoyed great conversation all through dinner and I loved being in his company, but I also knew that all evening there had been an undercurrent of sexual tension between us.

I nodded and bent my head to avoid looking into his eyes.

"I like you. I like you a lot, Grace. I like spending time with you."

My head shot up and I saw his intense dark eyes. "I like you too," I whispered.

He leaned forward and I felt his lips connecting with mine. His tongue slid inside my mouth as his kiss became deeper and more passionate. He stopped only long enough to remove the glass from my hand, and I felt my body heating up as Lucas coaxed me into a reclining position. His lips found mine, and as his hand skimmed over my breast I knew I was sliding toward that point of no return. A moan of desire filled the room, and I wasn't sure if it was me,

Lucas, or both of us, but I gently pulled back, my heavy breathing matching his.

Lucas held my face in his hands, and the look I saw in his eyes was pure desire. "I want you," he said, his voice husky with passion.

I gently touched my lips to his, willing my body to calm down.

"I think you want me too," he said, now stroking a fingertip over my lips.

I remained silent, a million thoughts swirling through my head.

Lucas shifted his position, and I felt his erection against my thigh.

"But we can wait," he said, sitting up and pulling my head to his shoulder. "We can wait until you are absolutely certain."

The kindness of his words brought tears to my eyes and catapulted me back to another time, another place.

I sat up straight so that I could face him. Maybe it was time— maybe it was time to allow my fears to come to the surface. I held his hand in mine. "Lucas, I need to tell you something," I heard myself say. "There are some things that you don't know about me." I attempted to swallow the lump in my throat. "The man that I had mentioned to you—Beau Hamilton—he was my lover for almost five years." I paused for a second. "And he was married."

"I see," was all that Lucas said, the expression on his face not changing as he waited for me to go on.

"The day that I met him I didn't know he was married. I didn't know this for about three months, and when he told me, it didn't matter. It didn't matter to me in the least—because it was too late. I had already fallen in love with him." I let out a deep sigh. "And during the first few years, it still didn't matter to me because we loved each other—and he did love me. I was certain of that. But it didn't matter because at the time I wanted to keep the single, independent lifestyle that I had. Oh, I never saw anybody else. Only Beau. But I traveled a lot with my aunt to Paris for the family business, and I had no desire to answer to anybody but myself. And with Beau's marital situation, it worked well for both of us."

I reached for the cognac on the table and took a sip. "After a couple of years, Beau said he wanted more. He wanted us to be a couple in public, and he started talking about asking his wife for a divorce. Their one son was grown and gone. He said he and his wife now had separate lives."

Lucas squeezed my hand. "And so he left her?"

I let out an exaggerated chuckle. "No, I'm afraid it wasn't that easy. Lila had a history of depression, and it only seemed to get worse during the last couple of years I was with Beau. I understood and didn't want to put additional pressure on him and so . . . I continued to wait, knowing that eventually we'd be together."

"But that didn't happen," Lucas said, putting his hand to my face.

I shook my head. "No. It didn't. Because I found out I was pregnant. We had always used protection, so at first I thought I was wrong. But I saw a doctor who confirmed it. I was secretly thrilled because I'd always wanted a child. I was about three months along and had planned to tell Beau that weekend, but I had a miscarriage before that happened, and the following day . . . I got a phone call from Lila. To this day, I have no idea how she found out about me because we were always so careful—meeting in Savannah or Jacksonville, never in Brunswick or around St. Simons Island, where he lived."

"And what did she say?" Lucas questioned.

"She told me she knew about us, knew I had been seeing Beau for quite a while, and then she laughed. She said, 'Do you think you're the only one he's been seeing all these years?' She claimed she could give me names to prove what she was telling me, and she wanted to make sure that I realized that she would never grant him a divorce. Never. She knew about his affairs and was prepared to live with it."

"And you believed her?" Lucas asked softly.

I nodded. "I did. I doubted myself and everything I had shared with Beau enough to believe her." Swiping at the tears that now fell down my face, I went on. "That was when I made the decision to leave Brunswick. Permanently. Aunt Maude helped me, and never revealed to Beau where I was."

"He never knew you were pregnant? You never told him?"

"No."

"And he's still in Georgia with his wife?"

I let out a deep sigh. "Beau still lives in St. Simons Island, but... Lila passed away a few months after I left the area. Suicide. An overdose of pills." All of the hurt, the pain, and the guilt came rushing back. Tears now coursed down my face as sobbing convulsed my body.

Lucas pulled me to him. I felt his hand on the back of my head as he murmured soothing words. "It's okay. It's okay," he whispered. "Yes, love can be very difficult. But also very beautiful. And so... you want to be sure this time. You want to be certain that what you and I have will not hurt you." He kissed the side of my face as he continued to hold me. "I understand that. I understand that very well. So... we will continue being very good friends until you are ready."

The kindness and compassion... and yes, possibly love, in his words only made me cry harder.

14

I felt a bit uneasy walking into the bookshop on Saturday morning after my episode with Lucas the previous night. But he looked up from the counter and sent me that killer smile, making me feel that nothing had changed between us.

The shop was empty, and he came from behind the counter to pull me into his arms. *"Bonjour, ma cherie,"* he whispered into my ear. "How are you this morning?"

I smiled. "Over my crying," I said, and he laughed.

"Ah, but confession is good for the soul." He leaned down to kiss me and then said, "We will be okay."

I hoped he was right. "Were you busy earlier?" He had insisted I not arrive until ten even though he opened at nine.

"Nothing I couldn't handle. But Second Street is beginning to fill up, so I think the tourists are out and about."

I turned to the sound of wind chimes. "I think you're right," I said, and headed to the coffee café. "So I'm reporting to work."

The morning had remained fairly slow, and I was glad I'd brought my knitting along. I had started working on a sweater for one of Monica's babies and removed it from my knitting bag. After a few minutes, I heard a familiar voice in the bookshop. Was that Chloe? And it sounded like she was flirting with Lucas.

"Well, I'll just have to invite you to Aunt Maude's so I can cook up a traditional Southern dinner for you," I heard her say.

What the hell? I got up and walked to the archway separating the two shops. Chloe had her back to me, and it was then that I noticed that she'd begun to lose some weight. She was definitely about ten pounds slimmer than when she'd arrived on the island. And had she changed her hairstyle?

"Chloe?" I said, causing her to jump and turn around.

"Oh, Gracie. I didn't realize you were here."

Hmm, obviously. "Yes, I'm helping Lucas out by covering the coffee café on the weekends."

"Well, you're just a Jill of all trades, aren't you?" she said, a hint of snarkiness in her tone.

Choosing to ignore this, I said, "I love your hair." And I did. She now sported a very chic style. Gone was the salt and pepper color. It had been replaced with a very soft brunette, chin length, with feathered bangs. Her frumpy look had disappeared. She was wearing a pair of nice-fitting jeans and a cotton pullover sweater in a shade of pale yellow that complemented her new hair color—all of it making her looks more youthful. "Did you just get back from Gainesville?" I asked.

"I did," she said. "I found a wonderful day spa there and had a great morning. I bet they could do wonders with those curls of yours."

I felt my hand go to my hair in defense. Okay, so curls could be difficult, but I happened to like them and wasn't about to get them straightened. At least not because my sister thought I should.

Before I could say anything, Lucas reached over and fingered a few curls. "Ah, but it is these curls that make Grace who she is, no?"

Chloe sniffed, letting out a sigh. "That could be, I guess. Well, I'm heading down to City Park. Any chance you could get me a double latte?" she asked, looking directly at me with any further thoughts of flirting with Lucas now forgotten.

"Sure," I said, heading back to the coffee café.

After Chloe left, both the bookshop and café got busy, preventing any further conversation with Lucas. Before I knew it, it was almost five. After cleaning the machines, I walked into the bookshop to find him turning the sign on the door to Closed.

"Busy day," I said.

"It was," he replied, taking my hand and leading me toward the back of the shop. Putting his arms around my waist, he nuzzled his face into my hair. "Don't ever get rid of these curls. I love them."

"Thank you. I'm rather fond of them myself."

Lucas bent his head to kiss me. Not quite as passionate as the night before—but not that tame either. This time it was him that broke away first.

"What are your plans for the evening?" he asked.

"Aunt Maude's cooking tonight, so I'll have dinner with her and Chloe and then . . . I think I'll just relax with some knitting. And you?"

"That sounds like a great idea. I'm reading a good book I'd like to get finished."

"Well, I think I'll head home, unless there's anything else I can do."

Lucas smiled and kissed my cheek. "No. You've certainly helped me more than enough. Have a good evening, Grace, and I'll see you in the morning."

That had such a nice sound to it.

I walked into Aunt Maude's kitchen and inhaled the wonderful aroma of lasagna and garlic bread as Annie came running to me.

I leaned over to scoop her into my arms. "I missed you all day, too, sweetie. Were you a good girl for Aunt Maude?"

My aunt turned from the stove and smiled. "Always. And I do believe that Lafitte is beginning to enjoy her company. They had a good time chasing each other around the house earlier."

I laughed. "You decided to work at winning him over, didn't ya, girl?" I placed her on the floor and helped myself to a glass of sweet tea from the fridge before sitting down. "Can I help you with anything?"

"No. I think I'm all set. Dinner will be ready in about a half hour. Your sister should be back from Gainesville soon."

"Oh, she's back. She stopped by the coffee café before heading to the park." I took a sip of tea. "Looks like she had a makeover at that spa. Completely new hairstyle, and it's very becoming. I think she's losing some weight too."

"That's good. I'm glad to see that she's taking an interest in herself again. She's been watching her food and walking a lot, so that accounts for the weight disappearing."

"Why is she jealous of me?" I blurted out.

My aunt spun around from the stove, her face showing surprise. "Why would you think that?"

"You heard her a few weeks ago when she got on that discussion about our parents. She thought I was the favored child, the one who got all the attention and reaped all of their love. Hell, I'm not sure they ever loved me, and yet she's jealous."

Maude wiped her hands on a towel and joined me at the table. "Oh, Gracie. Human nature can be so difficult to understand. First of all, it isn't that your parents didn't love you." She fingered the edge of the tablecloth and paused, as if forming her thoughts. "I always believed it was that they simply loved each other too much. That kind of love that they had—I'm afraid perhaps it didn't allow much to be left over to love children. And that was always very sad. I still remember when I got the phone call that they'd been killed in the automobile accident in France. My first thought had been, 'Thank God they went together,' because I don't honestly think one could have survived without the other."

"I never knew this," I said softly. All of a sudden many things made sense. "Then why on earth did they even have children? If they didn't have enough love to give them."

Aunt Maude sighed. "I don't think they ever realized this themselves, but they did love both you and Chloe. Don't ever doubt that, Grace. They just loved you in their own way up to their potential."

When I remained silent, my aunt said, "And I think the way that you and Chloe are now, as adult women, has to do with the abandonment issues you faced growing up."

"Abandonment issues? What do you mean? I never felt a sense of abandonment. I always had *you*."

Aunt Maude reached for my hand. "And I tried to do my best with both you and Chloe, but I wasn't your mother. I'm sure all of this had something to do with Chloe leaving us behind when she married Parker. And Gracie . . . you know yourself that until you got pregnant with Beau's child, you truly never wanted a solid commitment from him. The relationship you had worked very well. The terms of that relationship also enabled you to be free, because in being *free* you thought he couldn't leave you or hurt you. And he didn't leave you. In the end, you left *him*."

I felt moisture stinging my eyes. Was she right? Was all of what my aunt had just relayed true? I blew a puff of air through my lips and stood up.

"Why didn't you tell me any of this before?" I asked.

"There was no need to. But you asked if Chloe is jealous of you. Probably. But I don't think it's in a vicious sort of way. She mistakenly thinks your life has been so much better than hers. She's been pretending for years, making everybody think she was happy. She wasn't, and now she has to face that fact. That isn't always an easy thing to do."

I walked over to my aunt, leaned down, and kissed her cheek. "Thank you. Thank you for sharing all of this with me."

She reached up to grasp my hand. "Gracie, I won't always be here. And when I'm gone, you and Chloe will only have each other. You're sisters. Whatever it is that's caused the divide all these years—you both need to start working to mend it."

I knew she was right.

I was filling the salad plates when Chloe walked in the door. "I'm sorry I'm late," she said, her voice breathless. "I guess time got away from me." Tossing her handbag on the chair, she smiled at both of us. "So. What can I do to help?"

Was this the same Chloe that had dropped by the coffee café earlier? My aunt and I exchanged a glance.

"I'm in the mood for a glass of wine with dinner," my aunt said. "Why don't you grab a bottle of Beaujolais from the rack and open it."

Chloe did as she was told and then proceeded to pour some into the glasses. Was that humming I heard coming from her?

The three of us sat down to dinner, and before we began, Chloe raised her wineglass. "I just want to toast both of you," she said, that smile still on her face. "You're both remarkable women and I'm glad I'm here with you."

"We're glad you are too," my aunt said. "And that new hairstyle of yours makes you look ten years younger. I like it very much."

"Thank you. I think they worked a bit of magic on me at that spa."

It was either magic or happy pills, I thought.

We began eating and after a few moments, Chloe said, "Do either of you know Cameron Marshall? He owns the jewelry shop downtown."

"Sure," I said. "Cameron's lived on the island for many years."

I noticed she was pushing more lasagna around the plate than she was putting into her mouth. "Why?"

Was that a blush I saw creeping up her neck?

"Oh, well, I had a gold chain that needed to be repaired, so I stopped in there. After I left the coffee café," she said, quickly glancing up at me.

"That's good," I replied. "Yeah, Cameron has a nice shop."

"He does. I enjoyed browsing in there while he fixed the clasp on my chain." She took a gulp of wine.

Where was this heading?

"So, is he . . . um . . . married or anything?"

Oh, so *this* was where it was all leading. I laughed. "Chloe, stop beating around the bush. You're attracted to him, aren't you?"

She looked down at her plate and continued pushing the food around. "No. No, of course not. Don't be silly."

"Well, you know," my aunt said, getting into the conversation. "You will be a divorced woman in another month, so there's certainly nothing wrong with having a male friend."

"Right," I agreed. "And just for the record—no, Cameron is not married. He's been divorced for many years. Has a grown daughter who lives in California and one granddaughter. Oh, and I'd say he's late fifties, early sixties. And a very nice man. Anything else you need to know?"

Chloe looked up. A huge smile covered her face. "Hmm, no, I do believe you covered it all, *sis*."

15

I lit some lavender incense, arranged my crystals on the kitchen table, placed my tarot cards beside them, and poured myself a glass of wine. About to sit down to read my cards, I heard a knock on the door.

"Hey, Chloe," I said, surprised my sister had come upstairs for a visit. "Come on in. Would you like a glass of wine?"

"Sure," she said, seating herself at the table. "That was a nice dinner with Aunt Maude."

What was this all about? "It was," I said, sitting down across from her.

Her glance strayed to my crystals and cards. "I remember you doing this when you were a teenager. I didn't realize you still believed in this stuff."

I smiled. "Well, I guess I found there was a lot of truth in the cards. If we pay attention. Besides, the women in our family have been reading cards for generations."

"I guess I missed that gene," she said, taking a sip of wine.

And then she completely surprised me.

"Any chance you could read mine?"

"Well . . . yeah . . . I could. Are you sure?"

Chloe nodded emphatically. "Sure, why not? None of it will probably make sense anyway."

I slid the deck across the table. "Shuffle them as much as you want and when you feel ready, set them down."

Chloe shuffled the cards, never taking her eyes from them, and after a few moments, she laid them down and looked at me. "Now what?"

"Remove the top card and turn it over."

It was the Major Arcana, Number VII.

"What's it mean?" she asked, leaning across the table.

"This card represents *awareness*."

"Awareness? Of what?"

"Well, you need to figure that out. But the translation of this card is that you need to de-clutter your mind, get rid of the past and open your thoughts so that you can really live."

"Interesting," was all she said. "Should I turn over another one?"

I nodded.

The next card she chose represented The Outsider. "This one is the Outsider. It represents feelings of being left out." Although I knew what the cards were capable of, it still astonished me how eerily correct they could be, and I didn't want to piss Chloe off, so I chose my words carefully. "It means that there may be a gate in front of you, but it's not keeping you an outsider. The gate needs to be opened and walked through."

"I see," was all she said.

"One more card," I told her. "This last card will give you meaning into understanding of your issues."

She moved her hand toward the deck and slowly removed one.

"This is simply an action card. Fire. And it represents possibilities. In other words, don't be content with boundaries. The universe has a multitude of experiences waiting for you, so you need to try something different and move out of your comfort zone."

Chloe was quiet for a few moments and then blew out a breath of air. "Wow. I always thought this was just a bunch of hooey." She took a sip of wine, her expression reflective. "I'd have to say those cards were pretty insightful. Do you read your own cards?"

"Yup."

"Do you find them to be as interesting as mine were?"

I nodded. "Sometimes I can't figure out exactly what they're supposed to mean, but if I slow down and take more quiet time, the answers usually arrive. Not to say I always like the answers."

Chloe smiled. "Well, thanks. Thanks for reading them for me. You know ... I was ... kind of wondering ..."

I waited to hear what she was obviously having a hard time saying.

She cleared her throat and picked up the cards, forming them back into a single deck. "Well, you know how I'd mentioned Cameron earlier this evening? I was wondering if you thought it might be okay if I invited him to dinner."

My sister was asking my advice? For the first time I could remember, it appeared that she was.

"Ah, yeah, sure. What did you have in mind?"

"Well, that's where I'd need your help. When I was in his shop this afternoon, he seemed overly attentive to me. I mean ... I haven't dated in years, but I haven't forgotten what it felt like to know when a man was showing some interest." She took another sip of wine. "And I think he was. So ... I just thought it might be nice to invite him here for dinner. But I don't want to appear ... forward ... so I thought maybe you and Lucas and Aunt Maude could be at the dinner also. I'd do the cooking." She paused for a moment. "Oh, maybe I should just forget it. It's probably a silly idea."

I reached across the table for Chloe's hand and gave it a squeeze. "No, no. It's not silly in the least. I think it's a great idea, and I happen to know that Cameron isn't seeing anybody at the moment. He lives alone. I think he'd be flattered if you invited him."

"Really?" The look on my sister's face reminded me of an excited teenager.

"Really," I said. "And yes, of course we'll all be here to share the dinner with you and make it a little easier."

That huge smile I'd seen earlier covered my sister's face again.

"Oh, Gracie, thanks. Okay, then. I'll go down and see him tomorrow and extend that invitation."

I had a feeling that card had been correct—some interesting possibilities were around the corner for Chloe.

After she went back downstairs, I settled myself on the sofa with my knitting. The soft strains of Mozart's Symphony no. 40 filled the room, causing me to relax and let my mind wander as I knitted.

I must have dozed off, because suddenly my eyes flew open and I had a feeling I wasn't alone. The same kind of feeling that I'd had when I first moved in. My glance scanned the room. Nothing out of place, but the room felt exceptionally cold. Nobody here except me and Annie, and she was sound asleep at the foot of the sofa. It was then that I recalled what must have been a dream. Two little girls, unfamiliar to me, had been running down a road, holding hands, laughing. They came to an abrupt stop when they encountered a long brick wall. The laughing turned to crying—and that was when I woke up.

I sat up and placed my knitting on the table. *What the heck was that all about,* I wondered. Did the two little girls represent Chloe and me? I was a firm believer that dreams sent us messages while our mind rested. I shivered and got up to close the windows.

Overtired, I thought. *You're overtired, Grace, and need to call it a night.*

When I returned from helping Lucas at the coffee shop the following afternoon, I headed up to the loft in the carriage house. Walking up the stairs, I recalled my tumble from the week before and how concerned Lucas had been.

I'd now opened my heart to him by sharing a part of myself that I'd shared with no other man since leaving Beau. The surprising fact was that it hadn't seemed to diminish Lucas's feelings for me in the least.

I sat down at the computer and smiled as I checked for any e-mail inquiries on bookings. Two more. One from a woman in Boston saying she was interested in booking the last week in January and another from a woman in Tampa, requesting the same weekend.

If they decided to book, we'd have our six reservations. It had definitely paid off for me to do all the advertising that I'd done.

I called the first one, Tara Lesley in Boston.

"Oh, my cousin and I would love to come," she gushed. "I'll give you my credit card information now and we'll be confirmed. My cousin is flying over from England. We only recently found each other in the family tree, and we're so excited about getting together. Especially since we're both avid knitters. This will be a great celebration for us. Somebody will be doing that class on intarsia, right?"

I smiled. Another great story for two of the women attending. "Yes. Eudora Foster will be doing that all day Saturday. You'd like to sign up for that?"

"Yes and also my cousin, Julia Beecham. Put us both down for the class."

I took all of the information. "Any other questions?"

"I'll be coming with my dog. Can you recommend a place to stay?"

"The Faraway Inn is pet friendly and it's only a short walk from there to the carriage house."

"Great," she said. "I'll call them when we hang up."

Next I dialed the number for Riley Jackson in Tampa.

"Oh, yes, my friend and I love Cedar Key and we want to come for a Blue Moon Knitting Retreat. I'm afraid neither one of us are expert knitters though. Will that be a problem?"

"Not at all. We are offering an advanced class on Saturday, but you can just join the group and knit whatever you'd like."

"Oh, good, then we'd like to confirm. My friend's name is Devon Hall."

After taking the rest of her information, I hung up the phone and smiled. *Well,* I thought. *Not bad. Not bad at all.* And I had a feeling that before long we'd be fully booked for months at a time.

I was about to enter all the information into our Day Runner when the phone rang and I answered to hear Suellen's voice.

"Hey, girlfriend," I said. "How'd ya know I needed a break right about now?"

"I didn't, but I'm glad you're not busy."

Her voice lacked the usual animation. "What's up?"

Before she got any more words out, Suellen was sobbing across the line.

"My God, what's wrong? Are you okay? Is it Ashley?" I gripped the phone tighter.

"No, no . . . Ashley's fine. It's Miss Dixie . . . she passed away about an hour ago. There she was doing just fine since her heart attack last year, and boom, she had another one. . . ."

Suellen began crying again.

"Oh, no!" I said. "I'm *so* sorry. Another heart attack?"

"Yup, and this one took her off to the pearly gates. I'm the one that called nine one one. She called me around five, said she wasn't feeling so good, so I rushed right over to her house. The ambulance came, and I followed them to the hospital. Within an hour she was gone. The doctor came out and told me there wasn't anything they could do. He said her heart was just worn out . . . and she's gone."

I could hear the sadness and shock in my friend's voice. "Gosh, I'm so sorry, Suellen." Why were words always so inadequate at a time like this? "Is there anything I can do? Do you want me to come up there to be with you?" I knew how close Suellen was to Miss Dixie. The woman had been more like a grandmother to her.

I heard a hiccup come across the line and then she said, "You'd do that for me? You'd really come back to Brunswick?"

Without hesitating, I said, "Of course I would! That's what best friends are for. I could drive up tomorrow."

Her crying had subsided and I heard a smile in her tone. "No wonder you've always been my best friend, but no, sugar, you're busy enough there. I'll be okay. Really. Besides, Miss Dixie had no family, and she'd always told me she didn't want a service or anything like that. She used to say, 'Once the good Lord decides it's time for me to join Him, there ain't no need to prolong my time here on Earth.' I knew her heart was bad, but gee, I didn't think her time here was that limited."

I knew Miss Dixie was in her early eighties, and Aunt Maude

was a young and healthy seventy-two, but I was still uncomfortable with the fact that my aunt wouldn't always be with me either.

"I know," I told Suellen. "Gosh, are you sure you don't want me to drive up there?" And then another thought occurred to me. Her job. Where did that leave her position at the bed and breakfast?

As if reading my thoughts, she said, "No, really. There isn't anything you can do, but thank you for offering. I'm just wondering when I'll have to close the bed and breakfast. Miss Dixie had told me that since she had no family to leave it to, it would go up for sale as part of her estate and she wanted the money donated to a charity."

"Oh, cripe! So that means that you'll soon be out of a job?"

"I'm afraid so, but . . . I have experience running the Magnolia Inn, so hopefully it won't take too long before I find something else."

My thought was, *In this economy?* But I stayed positive. "Oh, I'm sure you're right."

"Everything okay with you? Has Chloe settled in all right?"

"Yeah, everything is fine here, and I think my sister is making an attempt to turn her life around. We're now fully booked for the first retreat in late January, and I'm really excited about all of it."

"That's great. Especially about Chloe. I still can't get over what Parker did to her. I mean, she could be difficult, but still . . . she gave him the best years of her life, and look what he did in return—she's left completely alone. Sometimes life's a bitch, huh?"

"Yup, it sure can be. But it also beats the alternative," I said, thinking of Miss Dixie.

As I hung up the phone, a brilliant idea occurred to me and I hoped I could make it happen.

16

I flipped the page of the calendar on the desk to November. I had been spending more and more time in my loft office, but Blue Moon Knitting Retreats was now booked through the end of May. I got up and walked to the coffeemaker to pour myself another cup, glancing at the clock. Just after five. Lucas would be arriving shortly.

I had continued helping him at the coffee café on weekends because he still hadn't found anybody to replace me. I loved spending time with him, but my own time was becoming more limited due to the increase in the knitting retreat business.

"I'm here," I heard him say, and looked over the railing to see him enter the carriage house. The excitement I always felt when I saw him hadn't declined at all in the past two months.

"Thanks for coming over. Come on up. Would you like some coffee?"

He laughed as he bounded up the stairs. "I think I've had my quota for today, but thanks. You said you wanted to speak with me about something?"

"Yeah," I said, sitting on the daybed and gesturing for him to join me. "I had an idea. Now I want you to be honest with me if you don't think it's a good one."

"Okay," Lucas said, his expression showing he was clearly interested.

"Well, you know my friend Suellen in Brunswick . . ."

"Yes. I met her a few times when she dropped by my bookshop there."

Right, I thought. *She was there checking you out so she could decide if you were suitable for me,* but of course I refrained from telling him this.

I nodded. "Well, I'm afraid Suellen is out of a job." I went on to explain her situation.

"So you'd like me to consider her as your replacement?"

"Yeah, and of course I'll be the one to train her with the coffee machines and everything. She's very dependable and a good worker. I don't think you'll be sorry."

"I trust your recommendation," he said, and then that slow, sexy smile crossed his face. "But I won't lie—I'll miss you there."

I leaned forward to place a kiss on his lips. "I'll miss you, too, but we'll just have to spend more time together away from the bookshop."

"It's a deal," he said, running his hand down the side of my face. "So she's planning to move to Cedar Key?"

I laughed. "Well, Suellen doesn't know it yet, but yes. She's single, her one daughter is off to college, she loves visiting here—I don't think it'll be a problem at all for her to relocate."

"That's great. Seems you've worked it all out."

"Thanks so much, Lucas. I think Suellen will be pretty excited about this."

And I was right.

"You're kidding me! You want me to come and work at Lucas's coffee café? I could live on Cedar Key? Be there all the time with you? We could be best friends again like when we were kids? No more just seeing each other once a year? We could share each other's secrets and we wouldn't have to . . ."

"Whoa! Hold on and slow down, Suellen," I told her, laughing into the phone. "Let me get this straight—you think you might be interested?"

I heard her laughter matching mine.

"Gosh, no, whatever gave you that idea? Of *course,* I'm interested! I can hardly believe this is happening. It was bad enough with Miss Dixie dying, then I lost my job, and in the past week I've had no luck at all trying to find a new one."

"Well, girlfriend, you have one now if you want it."

"I accept. When can I start?"

"That's entirely up to you, but the sooner the better. I'm getting swamped with work for the knitting retreats."

"Well, let's see . . . Miss Dixie's attorney told me to honor only the bookings through the middle of the month. I've called all the others, explained the circumstances, and the attorney is refunding their deposits. So it looks like I'll be free to leave here in about two weeks. How's that sound?"

"Perfect! You'll be here in time to share Thanksgiving with us. I can't wait. Oh, and you can share my apartment until you find your own place. I have the extra bedroom."

"That would be fun and one continuous pajama party, but I can afford to get my own place. Nothing fancy. Just a small cottage to rent. So ya think you could find me something before I get there? Then I could arrange to have my furniture delivered and wouldn't have to put it in storage. I'll take you up on your offer, though, and spend a night or two at your place till I get settled in."

"Sure. I'll start looking around for you. Aunt Maude will be so happy that you're coming."

"Wait till I tell Ashley about this. She won't believe it, and she'll be so excited for both of us."

I smiled. "And now she'll have to come here to visit you, which means I'll also get to see my goddaughter."

"Oh, hey, what's the latest update with Lucas? Anything new to report? And how's Chloe doing?"

"You sure you're not just coming here to get all the current updates on my love life?"

Suellen laughed. "Well, you have to admit, it's a hell of a lot more interesting than mine is."

"Not much to report, but maybe by the time you arrive I'll have something new to share with you. And I do believe Chloe has a new male interest in her life."

"Get outta here! Chloe?"

"Yup, and you should see the transformation she's made—lost some weight, new hairstyle . . . she's looking pretty chic."

"I'll be damned. Gee, maybe there's hope for me after all. Who's the new guy?"

I laughed and went on to explain about Cameron Marshall. "Thing is, I think she's a bit shy. She's wanted to invite him for dinner but hasn't done so yet. He takes her out for coffee, and she drops by his jewelry shop, but so far it hasn't progressed beyond that."

"Well, I hope that goes well for her. After what Parker did, she deserves a little pleasure in life—may he rot in hell."

That was one of the things I loved about Suellen. She told it like it was.

"I know. Listen, I've gotta run. I'll share the great news about you coming with Lucas and I'll tell Aunt Maude. I'll give you a call when I find a rental I think you might like."

"Sounds great. Love you. Oh, and Grace . . . thank you."

"The pleasure's all mine. Love you too," I said.

Suellen arrived on Cedar Key two days before Thanksgiving. The day before her arrival I was sitting in my great room attempting to finish up the baby sweater for Monica. A knock on the door preceded my sister calling out, "Are you home, Grace?"

"Come on in," I answered back.

Chloe walked in and bent down to pat Annie before settling herself in the chair across from me.

"What's up?" I asked.

"Well . . . I . . . I asked Cameron if he'd like to join us for Thanksgiving dinner. You said Lucas was also coming, so I thought it might be a good time to have him here."

My sister had finally decided to take some action. "Great. That'll be fun, and I'm sure Cameron was grateful for the invitation, rather than be alone."

"He was. Well, he seemed to be, but mine wasn't the only invitation. He said a few other people had told him to come by for dinner and then he said he was confirming mine."

"Right. That's just what people do on this island. Nobody lets anybody be alone on Thanksgiving, so dinner invitations are offered. Since he quickly accepted yours, I'd say he likes you, Chloe." I noticed a doubtful expression cross her face. "You don't seem convinced."

"Oh, yeah, he probably does. That isn't what I'm concerned about though," she said, leaning over to run her hands through Annie's fur.

"Then what is it?"

She continued patting Annie, avoiding eye contact with me. "Well, I was . . . wondering . . . if maybe . . . you could help me decide what I should wear that day. This seems like a date to me, and I haven't been on one of those in many years. I'm not sure what's appropriate."

I stifled a giggle. My forty-eight-year-old sister was stressing about what to *wear* for a simple Thanksgiving dinner? But then it occurred to me that she was actually asking for *my* advice. Something she'd not done my entire life.

"Well, I'm planning to wear a dress or maybe a skirt and blouse, so you can't go wrong choosing that."

"Right. Well . . . I was wondering if you could come downstairs and help me look through my closet. I've considered a few items, but I'd like a second opinion."

I smiled. And that second opinion was going to be mine.

"Sure," I said, getting up. "Let's go."

I walked into Chloe's bedroom to see various items of apparel spread out on her bed.

"I thought about this," she said, holding up a rather dowdy-looking gray dress.

"Hmm, let's see what else we can find." I walked over to the bed and began sorting through the clothes. "Oh, this would be really nice," I said, holding up a pretty burnt orange dress. With scooped neckline, three-quarter sleeves, and ankle length, it was casual dressy.

"Oh, I don't know," she replied hesitantly. "I'm not sure I've lost enough weight for that to fit me again."

I passed it to her. "Try it on."

Chloe slipped out of her jeans and top and pulled the dress over her head. It fit her perfectly.

"It looks great," I said. "Seems all that extra walking paid off."

She twirled in front of the full-length mirror on the closet door. A huge smile covered her face. "It *does* fit, doesn't it?"

"It certainly does. I think you found your outfit."

"Thanks, Gracie," she said, walking toward me and then pulling me into an embrace. "Thanks so much for helping me."

I couldn't remember the last time my sister had hugged me. Amazing what a little bit of happiness will do for a person.

17

I awoke Thanksgiving morning to the aroma of coffee and the sound of somebody tinkering in my kitchen.

I walked in to find Suellen removing sticky buns from the oven.

"Hey, keep this up and I won't let you move out of here," I told her as I headed for the coffeemaker.

"Well, I have to earn my keep for a few days. Since we're having Aunt Maude's dinner at two, I thought the buns would be good with coffee this morning."

I reached for one and sat down. "You thought right," I said, then took a bite. "Oh, yummy."

"Thanks." She joined me at the table. "Annie's out in the yard. Hope it was okay to let her out there."

"Fine. Like I said, I might not let you go."

Suellen laughed. "I can't thank you enough for finding that adorable little cottage for me. It's going to be just perfect."

"There was a method to my madness," I told her. "Having you just one street away, I figured we can do lots of visiting."

"You know we will, and I'll love living so close to you. Plus, I like the idea of walking downtown and not having to use my car. Monica lives in this area also, doesn't she?"

I nodded. "Yup, a short walk to First Street."

"Where is she going today, or is she having Thanksgiving at her house?"

I laughed. "Do you honestly think Adam would let her be on her feet cooking all day? Nope. They're going to Dora's home for dinner. And Sydney, Noah, and Saren will also be there."

"Oh, that's good. It's nice when families get together."

"Well, I'm glad you could be here with us, Suellen. You're certainly part of this family."

"I've always been happy about that. Oh, almost forgot to tell you—Ashley called me earlier. She and Jason arrived at his parent's home in Savannah last evening. She said the home is to die for and his parents have been very nice to her, so I think she'll enjoy spending Thanksgiving there."

"That's good. Do you think this is serious between them?"

Suellen got up and placed her mug and plate in the sink. "I don't know. They've been dating about six months now, so I guess only time will tell."

"Yeah, and she still has two more years of college. Is she still coming down here for Christmas?"

"Absolutely! And I can't wait to see her."

The longing for that mother–child bond flowed through me again. "Oh, did I tell you? Aunt Maude also invited Rachel, her cleaning girl, and her son, Max, for dinner."

"That was a nice thing to do, but then Aunt Maude wouldn't let anybody be alone today if she could help it. How old is her little boy?"

I smiled. "Max is six and really adorable."

"And no father or husband in the picture?"

I shook my head. "Nope. She lives alone with Max and she still hasn't told us much about her background."

I got up to let Annie inside and heard her say, "Yup, everybody has a story, don't they?"

I looked around Aunt Maude's dining room table and smiled. All of the people I loved and cared about gathered together to give thanks.

Chloe, sitting next to Cameron, looked positively radiant. The burnt orange dress had been a good choice, and from the look in Cameron's eyes, it appeared he thought so too.

My very best friend from childhood was chatting away with Aunt Maude and Rachel.

Lucas was having an entertaining discussion with Max about computer games.

A year ago I never would have thought this group of people would be together on Thanksgiving.

Aunt Maude's voice interrupted my thoughts. "Let's all join hands before we begin eating," she said. "I'll say a few words, but it was always tradition when Chloe and Grace were children for us to say what we're grateful for today, so perhaps each of us can do that."

I felt my hand being grasped by Lucas on one side and Suellen on the other.

"Lord," my aunt said, "bless all of us gathered here together. Thank you for allowing me to be on this beautiful island, surrounded by loving family and friends."

"Thank you for helping me to find my way here," Rachel said.

"I'm grateful to be with my aunt, my sister, and all of you today," Chloe replied.

Cameron nodded at all of us. "I'm thankful for a good life and to be a part of your celebration."

Suellen smiled. "I'm beyond grateful for my new job, my new home, and both my old and new friends," she said.

My turn. "It's been the best of times and the worst of times for me these past few months. I'm grateful to have all of you here, which proves to me that the good outweighed the bad."

I felt Lucas reach for my hand. "I'm very thankful that, like many of you, I also found my way to Cedar Key. Life has many twists and turns, and I'm grateful for that."

All of us looked at Max, who had been sitting quietly listening.

"I'm thankful that I get to eat turkey today, because I love turkey."

Laughter broke out around the table.

"Well," Aunt Maude said, "then by all means, let's begin eating."

* * *

Following dinner, Lucas and Cameron joined Max in the garden to toss his ball while the females helped Aunt Maude in the cleanup.

I saw Rachel staring out the window at them as she dried a dish.

"Max seems to enjoy playing ball," I said.

She pulled her gaze back to me. "Oh, he does. I sometimes feel bad that he has no male influence in his life."

"I take it you're divorced," Suellen said.

After a slight pause, Rachel replied, "Yes."

"I know what that's like," my friend went on. "I raised my daughter alone. It wasn't easy, but now looking back, I'm grateful he took off and left us alone. So Max's father doesn't visit him either?"

"No. He hasn't seen Max in four years."

"It has to be very difficult trying to raise your son with no help from family. Are you in touch with your parents at all?" my aunt inquired.

Rachel reached for another dish to dry. "No, I'm afraid not. My parents didn't agree with my choice of husband, and I guess they were right. They're up in New York—I haven't seen them or been in touch for eight years."

Chloe and I exchanged a glance.

"Gosh, maybe after all this time they'd want to hear from you," my sister said. "Especially since you're not with him anymore. They'd probably love to meet their grandson. Families can be very forgiving, you know."

Rachel let out a deep sigh. "Oh, I'm sure some families can, but I doubt mine would be that way. I'm an only child. Grew up in a pretty strict Jewish family. Education was everything, and I ruined that when I dropped out of college just before graduation to marry Max's father."

Suellen was right—everybody had a story.

"We certainly all do things in life that we regret," I said. Here was this young woman with a lot of potential now cleaning for a living to support herself and her son. Yup, Lucas was also right—life had many twists and turns.

"Well," Aunt Maude said, pushing the button on the dishwasher. "I do believe we did a great job, and we'll have dessert and coffee in a little while. Let's go join the fellows outside."

I walked out to see Lucas laughing at something Max had said. He seemed to be enjoying himself tremendously, which made me wonder why he had not had children when he was married. It was easy to see that he'd make a great father.

I pulled up a chair to watch Lucas and Cameron tossing the ball to Max as Rachel sat down next to me.

"Thank you so much for inviting us here today," I heard her say to Aunt Maude. "I honestly didn't know what I was going to do about cooking that turkey that Max wanted. The travel trailer doesn't have a kitchen equipped for large dinners."

"It was my pleasure. I'm glad you could both come and share the day with us. I think Max is having a good time."

After a few minutes, Lucas left the ball playing to Cameron and joined the women.

"All ready for your training session with Grace tomorrow?" he asked Suellen.

She laughed. "I sure am, and I have a feeling she's a tough teacher."

"Right," I said, a smile spreading across my face. "But I think you'll be a good student." I had just finished joking with Suellen when we heard sirens getting closer.

"Oh, my," Aunt Maude said, walking to the gate. "They're going down G Street. I hope it isn't anything serious."

We watched as an ambulance and fire truck roared past.

"Well, how about we go inside for some of those delicious pies that I made," she said, leading the way into the house.

Later that evening Suellen and I had settled down to relax with our knitting when the phone rang. I answered to hear Adam's voice.

"I'm afraid I have some bad news to share. Saren passed away this afternoon—we were all at Dora's house and he developed some chest pain. By the time the ambulance arrived, he was gone."

"Oh! God! I'm so sorry. How's Monica and Sydney?"

"Pretty upset, but they were both glad they were with him when it happened and he wasn't at home alone. I'm sure they're also both happy that they found each other five years ago. Some people go through life never knowing their father and grandfather."

I knew he was right, but I also knew that Saren Ghetti was going to be greatly missed, and not just by his family. The entire island would mourn his loss.

∾ 18 ∾

And I was right.

Cedar Key Cemetery was overflowing with people Saturday morning. Born and raised on the island, Saren had known everybody, and I couldn't think of a single person who hadn't loved him.

Standing beside my aunt, Chloe, and Suellen, I watched Adam tighten his arm around Monica while his other arm encircled his daughter, Clarissa. Beside them, Noah Hale stood with his arm linked through Sydney's.

I glanced at the granite marker that bore Sybile Bowden's name—Sydney's mother and Monica's grandmother. No, Sybile and Saren had never been married, but they had shared a lifetime love, and both had agreed that when the time came, they would be buried together.

And now, they're together for eternity, I thought. Looking to my left, I saw Lucas standing beside Cameron. He nodded and sent me a weak smile. I wondered about this relationship I had with him—was it destined to turn into something deep and everlasting like what Sybile and Saren had shared? Only time would tell.

Following Saren's funeral, I briefly stopped by Sydney's house to pay my respects and make sure Monica was doing okay. It worried me that she was pregnant and going through a stressful situation.

I found her sitting comfortably on the sofa, a cup of tea in hand, with Adam and Clarissa on each side of her.

"I'm okay, really," she assured me. "Saren lived to be a good age and had a good life. I'm just so grateful we had him with us these past few years."

I kissed her on the cheek. "I have to get to the coffee café, but if you need anything, you call me. I'll stop by to see you during the week," I told her.

Walking into the bookshop, I found Lucas standing behind the counter, looking at what appeared to be a small photograph in his hand. His head popped up as he stuffed it into his pocket.

"Hey," he said, walking from behind the counter to greet me. "I'm glad you got here a little early. I've missed you."

He pulled me into a tight embrace but remained silent.

"Is everything okay?" I asked after a moment.

Lucas let out a deep sigh, stepped back, and ran a hand through his curls. He nodded. "Yes. Fine. I just don't like funerals."

Having lost his wife at such a young age, I could certainly understand that. I reached out to stroke his face. "I know, but it was nice of you to be there."

"You and Suellen are still coming for dinner this evening, aren't you?"

"Absolutely," I said, as she walked through the door. "And there's my star pupil right now."

"Hope I'm not late. I ran home to change after the funeral, but here I am."

"You're right on time," I told her, heading toward the café. "Come on. Let's see what you learned from yesterday."

By five o'clock it was obvious that Suellen had learned quite a lot. She had managed to work the coffee machines all afternoon with no assistance from me.

"Good job," I said, as we cleaned up. "Think you're ready to fly solo tomorrow?"

"Well, I'm gonna miss you here with me, but yes. I think I'll be just fine. I also think I'm going to love working here."

"I'm glad," I told her, raising my hand in the air for a high five. "Well, here's to the new coffee barista. I officially bestow my former title on you."

Suellen laughed as her hand connected with mine.

Later that evening Suellen and I sat at Lucas's dining room table.

"That dinner was superb," she said. "I think you're a candidate for a French cooking show on the Food Channel."

I laughed. "Don't go there, Suellen. My aunt and I already tried to talk him into being a chef, and it didn't work."

Lucas took a sip of coffee and smiled. "No, I'm afraid I enjoy cooking only for pleasure, not as a business."

"Speaking of business," Suellen said. "Are you planning to do anything with the property where your coffee shop was?"

I shook my head. "No, I don't think so. There isn't anything I want to build on it. Real estate sales are so bad right now; I think I'll just let it sit there."

"Probably a good idea," she said, glancing at her watch. "Oh, if you guys don't mind, I'm going to scoot on home. I told Ashley I'd give her a call this evening. She's due back from Savannah."

"I'm glad you could join us," Lucas said, standing up.

"Well, thank you for inviting me. I really enjoyed it, Lucas." Suellen leaned over to place a kiss on my cheek. "And don't you hurry home," she whispered in my ear.

I smiled. "If you're in bed when I get home, I'll see you in the morning," I told her.

"We can take our coffee outside to the deck," Lucas said.

"Sounds good." I followed him through the French doors. "What a great night. There's even a nip in the air."

I settled myself on a lounge as Lucas went back in the house and returned with a warm afghan.

"Here," he said, placing it around my shoulders.

I looked up and smiled. "Thank you." This man definitely had an abundance of good qualities.

We sat in comfortable silence sipping our coffee, and I felt his hand reach across for mine. This was nice. Very nice. The way I had always imagined it should be with couples who cared for each other. A certain amount of passion balanced with quiet, contemplative moments. My thoughts drifted to what it might be like to have a relationship like this along with a child in the equation. Having observed Monica and Adam, I knew that it didn't get much better than what they shared, and my old longing began to surface.

"You seemed to really enjoy playing ball with Max the other day," I said, breaking the silence.

I turned to catch the smile that crossed Lucas's face and saw him nod.

"I did. He's a great little boy. Personable and very well behaved."

"Maybe someday you'll have a son of your own," I said, and was immediately sorry I'd been so bold.

Lucas remained silent for a moment. "Oh, I don't think so."

What he said surprised me. He was only forty-six, certainly still young enough to father and enjoy a child. Maybe there was a reason he couldn't have any?

"And how about you, Grace? Is having a child very important to you?"

I was going to say no, but I let out a deep sigh and then said, "Yes. Yes, it's important. I'm certainly not one of those women who feels it's imperative to experience motherhood. I don't feel it would validate me as a woman. But . . . I think it's always been something I wanted. And I think I knew this even more when I miscarried. I could certainly live the rest of my life childless and be happy . . . I just hope that I won't."

Lucas was quiet again for a few moments and then said, "I see."

I felt I was treading into an area where perhaps we disagreed. "So you don't want children at all? You and your wife made a decision not to have any? And you're comfortable with this?"

"No, no. That isn't what I said, Grace. I just said I didn't think I'd have any. And you . . . if you were not in a relationship, would you consider an alternative means to have a child?"

I swung my legs to the side of the lounge in order to face him better. "You mean like a sperm donor?"

He nodded, and in that moment I knew immediately that, yes,

as my biological clock ticked away, I *would* consider this option. I cleared my throat. "I haven't given this any serious thought, but yes . . . I certainly would not rule out the possibility."

I saw the look of surprise that crossed his face. "So you're prepared to raise a child alone, with that child growing up to never know who the father is? You've considered all the aspects, not just for yourself but for the child as well? And do you not consider this to be a bit selfish on your part? The child, of course, has no choice. But in order to fulfill this *longing* that you say you have . . . you're willing to deprive a child of its father?"

Frankly, I had considered very little because only in the past few minutes had sperm donation seemed a realistic option, but what was totally baffling to me was Lucas's reaction to all of it. While I couldn't say he was displaying anger, it was apparent that he was upset with my thoughts on the subject.

And while I wasn't exactly angry, I did feel myself leaning toward irritation that a man I hadn't even made love with should be upset about how I might choose to produce a child.

Dropping his hand, I stood up, letting the afghan fall to the lounge. "Actually, Lucas, I don't think we should discuss this any further. And I'm very sorry I raised the subject at all. It's getting late and I think I need to get home."

Lucas jumped up and pulled me into his arms. "I'm sorry," he whispered into my neck. "I had no right to say what I did. Please forgive me."

"There's nothing to forgive. You're entitled to your own opinions."

"But I've upset you and I didn't intend to do that. Please, stay and have a glass of wine with me."

"No, I really need to get home. I'm not upset with you."

"I'll walk you," he said, taking my hand and leading me into the house.

"That's not necessary, Lucas. Really. I'll be fine walking the short distance."

"Please. Allow me to do this."

I reached for my handbag on the sofa and nodded. "Okay," I said, heading to the door.

Both of us remained silent as we walked along F Street. Lucas followed me up the stairs to the deck. As I reached for the doorknob, he turned me toward him and pulled me into an embrace.

"I like you, Grace. I hope you know how much I like you," he said, as his lips found mine.

I returned his kiss as my mind filled with the thought, *You like me? But you consider me a selfish person if I were to bring a child into this world by artificial means.*

"Good night, Lucas," I said, and walked inside, leaving him standing on the deck.

❧ 19 ❧

I had awoken earlier than Suellen the following morning, and she found me at seven o'clock sitting on the back deck, sipping my coffee. In a total funk.

"Good morning," she said cheerily as she pulled up a chair to join me.

"Hmm," was my only reply.

"Or not. What's up?"

I let out a deep sigh. "I'm beginning to think I'm just not destined to have a partner in this lifetime."

"Uh-oh! Trouble with Lucas?"

"More like trouble with *me,* I think. We had a bit of a heated discussion last night after you left," I said, and went on to fill Suellen in on the details.

"Gosh, I never knew you were considering sperm donation," she said, with surprise in her voice.

"I'm not. Well, I didn't think I was. I've never given it much conscious thought at all . . . until last night. The idea just seemed to pop into my head, and the thing is, I'm not sure at all if I'd seriously consider something like that."

"Oh . . . I see," was all Suellen said.

"What do you mean?"

"Well, maybe it's not the subject of sperm donation that irritated you as much as the fact that Lucas seems to be totally against it. In other words, he wasn't supportive at all, nor did he consider the fact that you're free to make a choice like that if you want to."

"So you think I'm being stubborn about it?"

"I didn't say that. Grace, you've always lived your life on your terms. Which is only natural. When there's no husband or partner involved, any choices you do make are completely *yours*. But . . . that changes when you allow somebody else to share your life. It's called compromise. You're not used to this. Even with Beau, you have to admit, you were your own person due to the circumstances, and he knew that even if he disagreed with you on something, bottom line was that he had no rights to object or interfere."

Maybe Suellen had a point. "And . . . I liked it that way."

"For the most part, I think you did. But when you got pregnant, all of that changed. At least it should have. You didn't even tell him you were pregnant and you were three months along. Technically, he had a right to know. Any decisions should have been shared together."

"And they weren't," I said quietly. "Well, it was a bad situation with him being married. I didn't want to back him into a corner. Any input from him would have been limited, and besides, I was going to tell him that weekend. I had just needed time to figure out what *I* was doing."

"That's my point, Grace. *You* wanted to solve the problem first before sharing any of it with Beau."

I took a sip of coffee while digesting what Suellen had said. "But wait a sec. The relationship I had with Beau and what I have with Lucas are way different. I mean, God, I really don't even know what I have with Lucas, beyond being friends. So why shouldn't I be entitled to have thoughts about sperm donation? And he pretty much said he's not interested in ever having a child of his own, so . . ."

"That's the point I'm trying to make," Suellen cut in. "You just got all annoyed with him because he didn't seem to understand where you were coming from. You didn't take the time to go more in-depth on his feelings or why *he* feels the way he does. I'm not saying you could change his mind. I'm just saying maybe you should have given a little more consideration to discussion rather than forming your own conclusions."

"Which brings me back to the fact that maybe I'm better off alone. There's certainly no rule books for the great and lasting relationship. Maybe it's just luck, and right about now I feel mine's a quart short."

Suellen stood up laughing and leaned down to give me a hug. "Hey, you've always been an optimist. Don't change now. I'm going to hop in the shower. Have to be at the coffee café for ten." Just before walking inside, she paused to look at me. "Anything you want me to say to Lucas for you?"

"Yeah, tell him I think Frenchmen are hardheaded."

"Right," Suellen said. "I won't say a thing to him."

Later that afternoon I was upstairs in the loft of the carriage house checking on e-mails when I heard Aunt Maude holler to me from below.

"Time for a break?"

I looked down to see her place a tray with teacups and cookies onto the table.

"Sounds good," I said, logging off the computer and going down to join her.

"How's it going with the bookings?" she asked, passing me a mug of tea.

"Great. We're now getting some inquiries for next fall. I have to say, I thought we'd do well, but even I'm surprised at how our weekend retreats are catching on. I think a lot of it is word of mouth. Women telling women."

"There's a lot to be said for that. We're a powerful force, you know," she said, with a smile on her face.

"Do you think sometimes women can be too self-sufficient?"

My aunt looked surprised by my question. "Well, I'm not sure I know what you mean. In which way?"

"You were part of the sixties rebellion by women. You know, burning bras and all that. Fighting for equal rights. Do you think it was worth it?"

Aunt Maude took a sip of tea before answering. "I'm not sure about the bra burning," she said, laughing, and then her tone grew serious. "But yes, I've always felt women should be considered equal in all ways. The same way that I feel that ethnic groups should be equal. It shouldn't matter the color of your skin or where your ancestors came from. All of us, as human beings, should be judged on our character. On our potential. On who we are *inside*."

I nibbled on an oatmeal cookie. "So you don't think a woman can be too strong? In her values or convictions?"

"As long as she's not hurting anybody else? No, I don't think she can be too strong. You have to remember, Grace, women only got the right to vote in 1920. I'm still appalled when I think that prior to then, women were not even supposed to have their own political views, and if they did, they were forbidden to exercise them. So yes, I feel women are fully entitled to stand by their views and convictions. But what brought up this subject?"

"Oh . . . I've just been giving some thought to various things." I took a sip of tea before going on. "How do you feel about sperm donation? About a single woman using that as a means to have a child?"

I saw the look of surprise that covered my aunt's face, but not a trace of it was revealed in her words. "I think it's entirely up to the woman involved. It must be her decision—like any other decision involving the woman's body."

"So you wouldn't be against it?"

My aunt laughed. "For myself? Most definitely. My childbearing days are over. But no, of course not. I'm not here to judge other females and what may be right for them."

"Are you sorry you never had children?" I knew I was heading toward a discussion my aunt and I had never had. Not because of my aunt's reluctance to discuss subjects with me. That was something she made sure I understood as a child—no subject was taboo, and she would always be honest with me, but up until this very moment I had never been concerned about her personal life.

"Ah, that's a tricky question, Grace. Yes and no. Until your parents died, I think I was sorry. But maybe *sorry* is the wrong word. I think perhaps *wistful* is a better word. I certainly had a full life, with the antique business and all the travel involved, but I'd wonder if maybe in my old age I'd be lonely. Yes, I always had you and Chloe, but I knew you'd grow up and have your own lives, and that's when it occurred to me so would my own child. And then your parents were killed and I had you with me full time, so I never gave it another thought."

I never knew this about my aunt, which made me realize there were other things I also didn't know. "How about a man in your life? I mean, I can't ever recall you going out on a date when I was little, and I know you didn't when I came to live with you permanently."

My aunt remained quiet for a few moments, and I worried that maybe I'd overstepped my bounds with this question.

But she reached over and squeezed my hand before saying, "Maybe the time has come to tell you my story. We all have a story, Grace. I've always felt that to not have a story is to not live life, and I did live my life to the fullest. I still do. Every single day." She reached up to secure a pin in her French twist before going on. "You're right. I didn't date when you were little. I didn't see the need to . . . because I had lost the love of my life eleven years before you were born."

"What?" I gasped. "I never heard about this. Did my parents know?"

My aunt shook her head. "No, the only one who knew was my very close friend, Bonita."

"I remember her," I said, as I recalled the exotic-looking stylish woman with mocha-colored skin. "She passed away when I was about ten."

"She did, and I've missed her every day since then. She developed cancer, and within a year she was gone. Actually, my story begins with Bonita. She was a black girl from Savannah and came from a fairly well-to-do family—her father owned a company that dealt with European antiques, and of course your father owned the antique business I worked for in Brunswick, so that's how I came to meet Bonita. Your father also had a shop in Savannah, and I pretty much ran that one and relocated there in the late fifties. Bonita and I became instant friends. It was a difficult time in the South between blacks and whites, but because of her father's business and social standings it was a little easier for Bonita. She invited me to their lovely home for dinner and that's how I met Oliver—her brother."

"Oh, wow. So you fell in love with her brother? A black man?"

My aunt nodded. "People joke about love at first sight—but I can attest to the fact, there truly is such a thing. From the moment we met . . . we *knew*."

"I can only imagine how difficult that was for both of you because of racism."

"Exactly. Oliver was a wonderful musician. Extremely gifted. He played the saxophone. During the day, he worked in the family business, but he was able to fulfill his passion in the evenings when he played at various clubs and hotels. One of his favorites was the Partridge Inn in Augusta, Georgia. So Bonita and I would book there for each weekend he was appearing, and in the Savannah area we were always at a front table wherever he was playing."

"And he was the love of your life? What happened? Was it the difference in race that caused you to separate?"

"No, although that made our love much more difficult as far as trying to arrange time alone together. We were very discreet because we knew the problems a white woman and a black man could cause, especially in the South in the early sixties. We were fortunate though—because of the business in both of our families, we were able to travel to Paris a lot, where color didn't matter. We would spend weeks at a time there together—allowed to be who we really were, simply a couple in love. Paris was where I'd grown up, so I truly felt at home there, especially with Oliver. We had been together four years when he asked me to marry him. We were going to reside permanently in Paris, where we would be accepted. He knew he could run an office for the business there and also continue his passion for music by playing the jazz clubs that were so popular. However . . . it didn't work out that way. It was 1964 and he was drafted to go to Vietnam—where he died six months later."

I felt the tears stinging my eyes as I got up to hug my aunt. "My God, I had no idea. I'm so sorry, Aunt Maude. So very sorry."

She brushed the tears from my face. "No, don't be sorry, Grace.

I've always been grateful for the experience—for the experience to fully understand what true love is. The deep lasting love that truly never dies. So I have no regrets—my one regret would have been not having Oliver come into my life, even for a brief time."

I suddenly understood so much more about my aunt. Not as my aunt, but as a woman.

"Now," she said, clearing her throat. "All this talk about sperm donation—does it have anything to do with Lucas?"

I felt a smile cross my face. "You really *are* psychic, aren't you?"

"I just know you very well, Grace. Sometimes better than you know yourself."

"Yeah, I guess it does have a little to do with him. But after hearing your story, maybe I need to do some more thinking before we discuss it."

"Perfect idea," my aunt said, standing up and putting the empty teacups on the tray. "When we allow ourselves to *think,* that's when we discover the answers."

❧ 20 ❧

The following day Suellen was moving into her rental cottage and I had agreed to meet her there at two, when the movers would arrive with her furniture. Walking over to Fourth Street, I reflected on how I still had not heard from Lucas since we parted Saturday night.

I approached the walkway of the little cottage with gingerbread trim and smiled. This place was so ideal for Suellen. Two bedrooms, two baths, with a small living room and kitchen.

"Hey," she said, opening the front door wide. "Welcome to my empty abode."

I laughed as I walked inside. "It won't be empty for long."

"I know. Oh, Gracie, I just love this place. I still have to pinch myself that I'm really here with you so close."

We both turned toward the street at the sound of a truck pulling up out front. "And here comes your furniture," I said. "Right on time."

Three hours later we were sitting on her small back deck sipping glasses of white wine. "Here's to your official welcome to the island," I told her, touching her glass with mine. "May you always be happy here."

"Thanks. And thanks so much for all your help this afternoon arranging furniture and unpacking some of the boxes."

"Well, you still have more to do, but at least we got your bed made up and the essentials put away. How was work today?" I asked, and felt certain Suellen would interpret my question as, *Did Lucas mention me?*

"He still hasn't called you?"

I shook my head and took another sip of wine. "Maybe he never will again."

"Oh, Grace, I seriously doubt that. You just had a misunderstanding, that's all. He'll get over it. He likes you—a lot. Can't you see that?"

I shrugged my shoulders and reached for a pretzel.

"Can I ask you something?"

"What?" I said, shifting in my chair to see her better.

"Are you really considering sperm donation?"

"I honestly don't know, Suellen. Like I told you yesterday, I've never really given it a lot of thought, but . . . maybe it's something I should look into. Do some research."

"But . . . well, what if you did that and then . . . well, you know . . . you and Lucas got quite serious, like fall-in-love serious. Then what? I mean, there you'd be, with some anonymous man's baby, when . . . had you waited, you might have had a child with Lucas."

"True," was all I said.

"Do you think you'd be okay not ever having a child, Grace? Have you thought about that?"

I nodded. "I have. Many times. And yes, I think I'd be quite fine, to be honest with you. I'll admit, being a mother has never been this huge burning desire inside of me. And yet, I was never like Monica either—fairly convinced I didn't want to have a child. So I guess I've always been in the middle on this subject. Believe me, I do not need to have a child to validate myself as a woman. If I do have one, it will be because I truly want to bring a child into the world to share my life. And . . . I don't know, the thought of this seems to have gotten stronger since Monica became pregnant. Seeing her so happy just kind of nudged a longing inside of me."

"Maybe that longing has to do more with love in general. Not

necessarily a child per se. Maybe you're simply searching for a connection to another person?"

I thought about this for a moment and then laughed. "You
could be right, Doctor Suellen, and when are you hanging out your
shingle?"

She joined my laughter. "I don't mean to sound like a shrink.
I'm just trying to help you sort it all out—without making a major
mistake in the process."

"Like losing Lucas?"

"Like losing Lucas," she said.

A soft mewing sound caused both of us to stand up and look
over the deck railing. Looking up at us with the most sorrowful-
looking green eyes was a gorgeous gray and white kitten.

"Aww," Suellen said. "How sweet. I wonder who he belongs to?"

I laughed. "Probably you. We have a lot of strays on this island. It's a fishing village and attracts cats. Most of the residents
keep food outside for them and so do the merchants downtown.
We have the TNR program here—trap, neuter, return. The owners
of the Faraway Inn began the program a few years ago, and to
date over seven hundred cats have been done. They trap them in
cages, get them neutered by the vet, get their injections, and when
they're recovered, they're released right back to where they were
picked up."

"Oh, wow. What a great thing to do!"

"It is, and the way you can tell if the cat has been done or not is
the ear. This one has been. See how his one ear is notched? He or
she has been spayed or neutered."

"It's a great way to control the population of unwanted cats.
Who pays for all of this?"

"Donations from the community. Cedar Key is very pet friendly,
and most people want to help out. Many times the cats find their
way to somebody's back door, and if the person doesn't officially
adopt them and make them an inside cat, they do set out bowls of
dry mix and fresh water for them every day."

Suellen set her wineglass on the table. "Come on," she said,
heading inside.

"Where're we going?"

"To the Market to buy cat food, of course."

We returned twenty minutes later and the little kitten was still sitting in Suellen's backyard. She raced back inside and returned with a bowl filled with dry cat food. I stood on the deck and watched as she inched her way down the steps, crooning to the kitten.

"Come on, little fella, I have food for you." She placed the bowl a few inches from the kitten and made her way back up the steps. "Oh, look," she said, excitedly. "He's eating!"

I smiled. Another Cedar Key cat had found a home.

After we watched the kitten consume his supper, I stayed and joined Suellen in a frozen pizza dinner. By the time I walked in the back gate and was heading up to my apartment, it was just past eight o'clock. Aunt Maude opened her door.

"Did Suellen get settled in okay?" she asked.

"Yup. The furniture arrived and I helped her get some stuff unpacked. I think she's going to love it there. Has Annie been okay?"

"Just fine. I let her outside about an hour ago. She's back upstairs. You had a delivery while you were gone."

"A delivery?"

"Yes. You might want to go up to the loft. It's up there."

I knew my aunt wasn't about to divulge one more word, so I headed to the carriage house. I walked up the stairs and sitting on my desk was a huge crystal vase filled with the most exquisite arrangement of red roses. I felt a lump in my throat as I walked over and inhaled their sensuous fragrance. A white envelope lay beside them. I removed the card inside, which read, *Grace, I was wrong. Please accept my apology. With much affection, Lucas.*

I let out a deep sigh. In that moment there were two things I knew for certain—Lucas was a very special man and my *fondness* for him had notched up another level.

Without hesitating, I picked up the phone and dialed his number. When I heard his deep, sexy voice, my heart melted. "Lucas? I accept your apology. Can we talk?"

"Yes, in person. I'll be right over," he said.

"I'm in the carriage house," I told him, and then heard the click of his phone.

Within five minutes, I heard him holler, "Grace?"

"Up here," I said, and watched him jog up the steps.

I stood up to greet him and felt myself being pulled into his arms. God, his arms felt good.

"I missed you," he whispered in my ear. "I missed you a lot."

"I missed you too. I wasn't sure I'd hear from you again."

He held me away at arm's length and stared at me with intense dark eyes. "Because of a disagreement? You are serious?"

I smiled and realized that when Lucas got excited his accent seemed to thicken. "Yeah," I said.

He pulled me close again, *"Non, ma cherie,"* he said, stroking my back. "It was a disagreement—not a parting."

A feeling of relief surged through me. "Well . . . I'm also sorry. You have a right to your opinion on certain matters."

His lips met mine, sensuous and passionate. I pressed closer to his body as desire filled me. I definitely wanted this man and yet . . . I knew I wasn't quite ready to take this step. Pulling away, I heard a deep sigh escape me, which matched Lucas's.

"The flowers," I said, pointing to the vase. "That was incredibly kind of you, but not necessary."

"But you like them?" he asked, his voice still husky.

"I love them, so thank you."

"That is what matters. They made you happy."

I couldn't help but wonder when the last time was that a man had truly cared about my happiness.

"I brought some wine," he said, indicating the bag he'd placed on my desk. "Shall we enjoy a glass?"

"Absolutely," I said, reaching for the corkscrew and two glasses from the credenza.

After he poured the deep red liquid, he lifted his glass and touched mine. "Here is to us," he said, never taking his eyes from my face. "To the present and the future."

He thought we had a future? I liked the sound of that. A lot. And did this mean he also felt perhaps we'd moved a bit further up that friendship scale?

"To us," I repeated before taking a sip. "Another great wine," I said.

"I'm glad you like it. So, tell me . . . did you help Suellen move into her new place today?"

"I did, and I think she'll like it there a lot. Is she doing okay at the coffee café?"

"Perfect, but then she had the best teacher."

I smiled and leaned over to brush my lips against his. "Thank you."

He took a sip of wine before placing it on the table and reaching for both of my hands. "May I ask you a question?"

"Yes, of course."

"Having a child . . . Is it so important to you?"

I would have preferred not going there again, but recalled what Suellen had said about discussing things. I looked down at my hands encircled in his. It looked so right. It *felt* so right. "I'm not sure, Lucas. I'm honestly not sure," I said, and felt that perhaps it was not so important to him.

He squeezed my hands. "That is an honest answer. Will you promise me . . . when you do decide and you know for sure, you will tell me?"

I nodded as the realization hit me that should I allow myself to fall in love with Lucas, I also could be giving up the possibility of motherhood. But little did I know then that even though my head wouldn't admit it, I had already fallen in love with Lucas Trudeau.

~ 21 ~

I awoke with a strange feeling—that same sensation I'd had before that I wasn't alone in the room. Opening my eyes, I allowed them to adjust to the semidarkness. Feeling chilled, I reached for the blanket, bringing it to my neck, and that was when I saw her—a misty, cloudy vision of a woman. Standing near the window wearing a beautiful, long, white, filmy dress. Her hair was pulled up and secured at the top of her head, and when she turned sideways it was then that I thought she looked vaguely familiar and I saw the bulge across her middle. Before I even had a chance to become frightened or begin to comprehend what was going on, she was gone. Just like that.

My glance flew to the bedside clock and I saw it was a few minutes before five. I hadn't realized I'd been holding my breath and now let out a swoop of air between my lips. I felt Annie at the bottom of the bed, curled up against my legs.

A dream, I thought as I became more awake. It was simply a dream. *Wasn't it?* Of course it was. All this recent talk about babies and sperm donation, no wonder I was dreaming of pregnant women. But something inside of me didn't agree.

Getting up to use the bathroom, I decided to just stay up rather than grab another hour of sleep.

Padding into the kitchen, I switched on a lamp and began preparing the coffeepot. The dream or whatever it was still bothered me. I'd never seen a ghost in my life. I wasn't even sure I believed in such a thing. But I did know that I was highly sensitive when it came to things of an occult nature. I recalled that once when I was in college our psychology professor had hypnotized the entire class as an experiment. Apparently, I had gone under so quickly that the professor called me aside when the class ended. He told me to be careful in the future if I ever went for hypnosis, explaining that I was highly sensitive to the suggestion and somebody could take advantage of this. I wondered now if my ability to be so *open* may have encouraged a ghost to appear.

"Silly," I said, pouring coffee into my mug. "You're being downright silly, Grace."

But I jumped when Annie trotted into the kitchen a minute later and startled me. I had to admit I did feel a bit edgy.

After showering and getting dressed, I clipped on Annie's leash and we headed downtown. Walking along Second Street I knew Christmas was in the air. Not only had our climate changed to a wintry feel but all of the shops were decorated with red bows and strands of garland. The large nativity scene was set up in front of city hall and the festiveness of the season had arrived on the island. When we reached City Park, I saw the huge cedar tree all decorated. During the holiday season the tree became the focal point of the park area.

After allowing Annie to run around for a while I hollered to her. "Come on, girl. We're going to pay a visit to the library."

My dreamlike visitor had continued to plague me, and I thought perhaps I could find some answers from Miss Edith, our librarian and town historian.

Picking Annie up into my arms I walked inside to find Edith behind the desk working on the computer.

"Grace," she said, looking up with a smile. "Good morning. Anything in particular you're looking for?"

Yeah, I thought. *Answers about a possible ghost.*

"Well, I know you have a lot of knowledge about town history. I was wondering if maybe you could tell me something about the people that have occupied Coachman House over the years."

"That's right. Your aunt bought the old place and you're both living there now. Well . . . I'm sure you know that it's a tabby structure and all that. But it's the people you're curious about? After it was built, Ben Coachman purchased it. That was the late eighteen hundreds. Then later EJ Lutterloh made it his home. He was the manager of the Florida Town Improvement, which was a branch of the railroads town management. I believe a few other families occupied the house after that."

"Hmm," I said. "And did you ever hear any . . . ah, you know . . . odd stories about the house itself?"

Edith began clicking the retractor on the ballpoint pen she was holding. "Like what?" she questioned.

"Oh, I don't know. Like . . ."

"Ghosts?"

I found myself gripping Annie a bit tighter and nodded. "Yeah."

"Well, as you probably know, in many old towns there are always legends of that sort."

"And was there a legend connected with Coachman House?"

"There was, although it's been so long now not many people ever talk about it anymore. But it was even mentioned in some writings. Journals that a lot of the old timers had written and passed on in their family."

"What did they say about Coachman House?"

"Actually, it was quite a tragic event that occurred. Ben Coachman was newly married when he purchased the house. At that time it was one large home, not the two apartments that it is today. I'm sure that he and his wife, Bess, were planning to fill the rooms with many children. But that didn't happen. Seems she wasn't able to conceive. However, about twelve or so years later, Bess did finally get pregnant. The terrible thing is, a couple months before she was due for the baby, she drowned. Just off shore of Cedar Key."

"Oh, gosh," I said, feeling overcome with sadness. "That *is* tragic."

Edith nodded. "So poor Ben lost both his wife and his unborn child. Bess had taken their boat out that afternoon, and although she was fairly proficient on the water, one of those storms came up that quick, before she had a chance to get back to shore. Nobody knows exactly what happened. Some say she fell overboard and hit her head. Others say she was struck by lightning. But . . . her body was never found."

The sadness I'd felt from a moment before was now replaced with a sense of eeriness. I rubbed the goose bumps on my arms. "So is she supposed to be the ghost at Coachman House?"

"Well, who really knows? It seems a few of the families that lived there after Ben sold it claim they've heard a woman crying, some have actually said they saw a pregnant woman wandering about, and a few have said odd things happened in the house. Oh, nothing bad or scary. All very benign, like clocks stopping, items being misplaced, that sort of thing. It could all just be part of some island folklore, and the strange thing is that people who claim to have seen her all describe her differently, almost as if this spirit takes on a different form depending who sees her. So it's all quite odd, but the theory is, for those who believe in ghosts, that Bess or *some* woman is searching for that unborn child."

"Hmm, I've lived here ten years. Strange I never heard about this before."

"Well, legends come and go. Sometimes people just forget the stories. And supposedly there are other ghosts around the island, so I think many times people tend to just get used to the stories and they lose their appeal."

"Hmm, could be," was all I said.

Edith looked up and held my gaze. "Why, Grace, is there any chance you may have been paid a visit by Miss Bess or somebody?"

"Nah," I told her. "I'm afraid it's only Annie and me in that apartment." If Bess Coachman or whoever it might be *was* sharing my residence, I wanted to keep her all to myself.

* * *

I returned home to find Chloe sitting on the back deck working on the *USA Today* crossword puzzle.

"Hey," I said. "What's up?"

Before she had a chance to answer, Annie spotted a squirrel in a tree and began barking.

"Must that dog bark constantly?" she asked. "God, she's so annoying."

Truth be known, Annie really wasn't a yapper dog. Well, except when squirrels were around.

Rather than reprimand my pooch, I said, "Grumpy today, are we?"

"In a pissy mood would cover it."

Annie had given up on the squirrel and come to lie beside me. "What brought this on?" My sister had been with us for two months and I had to admit this was the first time I'd seen her revert back to her nasty mode.

"My divorce became final yesterday and I guess not a moment too soon. Got a phone call this morning from one of my so-called friends. Seems Parker's girlfriend delivered a baby girl last night."

Ouch! Even though Chloe knew both of these events were going to take place, I guess the reality of it didn't soften the blow.

"I'm sorry," was all I could think of to say.

Chloe flung the newspaper and ink pen across the table. "Well, I guess that's officially the end of my life as I knew it."

I refrained from reminding her that she had retreated to Cedar Key to physically get rid of that life. "I know this isn't easy for you, Chloe. Is there anything I can do?"

"No."

I never claimed to be good in the coddling department, but I tried once more. "Okay, look, it isn't going to change anything by sitting around here being angry. How about the two of us go out for dinner tonight?"

Chloe looked at me with interest. "Really? I'm not sure I'll be very good company."

"Yeah, you will. I'll make damn sure of it. Get your dancing shoes out, sister. We're going to Frogs for dinner and then we're staying for the music and dancing. I'll give Suellen a call and maybe she'll join us. Girls' night out—to celebrate your freedom."

"Well . . . I'm not sure . . ."

"I won't take no for an answer. Get yourself all glammed up and I'll be down at six to get you."

Without giving her a chance to say no, I headed upstairs with Annie close at my heels.

Suellen had just told us about the time she got a phone call from a prospective customer at Miss Dixie's bed and breakfast and both Chloe and I couldn't stop laughing.

"No way!" I said, trying to control my giggles.

"Yup. He had to be sure the beds had headboards. At first I didn't catch on, and when I did, I lied and told him we were fully booked."

"So you think he wanted the headboard to tie up his girl-friend?" Chloe was about doubled over with laughter.

Suellen nodded. "I'm positive he did. Hey, I don't have a prob-lem with kinky sex, but geez . . . not in Miss Dixie's bed and break-fast."

I shook my head, still laughing. Leave it to Suellen to lighten up Chloe's mood. When I put out the distress call for her to join us at Frogs, she didn't hesitate, and now it seemed she had managed to bring forth some laughter from my sister.

Except for one toast to Chloe's new freedom, Parker, his mis-tress, and their new addition had not been mentioned at all.

The band had been tuning up and now launched into a great rendition of Kool & the Gang's "Celebration."

"Did you request that?" Chloe said with a smile on her face.

"I didn't. Honest. But it's certainly appropriate. Come on, sis. Let's dance," I said, taking her hand and pulling her up to the small dance floor.

We laughed our way through all the gyrations, and I knew it had been ages since I'd had that much fun. Making it extra special when the song ended, we got a standing ovation from the other patrons with lots of clapping and hooting. From the look on Chloe's face, I'd say the evening we'd just shared had been exactly what she needed.

22

When the week before Christmas rolled around, I knew we had to start planning a baby shower for Monica. She wasn't due until March, but the doctor had already indicated the triplets would most likely arrive early. I decided to give Dora a call and see if she might have some suggestions.

"Good idea," she told me. "I've been thinking about it, but I've been so busy trying to do double duty at the yarn shop and with the holidays just around the corner . . ."

"Well, I'd be more than happy to begin arranging something. And I know Suellen and my sister will want to help."

"That would be wonderful. I was scared the time would get away from me and those triplets would arrive before poor Monica had her baby shower. Well, first of all, let's choose a date. I spoke with Monica yesterday. She'd just seen the doctor and it seems she could be delivering in early February, rather than March. The doctor has her on modified bed rest right now, so maybe we should think about having it right after the first of the year. I'd hate to think she could end up on full bed rest and miss her own shower."

I reached for the calendar on my desk and flipped the page to January. "Well, how about Sunday, the twenty-second? That will give us a good four weeks to prepare, and it will be the weekend before our first knitting retreat."

"Yes, that sounds perfect. Oh, and by the way, let's have the shower here at my house. I have plenty of room, and we can just fib and let Monica think she's coming over for Sunday dinner."

I laughed. "Sounds like a plan. Okay, I'll get with Suellen and Chloe and we'll come up with a guest list and ideas for decorating and all that stuff."

"Let's make it a luncheon, and I'll do some crab salad sandwiches and make the cake."

"And all of us will pitch in with making other dishes and desserts. Okay then, I'll get back to you with more details after I get together with Suellen and Chloe."

I hung up the phone and sat staring out the window of my upstairs loft. After a few minutes I booted up the computer and typed the words *single mothers* and *sperm donation* into Google search. I was astonished at how many pages popped up.

I was also astonished at some of the statistics. According to Mikki Morrissette, founder of the Minnesota-based online forum Choice Moms, it is estimated that fifty thousand women a year start families on their own. *Wow,* I thought, *I had no idea!*

I went on to read that Jane Mattes, a New York psychotherapist and founder of the support group Single Mothers by Choice in 1981, explained the trend has roots in the 1970s feminist movement, which opened doors to better, higher paying jobs for women and the means to support a family.

Having never before pursued this line of research, I was amazed at how much information was out there in cyberspace available to women like me—contemplating having a child with sperm donation. When I went to the Single Mothers by Choice website I found a multitude of information available. Members of the group were scattered across the country. According to their site, the average age of members was thirty-five and nearly all had completed college or beyond. The site stated that almost half of the members are "thinkers"—women who have not yet decided whether they want to become single mothers. *Well, I certainly fit into that category.*

I read over their philosophy and strongly agreed with number six, where it stated the word *choice* had two implications. That a woman had made a serious and thoughtful decision to take on the responsibility of raising a child alone and the woman had chosen not to be in a relationship rather than be in one that does not seem satisfactory.

You would think that would go without saying, but I knew of so many women who married for all the wrong reasons. Although I still wasn't sure at all that I wanted a child enough to resort to sperm donation, I *did* know one thing for sure. I was very comfortable with the fact that I was thirty-six, single, and childless. My relationship with Beau had proved to me that sometimes it's better to be alone than involved in a stagnant or toxic relationship.

"Well," I said, as I logged off the computer. "You've certainly given yourself a lot to think about."

I walked out of the carriage house and found Aunt Maude sitting on her deck knitting. Attached to her needles was a gorgeous pink and white baby blanket. The eyelet lace pattern gave it the quality of an heirloom piece.

"Oh, that's beautiful," I told her, pulling up a chair. "For Monica's baby?"

"Yes. I've completed a blue one and have another blue one to go. Imagine needing three of everything for an impending birth."

I laughed. "I know. Monica may have doubted her mothering ability for a while, but she sure made up for it when she got pregnant. I have two sweaters finished and I'm working on the pink one now. Oh, I spoke with Dora a little while ago and we've made plans for Monica's shower." I proceeded to fill my aunt in on all the details.

"That's great. I know she'll enjoy that."

"I did some research a little while ago. About sperm donation."

Aunt Maude looked at me with raised eyebrows. "Did you now?" was all she said.

"Yeah, I wanted to learn more about it. According to some of the research, ten to twelve thousand single women a year visit a sperm bank. The nation's largest one is California Cryobank in Los

Angeles. Frankly, I was surprised that so many single women have chosen to go this route."

"And is this the route you might choose to go?" she asked, continuing to work away on her yarn overs and knit two togethers.

"Oh . . . I honestly don't know. I think at this point I was more curious than anything. But, I can't help but think what Suellen said. What if I decide to do this and then . . . something serious develops between Lucas and me?"

"Very good point."

"Right. Which means I certainly don't see myself rushing off to a sperm bank any time soon. I'd have to give this a lot more thought and consider all possibilities. But I can't help but feel that for a woman who's done all the research, considered the positives and negatives, is at a place in her life where she's responsible and financially stable, but Mr. Right hasn't come along—she has the *choice* to bring a child into the world and raise that child with love. Even though she's single."

"I very much agree with you," my aunt said. "Choice is a very valuable asset—an asset that every human being should be entitled to experience."

"I always feel good after talking with you," I said, standing up and placing a kiss on my aunt's forehead. "Guess I should get upstairs and feed Annie. Then I plan to have a relaxing evening knitting and watching television."

After I got Annie fed, I heated up leftover tuna casserole, poured myself some sweet tea, and was about to sit down to eat when the phone rang.

"Could I interest you in a nice grilled eye of the round?" I heard Lucas ask.

I laughed. "If you had caught me fifteen minutes earlier, yes. I was just about to sit down and eat."

"Oh, that's too bad. I was late closing the shop today, so I just got home. Our local author, Shelby Sullivan, had stopped by to sign some stock and we got carried away talking."

"She has another release coming out after the holidays, doesn't she?" Shelby Sullivan was Cedar Key's *New York Times* best seller and lived out by the airport. She wrote romance novels and had fans across the country.

"Yes, and before I forget, she said we must make a point of driving by her house to see the elaborate Christmas decorations."

"Oh, she's right! This is your first Christmas on the island, so you've never seen it. Her home is the one out on the point by the airport. She's right about the display being elaborate. She does it every year—it's like her Christmas gift to the island."

"Well, then, why don't I plan to cook dinner for you tomorrow evening and afterward we'll take a drive over there."

"Lucas, you're really going to spoil me with all your wonderful home cooking."

He laughed across the line. "Precisely. That's what I'm hoping. Come over tomorrow about five-thirty and let me spoil you."

"I'll be there," I said, hanging up.

Glancing at the plate of tuna casserole waiting for me, I realized how pathetic my cooking skills were.

After cleaning up the kitchen, I let Annie out in the yard while I went to find my knitting bag. It was on the desk in my bedroom. I picked up the tote and began to walk out of my room when I realized something was amiss. Where were the two finished baby sweaters? I knew I had placed them in a plastic zippered bag and yet . . . they were gone. I opened up the desk drawer and my bureau drawers, and looked around the room. No baby sweaters.

"Oh, this is insane," I said, standing in the middle of my bedroom as confusion washed over me. "I *know* I left those sweaters on the desk." But they were nowhere to be found.

I took the tote and walked slowly into the great room. This just couldn't be possible. Could it? I recalled a similar incident happening to Monica. Items in her house kept getting misplaced. Despite her lack of belief, she had questioned me about the possibility of the spirit of her grandmother, Sybile, hovering about. When she explained the incident, I had a strong feeling that her deceased grandmother could indeed be the culprit.

So why was I now doubting the possibility that I had a spirit lurking around my apartment? Why was I not willing to consider that somebody could be paying a visit to share a message with *me?* Maybe I didn't want to *hear* what she had to say?

Great, just great, I thought. *Bad enough I might have a ghost invading my space, but my ghost could also very well be a thief.*

❧ 23 ❧

The last time I had experienced a wonderful Christmas had been the year before my parents died, but this one was even better.

The week leading up to Christmas had been busy with parties given by the Historical Society, the Garden Club, and an open house at the bookshop and coffee café that Lucas had hosted. Christmas Eve had been spent with Lucas as we drove around the island delivering gifts to Monica and her family, Dora, Sydney, and Noah. Christmas Day was filled with good food, a gift exchange, and lots of laughter with my aunt, Chloe, Lucas, Suellen, Rachel, and Max. Being surrounded by people I loved was a true gift. What made all of it even more meaningful was having a little boy in our company. Christmas truly is about children, and Max was a delightful addition.

I picked up the gorgeous white gold bracelet from my bureau and fastened it around my wrist. Cultured pearls were spaced along the strand, and I smiled as I ran my finger over them. Lucas's Christmas gift to me. I loved it and admired his exquisite taste in jewelry.

It was New Year's Eve and we'd be welcoming in a brand-new year together. Chloe and Suellen had opted to attend the dinner and party at the Island Hotel, and Aunt Maude was going to have a quiet evening with Lafitte while she watched television.

Lucas was due to arrive in ten minutes. I took one last peek in my mirror and smiled in approval. I had finally gotten to Gainesville the week before and done some serious shopping. For tonight, I'd chosen to wear a three-piece, dark green velour outfit—slacks, tank top, and jacket. The gold sandals were perfect to complete the semi-dressy look I was aiming for.

I walked into the great room and looked around. All seemed to be in order. My small tree on the table glittered with lights. Pillar candles flickered on the fireplace and tables. Pine incense filled the air, and Perry Como crooned a Christmas carol on the CD player. Lucas had purchased French champagne the day we went to Gainesville, and a bottle was now cooling in the ice bucket.

Annie was curled up at the end of the sofa happily chewing away on a new bone Santa had brought her. With a red bow around her neck, she looked like she belonged on a Hallmark Christmas card.

I heard a knock on the back door and opened it to find Lucas looking exceptionally handsome wearing a navy blue blazer, open-collared shirt, and dress slacks. He leaned in to kiss me.

"You look like Little Red Riding Hood with that basket," I joked with him.

"My supplies for the feast I'm about to prepare for us," he said, placing the basket on the counter. He removed his blazer, hanging it on the back of the chair.

He then pulled me into his arms for a kiss that was more passionate than the one he greeted me with.

"How nice," I murmured against his ear.

He smiled that wonderful smile as he stood back and allowed his eyes to slowly scan down my body. "You look stunning. The color of that outfit is perfect with your hair."

Exactly the reaction I'd been hoping for. "Thank you."

"And I see you're a very good chef's assistant," he said, pointing to the champagne bottle.

"Oh, yes. I don't want to lose that position, so I started chilling the champagne a couple of hours ago as you instructed."

"Very good," Lucas said, putting an arm around my waist. "And now we can enjoy the results."

He removed the bottle and blotted the bottom with a towel. With the expertise of the finest sommelier in France, he uncorked the bottle without spilling a drop. After pouring the gold, bubbly liquid into two flutes, he passed one to me. Picking his up, he touched it to mine.

"Here's to us. I am so very happy these past few months to have you in my life, Grace. You mean a lot to me. Happy New Year."

The bubbles in the flute seemed to match what I was feeling—effervescent. I felt exhilarated and alive. "Here's to us," I repeated. "And I am very glad you walked into my coffee shop last spring. Happy New Year."

We exchanged another kiss and then I perched on the stool as Lucas took over my kitchen. Wonderful aromas filled the room as he prepared shrimp scampi for us. A few minutes later, I removed the rice pilaf and salad from the basket that he'd prepared at his house. I placed the bowls on the table, which I'd covered with a white tablecloth. Lighting the candles I'd placed there earlier, I watched Lucas create his magic and smiled.

After walking over to the stove, I placed an arm around his waist and kissed his cheek. "It smells heavenly," I said, inhaling the aroma of garlic.

When it was ready we sat down to enjoy our first meal to welcome in a new year together.

"*Bon appétit,*" he said, reaching across the table to squeeze my hand.

"*Bon appétit.*" I smiled and returned his squeeze. Taking a bite of the scampi, I moaned. "This is superb," I said, while trying to curtail further moaning. But I did have to admit that Lucas's cooking bordered on orgasmic.

Following dinner, Lucas and I cleaned up the kitchen together. Then I prepared coffee in the French press, which we took into the great room along with the champagne.

Lucas settled himself on the sofa. I slipped off my sandals and curled up beside him.

"That was nice," I said. "Thank you."

"Ah, but it was my pleasure. I like spending my time with you."
He leaned down to brush his lips with mine.

"I will have to make a trip back to France next year," he said.
"There's business there that I still have to attend to."

My heart fell as a surge of emptiness went through me. I didn't
like thinking about him way over there—and me over here.

"You have a passport, yes?" he questioned.

I sat up straighter to look at him and nodded.

"Good. Then perhaps you will accompany me when I go?"

"Really?" I could feel the emptiness ebbing away.

"Yes, really," he said, laughing. "I think it would be nice for the
two of us. I no longer own my place over there, but my cousin,
Jean-Paul, he has an apartment in Paris, in Montparnasse, that he
lets me use when I'm there. You would like to go?"

Without a second's hesitation, I said, "Yes. Oh, absolutely! I'd
love to."

"Then it is definite. I'm not sure when. Perhaps in October.
That's a lovely time to be in Paris."

"I remember. I loved going there in the fall with my aunt."
Lucas may have been reluctant when I'd first met him about us dating and being together, but all of a sudden it seemed like he was attempting to forge some kind of commitment between us. And I
liked it.

"I will enjoy showing you Paris through my eyes," he said. "And
in return, seeing it through yours."

I could only imagine how much fun that would be. Standing on
Pont Neuf, overlooking the Seine—kissing. Walking the streets of
the most romantic city in the world, holding hands with somebody
you truly cared about. Sipping wine at a sidewalk café, talking for
hours, watching the world go by. How many times had I dreamed
of all this?

"Oh, Lucas," I said, excitedly. "I can hardly wait. Do you ever
miss not living there anymore?"

A solemn expression crossed his face. "Sometimes, yes. But that
was another lifetime. Besides, had I not left there, I never would
have met you."

I never would have met you. His words warmed my heart. I reached up to stroke his face. "And I'm *so* glad you did."

"Then I would like to ask you something." He paused for a moment. "Do you have interest in seeing anybody else?"

His question caught me by surprise. "Do you mean like date another man?"

He nodded.

"No. I haven't given that any thought whatsoever. I like being with you. I think we have fun together and I enjoy your company."

A huge smile covered Lucas's face as he reached for my hand. "Good. Because I feel the same way." He shifted on the sofa to face me directly. "I was wondering . . . you had told me about this other man . . ."

"Beau?"

"Yes. Did you ever consider marrying him? What I mean to say is . . . had he not been married, do you think you would have considered this?"

Nobody had ever asked me this question. Not only that, I realized in that moment that I truly had never really given this any thought myself. "I'm not sure," I said, while still thinking about his question. "I mean . . . it's hard to say, since it was impossible for that to happen."

Lucas nodded. "I understand. Perhaps what I meant to ask was . . . you had mentioned that you were satisfied with the relationship with Beau, because you wanted to keep the single, independent lifestyle. You said that relationship with him worked well for both of you."

"Yes," I said, unsure where he was headed.

"Do you think you will always feel this way? Wanting to stay a single woman? Do you ever have a desire to someday be married?"

Our conversation had certainly morphed into extremely serious territory, and he was touching on subjects I'd never discussed with another man before. I wasn't sure how to answer, because quite simply, I wasn't sure I *had* an answer.

I ran a hand through my curls and let out a deep sigh. "Well . . . if you're asking if I'm against marriage, the answer is no. Of course not. However, with the divorce rate at fifty percent, I feel one has to be cautious. I certainly have never believed that a woman must be married in order to complete herself as a woman." *Like my sister,* I thought. "But yes, if a couple meet and feel they are right for each other, then yes, it could ultimately lead to marriage."

Lucas remained silent for a moment and then asked, "And you don't feel that marriage would result in a loss of freedom?"

"Well, no. But I also don't feel that two people should have to give up their own identity when they become married. Hopefully, the traits that one admires and respects in a person when they are dating will continue after they marry." I recalled what Suellen had said about compromise. "Perhaps it's a matter of learning to compromise? When somebody is alone . . . they never have to compromise," I said, slowly beginning to understand what Suellen had been saying to me. "With a partner, I think compromise is inevitable."

Another smile crossed Lucas's face and I foolishly felt like I had passed some sort of test. "Compromise is the magic word, but it's not always an easy thing to do."

Did he know this from his own previous marriage? I couldn't help but wonder if a man who seemed to understand the importance of the word was willing to compromise about having children?

"And so . . ." he said slowly. "What do you think allows this compromise to even be possible?"

Without hesitating or thinking about it, I said, "Love. I've always felt that *love* is the strongest emotion we have."

Lucas brought my hand to his lips and nodded as his intense gaze consumed my very soul. He had not uttered the words. No. But I knew, without a doubt, in the depths of my soul that Lucas loved me. And for the first time I allowed what I also felt to be acknowledged in my mind.

~ 24 ~

Dora Foster's house was a bustle of female excitement. I had arrived early along with Suellen and Chloe to do the decorating. Standing on a step stool, I reached up to secure a cluster of pink and blue balloons to the wall. I continued to work my way around the room until all the balloons had been placed.

Standing back, I smiled appreciatively. "Okay, what's next?" I asked.

Dora came out of the kitchen to place a bowl of shrimp dip on the table she'd set up in the great room. "Oh, nice job," she said, looking around the room.

Suellen and Chloe were finishing up hanging pink and blue streamers of crepe paper around the doorways.

"I think that will complete the decorating," Dora said. "Perhaps you girls can help me to bring more of the food from the kitchen."

I picked up two platters of crab salad sandwiches, while Suellen and Chloe brought out potato salad and coleslaw.

"I'm here," Aunt Maude hollered from the front door, trying to balance a gift bag and plate of cocktail meatballs.

"Here, let me help you," I said, running to assist her.

A minute later Monica's mother-in-law, Opal, showed up with Sydney right behind her.

"Ah, your famous key lime pie," Dora said, taking two pie plates from her. "And Sydney, I'm so glad you made Sybile's traditional cheesecake."

"Here we go," we heard Opal's friend, Charlie, say as he maneuvered his way through the door carrying a maple cradle.

"Oh, Opal," I said, going over to run my hand along the smoothness of the wood. "This was Adam's?"

"Yup," she said, beaming. "It sure was. Slept in there his first couple months and now my firstborn grandson will use it."

"Be right back," Charlie said, and returned with two large gift-wrapped packages under each arm. "The other two cradles. Brand new ones, but each baby will have their own."

I smiled as I helped him lean them against the heirloom cradle. By the time two o'clock arrived all the guests were seated, the gifts had been placed inside and around the cradle, the food was all arranged on the table, and we waited for our guest of honor's arrival.

A few minutes later we heard a car pull up out front. Dora ran to the window. "Shhh," she said. "Here she comes."

The door opened and Monica walked in, with Adam and Clarissa right behind her, as all of us shouted, "Surprise!"

Monica's hand flew to her mouth as she began laughing. "Oh, you guys! I thought maybe I'd escape this," she said, making her way to the chair we'd decorated in her honor.

I ran over to give her a hug. "Are you kidding? Did you really think we'd miss an opportunity for a party?"

Poor Monica attempted to get comfortable in the chair, which wasn't an easy feat considering the huge size of her stomach. Adam leaned over to kiss her. "I think you're in very good hands," he said. "Time for this male to get outta here."

We all laughed as Suellen said, "Right. Females only."

"Here, Clarissa," Dora said, pointing to the chair beside Monica's. "This is your place of honor. You'll be the one to get each gift and pass it to Monica to open."

"Really?" The ten-year-old positively beamed with pride. "Okay," she said, taking her seat. "Thank you."

After all of the gifts had been opened, Monica became overcome with emotion as she attempted to thank all of us. "I really can't thank all of you enough," she said, looking around at the baby outfits, car seats, triplet carriage from Sydney, beautiful hand-knitted baby items, and so many other beautiful and necessary gifts. "I never expected all of this. So, thank you," she said, as tears glistened in her eyes. "I love each and every one of you."

Much to my aggravation, I never did find those two baby sweaters. So I'd had to resort to quickly knitting two more—both blue this time—to go with the pink one.

"Well, then. Maybe you can finally share with us what the names will be for my new grandchildren," Opal said.

Monica laughed. "Yes, I think it's time to share that with all of you." She put her arm around Clarissa. "It was a family decision. The three of us spent a lot of time trying to decide. And ... the first-born boy will be named Saren, in honor of his great-grandfather."

Oohs and ah's filled the room. "Oh, how nice," Dora said. "Saren and Sybile would be so proud."

"I think so," Monica said. "And the second boy will be named ... Sidney. Spelled the male way with the 'i' and named for my mother."

Sydney jumped up in excitement and ran to her daughter. "Oh, wow. I'm so flattered. Thank you," she said, placing a kiss on Monica's cheek. "Imagine, a grandson named after *me*."

All of us laughed as we gave Sydney a huge round of applause.

"And the girl?" Suellen questioned. "What name did you choose for her?"

Monica smiled as she pulled Clarissa close. "Clarissa chose her name and I'll let her tell you."

"My new sister will be called Candace Opal Brooks," she said, with excitement and pride. "I like the name Candace and I wanted her to also have the initial of 'c,' and her middle name is for our grandmother."

"Lord above," Opal said, rushing over to pull Clarissa into an embrace. "I'm so honored. Thank you. You're such a special grand-daughter."

Another round of applause followed.

"Well," Dora said. "I think it's safe to say that all of us here approve of your choices, and now we can't wait to meet Cedar Key's newest additions. Time to celebrate with food."

When the shower ended, I went with Suellen to her house to borrow a pair of number seven knitting needles.

"How about some coffee," she said, as we walked into her kitchen.

Before I could answer I looked down to see the little stray gray and white kitten scampering toward me. I leaned down to pick him up and cuddle him.

"Obviously, you know you have a kitten in your house?" I said.

Suellen laughed. "Yeah, the little guy won me over. Meet my new companion, Freud."

"Freud, like the psychiatrist?"

"Yup. The evening he showed up in the yard you and I were having a discussion, remember? And you kidded me about hanging out my shingle. So . . . I thought Freud was appropriate."

"I love it," I said. "And he's such a cutie."

"He's a great little kitten. And he is a *he*. I brought him to the vet for a checkup and he confirmed it. So Freud has had all his shots and now he's an indoor cat."

"That's so great," I said, placing the kitten back on the floor. "I'm really glad you found each other. And yes, I will have some coffee."

After she'd prepared it, we both sat at the kitchen table. "So I take it things seem to be going very well for you and Lucas?"

I nodded. "Yeah, ever since New Year's Eve, it's like we turned a corner, or maybe moved ahead is more accurate."

"That's great. Maybe Lucas just needed time to be sure. Didn't want to get into a relationship before he knew what he was getting into."

"I think you could be right. We had a very in-depth discussion about how we felt concerning important issues in a relationship. I think we both ended up coming to know and understand each other much better."

"I've always felt that's how a solid relationship develops and grows. You start off as friends and you always remain friends. Of course, there's passion and a chemistry that goes with it. But the core of the relationship is rooted in both love and a genuine understanding as friends."

I nodded. "And . . . I *do* love him, Suellen." That was the first time I'd actually verbalized those words out loud.

"No kidding," my friend said.

My head shot up in surprise. "You knew this?"

Suellen laughed. "Hey, I haven't known you since first grade for nothing. Of course I knew. I think you did too. You just wouldn't admit it."

"Neither one of us has said it out loud yet."

"You don't have to. You both *know* and when the time is right, you'll say it."

"Tell me something," I said, and then paused to think about my question. "Do you see a difference between me and Lucas from me and Beau?"

"A world of difference," she said, without hesitating. "I mean, first of all, it's an entirely different situation, Grace. With Beau, there were all the secrets and being discreet. That's not needed with Lucas. But beyond that, there's another difference. And the difference is *you*. You're relaxed with Lucas, more mellow, more the person you really are inside."

"Interesting," was all I said.

"I'm not sure you ever truly loved Beau."

"Are you serious? Of course I did."

"Well, I've always felt there are various kinds of love, so maybe you're right. You might have loved him . . . but not in that deep, forever kind of love. By the way, during your discussion, did the subject of children or sperm donation come up?"

I shook my head. "No. Actually, I did a lot of research on sperm donation. I think it's a wonderful option for a lot of women. However . . . I'm not so sure now that it's for me."

Suellen smiled.

"Okay, Doctor Sue, what's the smile for?"

"Like I said, there are various kinds of love, and honey, I think you're pretty damn fortunate. Because I think you've found the lasting kind."

I took the last sip of my coffee. "Still say you need to hang that shingle out, but in the meantime, go get my needles so I don't go home without them."

❧ 25 ❧

Two surprising events occurred a few days before our first knitting retreat began.

Rachel had asked Aunt Maude if she could meet with both of us on Wednesday morning.

I walked into my aunt's kitchen to find her removing banana bread from the oven.

"She's not here yet?" I asked.

"No, but she should be along shortly."

"What's this about? Do you know?"

My aunt shook her head as she scooped coffee into the filter. "No. Not a clue."

There was a knock on the back door and Rachel walked in, a smile on her face, so I assumed the news wasn't going to be too bad.

"Good morning," she said, pulling up a chair.

Maude placed the sliced bread on the table along with coffee mugs. "Good morning, Rachel. Is everything okay with you?"

"Oh, yes. Fine, actually. But I needed to discuss something with you."

My aunt poured the coffee as we waited.

"Well...uh...I wasn't all that truthful with you when I first came here. What I mean is, I'm actually not divorced. Not yet, anyway."

I took a sip of coffee as Aunt Maude sat down. This didn't seem to be earth-shattering news.

"You see," Rachel went on. "My husband . . . well . . . he's actually in prison."

I tried not to let my surprise show too much. "Oh," was all I said, as my aunt remained silent.

"I guess I should start at the beginning. I met Dean when I was at college in North Carolina. He was from that area. My parents had met him and didn't like him at all. But . . . of course, I wouldn't listen. So Dean and I eloped, and after we got married we moved to the Miami area. He really had no special skills and hadn't been to college, so it was difficult for him to find a job. I was able to pick up a low-paying office job, but the only thing Dean could find was working for a company doing landscaping. And then once I had Max, I wasn't able to work."

I couldn't help but think—typical story, girl meets wrong boy, girl falls in love, and girl spends years regretting all of it.

Rachel took a sip of coffee. "So it was a pretty rough time, but then all of a sudden Dean began bringing more money home. He told me he got a promotion at work and . . . I believed him. I just knew that financially it was getting easier. We were even able to purchase a very nice home in a very nice neighborhood." She let out a deep sigh. "Life really did get much better. We had a new car to drive, we were able to take weekend trips with Max in the travel trailer, but even though we were doing well my parents still wanted nothing to do with me. I had tried a few times to contact them after Max was born, but it didn't work out."

"That's really a shame," Aunt Maude said as I nibbled on a slice of banana bread wondering where Rachel's story was going.

"I missed them. A lot. But they refused to give Dean a break at all. And then . . . one evening the cops showed up at our front door looking for him. I thought it had to be some kind of mistake . . . but it wasn't. Dean was a drug dealer."

"Oh, my God," I said, leaning forward in my chair. "And you never knew this?"

"Not at all. He handled the money, so I had no idea exactly how much we had. I just knew it was enough to have a good lifestyle. Stupid me."

Not as stupid as you might think, I thought, as I recalled Sydney Webster's story and so many others like her.

"And so . . . they did find Dean, arrested him, and he didn't make bail. He was found guilty at the trial and sentenced to five years. I was so horrified and embarrassed by all of it, I took Max and the travel trailer and I left."

"Oh, wow," I said. "So that's when you came here to Cedar Key?"

Rachel nodded. "Right. And . . . Dean has no idea where we're at."

"So you ran away with your son?" Aunt Maude said.

"I did. Not that he'd miss either one of us. I'm certainly not excusing the fact that what I did was probably wrong, but Dean was never at home during that last year. Max really needed a father around and he wasn't there for either one of us."

"Sounds like a case of survival to me," my aunt said.

"That's what my dad said when I called him last week."

"You called your parents?" I asked.

Rachel nodded. "I figured, what did I have to lose? So I told my dad the truth about Dean, admitted that I'd made a terrible mistake, and that's what he said. When he found out that I'd taken his grandson and gotten away from that situation, it seemed he was proud of me. He said something about always knowing I'd survive."

"That's wonderful," I said. "So now you have contact with your parents again?"

"It's even better, and that's what I wanted to talk to you about. My dad asked if I wanted to come home. He said Max and I were welcome to come to New York and stay with my parents till I got on my feet. He also said he'd handle getting an attorney so I could divorce Dean and start over."

"That *is* wonderful," Aunt Maude said. "So you'll be leaving us?"

"Well, not right away. I told my dad I hated to take Max out of school midyear, and he agreed. But yes, I'll be going to New York in May when school finishes, and my parents are planning a trip down here next month so that they can finally meet their grandson."

"I'm so happy for you," my aunt said. "We're certainly going to miss you, but how great for you and Max."

"Gosh, I agree," I told her. "We'll miss you, but this is great news."

"So I wanted to let you know right away. You know, so that way you could be looking for another cleaning girl."

"That was very thoughtful of you," my aunt said. "But you're not to worry about that. I'm sure we'll find somebody."

"Thank you for being so understanding," Rachel said, getting up to give my aunt a hug.

The second piece of news came that evening from my sister. My aunt had made a New England boiled dinner and insisted I join her and Chloe.

I walked in to find Chloe setting the table. "Hey," she said, looking up with a bright smile on her face. "Could you uncork that Cabernet I just brought home?"

"Sure," I said, reaching for the bottle. "Where's Aunt Maude?"

"In the other room on the phone with somebody from the Garden Club."

A minute later she joined us and I passed her a wineglass.

"Thanks," she said, before taking a sip. "I just have to get this smoked shoulder sliced, so if one of you could start removing the vegetables into bowls, we'll be eating shortly."

I began spooning potatoes, carrots, turnips, and cabbage into the serving bowls.

The three of us sat down, and I noticed Chloe seemed to be unusually happy.

"How's Cameron?" I asked.

"Oh, he's good. He's leaving next week to fly out to California to visit his daughter and grandchild, but he'll be back mid-February."

Well, that couldn't be what was making my sister seem perky.

"I got some interesting news today," she said, and both my aunt and I looked up with interest. "I was at the yarn shop—oh, have you seen the new sugarcane yarn that Monica got in? It's really scrumptious. I got the prettiest shade of green to make a scarf. Anyway, while I was there, Dora told me that Monica's thinking of selling the yarn shop."

"What?" both my aunt and I said at once. This was the first I was hearing about this.

"Yeah, but listen," Chloe said. "Monica feels that once the triplets arrive she really won't have enough time to devote to the shop. But she doesn't want to just close it or let it go out of the family. So . . . she's offered to sell it to Dora."

"Oh, thank goodness," my aunt said. "I think we're really spoiled having the yarn shop here on the island."

"Right," Chloe continued. "So Dora was telling me about this and she said it had always been her dream to own a yarn shop, but she doesn't feel she could run it alone. And so . . . she's asked me to be her partner."

"Are you serious?" I said. Now I understood the reason for my sister's perkiness. "Are you going to do it? That would be great."

"I think I am," Chloe said. "Maybe it'll give me a chance to finally use that degree I got in college so many years ago. Hey, I have the money to invest in the partnership, so why not?"

"Oh, Chloe," my aunt said. "I'm so happy for you. I agree. I think it would be a wonderful opportunity for both you and Dora. You like each other, you're both expert knitters, and it would enable each of you to have some time off when you needed it. I'd say this is a win–win situation."

Chloe smiled. "I think so too. Gosh, it's hard to believe how miserable I was just a year ago, and now . . . I'm going to be part owner of a yarn shop." She held up her glass of wine and tilted it toward me and my aunt. "I'm really glad I'm here. You've both helped me through a really tough time."

"I'm glad too," I found myself saying. And I meant it.

"That's what family's for," my aunt said, sending a wink in my direction. "I'm proud of both of you. You've both managed to walk through some difficult times and get to the other side."

"So when do you think that you and Dora will be the official owners of the yarn shop?" I asked.

"Monica said we're free to run it together now, but we'll do the official paperwork after she delivers the triplets. So probably around May when she gets back on her feet."

"Are you planning to change the name of it?" my aunt questioned.

"No. Dora and I discussed that. We like Yarning Together, and besides, yarning represents the cute word that Clarissa used to call knitting, and Yarning Together is still appropriate."

"Oh, good," I said. "I liked Spinning Forward, the name Sydney called it, but Yarning Together is different."

"Oh, I have some other news," Chloe said. "You just might finally be getting rid of me. I stopped in at Pelican Realty today to see what was for sale on the island. The Hale Building on Second Street is available . . . and I think I'm interested. The two apartments upstairs are vacant, and I could live in one of them and rent the other. Tony's Restaurant downstairs has a lease, and I'm sure somebody might be interested in leasing the small shop next door."

"Wow! You're just full of surprises," I said. "So you'll be a yarn shop owner and landlord to a couple of businesses. That's great."

"That *is* great, Chloe. I think that would be an ideal situation for you, and you could walk to work from your apartment," my aunt told her.

"Yeah. I'm going to go take a look at it tomorrow. Who knows, maybe I'll end up being a bona fide part of this community."

I laughed. "This island has a way of making that happen. A lot of us come here as a *retreat,* but we end up settling in and never leaving."

"Are we all set for the knitters to arrive on Friday?" Chloe asked.

"Yes, I believe we are," my aunt said. "I think we have a great group of women coming for our debut weekend. I'm looking forward to getting to know them."

"And the weather looks like it'll be great for the Blue Moon ceremony Sunday evening on the beach," I said.

Chloe got up to clear the plates from the table and begin stacking them in the dishwasher. "As much fun as I'm sure the original ones were, I'm rather glad we won't be sleeping all night on the beach."

I laughed as I helped her to clear the table. "Yeah, the one I attended with Monica was fun, but I agree. I think we'll be able to accomplish what we hope to from five till seven. It'll be a nice way to finish off the weekend."

My aunt began wrapping up the leftovers. "And you both have chosen a quote to read Sunday evening?" she asked, sounding like a parent checking on a child's homework.

Chloe and I both laughed. "Yes, Auntie, I have mine."

"Me too," I said. "And Suellen has been tuning her guitar, so we'll have some music. Oh, do we have the candles?"

"We do," my aunt said. "I found some nice ones in Gainesville."

"Then the only thing left is the arrival of the ladies on Friday morning." I had to admit that I was excited about the upcoming weekend.

❧ 26 ❧

I was up by six Friday morning, took Annie for a quick walk, got myself together, and was in the carriage house by eight, but Aunt Maude was already there preparing coffee when I walked in.

"Good morning," she said, a huge smile on her face. It was obvious that she was in her element and was going to enjoy these weekends.

"Aren't you the early bird? What can I do to help?"

"I have muffins and bagels. Maybe you could start putting those out on a plate. Chloe will be over shortly to help."

Just before nine, the table was arranged, Dora and Suellen had arrived, and soft music was playing on the CD player.

"Hello," somebody hollered from the doorway. "Do we have the right place?"

I looked over to see two women who appeared to be in their early thirties. Both were tall and slim, wearing jeans and sweatshirts. One was exceptionally attractive with blond spiky hair that had a strip of green, a nose ring, and a tattoo of a butterfly on her lower arm. The other was more subdued, with little makeup and long dark hair that hung in a single braid down her back.

"Riley and Devon?" I asked, walking toward them with my hand outstretched.

"Yeah," the blonde said. "I'm Riley, and this is my friend, Devon."

"Welcome." My aunt gestured toward the table. "Come on in. We have coffee, juice, and some muffins and bagels."

"Great. I'm starved," Riley said. "We left Tampa at five this morning."

"That was Riley's idea," her friend replied. "I told her I'd pay for the extra night to come yesterday, but she wouldn't hear of it. She's been frugal since kindergarten."

Suellen and I looked at each and laughed. "Ah, yes," she said. "Being childhood friends allows you to really know each other." She went on to explain that we'd also been friends since we were little.

A minute later the final four women arrived.

"Everybody help yourselves to some coffee and food. I'm Maude Stone," my aunt said, and then introduced the rest of us. "Find a nice cushy seat and then we'll all get to know each other."

After we got seated, Riley and Devon introduced themselves first.

"I'm Tara Lesley, and this is my cousin, Julia Beecham."

Both women looked to be early sixties, with dark hair and a resemblance that bordered more on sisters than cousins.

"Oh, that's right," I said. "Julia, you're from England, aren't you?"

"Yes. I flew to Boston last week to stay with Tara for a few days before we drove down here."

We looked at the other two women sitting on the love seat.

"I'm Martha Bellingham, and this is my sister, Rebecca Chase. I live in Washington State but flew to Tampa last week to stay with Rebecca before we drove up here yesterday."

"Well, how nice that all of you could join us for the first knitting retreat weekend," my aunt said.

"I hope I'll leave here knowing how to knit better." Riley got up to refill her coffee mug. "I'd sure love to know how to knit cables."

"I'd bet anything that by the time you leave here on Monday, you'll be an expert," Suellen said. "How long have you been knitting?"

"Only about three months." She paused for a moment. "My . . . ah . . ."

"Her mother passed away last August," Devon continued. "I thought it might be good for her to learn how to knit, so we both signed up at a local yarn shop in Tampa."

What a caring thing to do for a friend, I thought.

"Knitting can be excellent therapy for many things," Dora said. "Well, don't worry, Riley. Suellen's right. You'll be making cables before the weekend's over."

Chloe and I got up to remove the empty plates and coffee cups. "Okay, ladies," I said. "Time to begin knitting. Let's see what everybody's working on."

Julia produced a few rows knitted in gorgeous self-striping colors of pale yellow, blue, and melon. "I just started this yesterday. We went downtown to Yarning Together to get some new yarn. This will be a jumper—well, in American terminology, a sweater— and is being done in mohair and wool from Plymouth Yarn Company."

"Gorgeous," I said, reaching over to touch the soft fiber. "And what do you have there, Tara?"

"A tunic that I began working on last month. The yarn is Cotton Fleece, and I just loved this shade of blue. As you can see, it has cables so I'd be more than happy to sit with Riley and teach her how to make them."

"That would be great," Riley said, reaching in her bag to produce a beautiful shade of soft pink yarn. "I was hoping to make myself a scarf."

"And I'm making a fairly simple afghan for my sister. She's getting married next year," Devon said, holding up a lovely piece of work done in blues, purples, and various shades of green. "The pattern is just knits and purls and easy to follow."

"I'm working on some mock cable dishcloths," Rebecca said. "No cable holder is required because it's not a proper cable stitch.

It's fairly easy to do. You just skip the first stitch on the left needle, knit in front of the second stitch, then knit the first one and slip both stitches off the needle at the same time." She held up squares in blue, beige, and yellow. "I donate these for different organizations and bazaars."

"How clever," Suellen said, getting up to take a better look. "I'd love a copy of the pattern."

"I donate preemie beanies to our local hospital," Martha said, holding up two that were done in a soft cotton yarn using three different colors. "The new moms really love these, and of course they keep the tiny heads warm."

"Oh, I like that idea," Chloe said, taking one of the caps to inspect it. "I'd like a copy of this pattern. This might be a nice project for our knitting night at the yarn shop." She removed a half-finished sweater from her bag in a deep navy color. "This is for one of my sons. It's done in a basket weave pattern, which tends to be masculine."

"And I'm working on some lacy socks for my daughter, Marin," Dora said. "She loves wearing hand-knit socks."

Aunt Maude held up a gorgeous afghan in a rippled pattern done in shades of brown, tan, and beige. "This is going to be a raffle item for our Women's Club fund-raiser."

"My daughter, Ashley, love shawls," Suellen said, holding up a work of deep purple lacy stitches. "So this is for her."

"As for me," I said, reaching into my tote bag. "I'm making a sweater . . . for the man in my life." I held up the beige sweater with diamond stitches. "It's actually fairly easy."

"Ooh, I love that!" Riley said. "How did you get those diamonds in the pattern?"

"With cables," I told her. "See what you'll be able to do as soon as you learn how to do those cables?"

Riley laughed. "Yeah, and I can't wait."

"Okay," Maude said. "Then let's get started. Dora, you're teaching the intarsia class, and I believe Tara and Julia signed up to take that. So perhaps the table will be the easiest place for you gals to sit.

And Grace, maybe you can help Riley with her cables since Tara is taking the class."

"Great," I said, getting up to sit next to Riley on the sofa.

"And the rest of us can just relax and knit."

I was shocked when I glanced at my watch and saw that it was already twelve-thirty. The soft buzz of conversation had filled the room for over three hours as all of us got to know each other better.

"Well, ladies," Aunt Maude said. "We'll be breaking for lunch shortly. I'd say it was a very productive morning."

"I'll say." Riley got up and stretched her arms above her head. "I think I'm getting the hang of these cables."

"You certainly are," I told her as I walked to the kitchen area to begin helping Aunt Maude, Dora, and Chloe set out plates, silverware, chicken salad sandwiches, potato salad, and coleslaw.

"Oh, Riley," Devon said, as her friend held up a few inches of her new scarf. "It's gorgeous. Now you'll have to teach me how to do those cables."

"If you have extra yarn with you," Chloe said, placing a pitcher of sweet tea on the table, "we could get you started while you're here."

"I don't. But I can leave here a bit early this afternoon and run downtown to the yarn shop."

"Who's covering the shop today?" I asked Dora.

"Sydney's there. She was the original owner," Dora explained to the group. "She's my niece, and now her daughter, Monica, owns the shop."

"But not for long," I said, laughing.

Chloe nodded. A smile covered her face as she explained about the upcoming plans for her and Dora.

"Isn't that great," Martha said. "Keeping it in the family. I really like that."

"Oh, me too," Rebecca piped in. "And how nice that you all live here near each other. Martha and I have to resort to visiting a few times a year."

"But it sounds to me like you really make those visits meaningful. Why don't you tell everybody why you planned this visit to Cedar Key," I said.

"Well," Martha explained, "my sister and I are both breast cancer survivors. And once a year we plan a trip somewhere together—to celebrate life."

"Oh, that's so cool," Riley said, reaching for a sandwich. "With my mother gone, I really don't have any family left. I'm an only child and my father and I . . . well, we don't see eye to eye on a lot of things. He didn't approve of me leaving Florida five years ago to pursue my acting career in California."

"Oh, you're an actress?" Suellen asked.

Riley shook her head. "Nah, just a wannabe. I tried. Had some auditions, but . . . they didn't lead anywhere. Trying to get a break is downright impossible. Then my mom got sick with cancer and I came back home last year. She always supported me though. She was always my strongest ally—when I put the green strip in my hair, she laughed. When I got a nose ring, she said, 'On you, it looks cute.' And when I got my tattoo"—Riley skimmed her fingers across her forearm—"she said 'Ouch!' So I really miss her support. My dad thinks I'm a complete screwup, but he's never taken the time to understand me."

"That's a shame," Aunt Maude said. "Family is very important. People might not always agree and see eye to eye . . . but in the end, family is what sustains us."

I glanced up to see my aunt's gaze on me, a smile on her face.

"And sometimes one doesn't even realize the family they have," Julia said.

"What do you mean?" Dora asked.

Tara laughed. "Do you want to tell our story or should I?"

Julia's laughter joined her cousin's. "I think it's your turn."

"Well," Tara began, "my father had a brother and they both served in World War Two at the same time, stationed in England. I grew up always hearing my mom tell the story that my dad was actually engaged to a woman in England during the war, but he came home, met my mother, . . . and ended up sending a telegram to this other woman saying he'd changed his mind. He was marrying somebody else."

"Oh, that's sad," Chloe said.

"Yes, except if that hadn't happened, I wouldn't be here telling you this story," Tara said, causing us all to laugh.

"His brother, who is my uncle, was married before he left for the war. Now fast forward to over sixty years later, and I receive an e-mail—from a girl in England asking if I'm the daughter of so and so, from Salem, Massachusetts. I was. The e-mail went on to say that she had reason to believe we were related and from the same family."

"Oh, my gosh!" Devon exclaimed. "What an amazing story."

"It gets better," Tara said. "Come to find out, the girl writing the e-mail was Julia's daughter, Sally. I wrote back right away, and pieces of the puzzle began to fall into place. But for a little while, I questioned if perhaps Julia was my *sister* and not my cousin, because of that woman my father had been engaged to."

"Oh! Wow!" Riley said, leaning across the table fully engrossed in the story. "But you're cousins, right?"

Tara nodded. "Yes, and the evidence that proved it was due to the fact that Julia's father had to have been in England in November of 1944, because she was born in August of 1945. My father was part of the Normandy Invasion and therefore left England late May 1944, according to a diary he had kept. So of course, he wasn't there when Julia's mother became pregnant. But my uncle was, and it was his name on Julia's birth certificate anyway. Julia never saw the official copy of her birth certificate until a few years ago when her son and daughter began working on a family tree and genealogy, after her mother died."

"Did your mother ever share any of this with you?" Aunt Maude asked.

"No. She always refused to talk about it. All she'd tell me was that my father was an American but had been killed in the war."

"Do you think he knew about you? And you never got to meet him?" Dora questioned.

"That's part of the puzzle we'll never have an answer to—whether he knew about me or not. And no, unfortunately, I never got to meet him. That's why I'm so grateful to have at least found my cousin." Julia reached over to give Tara's hand a squeeze.

"And I'm just as grateful," Tara said. "I was the only girl on my dad's side of the family—all boy cousins. It took over sixty years, but I finally have my female cousin. And—our grandmother's name was *Julia*. Julia was named after our grandmother."

"That is such a cool story," Riley said.

Aunt Maude shook her head. "And I think it only proves once again that truth is definitely stranger than fiction."

Over dinner that evening Chloe informed my aunt and me that she'd looked at the building and apartment on Second Street, fallen in love with it, and had made an offer.

"That's great," I said. "When do you think you'll hear something?"

"By Friday. So I'm hoping they'll accept and I'll have a place of my own."

"I've loved having you here," Maude said. "But yes, we all need our own space. Especially women, according to Virginia Woolf."

"Right," I said. "According to her, a woman is to have money and a room of her own if she is to write fiction."

Chloe laughed. "Well, I'm not planning to write anything, but it'll give me some personal liberty. Something I've never really had."

"Tony's Restaurant is downstairs, but what do you plan to do with the empty shop next door?"

"I'm not sure yet. I think I'll advertise for a tenant. Somebody might want to open a small business there."

"Well, look at you—my sister, the new land baron on Cedar Key. Good for you, Chloe. I'd say you're coming into your own."

Chloe laughed. "Yeah, at age forty-eight, guess it's about time."

Our conversation then drifted to how well our first knitting retreat had gone.

"Such nice ladies," my aunt said. "All six of them."

"I know, and I love how they're sharing about themselves and telling their stories." I reached for another delicious biscuit my aunt had baked.

"I think they all represent the embodiment of women." Maude took a sip of sweet tea. "The sisters went through a scary and life-changing ordeal. The cousins had a delightful story of finding each other and proving life is full of surprises, and I think Riley and Devon are on a good path for their own destinies. They're both young, but I think they're both willing to face life head-on."

"It was a lot of fun," Chloe said. "I really enjoyed it—way more than I thought I would—and now I'm really looking forward to the Blue Moon ceremony Sunday evening."

When I went upstairs later I realized it had been a while since I'd done a tarot reading for myself. After lighting some sage and cedar incense, I sat at the kitchen table with the deck in front of me.

I let my mind wander and then removed three cards. Turning over the first one, once again the card representing Beau Hamilton stared up at me. *What is it with his card now appearing regularly?* Before turning over the next card, I allowed myself to think about him—something I seldom did.

I wondered if he was happy and if his life was going well. Beau was a decent person. So was I, and neither one of us had entered that relationship with the intention of hurting the other. Those things just happen.

I fingered the cards as Lucas came into my mind and found myself comparing what I felt for him with what I'd felt for Beau. Similar, but very different. I had loved Beau, and yet—it wasn't a forever kind of love, which I was beginning to think I had found with Lucas. My entire relationship with Lucas was different. The one word that came to mind was *free.* I was free to be exactly who I am. With Beau, due to the circumstances, I always felt on guard. Always concerned that we might be seen together, that his wife would find out, and the guilt that I tried to push down was always simmering just below the surface. Certainly not good qualities to forge a lifetime relationship.

I let out a deep sigh and pushed the cards aside. Maybe Lucas's grandmother was right. Maybe one should look beyond cards for the answers in life.

I awoke Sunday morning filled with anticipation about the Blue Moon ceremony that evening. Milky blue light was filtering through the blinds. I felt Annie curled up beside me. As I reached out to stroke her fur it was then that I glimpsed a vision in the corner of the room. Misty at first, the form took on shape, and I realized it was the same woman I'd seen before—but this time she wasn't pregnant. She was wearing the same long white dress, which now reminded me of an old-fashioned wedding gown. Her figure was slim and willowy. I attempted to adjust my eyes to see her more clearly and saw her smile at me.

I heard the soft words, "You are learning to find your own answers. Do not question them. Listen to your soul and follow your destiny."

I blinked and saw the form begin to fade. She disappeared so quickly I now questioned if she had really been there. And did I actually *hear* her say that? Or did I only hear those words in my head?

What the hell is going on?

Annie stirred and I swung my legs to the side of the bed. Getting up, I slowly walked to the corner of the room, which was empty. Looking down at the oak floor, I gasped. There, neatly folded, lay the two baby sweaters that I had knitted for Monica's baby—and had misplaced.

I bent down and tentatively reached out my hand to touch them. They were real. The exact sweaters that I had searched for and been unable to find. I clutched them in my hand, feeling the soft fiber, wondering yet again about a possible other dimension we had little knowledge of.

Later that afternoon at the carriage house all of us were knitting away when Riley brought up the subject of ghosts.

"Do you all believe in them?" she asked.

I got the feeling that Riley had no qualms about being different both in her manner of style and her philosophies.

After a few moments of silence Aunt Maude said, "Well, I don't *not* believe in them. Have you ever witnessed any?"

"No, not exactly. But . . . I sometimes have *feelings*. And I think it's my mom and she's with me. It's almost like she's trying to tell me something."

I decided to bite the bullet and was prepared for laughter and disbelief from the group. "Well, I happen to have a *visitor* in my apartment. She's appeared to me twice," I relayed, and went on to explain about the possibility of Bess Coachman or another spirit.

There was no laughter, and all six women leaned forward, putting their knitting in their laps.

"What do you think she wants?" Martha questioned.

"I'm not sure she wants anything," I said. "I'm beginning to think maybe she's trying to guide me, force me to figure some things out in my life."

"Wow, that's amazing," Devon said. She turned toward her friend. "See, Riley, I told you you're not crazy. You really *could* be feeling your mom near you."

Julia nodded. "Oh, yes, definitely. I'm sure all of you know that England is famous for having many spirits hovering about. Be open to it, Riley. Don't discount an experience that could be beneficial to you."

"I agree," Aunt Maude said. "I think many times if we pay attention, much insight is gained."

"Gee," Chloe said, picking up her knitting. "I wonder if there'll be a ghost in the building I might be purchasing downtown."

"I wouldn't doubt it," Dora said. "That's a pretty old building, just like Coachman House is, and that's where they seem to hang around." She cleared her throat. "Well . . . that is, if you believe in that sort of thing."

Chloe smiled. "And I have a feeling you do, Miss Dora. Hmm, maybe I'll be lucky and it'll be a male ghost. Tall, dark, and handsome. Oh, and a wonderful housekeeper and chef. He'll cater to my every whim."

The room erupted in laughter.

"You wish," I said, shaking my head. I liked this new sister of mine. I liked her sense of humor and the mellowness that now seemed to surround her.

By the end of the afternoon, Riley had perfected making cables, Tara and Julia had learned intarsia, other knitting projects had been completed and new ones begun. But most of all, eleven women had bonded in the age-old ritual of female friendship, which would be further cemented during the Blue Moon ceremony.

28

At five o'clock that afternoon as the sun was descending in the western sky, all of us gathered on the beach at City Park.

Chloe and Aunt Maude were uncorking bottles of wine while I poured and passed each woman a glass. Riley was playing a haunting New Age melody on her flute while Suellen was strumming similar chords on her guitar.

"Okay," I said, after the wine had been distributed and I was holding up my glass. "I want to propose a toast to the first knitting retreat weekend. May you take away what you need and leave the rest behind. The six of you will always be extra special to us because, well . . . you were the first."

"Here, here," the crowd said, as all of us touched glasses together.

After taking a sip, Suellen placed her glass on the table and picked up her guitar. This time the sound was lively and upbeat, and I recognized the music from the song by Sister Sledge, "We Are Family."

Shoes were removed as Suellen proceeded to lead us along the edge of the shore into the water, playing her guitar, our voices singing the lyrics, as each woman held the hand of the woman in front of her.

"That was great," Chloe said, attempting to catch her breath.

"It certainly was," Dora replied, still laughing.

"I don't think I'll ever forget this weekend." Tara plunked down onto the blanket.

"Me either," Julia said, joining her.

"You know," Dora said, looking at Riley. "I think we need to hear 'Amazing Grace.' That was one of my sister Sybile's favorite songs, and it was the two of us that had the first Blue Moon ceremony here on the island. Think you could play that?"

Riley nodded, and the lilting sound of the music filled the air as we all quietly listened.

When she finished, a round of applause followed.

"That was very appropriate," my aunt said. "Thank you, Riley. And also thank you to you, Dora, and Sybile—who I have no doubt is right here with us."

"Okay," I said. "Let's all form a circle and hold hands."

Once everyone had done this, I said, "Now let's close our eyes. Focus on sounds and smells and energy surrounding you. Allow yourself to become one with the water, the sky, and the beauty of the island. Take in some deep breaths and slowly blow them out. Think about what you might want to bring into your life and what you might want to discard."

I closed my eyes and did exactly that. I thought about Beau Hamilton, and for the first time in ten years I wasn't consumed with guilt. Or regret. Or thoughts of what might have been. Instead, I saw Lucas's face. Although he had never uttered the words, I felt his love. I felt it deep in my soul, because it matched the love I felt for him. I inhaled deeply and blew out a breath. It was finally time to discard what I had shared with Beau. Beau was meant to cross my path for many reasons, but he wasn't meant to remain in my life. I was almost certain that Lucas Trudeau was. I took in another breath, exhaled it, and knew deep inside that the time had come to discard Beau completely and focus on a lifetime with Lucas.

I opened my eyes to see the vivid pinks and purples, red, and orange of the setting sun and sky.

"Does everyone have their candles?" I asked.

Heads nodded as the women retrieved them.

I went around and lit each one before rejoining the circle and lighting my own.

"Okay, it's now time to read the verse that you've chosen and explain how it pertains to you and why you chose it." I reached into the pocket of my long, gauzy skirt and removed a slip of paper. "I'll go first," I said, clearing my throat. "I chose a verse by one of the most influential writers of the French Renaissance, Michel de Montaigne. 'If a man should importune me to give a reason why I loved him, I find it could no otherwise be expressed, than by making answer: because it was he, because it was I.' " I blew out a breath as my gaze locked with my aunt and then Chloe. "I've come to believe that certain people cross our path in life for different reasons. Some are meant to stay. Some are not. I have learned from both."

Aunt Maude nodded and smiled. "Indeed, Grace, indeed. Who would like to go next?"

"I will," Riley said. "I chose my verse, which is a Yiddish proverb, because . . . well, because I believe it to be true. 'About being oneself, if all pulled in one direction, the world would keel over.' "

"How very true," Dora said.

"I agree," Tara said. "My quote is from Ralph Waldo Emerson. 'The age of a woman doesn't mean a thing. The best tunes are played on the oldest fiddles.' "

Laughter filled the air. "I'll second that," my sister said.

"And the reason I chose it . . . is because I believe it. The best is yet to come, I always say."

"My feeling precisely," Martha said. "My quote is from Jack London. 'Life is not a matter of holding good cards, but sometimes, playing a poor hand well.' I chose this quote because I also have found this to be very true and each day I try to play those cards the best that I can."

"Bravo," her sister said. "It's probably ironic that I chose a similar quote, but mine is from Emily Dickinson. 'Find ecstasy in life, the mere sense of living is joy enough.' The older I get, the more I find that life truly is a journey, not a destination, and I soak up each and every moment."

"As do I," Dora said. "Which is the reason I chose my quote from Mohandas Gandhi. 'Happiness is when what you think, what you say, and what you do are in harmony.' A life of balance is what I strive for."

"Well, my chosen quote is along the same lines," Suellen said. "I fully believe the words, and that's why I chose it. 'Life is a song, sing it. Life is a game, play it. Life is a challenge, meet it. Life is a dream, realize it. Life is a sacrifice, offer it. Life is love, enjoy it.' The quote is from an Indian guru who died in 1918. He taught a moral code of love, forgiveness, helping others, charity, and inner peace."

"I really like that quote," Devon said. "My quote is from *Walden* because, like Riley, I've always believed this to be true. 'If a man does not keep pace with his companions, perhaps it is because he hears a different drummer. Let him step to the music which he hears, however measured or far away.' I think this quote is so popular because of the meaning."

"I agree with that," Julia said. "And my quote is from Benjamin Franklin. 'At twenty years of age, the will reigns; at thirty, the wit; at forty, the judgment.' I chose this quote because I feel that life is a continual learning process and all of us keep growing and changing."

"Isn't that the truth," Chloe said. "Well, my quote is from Albert Schweitzer, and I think the reason I chose it will be obvious to Aunt Maude and Grace. 'Sometimes our light goes out but is blown into flame by another human being. Each of us owes deepest thanks to those who have rekindled this light.'" Chloe paused to swipe at her eyes. "I owe deepest thanks to both my sister and my aunt . . . so thank you."

I swallowed the lump in my throat as I glanced at Aunt Maude and saw her eyes were also glistening.

"Thank you, Chloe," Maude said. "And thank you to all of you that came for our first knitting retreat. I hope you'll return home with more than just new knitting techniques. My quote comes from Anaïs Nin, because I felt it was very appropriate for our gathering. 'Each friend represents a world in us, a world possibly not born until they arrive, and it is only by this meeting that a new world is born.' I believe our weekend together has formed a new world."

Cheers rang out as all of us extinguished our candles and reached for our wineglasses to lift them high.

"Here's to friendship and female bonding and finding our paths on this journey," Suellen said.

"And here's to knitting," Dora chimed in.

"Amen to that," Martha said.

"And here's to no dropped stitches." Rebecca held her glass high, as we all nodded and laughed.

Riley picked up her flute and began playing the melody of "Let It Be."

"I'd say this was a very successful retreat and Blue Moon ceremony," my aunt said.

I looked out across the water just as the huge orange globe slipped from the horizon and felt a sense of serenity envelope me.

Chloe came to stand beside me. I pulled my aunt into an embrace and then turned to my sister.

"I'm glad we found each other," I said. "I love you, Chloe."

"I love you too, little sis."

29

That first knitting retreat weekend would be extra special to us because it was our first, but over the next few weeks the ones that followed were just as enjoyable. The women ranged in age and each one had a story to share with us. Being in the group bound us together as much as the stitches we knitted.

I was in the carriage house with Aunt Maude getting things ready for the upcoming weekend when I heard Rachel's voice in the doorway. I turned around to see her with a middle-aged couple and Max.

The man was tall and slim, casually dressed in polo shirt, jeans, and loafers. He reminded me of a professor I'd had in college, and he was clutching Max's hand. The woman was very attractive, and I saw a striking resemblance to Rachel.

"I hope you don't mind," she said. "But I wanted my parents to meet you."

"Of course not." Aunt Maude walked toward them, hand outstretched, and introduced herself.

"And I'm Maude's niece, Grace. Come on in. How about some coffee, and Max, I bet you'd like a glass of lemonade?"

"That would be great," Rachel's father said. "I'm Jake Kaplan, and this is my wife, Tess."

The four of them sat at the table while my aunt prepared the coffee and I poured lemonade for Max.

"When did you arrive on the island?" Aunt Maude asked.

"Just yesterday," Tess replied. "And I can already see why my daughter came here. Not only is it beautiful, the people are so friendly."

"Where are you staying?" I asked, putting some cookies on a plate.

"We'll be here for a month, and we drove down with our dog, so we're booked at the Faraway Inn," Jake told us.

"Good choice," I said. "You got one of the cottages?"

Tess nodded. "Yes, and it already feels like home."

"My wife and I want to thank you . . . for looking out for Rachel and Max. She told us how you gave her the cleaning job with no experience and how she spent the holidays with you. That was very kind."

"It was our pleasure," my aunt told them. "Rachel's a fine girl and a wonderful mother. You should be proud of her."

When neither parent replied, Maude said, "You know, many times in life we make bad choices, but when we fix those choices and go on, that's what counts. The end result."

"You're right," Jake said. "My wife and I can see now that maybe we were a bit rash these past years."

I saw his eyes move to Max, and there was no doubt this man was filled with love for his grandson.

"And I have a grandpa and nana," Max said, his face showing excitement. "I never had a nana and grandpa before. And I like it."

We all laughed as Rachel tousled her son's hair.

"Well, you've always had grandparents, Max. But now you'll get to know them."

Max nodded emphatically. "And we're going to live with them in New York and ya know what?" Before waiting for an answer, he said, "They told me I could get a puppy. A puppy! I've always wanted one of those."

I leaned over and squeezed Max's hand as I felt my eyes moisten. "I'm so happy for you, Max. That puppy will be very lucky to have you as its owner."

Aunt Maude poured coffee into mugs and joined us at the table. "I'm very happy for all of you. This couldn't have worked out better, and Rachel, I have no doubt you'll do very well in New York."

"I think so. I'm going to begin college in the fall. Finish off that degree from before Max was born."

Jake smiled. "We have quite a large home, so Rachel and Max will stay with us until she finishes college."

"And I'm going to love having them with us," Tess said. She looked around the carriage house. "You have a lovely place here. Rachel told me about your knitting retreats. I think that's such a wonderful idea for women."

I smiled. "We think so too, and it's working out very well. Do you knit, Tess?"

"I do, and I was hoping there'd be a yarn shop on the island."

"There certainly is," I said. "My friend Monica owns it now, but very soon she'll be selling it to her aunt and my sister. It's called Yarning Together, right downtown on Second Street. You'll have to stop in. Oh, and we have knitting get-togethers on Thursday evenings, if you'd like to join us."

"I'll definitely stop by and stock up on some yarn, and yes, that would be fun and give me a chance to meet everyone."

"Have you found anybody to replace me yet?" Rachel asked.

"No, not yet," my aunt told her. "But you're not to worry about that. We have three months before you leave."

Rachel's parents asked us questions about the island and its history, and my aunt brought forth laughter relaying some anecdotes. By the time they were ready to leave, I knew it would all work out for Rachel, and I was glad she had reconciled with her parents. Like my aunt had said, it's the end result that counts.

Later that afternoon I took Annie for a walk downtown. I was running low on my merino silk yarn and needed to make a stop at the yarn shop.

"So your dream is about to come true."

Dora looked up from unpacking the most luscious skeins of lavenders, blues, and greens and laughed.

"Right. I hope it won't be a case of be careful what you wish for."

"I seriously doubt that," I said, reaching out to finger the exquisite softness of yarn she was placing on the counter. "I think you and Chloe will be a great team, and I think you'll be quite successful."

"Even at my age, I guess we all get a bit frightened of a new venture, but I have to admit, I'm very excited."

"You should be, Dora. This is something you've always wanted. Remember when Sydney first opened the shop? You were thrilled just to be working here part time, and now you'll be part owner. I'm really happy for you."

"Thank you. I do think it'll be a lot of fun. So how's everything with you?"

"Very good. I'm heading over to the coffee café to see Lucas, but I need some more of that merino silk."

I walked over to the wooden cubbyholes against the wall and removed two skeins of a soft shade of apricot.

"How's Monica doing? Any sign of those triplets making an entrance yet?"

"Oh, it won't be much longer now. She saw the doctor yesterday and they're concerned her blood pressure is going too high. They have her scheduled for a C-section next Tuesday, the fourteenth."

"On Valentine's Day? Oh, wow! Her three little sweethearts coming into the world on the most romantic day of the year. That seems appropriate. Is she feeling okay though?"

"She's very tired, and of course being so large, it's difficult for her to find any comfortable position. The doctor said all three babies should be a pretty good size, which is good. I know she'll just be glad to have them in her arms."

Dora rang up my purchase and passed me the small paper tote bag.

"Well, give her my best. Tell her I'll pop by this weekend before she goes into the hospital next week."

Annie and I made our way down Second Street to the coffee café. I walked in to see Suellen behind the counter.

"Hey, girlfriend," she said, a huge smile covering her face.

"How's it going?" I said, leading Annie to a corner table, where she promptly curled up beneath it. Another thing I loved about this island. If no food was served inside and the owners obtained the permit, the establishment was pet friendly.

"Going well. We've had a busy day. Lucas is over in the bookshop ringing up more sales. Double latte?"

"That would be great. Oh, hey, did ya hear? Monica's going in the hospital on Tuesday for a C-section."

"Really? She'll have her triplets. Oh, isn't that Valentine's Day?" I laughed. "Yeah, it is. Apropos, wouldn't you say?"

"With the love she and Adam share . . . very much so. That's great. I hope it all goes well for her. I bet she'll be glad not to have to carry all that extra poundage around."

"Dora said she's pretty uncomfortable. I bet the three of them are so excited now that it's almost here."

Suellen placed my coffee in front of me and joined me at the table.

"So what else is going on around town?" she asked.

"Hey, you're the one down here with everybody. You should get the gossip long before I do."

Suellen laughed. "Actually, it's been pretty quiet lately. Oh, I did meet Rachel's parents this morning. She dropped in with them."

"They came by the carriage house earlier, too, so we could meet them. Seem really nice. I think Rachel's going to do fine."

"I agree. I'm glad she got in touch with them. They'll be a huge help to her and Max."

We both turned toward the door as the chimes tinkled and I saw my sister walk in, a wide smile covering her face.

She struck a pose, one hand on her hip, head tilted up toward the ceiling, and said, "Well, girls . . . meet the new owner of the Hale Building across the street."

"No!" I said, jumping up to grab her in an embrace. "You made an offer?"

"I made an offer and just found out it was accepted."

"Hey, you go, girl!" Suellen said, jumping up to join us in a circle as the three of us danced around like five-year-olds. "Congratulations!"

All the whooping and hollering drew Lucas from the bookshop over to the coffee café. He stood in the doorway, a perplexed expression on his face watching three grown women being kids again.

I ran over to give him a huge bear hug. "Chloe made an offer on the building across the street and they accepted. It's hers! She'll be the new owner of the Hale Building."

Lucas burst out laughing. "Congratulations, Chloe. I wondered what you ladies were so excited about."

Chloe threw her hands up in the air, joining Lucas's laughter. "I know. I can hardly believe it. I've gone from depressed housewife to an entrepreneur."

I ran over to hug her again. "And I'm so happy for you."

"I hope you really mean that, because I'm going to need some help moving into that apartment upstairs."

"Of course I'll help you. When are you moving?"

"Two weeks."

"Not a problem. You can count on me."

"Oh, me too," Suellen said.

"And I'll help as well," Lucas chimed in.

"Have you told Aunt Maude yet?"

"Not yet. I need a nice strong coffee and then I'll head home."

"Coming right up," Suellen said, going behind the counter.

ஒ 30 ஒ

The next two weeks flew by. I took a few trips into Gainesville with Chloe to make some household purchases, and by the time moving day arrived, my sister's level of excitement was at a high.

She'd hired a moving company to transport her furniture from the storage unit to her new apartment, but she needed help getting everything arranged.

I stood in the middle of my sister's front room and looked around. "This is a good-size room, and I love how it leads right out to that porch overlooking Second Street."

"Yeah," Suellen said. "Imagine the gossip she'll gather from up here. I want all the details of what you see going on down there."

Chloe laughed as she pushed an expensive-looking, beige leather sofa against the wall. "Right. Like I'm going to have time to just hang out there and soak up what everybody's doing. I'll be busy down the street at the yarn shop."

I saw Lucas smile.

"What is it about women and gossip? I remember my grandmother and her friends in the village. They prided themselves on knowing what was going on with everybody."

"Aw, come on," I said. "You can't tell me males don't do the same thing when they get together. Look at that juicy gossip you told me last week about that guy who's renting a place here on the island for his mistress. And *that* was told to you by another man."

"What?" Suellen nudged my arm. "And you didn't share this with your BFF?"

"No, I didn't. Because you don't know the people involved. Chloe, want me to start unpacking that box of dishes in your kitchen?" I said, changing the subject.

"That would be great. I'll tackle the box of linens. Maybe you could help me with that, Suellen, and Lucas, if you don't mind maybe you could get my full-length mirror hung on the back of my bedroom door. All the hardware for it is here," she said, holding up a bag.

"Cripe, your sister's quite the task master," Suellen joked, and headed for the bathroom.

I walked into the small kitchen off the front room and began carefully unwrapping dishes. No doubt about it. My sister had excellent taste with décor. I flipped over a plate and saw the imprint of a pricey china manufacturer in England. The pattern was a beautiful blue willow, and I wondered if these would be her everyday dishes. Four more boxes sat piled up on the floor labeled *kitchenware.*

An hour later Chloe's cabinets were filled with two sets of dishes, crystal, and cookware. It was a good thing the boxes were empty, because I'd run out of space.

I walked into the bedroom off the front room to find Chloe and Suellen emptying the last of the box of linens and towels. All of it had been neatly arranged in a large closet in the bathroom.

"You have a good-size bedroom, too, Chloe. Your bedroom set fits in perfectly and still gives you plenty of room for that cushy chair in the corner."

My sister stuck her head out from the bathroom. "I know. The rooms are very spacious and I love that. It doesn't feel cramped at all for an apartment. That chair will be perfect for curling up with a good book. That's why I put the floor lamp beside it. And my roll-top desk fits well in the living room. Plus, I like having the extra bedroom and bath in case I ever have guests."

Suellen emerged from the bathroom swiping a strand of hair from her face. "Well, that's it for towels and linens. Done. This really is an ideal place for a woman alone. I love it, Chloe. If I didn't have a lease on my cottage I'd be asking to rent that back apartment from you."

"Anybody interested in that?" Lucas asked, closing the bedroom door to show us the installation of the mirror.

"Oh, that looks great, Lucas. Thank you so much. No, I haven't had any inquiries yet. I'm not in a huge hurry to rent it, but eventually I might put an ad in the paper."

"I'd bet anything you won't have to. Around here, somebody will hear about it from word of mouth."

I looked at my watch and was surprised to see it was six o'clock. No wonder my stomach was growling.

"Hey, guys. I'm starved. Why don't we order a pizza?"

"Great idea," Lucas said. "My treat. To welcome Chloe into her new home. I'll run over to Island Pizza. How's mushroom, green pepper, and extra cheese sound?"

"Perfect," Suellen, Chloe, and I said in unison.

When Lucas returned with the pizza, Chloe produced a bottle of Cabernet, which she uncorked and poured into quite elaborate wineglasses.

"Geez," I said, taking mine. "I'm almost scared to use this. It's gorgeous crystal, Chloe."

"Yeah, got it on a trip Parker and I took to Paris years ago. May he rot in hell."

Suellen and I laughed.

"Not a forgiving soul, are ya, sis?"

"Hey, I'm in a good place now. I could care about him. And don't be scared of breaking the glass, Grace. One thing I learned years ago—beautiful things aren't meant to be locked away. They have to be used and enjoyed."

"Aunt Maude always said that," I told her. I lifted my glass high. "Well, here's a toast to you, your new apartment, and your new life."

"Many years of happiness," Suellen said.

"Bonne chance." Lucas touched his glass to Chloe's.

"Thank you all so much. You were a huge help to me, and I really appreciate it. Let's take that pizza out to the patio table on the porch."

After finishing two slices of pizza and a glass of wine, I stood up and stretched. "Well, this was fun, but I have to get home and take Annie out."

Chloe jumped up to pull me into an embrace. "Thank you, Grace. For everything. I'm so glad I have you to share good things with."

The years fell away and I recalled the last time my sister hugged me when I was a child. The day she left for college. I realized that prior to that, while she may have been remote in the way an older sister might be, I had felt she loved me. But it wasn't the same sister that returned four years later. Strange how I hadn't given this any thought over so many years.

"It was my pleasure, Chloe," I told her, placing a kiss on her cheek. "I'm glad you're back in my life."

"I have to walk Duncan also," Lucas said. "Would you like to join me over at the Black Dog for a glass of wine?"

"Great idea. I'll go home and get Annie and meet you at your house."

An hour later Lucas and I were sitting on the back deck of the Black Dog Bar and Tables, a wonderful glass of Cabernet in my hand and the gorgeous vista of the Gulf spread out before me. A few lights twinkled from boats anchored off shore, and the balmy air completed my sense of well-being.

I looked down at Duncan and Annie curled up beside each other and smiled.

"It's nice that we can take them here with us when we want to relax with a glass of wine, isn't it?" I said.

Lucas nodded. "Very civilized. Much like France."

"I think Chloe will be very happy in her place. Thank you for helping us."

"I enjoyed it, and yes, I believe she is finding her way."

"Finding her way," I said. "You know, when she hugged me earlier I remembered that until she left for college, she was a pretty good sister to me."

"You think something changed after that?"

"I'm not sure. But yes, I get the feeling that something happened during those four years she was away."

"What do you mean?"

I shook my head and took a sip of wine. "I don't know," I said after a few moments. "It's a *feeling* I have—and whatever it was, I don't think it was good."

"She met her husband in college, yes?"

"Yeah, she met Parker her senior year and they married right away, that summer after she graduated. I know she had abandonment issues concerning our parents, and I also think there was some jealousy there concerning me—but I think there's more. Something she's never talked about."

Lucas sighed and reached for my hand. "Ah, to have secrets is probably human. Maybe someday she will share hers with you."

I nodded. "Maybe," I said, and wondered if Lucas still harbored some secrets.

❧ 31 ❧

When the first week of March arrived, Monica was home with her triplets, and although I'd gone to Gainesville to visit her and the babies, I was anxious to see them without glass separating us.

I knocked on Aunt Maude's door and hollered, "All set to go see those babies?"

She opened her screen door holding a beautiful bouquet of fresh-cut flowers. "I am," she said. "I bet they've already grown since we saw them in the hospital."

"You're probably right," I told her, heading to the golf cart.

Monica looked tired but she was glowing when she opened the door. "Oh, I'm so glad you came by."

"I bet it's good to finally be home," I said, following her into the great room.

"Oh, you have no idea. Sleeping in my own bed last night was pure joy. Well, sleeping in between feedings, that is."

My eyes went to the three identical baby seats lined up on the sofa with three small, identical babies cuddled inside.

"Oh, Monica," I said softly while walking closer for a better look. "My God, they're beautiful! And they certainly look alike."

"What precious little angels." Aunt Maude stood beside me, a look of awe on her face.

"I know. I can hardly believe they're mine. Adam and Clarissa are over the moon with excitement. I had all I could do to scoot them both out the door this morning for school."

I laughed and noticed a large piece of cardboard on the coffee table that looked like a graph with names on it.

"What's that? People signing up for baby duty?"

Now Monica laughed and nodded. "That's exactly what it is. My mother's idea. While I was in the hospital, she went around recruiting people to come by for a couple hours at a time to help out."

I shook my head. "Leave it to Sydney. Always organized."

"That's a very good idea," Aunt Maude said. "Lord knows you're really going to need some extra hands with three babies. But she didn't contact me."

"I think she thought with your knitting retreats you might be too busy yourself."

"Nonsense," my aunt said, picking up the cardboard. "I can certainly volunteer a couple hours on a Tuesday or Wednesday." She removed an ink pen from her handbag, wrote in her name, and said, "There. I'll be here next Wednesday from nine till eleven in the morning."

"Thank you so much, Maude. I really appreciate it."

"I don't know a thing about babies," I said, taking the cardboard. "But I'd be more than happy to come over and do your laundry, vacuum, that sort of thing."

"Oh, Grace, you don't have to do that."

"No, I want to." I proceeded to fill my name in for two hours the following Tuesday.

"That's really nice of you. Would you both like some tea or coffee?"

"No, no," my aunt said. "We don't want you waiting on us. We only wanted to stop by to welcome you home, and I picked these for you from my garden." She passed the bouquet to Monica.

"Thank you again. They're lovely."

The doorbell rang and we turned around to see Polly.

"Here I am," she said. "Reporting for baby duty. I have a feeling I'm going to enjoy this way more than working in my hair salon."

We laughed as she leaned over to look at the sleeping infants.

"We need to get going," I said. "I can see you're in very capable hands."

"Oh, she is. Now I want you to go take a nap, Monica. That's why I'm here, so you can rest."

"I have a feeling you guys are going to spoil me rotten."

"You're absolutely right," I told her, heading to the door with my aunt. "See you on Tuesday."

After we left Monica's, Aunt Maude needed to stop at the Market for a few items and I decided to pay a visit to Chloe.

I loved the walled courtyard that led upstairs to her apartment. When I reached the top of the staircase I could hear the strains of a Mozart symphony coming from inside and gave a knock on the door.

"Hey," Chloe said, opening the door and looking happy to see me. "Glad you stopped by."

I followed her into the living room and was amazed at how much she had accomplished in just a week. Pictures were hung on the walls, furniture was arranged, fresh flowers were in a vase, and all of it had a cozy, lived-in quality.

"Your room looks great," I said. "You've sure been busy."

"Yeah, but I've really been enjoying it. Do you realize—here I am pushing fifty and this is the first time I've had a place of my own? At college I had a roommate, and I went from there to the house with Parker. I've always lived with somebody else and their decorating ideas."

"Well, you certainly have an eye for style," I said. "It looks gorgeous."

"I love it here. I'm so glad I bought this place. Hey, I was just going to pop over to Lucas's for coffee. Wanna join me?"

"Sure. Great idea." I took another look around the apartment before we left. "Oh, there's one thing missing here though."

"Really? What?"

"A nice cat."

"Funny you should say that," my sister said, following me down the stairs. "I was at the yarn shop earlier and Dora told me that somebody on the island died recently and she had about ten cats. Now they all need homes. I was thinking of going over to see them. Maybe I'll take one home with me."

"I bet you won't be sorry," I told her as we crossed the street to the coffee café.

"Hey there, you two," Suellen said. "What's up?"

"Well, I popped by to see Monica and the triplets. They're all doing great. And Chloe here just might be getting a cat for her new apartment. Oh, and I'll have a double latte, please."

"Just regular black coffee for me," Chloe said.

"I think a cat's a great idea. I just love my little Freud. He really keeps me entertained. Do you know they've done studies on cats? And just by sitting there stroking them, it can lower your blood pressure."

"Animals are amazing," I said, joining my sister at one of the tables. "I don't know what I'd do without my Annie. Has Lucas been busy over on the bookshop side?"

"Not too much. He's been on the phone a lot this morning doing orders, and don't tell him I told you, but I think he's giving some thought to having some author signings."

I reached for the latte Suellen passed me. "Really? I think that's a great idea. I'd mentioned that to him when he first opened."

"Well, Josie's mom, Shelby, came by earlier and I overheard them talking. Sounded like she was interested in setting something up."

"That's great," Chloe said. "I'd definitely attend. I've read all her books."

I looked up as the chimes tinkled and another customer walked in. She didn't look familiar, and I knew she was a tourist.

"Hi there," I said, and saw the look of surprise on her face that I'd spoken to her.

"Oh, hi."

She might be a tourist but her funky style of dress fit the island. Wearing a long woolen purple cape, tight black jeans, knee-high black boots, and a wide streak of purple through the side of her long black hair, she looked to be mid-forties.

"Do you have lavender tea?" I heard her ask.

"I do," Suellen said, returning to the counter to prepare it.

I smiled. This woman seemed to have a thing for the color purple.

She sat at the table across from Chloe and me.

"Are you visiting the island for the day?" I asked with my usual friendliness.

"Actually, I'm here for a few days. I'm staying at the B and B."

"Oh, that's nice," Chloe said. "Where're you from?"

"Salem, Massachusetts," she replied, while removing a cell phone from the oversized black leather bag she'd placed on the chair next to her.

My ears perked up. "Wow! The Witch City?"

The woman laughed. "Yup. I was born in Maine, but we moved to Salem when I was about five. And yes, in case you're wondering, I do follow some of the Wiccan traditions."

Suellen placed the mug of tea in front of the woman. "Oh, I've always wanted to visit there. It seems like such an interesting place."

After taking a sip of the tea, she said, "Very good. Yeah, Salem is quite interesting. The problem is since the town started capitalizing on the witches it's become too crowded for my liking. Constant tourists visiting all the psychics and witch shops. And Halloween—you don't even want to be within fifty miles of there. It's not the Salem I grew up in. Way too commercialized now."

"That's a shame," I said, praying that Cedar Key would never resort to something like that.

She took another sip of tea and nodded. "That's why I'm on a mission. To find a place to relocate. Someplace where my soul can breathe and I can be one with nature. Do you know what I mean?"

Chloe, Suellen, and I looked at each other and smiled.

"Well, honey," Suellen said. "You just may have found it."

"I did a lot of research on the Internet before I came here, and I'm thinking you could be right."

"What type of work do you do?" Chloe asked. "Do you have an idea how you'd make a living?"

"Oh, I don't need much, but yeah, in Salem I own a shop. It's a chocolate shop, but I also sell gems. You know, crystals and that sort of thing. Kinda eccentric combining chocolate and gems, huh?"

I laughed. "On this island? Not at all."

"I also own a few alpacas so I spin the fiber and sell the yarn on my website."

"You also knit?" I asked. A woman after my own heart. "Wow, I don't think I've ever met anybody who has their own alpacas. That's really cool."

She nodded. "Oh, yeah, I'm a compulsive knitter. I keep my alpacas at a friend's place in Hamilton. Jill has plenty of room for them on her property, and it's only about ten miles from Salem."

"I like you gals," she said, getting up with her hand outstretched. "I'm Berkley. Berkley Whitmore."

And I liked this woman's upfront openness.

"Nice to meet you," we all told her.

"Berkley. That's a very unusual name. I like it," I said.

She waved her hand in the air. "What can I say? My parents were students at Berkeley when I was conceived, and my mom was a product of the sixties. Through and through."

"So do you have a husband or family?" Chloe asked.

"A few bad relationships, but no husband. I just have my mother now, but she moved to the Cape after my grandmother died last year—but we've never been that close, if you know what I mean. So it's just me and my twenty-pound black cat, Sigmund."

This woman was getting more and more interesting. She had a cat named Sigmund, and Suellen's cat was named Freud. When she mentioned her mother, Chloe and I exchanged a glance.

"So what do you think of our island so far?"

"I like it. I like it a lot. Off the beaten path but still close enough to larger towns." She looked out the window of the coffee café to the empty shop across the street. "Who owns that building over there?"

"I do," Chloe said.

"No shit?"

Chloe laughed. "No shit. I just purchased it a few weeks ago. I moved into one of the apartments upstairs. Tony's Restaurant is there. World champion for clam chowder in 2009."

"You mean to tell me he beat out New England?" Berkley said.

"I'm afraid so," Chloe told her.

"So what's that empty shop next door to Tony's?" Berkley gestured across the street.

"Just an empty shop. Waiting to be leased."

Berkley remained silent, taking another sip of her tea.

"Hmm," she said. "Any chance you could show it to me? And do you happen to know of an apartment or cottage for rent on the island?"

Chloe laughed. "Not only could I show you the space, I have an empty apartment upstairs next to mine."

"I'll be damned," Berkley said. "Guess those cards were right after all."

"You do tarot?" I asked.

"Among many things, and I can see by your aura that you also have a gift."

Yup, this woman was definitely interesting.

"Okay," she said, standing up and reaching for her wallet. "Let's roll. I wanna see that shop and the apartment."

I waved my hand in the air. "The tea is on the house. My boyfriend owns the shop. Our little welcome to you."

"That's really sweet," she said, and then followed my sister out the door.

❧ 32 ❧

I was awakened the next morning at six to the sound of Suellen's desperate voice on the phone.

"Grace! I need your help. I'd never ask you if it wasn't an emergency. You know that. And you know that Lucas is up in Brunswick for a few days and I don't know what I'm going to do. It all happened last night and you know I have to be there for Ashley and I really hate . . ."

"Suellen," I yelled into the phone. "Slow down! What on earth are you talking about? What happened to Ashley?"

I heard the intake of a deep breath across the line. "She . . . she fell down the stairs at her dorm. She's in the hospital. It's a compound fracture to her arm. They have to do surgery and I . . . I *have* to be there with her."

She ended her sentence with a hiccup, and I knew she was crying. I sat up in bed. "Of course you have to be there. It's not a problem. I'll go over to the bookshop and café at ten and open up and stay there till five."

"Oh, Gracie, thank you. Thank you so much. Oh, and do you think you could come by here this evening and feed Freud for me? I'll probably be gone a few days."

"I'll feed him every day that you're gone. Suellen, do you want me to drive up there with you? Maybe you shouldn't be driving alone."

I heard another deep breath come across the line. "No, no. Really. I'll be fine. It's just that she only called me a little while ago and I guess I'm still upset. But I'm going to calm down. Then I'll pack a bag and head up to Georgia. I'll call you later this evening, okay? And Gracie, thanks again."

"You drive safe and give my love to Ashley. Stay there as long as you need to. I'll look after Freud for you and I'll cover at the café."

"Okay. Love you," she said before hanging up.

I sat on the edge of the bed and yawned. Well, the day wasn't going to be the relaxed one that I'd planned. Oh, well, maybe the bookshop and café wouldn't be too busy and I could still get some knitting done.

I managed to handle the morning rush pretty well on my own, and by early afternoon I was sitting working on a gorgeous lacy pattern scarf in a soft fiber of bamboo in shades of green.

I looked up as Chloe walked in.

"Hey," I said. "How'd it go yesterday with Berkley?"

She pulled up a chair to join me.

"Very well. I'd say we have a new resident and merchant moving to the island in the fall."

"Really? That's great. So she was interested in the apartment and the shop?"

"Yup. She said the shop was the perfect size and would be ideal for what she wanted. Isn't that a riot? That she sells chocolate and gems? She showed me a couple photos of her shop in Salem, and it's very nice. That woman has a gift for presentation. Her store window was gorgeous. And she loved the apartment. Said it would be ideal for her and Sigmund."

I laughed. "I have a feeling Berkley will fit in quite well on this island. She seems really nice. I'm glad this all worked out for both of you."

"Me too. We ended up going to Frogs for dinner last night so I had a few hours to get to know her. She's a bit funky, but I like her."

"But she's not coming down to stay till the fall?"

"Yeah, she has a lease on her place up there, and then she has to arrange to get everything moved down here. She makes her own chocolates, you know."

"No, really? I just assumed she ordered them from a distributor."

"Nope. She's a bona fide candymaker. Said her mother and grandmother were too, and that's how she learned the craft."

"Wow. She's quite an interesting woman. I'm glad she found her way to Cedar Key."

Chloe nodded. "Another one who will find our little island to be her retreat. Listen, I've got to run," she said, standing up and ruffling her hand through my hair. "Oh, why are you here? Where's Suellen and Lucas?"

I filled her in on Ashley's accident and explained that Lucas had to go to Brunswick for a few days to tend to bookshop business.

"Well, it looks like you have everything under control. See you later."

Within three hours I would find out that I had nothing under control and my life would be turning upside down.

I had just finished wiping down the counters and getting ready to close the café and bookshop for the day. My back was turned to the door, and when I heard the chimes I thought perhaps it was Chloe stopping by again.

And then I heard his voice.

"Grae?" he said, and my heart fell. Only one person in the entire world had ever called me *Grae*.

I turned around slowly to see Beau Hamilton standing inside the coffee café. After ten years—ten years of going out of my way to avoid him, ten years of recriminations, sorrow, guilt, and finally acceptance, he had found me.

I saw him walk toward the counter as if in a dream. The years had been very kind to him. He was still tall and exceptionally good looking. The only difference I quickly noted was the silver along his temples. Other than that, he looked like that same man who entered my antique shop years before. I gripped the side of the counter, feeling the perspiration dotting my forehead, and remained silent.

"I saw you through the window," he said in that same sexy voice that I thought I'd long forgotten. "And I thought it was you. You haven't changed at all, Grace. Just as beautiful as ever."

Oh, but I have, I thought, trying to collect my thoughts.

I finally found my voice. "Beau," was all I could manage to say.

"It's been a lot of years," he said.

"Ten. Ten years since I left Brunswick. What are you doing here? On Cedar Key?" I knew I sounded like Cedar Key was the end of the earth, but I didn't care. My thoughts were so jumbled I wasn't able to form a coherent sentence.

"Just came for a few days. Had read about it in a travel magazine . . . and decided to visit." He ran a hand through his hair in the way I remembered and caused too many long-buried memories to surface. He then cleared his throat, and from knowing him so well, I knew he was nervous, but I still remained silent.

"Look, Grace," he said, leaning across the counter. "Is there any chance we could talk? I mean, since I'm here . . . I . . . ah . . . I'd like it if we could talk about what happened ten years ago when you left." After a pause, he said, "Please."

My stomach was churning. I wasn't sure if it was from the shock of seeing Beau, especially on my territory, or if he had somehow managed to stir up all of those feelings that I once had for him. At that very moment, I wasn't sure of anything at all. I blew out a deep breath and realized that perhaps the time had come. The time for me to face my demons once and for all.

"Okay," I said, before I even knew what I was saying. "Okay. We'll talk. But not here. And not at my place. . . ."

"Can I take you out for dinner or a drink?" he asked, and I saw the pleading in his eyes.

I nodded. "Give me ten minutes to close up here. I'll meet you at the Black Dog, over on Dock Street. If you get there first, grab a table outside on the deck. It'll be more private to talk."

The smile that crossed his face caused me to feel . . . what? Guilt for the way I'd left him ten years before.

"Okay," I said, before I could change my mind. "I'll meet you there shortly."

Without another word, Beau turned and left.

It wasn't until he walked out that I realized I'd dug my nails into the palms of my hands. I walked over to the sink to wash them and saw my hands were shaking. All I could think was, it's so true what they say about your past. You are never totally rid of it. Not ever.

I went into the restroom, ran a hand through my curls, applied some lip gloss, and took a deep breath. *Well, this is it, girl. Time to face what you never wanted to face.* It was then that I thought of Lucas. How ironic that he should be gone when Beau showed up.

I crossed the bridge over to Dock Street, and by the time I arrived at the Black Dog, I had resumed a semblance of calm.

I found Beau on the back deck, two glasses of Cabernet on the table.

"I wasn't really sure you'd come," he said, pulling the stool out for me.

"I wasn't either," I told him.

33

Sitting down across from Beau, I took a gulp of wine and glanced out to the western sky where the sun was beginning to go down.

"Can we start at the beginning?" he asked.

I looked across to the face that I'd once known so well and nodded.

"What happened? What happened with us, Grace?"

I let out a deep sigh. "What happened was that we never should have been."

"I'm not sure that's true," he said, softly. "We fell in love—almost from the moment we met. There's no way to control something like that."

"That's true. But had I known when we met that you were married, I'm not so sure I would have acted on that love." Or would I still have allowed myself to get involved?

"I was wrong."

I looked up and saw the expression of regret on his face.

"I was wrong in many ways. I should have told you right away that I was married and then . . . as the years passed, I should have made a decision. To either leave Lila or . . ."

My head shot up. "Or leave me?"

"I was a coward. I knew I couldn't leave you. It damn near

killed me when you took off. Let's face it, circumstances were lousy.
Lila had a history of depression, and I didn't want to be responsible
for what she might do. And in the end—that's probably exactly
what she did."

Was he saying Lila committed suicide? "So the rumors were
true?" I asked, and felt my own heart constrict.

"We're not sure. The doctor determined it was a heart attack,
but she also had an excess amount of narcotics in her. Lila was a
very complex person." He took a sip of wine and began fingering
the stem on the glass. "I can understand you wanting to get away
from that situation, Grace. I really can. But did you have to take off
like that without letting me know where you were going? Without
letting me know you were okay?"

I took a sip of wine while forming thoughts in my head. "I wasn't
okay, Beau. That's just it. I wasn't okay at all. And I was still so fragile that I knew if you followed me . . . and if you asked . . . I probably wasn't strong enough to resist you. I had to make sure it was a
clean break."

He nodded, and when he looked up I saw the pain in his eyes.
"It was the phone call, wasn't it? When Lila called you—that's
what put you over the edge."

"You knew about that phone call?" I asked in surprise.

"Not until about a month after you left. Lila had been drinking
and was in an especially foul mood. She told me she took pride in
the fact that she'd run you out of town. That was why you left?
What exactly did she tell you?"

All the pain of that day come rushing back as moisture filled my
eyes. When I remained silent, I felt Beau's hand come across the
table and grasp mine. I glanced down through my tears at the hand
of my former lover—the hand that had brought such pleasure to
my body and had taught me how to love.

"Yes," I said, and nodded. "That was part of the reason why I
left, because of what she told me." I paused and swiped at my tears.
"She told me that I was only one of many. That I wasn't the first one
you'd run around with and probably wouldn't be the last."

"Oh, my God, Grace! And you believed her? Surely you knew
how much I loved you. You had to know that I'd never been un-

faithful to Lila until I met you. There was never anybody else. Not ever."

I looked up through my blurry vision at Beau's handsome face. "But, see. That's just it. The other woman—she never knows anything with the utmost certainty. She doesn't have a right to. So I guess there're always doubts." I reached for a tissue in my handbag and dabbed my eyes. "But there was more to it, Beau. The reason I left." I took a deep breath. "I was pregnant with your child."

"What?" Surprise covered his face. "We have a child? You never told me?"

"No, we do not have a child. I miscarried the day before Lila had called me, and no . . . I hadn't told you at that point, but I had planned to. When I lost the baby—there just seemed no reason for you to know."

When I glanced across the table, I saw that it was Beau's eyes that were now filled with tears.

"I'm *so* sorry," he said, so quietly I barely heard him. "I'm so sorry, Grace. I had no idea."

After a few moments, he jumped up, threw some cash on the table, grabbed my hand, and said, "Come on. I need to walk."

I walked beside him down Dock Street over to City Park with neither of us saying a word. He chose a bench overlooking the beach, and I sat down next to him, inches separating us. Still neither of us spoke.

As I sat there waiting for Beau to digest all that I'd told him, I realized that something had shifted deep inside of me. Something I hadn't even been aware of. A bitterness that I'd managed to push down for so many years resurfaced, and then, like doves being released from a cage, my heart swelled with love and the bitterness was replaced with forgiveness. I had finally forgiven Beau, and in doing so, I had forgiven myself.

I felt him reach for my hand and allowed him to hold it. It felt good. But not in the same way as when I held Lucas's hand.

"We can't go back, can we, Grace?" he finally said.

I shook my head. "No. I'm afraid there's never any going back in life. And that's probably a good thing, Beau. We were meant to cross each other's path—we just weren't meant to spend our entire lives together." I leaned over and kissed his cheek. "I'm glad you came into my life."

"You were everything to me," he said, squeezing my hand. "You always will be, you know."

We both stared out to the ocean and then he said, "I'm afraid I told you a fib, and since we're finally being so honest, I want you to know."

I looked at him, wondering what he meant.

"I didn't find out about Cedar Key in a travel magazine," he said. "Chloe told me where you were last June when I bumped into her."

Now it was my turn to be shocked. What the hell was he talking about? Chloe saw Beau last June and never told me?

"What?" I gasped. "What do you mean? You saw Chloe? Where? What did she say?"

"I saw her at Publix one afternoon. She told me that she and Parker were separated and getting a divorce. She was really upset and kept apologizing to me. Kept saying, 'I'm really sorry.' I didn't know what she meant at the time, and then she blurted out, 'She's in Cedar Key, Florida, you know.' I knew she meant you—and it's taken me almost a year to get up the courage to actually come here."

I was astounded by this information and my mind was swirling. Why would Chloe be sorry and apologize to Beau? Then it hit me!

"Oh, my God! It was *she*. It was she who called Lila that day, wasn't it? She must have seen us somewhere together. Oh, my God! My own sister betrayed me!"

Beau stood up and pulled me to my feet. "I wasn't sure if I should tell you, Grace, but I think you have a right to know, and yes, based on what Lila told me, I'm now positive it was Chloe who made the phone call that day."

I felt the tears streaming down my face. Both from hurt and from anger. Beau's arms went around me, and like so many other times, he held me tight until I regained my equilibrium.

The entire afternoon and evening was beginning to feel surreal. I moved away from Beau's embrace, staring out at the water. I felt numb. Why would my sister do such a mean and nasty thing? Why would she intentionally hurt me in that way? Did she really hate me that much?

"Are you going to be okay?" I heard Beau ask.

"Yes," I said, and recalled what Jake Kaplan had said about his daughter. "Oh, yes. I'll be fine. After all, I'm a survivor."

"I'm leaving the island in the morning, Grace. Thank you so much for seeing me. You have a special person in your life, don't you?"

I nodded.

"He's one hell of a lucky guy. I hope he knows that."

I knew that a part of my heart would always love Beau Hamilton and that we had come full circle.

"Thank you," I said, as he pulled me into his arms for a final embrace. "I'm glad you finally found me."

He kissed my cheek and stepped back. It was in that moment that I saw Lucas standing on the sidewalk, holding Duncan on his leash, staring at me and Beau. He turned quickly and headed up Second Street.

"So long, Grace," I heard Beau say as I took off running toward Lucas.

By the time I caught up with him he was almost to his house.

"Lucas," I called. I knew he heard me, but he only walked faster. He had picked Duncan up in his arms to accomplish this.

Christ almighty, I thought. I had to explain to him about Beau.

I finally reached him in front of his house. "Lucas," I said, panting and trying to catch my breath. "Let me explain. Please. That was Beau."

"*Explain?* I believe what I just saw explained everything—the old lover finally found you." He turned on his heel and began walking toward his front door.

"No, no," I said, feeling a sense of fear. "It wasn't like that at all. You don't understand."

Lucas spun around and I took a step back. I had never seen him so angry.

"Oh," he said, his voice quivering. "I understand *perfectly* well.

You have no idea how *well* I understand. Leave me alone, Grace. Go away."

I watched him open the front door and slam it shut as I stood on the sidewalk with tears streaming down my face.

After a few moments, I began walking home. And for the first time in my life, I knew what it felt like to have my heart broken—and what I thought I'd felt for Beau Hamilton years ago paled by comparison.

❧ 34 ❧

I faked a flu over the weekend and managed to escape the knitting retreat, Aunt Maude, and Chloe. By Monday morning I was still in the same nightgown I'd worn for four days, having never bothered to get dressed. I had been sneaking outside in my bathrobe early mornings and after dark so Annie could do her duty then hunkering back down in my apartment, turning my cell phone to off and my house phone to Do Not Disturb.

But by Monday morning I knew I couldn't remain a recluse forever. Aunt Maude was about at her limit with me refusing her entrance. Each time she'd attempted to come to my door, I hollered that I didn't want her catching what I had and that I was fine. I knew she'd only believe that for so long.

And when she knocked again around eleven Monday morning, I let her in.

"Well," she said, looking around at the disarray in my kitchen. Dirty coffee cups, plates, empty donut boxes, and newspapers littered my counter. "Enough of this, Grace. What exactly is going on?"

"What do you mean?" I said, and hated the whiny tone in my voice.

"What I mean is you're acting just like you did when you were thirteen and didn't make the cheerleading squad. You can't hole up here forever. So—what's going on?"

Where did I begin telling my aunt how my life had so easily fallen apart in a matter of a few hours the previous Thursday?

I started at the beginning, with Beau walking into the coffee shop, and finished by saying, "So I think we've come full circle."

Maude nodded. "Yes, it sounds like you have. But I still don't think that's why you've hidden out all weekend. Where's Lucas?"

Just hearing his name caused my heart to flip over. "I don't know," I said, and went on to explain what he had witnessed.

"Oh, I see," was all she said, which caused my head to snap up.

"What? Have you seen him?" I asked.

"No, I haven't, and I'm a little surprised at his reaction, to be honest. I thought Lucas knew how you felt about him and that you'd made a commitment to each other."

"Apparently not," I said, feeling more miserable than ever. "And that's not all." I got up and began pacing the kitchen floor. "Do you know *how* Beau knew I was here on Cedar Key? Do you know who made that phone call to Lila ten years ago? Do you?" I could feel all of the anger returning.

After a few moments, she said, "Chloe."

I spun around to face her. "What? *You* knew? You knew it was her and never said anything to me! So you betrayed me too."

"I did no such thing, Grace. Shortly after Chloe moved here, she confided in me. I told her right away that I felt the best thing to do was for her to be honest and tell you yourself. She didn't listen. It wasn't my place to tell you."

"Right, and *she* never did."

"It's pretty obvious why she didn't, Grace. You and she have become close over these months since she moved here. Chloe told me more than once how happy she was about that. I don't think she wanted to risk losing what the two of you were building on."

"Yeah? Well . . . that's over now! Completely over. I don't ever want to see her again. What kind of sister would do such a hurtful and mean thing to her own sister? She hasn't changed at all. She's a resentful and jealous person, and I don't want her in my life."

Aunt Maude remained silent for a few moments. "You may not want her, Grace, but you might come to see that you *need* her."

"Never," I said, stomping off toward the bathroom. "And as a matter of fact, I'm taking a shower and I'm going to finally confront her. Once and for all. I'll get this out in the open and that will be the end of it—and the end of having a sister."

An hour later I found myself stomping up my sister's back stairs to her apartment. She didn't seem surprised to see me when she opened the door. I had a feeling she'd received a call from Aunt Maude.

"We need to talk," I said, pushing past her into the living room. "And so," I yelled, pacing her oak floorboards. "Perhaps you might tell me why—*why*—you saw fit to stick your nose into my private life ten years ago? Were you that miserable and jealous? How could you! How could you call Beau's wife? You had no right to do that. None." I only stopped long enough to catch a breath. "You've always been a bitch, Chloe, but even more than I ever realized. And where the hell did you see us anyway?"

I forced myself to look across the room at my sister. It was easy to see that her anger level was matching mine.

"Why? Because every wife has a right to know, that's why. When I saw my sister coming out of a hotel in Jacksonville with a *married* man, I felt it was my duty to tell his wife."

I laughed. "Duty? No, it wasn't your duty. You just wanted me to be as miserable as you were. But you didn't succeed, because I'm not *you* and I never will be. I'm not a doormat like you always were for Parker. I took risks in my life—something you were always too fearful to do. I've made my own way without depending on a man to get me there. So what you did had nothing to do with *duty*."

The tears that flowed down my sister's face matched my own.

"You're right," she said, her voice rising. "Miss Perfect Gracie. Always right. That's you. And yes—I wanted what you had. I *always* wanted that and never had it. Not ever."

There. She had said it—what I'd always felt but never admitted. And now, Chloe had confirmed it.

"That's because you had no clue how to go about getting it.

None whatsoever! It was much easier for you to bitch and complain about what you didn't have rather than putting forth the effort to get it *yourself.* You're damn right I'm right—you're consumed with jealousy for what I've accomplished. You haven't changed at all, and I don't ever want to see you again."

She didn't try to stop me as I headed to the door and slammed it behind me.

Over the next month I discovered that it wasn't an easy task trying to avoid certain people in a town of only nine hundred residents.

I had to plan my visits to the yarn shop when I knew Dora would be there rather than Chloe. I hadn't returned to the coffee café and bookstore since Beau had showed up.

I admit I felt pretty lonely most days, but I'd severed my ties with Chloe and the ball was in Lucas's court. Which only left Suellen to commiserate with. I was grateful for the supper invitation she'd extended to me. I grabbed the bottle of Cabernet and my handbag.

Annie looked up from the sofa. She'd been my constant companion through all the recent upheaval.

"Be a good girl," I told her. "I won't be late, but mommy needs a little people company."

"Hey, come on in," Suellen said, opening the door. "How're ya doing?"

"Fair to shitty would cover it." I passed her the wine.

"Thanks," she said, heading to the kitchen for the corkscrew.

She returned a minute later, two wineglasses in hand.

"Here ya go, girlfriend. Better days ahead."

"Yeah, right," I mumbled, and took a sip.

We both curled up on the sofa.

"Still no word from Lucas, huh?"

I shook my head. "Nope. Maybe I'll never hear from him again."

"Oh, Gracie. I seriously doubt that. He loves you. He really does."

I looked over at my oldest friend on the planet. "And *you* would know this how?"

"I would know this because I am one of the biggest romantics in the world. We just know stuff like this. He's just pissed. Give him time to cool off."

"Till when? When we're in that nursing home together drooling?"

Suellen laughed. "Glad to see you haven't lost your sense of humor."

"That's about all I have left."

Suellen took a sip of wine. "Well, you have to admit, Grace. I'm sure it was pretty surprising to him. He comes back from Brunswick a day early, is out walking his dog and finds you in the park necking with some other guy."

"Necking? Does anybody even use that term anymore? And we were not *necking*. Beau was simply giving me a good-bye hug."

"Yeah, but Lucas sure didn't know that, did he? Just think what it must have looked like to him. And then think how you would have felt if you'd witnessed the same thing."

Suellen was right. Like always.

"So . . . things are really resolved between you and Beau?"

"Yes. Totally. And it feels good. Like a weight has finally been lifted. It was sad, telling him about the baby, finding out that he truly did love me. But it also made me realize even more that what we shared wasn't that forever kind of love."

"Like what you have with Lucas."

I didn't answer. Because it hurt too much to think about it—and what I'd possibly lost.

"Life can be a bitch, huh?" my friend said.

I took a gulp of wine. "You think?"

"And do I dare ask about Chloe?"

"Hey, can you blame me for being pissed? My God, I still can hardly believe it was *she* who called Lila. It's also crossed my mind how different my life may have been if she hadn't interfered."

"Oh, don't even go there. What-if's get you nowhere. You know that. And no, I don't blame you at all for being pissed at her. It was a really nasty thing to do. But . . ."

I sat up straighter on the sofa and turned to face Suellen. "But what?" I said, hearing the edge in my tone.

"Well, I think you're very right about the way Chloe was all those years. Hell, I knew her, too, don't forget, and she *was* a bitch. Difficult. Demanding. Snooty. But I have to be honest here, Grace. I also think she did a one eighty when she moved here to the island. She was really sincere in wanting a relationship with you."

"So . . . what? You're saying I should just forgive her and everything will be honey and roses again? No. I'm afraid I can't do that." I finished off the last sip of wine. "Out of the question. I mean, come on, she finally came out and admitted the jealousy she's always had for me. Saying that she wanted what I had."

Suellen was silent for a few moments. "Did ya ever think that was a compliment to you? She admired you. Yeah, she wished she could have what you did, but years ago she had no clue how to go about getting it. That doesn't mean she's a bad person, Gracie. Just like you and Beau weren't bad people."

Damn. Why did Suellen have to make such logical sense?

❧ 35 ❧

When it reached six weeks since I'd heard from Lucas, I was convinced it was over. And I won't lie, I was miserable without him in my life. I hadn't even bumped into him anywhere on the island. Not once. I did think I caught a glimpse of him one morning when I was at the end of Second Street walking Annie, but it was only a glimpse.

Since Chloe and Dora were now the official owners of Yarning Together, my sister worked there three days a week full-time. Therefore, she explained to Aunt Maude that she was going to back out of the knitting retreats. So this enabled me to partake of the gatherings once again, and I did wonder if Chloe had done this for that reason.

I was up in my loft office working on bookings for upcoming retreats when I sensed a presence downstairs in the carriage house. I looked down to see Lucas standing in the doorway and felt my heart skip a beat. Damn, he was handsome. I saw his curly dark hair, his tanned skin, and I remembered the first time he'd walked into my coffee shop. Our eyes locked as he stared up at me.

"Hi, Grace," he said, as I stood up and made my way downstairs.

I felt awkward and unsure of myself, but I walked toward him. "Hi, Lucas."

He shifted from one foot to the other, and I realized he was as nervous as I was.

This is it, I thought. *He's come in person to let me know we're finished.*

"I was wondering," he said, clearing his voice. "I would . . . ah . . . like to cook dinner for you this evening. Is there any chance we could talk?"

Beau had uttered those exact same words. And that had worked out well.

"Over dinner," he added.

I felt like I was getting a reprieve. I felt giddy and like a teenager being asked out on her first date. And I felt a smile cross my face as I said, "Yes. Yes, I'd like that, Lucas."

His smile matched mine. "Good. Would six o'clock be okay?"

"That would be great," I said, as he turned to leave. "Oh, and Lucas . . ." He paused to turn around. "Thank you."

That killer smile that I loved and had come to know so well covered his face.

I showed up at Lucas's door a few minutes before six and hoped my choice of black cropped pants, emerald green silk tank top, and black leather flip-flops would make me appealing in his eyes. I'd even added a spray or two of Magie Noire.

Lucas opened the door with Duncan dancing in circles at his feet. I registered a quick look and knew he certainly appealed to *my* eyes before bending down to pat Duncan.

"Come on in," he said, gesturing toward the living room.

Was it my imagination or did Lucas seem more reserved than usual?

Two glasses of red wine along with a cheese platter were on the coffee table. Before I had a chance to say anything, Lucas passed one of the glasses to me.

"*Santé,*" he said.

I nodded and took a sip. "Very nice."

Lucas sat beside me on the sofa, and the close proximity of his body made me realize even more how much I'd missed him.

"You've been well?" he asked as if having a conversation with one of his bookshop customers.

"Yes, and you?" The formality between us was almost comical.

"I have," he said, placing his wineglass on the table to turn and face me. "But I've missed you, Grace. A lot."

My heart turned over. "I've missed you, too, Lucas." I wasn't sure what to say next.

"But I've needed these weeks to think. I've had a lot of things to resolve in my mind."

When he didn't go on, I questioned, "And have you resolved them?"

"I think so, but there is a part of my life that I need to share with you. A part you know nothing about. And if we are to go forward together—you have to know."

The joy I'd been feeling since Lucas showed up earlier at the carriage house was now being replaced by fear. Was his wife not really dead? Was he still married? Did I not know this man at all?

Lucas reached for my hand and let out a deep sigh.

"I had told you that my wife was killed in an automobile accident . . ."

I held my breath and nodded.

"Yes, that is true." He looked down at our clasped hands, and then his deep brown eyes focused on mine. "What I neglected to tell you . . . is that my daughter was also killed in that accident."

A wave of dizziness and nausea hit me at the same time, and I felt myself gripping Lucas's hand tighter. *Daughter?* Lucas had a *daughter?*

"I know this is quite a surprise to you, and I understand if you're upset because I never shared this with you. But . . . it is very painful. Genevieve was six years old when I lost her—and she was the light of my life."

My God, I had no idea that Lucas had dealt with the tragic loss of a child. I gripped his other hand. "I'm *so* sorry. So terribly sorry."

He nodded in understanding. "Yes, it was difficult enough to lose Genevieve, but there's more to the story, I'm afraid." He took a deep breath and went on. "You see, when the accident occurred . . . Danielle, my wife, she was on her way to meet her lover. She was leaving me—and taking our daughter with her."

Lucas was right—there was much more to his story that I had no knowledge of. He hadn't been grieving the loss of a devoted and loving wife, as I'd been led to believe. It was the loss of his daughter that had torn his life apart.

"Oh, dear God," I said, feeling moisture fill my eyes. "Did you know? Did you know about her lover and that she was leaving you?"

"I had suspicions about the lover but no proof, and no . . . I had no idea that her plan was to leave, go to him, and take Genevieve."

Lucas released my hands, reached for his wineglass, and took a deep swallow. I did the same and waited.

"I returned home to our apartment late that afternoon. The weather had been exceptionally bad. Heavy rain, high wind. I was surprised to find Danielle and Genevieve not home. When I walked into the kitchen I found Danielle's note on the table. She told me she was very unhappy, had been for many years. She explained that she'd had a lover since the time Genevieve was three and the time had come to go to him permanently."

Lucas took another swallow of wine. "God help me, but my first thought was not for Danielle. In my heart, I had known for a long time that our marriage was over. As I stood there reading her note, it was Genevieve that my heart was breaking for. And within a few hours, the police called to tell me they were both dead. Danielle skidded on the wet highway just outside of Paris. Doing a high rate of speed—in her haste to be with that lover—and she took my daughter with her."

It was then that Lucas broke down, face in his hands, as his sobs filled the room.

I don't think I've ever witnessed such anguish in another person. I pulled Lucas to my chest, rocking back and forth as tears poured down my face. I felt his pain, his grief, his anger, and allowed all of it to connect with his.

Sitting there, holding Lucas tightly in my arms, snippets of various incidents came into my mind—his reaction about me seeking out a sperm donor, his obvious fondness for Max but reluctance to have a child of his own, his hesitation in asking me out, his ability to *trust*. All of it was beginning to make more sense.

"Seeing me with Beau brought back memories of an unfaithful wife, didn't it?" I whispered.

He nodded, leaned over, and touched his lips with mine before getting up and heading toward the bathroom.

I took a sip of wine and realized at that very moment I was experiencing that same feeling of a weight being lifted as I had with Beau. I also realized that all along something deep inside of me knew there was more to Lucas Trudeau than he had chosen to share.

When he returned to the living room, he was composed and had a hint of a smile on his face. Sitting beside me, he took both of my hands in his.

"So . . . now you have my story and you can see I'm not a perfect human being. But maybe now you have a better understanding of why I have acted in certain ways."

I smiled and leaned over to kiss him.

"None of us are perfect, Lucas. Least of all, me. And yes, many things now make much more sense. I'm glad you told me about Genevieve. I love you, Lucas." There, I'd finally said it. And I said it because I *wanted* to, not because I expected a return declaration. "I love you with my entire heart and soul, and I will always love you."

In that moment I saw all of the love I was feeling reflected in Lucas's eyes. He squeezed my hands tighter as a serious expression crossed his face. "Grace, I've loved you from the first moment I laid eyes on you. I just had to be sure."

"I know that," I told him. And I did.

"I want to love you for the rest of our lives and spend all of our moments together."

I didn't utter a word—scared that maybe I'd misunderstood him. And then I heard those words that I realized I'd been longing to hear Lucas say.

"Will you marry me?"

As tears filled my eyes again, but this time from happiness, Lucas reached over to the drawer of the coffee table. He removed a small blue velvet box and looked into my eyes.

"Will you be my wife?" he asked.

I looked down at the most exquisite diamond ring I'd ever seen as tears continued to blur my vision.

"This ring belonged to my grandmother," he said. "And I would love for you to wear it."

"Yes. Oh, God, yes. I'll marry you and I'll wear the ring forever," I told him, holding out my left hand as he slipped the ring onto my finger.

I threw my arms around Lucas's neck.

"I love you, Grace," I heard him say. "I love you with all that I am."

I pulled away to hold my hand out and catch the dazzling sparkle that winked back at me before Lucas took me into his arms and his lips met mine.

Our love and desire rose to the surface as each kiss increased in passion.

"I want you, Lucas," I whispered in his ear. "I want you to make love to me."

"Are you sure?" he whispered back.

I felt my desire rising and nodded. "I'm very sure."

Lucas stood up, looked down at me with a smile, and reached for my hand. As I walked with him to the bedroom, I knew without a doubt that love *was* the most powerful emotion of all.

❧ 36 ❧

When I awoke the next morning, I felt momentarily disoriented. I heard Lucas's soft breathing beside me and smiled. Holding up my left hand, I felt my smile grow wider as all of the events from the night before came rushing back.

Making love with Lucas was everything I knew it would be. Falling asleep in his arms was pure bliss.

I shifted carefully so as not to wake him and stared at the handsome face of the man I had committed to marry. My heart constricted with sorrow as I recalled his loss of Genevieve, but I knew without a doubt that together we would always keep her memory alive.

Lucas stirred, opened his eyes, and smiled.

"I want to wake to that beautiful face for the rest of my life."

"You will," I said. "And I have the ring to prove it."

He laughed and reached for my breast.

I sighed as his hand slid slowly down my body, igniting the desire of the night before.

"You have to open the bookshop, don't you?" I mumbled.

"I'm the owner, and right now I'm going to make love to my fiancée."

Who was I to argue?

* * *

"I think I hit the jackpot," I said, taking a bite of the omelet that Lucas had prepared. "Not only are you handsome, witty, and charming, you're the best chef I know."

Lucas laughed as he refilled my coffee mug and joined me at the table.

"Oh, and by the way," I told him between bites, "I really *can* cook. Maybe not as well as you—but you won't be expected to do all the cooking in our house when we're married."

"I enjoy cooking, but yes, we will share the cooking if you like." He took a sip of coffee, then reached for my hand. "Grace, there's one more thing I wanted to discuss with you that I didn't get to last night."

What more could there be, I thought.

"About children," he began.

But I cut him off. "Yes . . . I know, and I know even more so now. It's okay, Lucas. Really. I understand why you don't want a child—and I'm okay with that. I really am. We have each other, and . . ."

Now he cut me off. "No, no. I also gave that a lot of thought over the weeks we were apart." He took a deep breath. "I love children, Grace. You have no idea how much. But losing Genevieve . . . well, it frightened me. The thought of having another child and something happening . . . well, I wasn't sure I could face that again."

"And now?" I asked.

"And now I know we have no control over those things, but to never take another chance would be an even bigger loss."

I swear I could literally feel my heart swell with even more love for this man. "And so, you mean . . ."

"I mean, let's see what happens. Is that agreeable to you?"

I jumped up to throw my arms around Lucas's neck and laughed when he pulled me into his lap.

"Yes," I said, stroking the side of his face. "Yes, that's extremely agreeable to me."

He kissed my lips and then gently pushed me up. "Okay, now be a good girl and go eat your breakfast or you'll have me dragging you off to bed again."

I laughed as I sat in my chair. "And that would be so bad, why?"

"Because I do have to open that bookshop by noon and you have to get home to poor Annie."

I glanced at my watch and saw it was eight-thirty.

"Right, but Suellen said she'd go over around seven this morning and let her out again for me."

"And when you called her last night, you didn't tell her we were engaged?"

I smiled. "Nope. I only told her I was spending the night here. I heard a snicker come across the phone line and would swear she was thinking, 'I told you so.' She was convinced we loved each other and would get back together."

Lucas laughed. "She was right."

"So I'm going to invite her over this afternoon and I'm going to tell her and Aunt Maude at the same time. God, they'll be ecstatic."

"And Chloe? Are you going to tell your sister we're engaged?"

During all of our talking the night before, I had told Lucas about the part that Chloe had played with me and Beau.

"If she finds out I'm engaged, it won't be from me."

We were gathered at Aunt Maude's kitchen table, and I looked across at two expectant faces waiting for me to say something.

"Okay." I let out a chuckle. "Knowing how you both thrive on good news, I wanted to share my very exciting news with the two people I love at the same time."

I whipped my left hand, which I'd been hiding under the table, out in front of them as I said, "Lucas and I are engaged."

"Lord above," Aunt Maude said at the same time Suellen jumped up so fast from her chair that she knocked it over and came to scoop me into her arms.

"I knew it. I just knew it," she kept saying in between bursts of laughter. "I knew you two were destined to be together."

Aunt Maude laughed. "Oh, Gracie. I couldn't be happier for both of you."

"Thank you, thank you," I said, standing to take a mock bow, glowing in the limelight.

Suellen righted her chair and sat back down. "Okay, now details. We want details as to exactly what happened. I take it all is forgiven about Lucas seeing you with Beau?"

"Yes, that's true. But I have a lot more to fill you in on and all of it isn't happy. Actually, it's quite surprising and sad."

I went on to tell them about Lucas's daughter, his loss, and the difficulty he had dealing with all of it.

"Oh, my goodness," Aunt Maude said, shaking her head. "It's no wonder Lucas was cautious. What a horrific ordeal to go through."

I saw the tears glittering in Suellen's eyes. "God, I can't even imagine what I'd do if something happened to Ashley. That poor man. Does anybody ever get over something like that?"

"Not easily," Aunt Maude said. "But it sounds to me like Lucas has worked through it and gotten to a good place. And Grace, I have no doubt you had a lot to do with that."

"Oh, gosh," Suellen said. "Well, it certainly makes sense now why he never wants any more children."

I smiled. "That's not entirely true. He feels he's ready to take another chance. He loves children, so who knows. We've both agreed to see what happens."

This caused Suellen to jump up again, rush over, and pull me into a tight hug. "Oh, girlfriend, I'm so happy for you. You and Lucas will make the best parents."

I laughed at her exuberance and confidence.

"So when's the wedding?" she asked.

"We haven't set an exact date, but we're thinking October."

"Oh, perfect time with the cooler air arriving."

"And, Aunt Maude . . . we were wondering if maybe we could get married in your garden? It's such a beautiful spot, and this house really feels like home to me."

"Grace, I'd be honored. The garden will be a perfect spot for a wedding, especially in autumn."

"I'm so excited for you," Suellen said. "My little first-grade friend—finally getting married." Tears filled her eyes again.

I laughed. "And romantic that you are, I'd love for you to be my matron of honor. And I'm going to need lots of help choosing a gown, doing decorations, and all that sort of thing."

She began laughing and crying at the same time.

"Really? Your matron of honor? Of course I will! And any help you need, just let me know. Oh, gosh, this is going to be so much fun. Hey," she said, reaching out. "Let me see that ring again. It's gorgeous."

I proudly displayed my left hand. "It belonged to Lucas's grandmother."

"It's really lovely, Grace," my aunt said. "Family heirlooms are so special."

It didn't escape me that neither my aunt nor Suellen had mentioned Chloe's name at all.

Lucas and I were relaxing with coffee after dinner in my living room. Both Annie and Duncan were curled up side by side at the end of the sofa.

I smiled. "I think they're both going to adjust very well to living together."

"I agree. They've always liked each other, which is nice."

"Oh, hey," I said, putting my mug on the table. "Gosh, we have so many things to discuss about getting married. Where will we live? Your place or mine?"

"Well, I did give that a little thought and it's really up to you, but I thought maybe here might be better. With you doing the knitting retreat weekends, you have your office out there in the carriage house and . . . besides, your place is larger. You know—just in case we need that extra bedroom."

I smiled and leaned over to place a kiss on his lips. "Yes, I know, and I like your way of thinking. Okay, so *here* it is. I have no doubt my aunt will be pleased to have us upstairs."

"See, that was easy. One thing settled. What's next on the list?"

"I mentioned to my aunt that we'd like to get married out in the garden, and she said that would be fine. I think she was thrilled that we'd chosen her prized garden for our wedding. Oh, maybe we should decide on a definite date?"

"Good idea. Got a calendar?"

I jumped up to retrieve the one from my desk. "Here we go," I said, laying it out on the coffee table.

Lucas thumbed the pages to October. "Well, do you want early or late October?"

I stared at the boxes and numbers. "Hmm. Well, we don't want it hot and humid, so maybe later October? How about the twenty-fourth?"

"Sounds good to me, and remember that trip to Paris that I'd mentioned? I'm taking you to Paris for a two-week honeymoon. If you would like that."

I threw my arms around Lucas's neck. "Like it? I'd love it! Oh, wait till romantic Suellen hears this. That will be such a special trip."

"It will be, and if you don't mind, I'd like to take you to Père Lachaise Cemetery while we're there—so you can meet my daughter."

"I'd like that, Lucas. I'd like that a lot," I said, placing a kiss on his cheek.

"You won't need me to do the shopping for a gown and that sort of thing, will you?" he asked.

I laughed. "No, you're excused from that duty, Mr. Groom. Suellen will be my assistant with that." This caused me to think of Chloe again.

"Forgiveness is hard, isn't it?" I said.

Lucas nodded and pulled me into the circle of his arms as if he knew what I was thinking and wanted to give me comfort. "Forgiveness can be very hard, yes. But . . . it's also very necessary in order to go on with one's life."

"Have you forgiven Danielle?"

Lucas didn't answer right away. "A part of me has," he then said. "But a part of me still blames her for taking my daughter away from me. Maybe that's natural. I don't know. But I do know that until I was willing to forgive her I was stuck. I was going nowhere, and that's when I made the decision to relocate to Brunswick. And now, I can't help but feel that move ultimately led me to you."

I smiled. "The same with me. Maybe I had really forgiven Beau long before I even realized I had. I've now come to understand that it was *me* I was having a hard time forgiving for all these years. But when I saw him again, spoke with him, I suddenly knew the time had come to also forgive myself."

"Sometimes we're much kinder when it comes to forgiving other people."

"Do you think Chloe is sorry for what she did? Calling Lila and telling her about Beau and me."

"I can't answer that, Grace."

And since I had no desire to confront her to obtain that answer, I might never know.

❧ 37 ❧

The end of April had me reflecting a lot on the previous six months. So much had happened that in some ways it felt like a lifetime. My coffee shop and residence had burned to the ground. Lucas and I began dating and became closer. My sister and I reconciled only to be estranged once again. I began working with my aunt doing the knitting retreat weekends. And—in six months I would be married. Something that six months before I wasn't sure would ever happen.

Lucas had gone to Gainesville for the day to do errands and I was covering the bookshop. I was arranging some new arrivals on the shelf when I noticed a gentleman waiting for my attention.

"Oh, sorry," I said, turning toward him. "Can I help you with something?"

He appeared to be mid- to late forties, streaks of gray in his dark hair adding a note of distinction, and he was well dressed in jeans and a polo shirt.

Pushing his wire-rim glasses farther up the bridge of his nose, he stammered, "Ah, yes . . . I wanted to know . . . ah . . ."

His hesitation made me wonder if perhaps he wanted to inquire if we carried porn books, so when he went on to say, "I wanted to know if you know the woman working in the coffee shop," I burst out laughing.

Geez, Grace, I thought, *get your mind out of the gutter.*

"Oh, Suellen?" I said, stifling my laughter. "Gosh, yes. We've been friends since first grade. Is there a problem?"

"Oh, no. Not at all," he said, shifting the stack of books he held in his hands. "I was just wondering . . . do you know if she's married?"

I was so stunned by his question it took me a moment to answer. "No, Suellen's not married. She's been divorced for years."

A smile crossed his face, which enhanced his nice looks. "Oh, I see. That's good."

He must have seen the confused expression on my face.

"I realize that was a pretty odd question," he explained. "But I've been staying here on the island for a few days and going into the coffee café. I've struck up a few conversations with her and . . . I'd like to get to know her better, so I just wanted to be sure. . . ."

Oh, wow, could this be possible? The queen of romance might be getting an interested romantic partner of her own? I figured the least I could do was notch up my matchmaking abilities and maybe help the process along.

"That's really nice of you to check first," I told him. "And listen, just because she's my best friend, I'm not going to enhance her qualities, *but* . . . Suellen is one of the sweetest, nicest, and most caring people I've ever met."

He nodded. "I think I already gathered that. Is she seeing anybody?"

"No. She had a nasty divorce years ago, raised her one and only daughter on her own, so she's a tad cautious with men. Ashley happens to be my goddaughter and she's in college in Georgia."

"I see," he said again, and then balanced the books in one hand in order to reach out with his other. "By the way, I'm Mitchell Thomas. Nice to meet you."

I returned his handshake and said, "Likewise. I'm Grace Stone. My fiancé, Lucas, is the owner of the bookshop and café."

His glance took in the room. "It's a very nice shop."

"Where're you from?" I asked.

"Originally, the San Francisco area. Gave up my high-profile job in the Silicon Valley and relocated to Tampa a few years ago. Now . . . I run a dog-grooming service."

Well, he must like dogs if he grooms them, I thought. *A couple points for him.*

"Is this your first visit to the island?"

"Yes, and I have to say I've fallen in love with it. As a matter of fact, I've extended my stay for another week."

I smiled. "Yeah, this town can be like a magnet."

"Well," he said, again juggling the books in his hands. "I've taken up too much of your time. Thank you so much for all the information. Maybe you could ring me up?"

"Sure," I said, walking to the counter. I noticed his taste in reading ran from Michael Connelly to Ken Follett to a new mystery that had recently hit the *New York Times* list.

I passed the tote bag across the counter. "Well, it was very nice meeting you, Mitchell. I hope you'll stop in again."

"Oh, I'm sure I will, and nice to meet you, too, Grace."

Instead of leaving from the bookshop door, he headed back over to the coffee café, and I couldn't resist standing in the archway to take a peek.

Suellen turned around as he came up to her counter. He must have said something humorous because I saw a huge smile cross her face and then she laughed. They talked for a few more minutes and then he left.

Hmm, interesting. Very interesting. I waited a few minutes and then sauntered over and perched on a stool in front of the counter.

Suellen looked up from scooping coffee into a filter. "Hey, Grace, what's up?"

I smiled. "What's up? Gee, I seem to recall another time, another coffee café where girl met boy."

A perplexed expression crossed her face. "What on earth are you talking about?"

Trying hard not to laugh, I said, "Mitchell Thomas."

Was that a shade of crimson I saw creeping up her face?

"Oh . . . him? The guy that just left? You know him?"

"Well, after he gave me the third degree about you, yeah, I'd say I know him fairly well."

"Me? He was asking you questions about *me?*"

"Ah, yup. Hey, could I have a double latte?" I loved dragging out information with Suellen. I'd been doing it since we were kids, and I knew how much it annoyed her.

She threw the coffee scoop down. "No way in hell are you getting coffee till you tell me what's going on."

My laughter finally broke through. "Well, Miss Romance, I do declare I think you have a real live romance of your own brewing. He specifically came over to the bookshop to ask me if you were married."

Surprise covered Suellen's face. "No way!"

"Yup. Said he wanted to get to know you better but wanted to be sure you weren't married or seeing somebody."

Now I was positive that was a deep crimson covering my friend's face. "So I take it you're also interested?" I asked.

"Well . . . ah . . . he started coming in here a few days ago and you know, we started talking, and . . ."

"And you're interested in him," I stated.

"Well, he's a good-looking guy and he seems intelligent and, yeah, I did enjoy talking with him, so maybe. Maybe I'm a little interested, but I don't know a thing about him. He only told me he lives in Tampa and is here for a few days visiting the island."

"Hmm, make that a week, honey. He's extended his stay."

Suellen's face lit up. "He has?"

"Yup, and he's originally from San Francisco. Worked in the Silicon Valley but sounds like he wanted to get away from the pressure, because now he runs a dog-grooming service."'

"He told you all this?"

"Of course. Once he found out we were best friends, I'm sure he had no doubt whatsoever that I'd relay it all to you."

"I'll make you that latte now," Suellen said. "Sounds like you talked me up to him. Thanks."

"Hey, what are best friends for? Did he ask you out?"

"No, but he came back over here to tell me he'd stop in again tomorrow morning."

"Ah, yes, it's only a matter of time until you, Suellen McSwain, have joined the ranks of the dating world."

And I was right. Suellen had her first date with Mitchell two days later. He took her to Gainesville for lunch and a movie. Tonight Lucas and I had invited them to his place for dinner.

I was slicing tomatoes for the salad and felt Lucas come up behind me. He kissed the back of my neck.

"So my little fiancée enjoys playing matchmaker, huh?" he said, pressing his body against mine. "Must be those French genes for romance and *l'amour*."

I laughed and jabbed him gently in the stomach. "Must be," I said.

Lucas lifted the cover on the large pot simmering on the stove, and the mouthwatering aroma of his cassoulet filled the kitchen. "I'm glad Suellen will have a companion," he said. "I think that will be good for her."

I laughed. "I might be the matchmaker, but you're the romantic at heart."

Suellen arrived a short time later with Mitchell at her side. I noticed she seemed to have a glow about her, and I couldn't have been happier for my friend.

The four of us enjoyed general conversation while we had a glass of wine with cheese before dinner.

When we sat at the dining room table, Lucas lifted his wineglass. "Here's to good times with good friends. *Bon appétit*."

The cassoulet was exceptionally good, with a mixture of various meats, beans, fats, and herbs.

"Oh, Lucas," Suellen said after her first bite. "You really outdid yourself with this one. It's wonderful."

Mitchell nodded. "I must say, I thought I cooked fairly well for a bachelor, but I can't compete with this. My compliments to the chef."

Lucas sent me a wink and smiled. "Thank you, but it's really quite easy, and I'd be happy to share my recipe with you."

"That would be great. So, Grace, in addition to helping at the bookshop, Suellen tells me that you and your aunt have a business doing knitting retreat weekends. That sounds like fun."

"Oh, it is, but I think we might have to slow down a bit."

Suellen looked across the table at me in surprise. "Oh, why's that?"

"I think every weekend is becoming a bit too much for Aunt Maude. She barely has time to relax and it's Friday again with more knitters arriving. I think she's looking tired lately, although she'd never admit it to me."

"You know," Suellen said, buttering her roll. "Now that you mention it, I saw Maude at the post office yesterday and I thought the same thing. She looked a little pale and well . . . just tired. So you could be right, but how on earth will you convince her to cut back a little?"

"I have no idea, but I plan to have a talk with her."

"Did she find a replacement for Rachel yet?"

"Yes, thank goodness. She found a nice girl from Chiefland and she'll begin the end of May when Rachel leaves. Mitchell, was there a reason you wanted to open a dog-grooming business? I'm always curious why people choose certain jobs."

He laughed. "Well, I have an Old English sheepdog, and Olivia has always required constant grooming. When she was a puppy I decided to purchase the equipment and do it myself. I found that I really enjoyed it, and over the years I taught myself how to groom various breeds. So when the time came for me to get out of the rat race, I thought, why not open my own business?"

"Very good idea," I said. "And it's obvious you enjoy it. Are the dogs well behaved for you?"

"For the most part, yes. Now and again I get one that doesn't want to cooperate, but eventually they get used to it and I think they even enjoy it."

By the time Suellen and Mitchell left a few hours later, I had decided that my best friend had found a male companion who was worthy of the good qualities she had to offer. I also decided that my matchmaking skills had probably paid off.

38

A few evenings later Suellen and I were sitting in her living room working on our knitting projects. I missed my weekly gathering with the women at the yarn shop, so I appreciated my friend suggesting we have our own evening of girl time and knitting.

"I heard the book signing with Shelby Sullivan went well," she said, not taking her eyes from the intricate sweater pattern she was working on.

"Oh, it did. A huge success. Lucas has already lined up some other Florida authors over the next few months. It's good for the bookshop and good for the authors, so he's pleased."

"Do we know yet who my partner will be at your wedding?"

"No, he hasn't made a definite decision yet on best man. He only has a few male acquaintances here on the island. Fellows he goes fishing with, but nobody that he's really close to. What he really wants is to have his cousin from France."

Suellen's head now popped up from her knitting. "Really?"

"Yeah, Lucas is an only child, and Jean-Paul has always been like a brother to him."

"So what's the problem?"

"Jean-Paul's wife is quite ill. Cancer. And Lucas doesn't want to put him on the spot—committing to be best man in October and not knowing what the situation will be then."

"Oh, that's too bad. Gee, I hope it works for him to be here."

"Me too. I can tell it really would mean a lot to Lucas."

"How's Maude doing? Did you have that talk with her?"

"She still looks tired to me, and yeah, I brought up the subject of cutting back on the retreats. To be honest, I was surprised she didn't fight me on it. We're booked through the end of this month for every weekend, but for June we only have one weekend booked right now, and she said maybe we should leave it like that. July and August are the same. She didn't say not to book if somebody calls, but I'm not going to. I think one weekend a month is plenty. Besides, I'm really a little concerned about her. I think she needs to slow down, and I'll feel better when she sees the doctor in a few weeks."

The next morning before heading to the bookshop I checked in with Aunt Maude. Knocking on the back door, I walked in hollering, "It's me." Lafitte greeted me in the kitchen with nonstop meowing.

I reached down to give him a pat. "What's your problem? Where's Aunt Maude? Aunt Maude, are you here?" I called, walking into the living room.

That was when I saw her. Crumpled in a small heap on the carpet in front of the sofa.

"Oh, my God!" I yelled, racing to her. "Aunt Maude, it's me, Grace. What happened?"

She opened her eyes slowly as she whispered, "Grace . . . I need some help."

I reached into my pocket, yanked out my cell, dialed 911, and quickly explained the situation to the dispatcher. I was told not to hang up, and I gripped the phone as I brushed the hair from my aunt's face.

"An ambulance is en route," I heard the woman say before I disconnected the call.

"Are you in pain? Did you fall?" I asked my aunt, kneeling

down beside her. I was stunned that she had seemed to age overnight. What had been pale skin the past few weeks was now pasty white. I took her hand and felt the clamminess.

"No . . . no pain. I felt . . . dizzy . . . last night . . ."

"Last night? Dear God! You've been lying here since last night?" Fear shot through me, and all of a sudden I felt like I was face to face with my aunt's mortality. *Where the hell is that ambulance?*

"I tried . . . I tried to . . . call you . . . but you didn't . . ."

"It's okay. Don't talk," I told her as I finally heard the wail of sirens coming closer.

The rest of what followed seemed like a blur. EMTs rushed into the house loaded down with equipment, and they immediately began working on my aunt. I heard the EMT say low heart rate, fly her to Shands, and the next thing I knew, Cedar Key's fire chief had his arms around me, once again consoling me.

"Grace, they're going to do everything they can for your aunt. I know you'll want to go to the hospital, but you're in no condition to drive. Do you want me to call Lucas for you?"

I nodded dumbly as I saw my aunt being lifted onto a stretcher. One EMT was on his cell and I dimly heard him talking with somebody about my aunt's condition and then heard him say, "We'll meet you at the helicopter pad on Twenty-four." I knew that for serious health injuries or accidents, residents of Cedar Key were brought via ambulance to State Road 24, just off the island, where they were met by the helicopter that would transport them to Shands in Gainesville, but I had never thought my aunt Maude would be one of those patients.

I stood beside her and took her hand in mind. "You'll be okay," I told her, although I had no way of knowing this. "They're going to fly you to Shands and I'll see you there. I love you, Aunt Maude." I leaned over to kiss her cheek and realized the wetness I felt was from my own tears.

"I . . . love you . . . too . . . Grace," she whispered before they took the stretcher out to the ambulance.

Jim Jacobs came back into the living room. "I just spoke with

Lucas," he said as the wail of sirens filled the air again. "He's on his way. Here, Miss Grace, come sit down."

He ushered me to the sofa where Lafitte came to rub against my leg. I lifted the large, fluffy cat in my arms, cuddling him, as sobs overtook my body. That was how Lucas found me a few minutes later when he raced in the front door.

"Grace, I'm here," he said, wrapping me in his arms.

"We have to go, we have to go," I told him, unable to control the tears.

"Yes, yes, it will be all right," he said, with more confidence than I felt. "Let me lock the back door and we will leave."

Returning to the living room, he said, "Okay, let's go," and put an arm around my waist to lead me out to the car. He passed me my handbag and closed the door. I heard him thank Jim Jacobs before jumping into the driver's seat and heading off the island.

During the one-hour drive, my left hand gripped Lucas's while my right one kept dabbing my eyes with a tissue. Except for Lucas's occasional words of reassurance, neither one of us spoke.

When we were on Archer Road with the stores and restaurants on either side, I knew it wouldn't be much longer until we were at the hospital.

"I can't lose her," I finally said. "I just can't lose her, Lucas." I was about to say *she's all that I have,* when I realized that was no longer true. I *did* have Lucas. But it was Aunt Maude who had been both mother and father to me since I was twelve, and the thought of losing her brought a fresh flood of tears.

I felt him squeeze my hand. "Do not think that, Grace. Your aunt is a strong woman."

But she hadn't looked strong at all when I'd found her on the floor. She'd looked so fragile and small. Two words I never would have used to describe my aunt.

"I'm going to drop you at the emergency room entrance and go park," I heard Lucas say as I looked up and saw the brick buildings on my left.

As soon as he braked, I yanked open the door to get out. "See you in there," I called over my shoulder as I ran toward the glass doors that automatically opened for me.

I raced over to the information desk. "Maude Stone," I said to the middle-aged woman sitting behind the glass partition. "I'm her niece, and she was flown here from Cedar Key. Can you tell me where she is?"

The woman adjusted the reading glasses perched on her nose and glanced down at papers in front of her. "Yes," she said. "She just arrived a little while ago. You'll have to have a seat."

"I need to know how she is. Can't I see her?"

"The doctor is with her now. I'm sure as soon as he knows something the nurse will be out to speak with you."

I could feel my patience disappearing quickly. "But I need to *know* if she's all right. Can't *anybody* here tell me anything?" I heard my own voice rising at the same time I felt Lucas by my side.

I'm not sure if it was the increased volume of my tone or the sight of a male next to me, but the woman coughed, cleared her throat, and said, "I'll call back there for you and see what I can find out."

"Thank you," I said, not entirely sure I meant it and still not budging from the information window. The window, which she had now effectively closed between us, preventing me from hearing her side of the conversation.

"Would you like some coffee, Grace?" Lucas asked as his hand reached for mine.

I shook my head. "No. Thanks," I said as I continued to stand there waiting for word on my aunt.

The woman finally hung up the phone and slid back the barrier. "The doctor is with your aunt. They're going to be conducting some tests. And a nurse will be out to speak with you very shortly. I'm afraid that's all I can tell you," she said in a kinder tone.

"Thank you," I told her, and this time I meant it.

I allowed Lucas to lead me to one of the chairs in the waiting room, and we had just sat down when a nurse came through a door and hollered, "Grace Stone? Is there a Grace Stone here?"

I jumped up and ran to her. "That's me. How's my aunt?"

"It appears she had an episode of what we call bradycardia, low heart rate. This is what caused her to be dizzy and pass out. We don't know if there're any other cardiac complications, so the doctor has ordered multiple tests. A CT scan, MRI, and possibly a cardiac catheterization. We're going to be admitting her, and we're waiting for a room now. You can come back for a few minutes to see her if you like."

"Oh, yes. Thank you so much." I glanced at Lucas.

"You go, Grace. I'll be waiting right here for you."

I nodded and followed the nurse through the door and down a corridor with curtained cubicles on each side. She turned into the last one on the left.

"Here you go," she said, pulling the curtain aside. "Miss Maude, your niece is here. Just a few minutes," she told me, leaving the area.

"Oh, Aunt Maude. How're you doing?" Except for the hospital gown, I didn't think my aunt looked any different than she had at her house. I reached for her hand and did notice the clamminess seemed to be gone.

"Tired. Just very tired, sweetie."

"Well, they're going to get you to a room and admitted and then do a lot of tests to find out what's going on. Lucas and I will be out in the waiting room, so we'll be here when they take you to your room."

"Oh, Gracie," she said, and it didn't escape me that even her voice sounded filled with fatigue. "I'm sure you both have things to do. You don't have to stay here."

I smiled. "Try and get us to leave."

A weak smile covered her face. "Okay."

The nurse returned and went over to pat my aunt's hand. "I'm afraid it might be a couple hours till we get you to your room. We'll be sending you for a CT scan first." She turned to look at me. "She'll be in three twenty-two, but you might want to go to the cafeteria for a while to kill some time."

"Thanks." I leaned over and kissed my aunt's cheek. "I love you, Aunt Maude. I'll see you up in your room."

I wanted to go before she saw the tears once again filling my eyes, and I retraced my way back down the corridor, through the door into the waiting room—and saw my sister, Chloe, standing there talking to Lucas.

39

I marched directly over to Chloe. "What the hell are you doing here?" I said before I could stop myself, and I instantly hated the nastiness I heard in my tone.

"She *is* my aunt, too, Gracie. I had to come."

Of course she did. What happened between Chloe and me didn't have a thing to do with our aunt.

"Is she going to be okay?" she asked, and I heard the fear in her question.

I let out a deep sigh. "I don't know. We don't know anything yet. They're going to be taking her to her room shortly and then doing a lot of tests. All I know is she had a low heart rate and that's what caused her to pass out."

Lucas had stood there quietly and now said, "Why don't we all go to the cafeteria and get something to eat or coffee until your aunt is in her room?"

Was he crazy? He expected me to *break bread* with this sister who had betrayed me?

I heard this sister immediately say, "That would be good."

I had no choice but to follow Lucas and Chloe to the elevator.

We wound our way through the counters of food and drinks. When we got to the cashier I saw both Chloe and Lucas had gotten a sandwich, and as she reached in her handbag to pay, Lucas held up his hand. "No, no," he said, holding out a twenty to the girl behind the register.

I took my coffee and headed to an empty table, filled with a million conflicting emotions. Lucas and Chloe joined me, and none of us spoke while they ate their sandwiches and I sipped coffee.

All of a sudden I heard Aunt Maude's words—telling me that someday she'd no longer be here and that Chloe and I would only have each other. I said a silent prayer that that day hadn't yet arrived.

Chloe wiped her lips with a napkin before taking a sip of her coffee. "You're the one that found her, Gracie? That must have been scary."

"It was." And then it suddenly hit me. "*Who* called you?"

I glanced up in time to see her look at Lucas, and he nodded.

"Lucas did," she said softly.

I now turned to directly face him, waiting for an explanation.

"It was the right thing to do, Grace. I called her from the bookshop as I was leaving," he told me, to which I said nothing.

I continued sipping my coffee and looked around the cafeteria. A few tables over, an elderly woman was being consoled by another woman who possibly was her daughter. A man in his forties sat by himself, a soft drink in his hand, deep in thought. So much sadness in the world, I thought. So many people facing terrible health issues either for themselves or for family members. A woman approached the man who had been sitting alone, kissed his cheek, sat beside him, and took his hand. *How do people get through these situations,* I wondered. But I already knew the answer to that—they get through it with each other and, most important, with love.

I glanced over at Chloe, who had her head bent and was fingering the spoon. Sitting across the table from Lucas and me, she looked alone. Alone and lonely.

"Come on," I said, getting up. "Aunt Maude should be in her room by now." I didn't want to sit there and dwell on my sister.

When we got to the room I let Chloe go in first but wasn't prepared for her reaction. She walked over to the bed, took my aunt's hand, and burst out crying. Typical of Aunt Maude, it was her that was comforting Chloe.

"There, there," she said. "I'm fine, Chloe. Beginning to feel much better."

But it took my sister another moment or two before she regained her composure.

"Aunt Maude, I'm so sorry. So very sorry," I heard her say, and couldn't help but wonder if she was only referring to just my aunt's episode.

"I'm glad you're here. I'm glad you're both here," my aunt said, and the meaning wasn't lost on me.

"Well, hello, Miss Maude. Feeling a bit better?"

I turned to the sound of a male voice I assumed belonged to the doctor.

My aunt managed a weak smile. "A bit, yes. These are my two nieces, Chloe and Grace, and Grace's fiancé, Lucas."

Handshakes were exchanged, and the doctor moved to the side of the bed.

"I'm glad you're all together. I just wanted to give you an update as to what's going on," he said, flipping through some pages he held in his hands. He turned toward my aunt. "What happened, Miss Maude, is that your heart rate fell dangerously low. We've gotten your records from your primary care physician. Normally your rate has been in the seventies. When you arrived in the emergency room it was in the low fifties and may have been lower when you actually passed out at home."

"What caused that?" my aunt asked.

"There's various reasons, but in your case your EKG shows that the strength and timing of the electrical signals passing through your heart is off. It showed us your heart is beating too slow and the rhythm is irregular."

"So this is dangerous?" I questioned.

"If left untreated, yes." He turned his attention back to my aunt. "However, we're going to do a few more tests today, just to be sure nothing else is going on. And right now I'd say my recommendation will probably be a pacemaker. Are you familiar with those?"

My aunt nodded. "Oh, yes. It's a little battery-operated generator that they place right here just under the skin." She pointed below her left clavicle. "And wires connect the generator to the heart, which controls the heartbeat."

The doctor smiled and nodded. "I'd say you're quite knowledgeable, Miss Maude. That's precisely what it does. So let's get the rest of the tests done, then we'll have a better idea what we're going to do. Any questions?"

"Yes," my aunt said. "When can I go home?"

All of us laughed as the doctor patted my aunt's arm. "My goodness, you've only been here a few hours. But if the tests go well, we can do the pacemaker insertion tomorrow afternoon, and I'd like to keep you overnight, just to be sure everything is normal. So you could reasonably go home the day after tomorrow. How's that?"

"Wonderful, and thank you."

When the doctor left, I moved to the side of the bed. "Is there anything I can do for you at home or anything I can bring you tomorrow?"

"You'll have to check on poor Lafitte for me and feed him. I'm sure he's quite upset with me gone."

"Oh, don't worry at all. When we leave here, I'm going straight home and I'll spend some time with him."

My sister stood on the opposite side of the bed while my aunt instructed me what to bring for clothes when she was discharged. I could be wrong, but I got the feeling that Chloe felt like an outsider.

As if picking up on this, my aunt said, "So are the three of you going out for dinner before you head back to the island? It's already five o'clock."

"Oh . . . no . . . I don't . . ." Chloe started to say at the same time Lucas said, "Yes, that's a good idea. We can stop at that deli that Grace likes on Archer."

Guess I don't get a vote in this at all, I thought, and said nothing.

"No, really," Chloe said. "We came in separate cars."

"That's not a problem," I found myself saying. "You can follow us." My tone may not have been enthusiastic, but I'd said the words.

I felt my aunt reach for my hand and give it a squeeze. "Very good idea, Grace. Now listen, I want all of you to skedaddle."

"Oh, but . . ." I started to say, and was cut off by my aunt.

"No buts. I'm tired and I'd really like to nap for a while in between those tests they have planned for me. I'll be just fine. I want you to stop for dinner and then go home. Give me a call in the morning."

I knew there was no arguing with my aunt and leaned over to kiss her good-bye. "Okay, now behave," I told her.

Chloe did the same and left the room with us. When we got down to the main lobby, Lucas explained to her where the deli was located and she said she'd meet us there.

Walking across the parking lot to the car, I exhaled a deep breath. When Lucas had dropped me off hours earlier at the emergency room entrance, the fear I'd felt was overwhelming. I'd been so scared of losing my aunt. I wouldn't feel entirely relieved until I had her back home, but at that very moment I certainly felt like I'd been given a very big gift.

❧ 40 ❧

I was having my first cup of coffee the following morning downstairs in my aunt's apartment. I'd been awake since five and had come down to check on Lafitte and feed him. No doubt about it, my aunt's cat might have a feisty streak but he was exhibiting definite signs of missing my aunt. I was giving him some extra attention when my cell went off.

I was surprised to hear my aunt's voice at six-thirty in the morning. "Is everything okay?" I asked anxiously.

"Fine, fine," she said, and her voice did sound a tad stronger to me. "I didn't want to wake you so early, so I called your cell to leave a message if it wasn't turned on. I wanted to let you know that the doctor came back last evening to let me know all the tests were okay and the diagnosis is, as he predicted, that I need a pacemaker."

"Oh, thank God!" I let out a sigh of relief. "So is he doing that today?"

"Yes, at one o'clock."

"That's great. I'm so happy this procedure will fix the problem." I'd had visions of bypass surgery or something equally involved requiring a longer hospital stay and recuperation. "So you should be home tomorrow."

"Yes, I'm pretty sure I will be. How's my Lafitte doing?"

I smiled. "He's in my lap as we speak. I came downstairs about an hour ago to spend some extra time with him. I think he's having a major case of loneliness. But he's really fine."

I heard a chuckle come across the line. "Yes, I'm sure he is."

"Well, I'll be at the hospital later this afternoon. By then you should be back in your room with your new little gizmo all in place."

"Yes, Grace . . . I wanted to talk to you about that. I need you to do me a favor."

"Of course, anything," I said, before realizing maybe I'd spoken too quickly.

"Well, I knew that both you and Chloe would want to come here later today and that's a lot—driving one hour each way. So I've . . . booked you both a room at the Holiday Inn down the street. This way you can stay there tonight and then come and get me in the morning without making that hour trip again."

"You what?" I gasped. And did I hear her say *a* room? Did she expect me to have a pajama party with my sister?

"Now, Grace . . ."

"Aunt Maude, I seriously doubt that Chloe's going to want to spend the night with me, in the same room no less."

"Actually, she's already agreed to it. She wants to talk to you, and she feels you both need to be someplace where you won't be interrupted." My aunt paused and then said, "Please, Grace, will you do this for me?"

My aunt asked extremely little of me. She knew it was darn near impossible to deny her infrequent requests.

I felt myself blowing air across the phone line and shaking my head. Maude Stone's heart might be weak until that pacemaker was inserted, but she was still one very strong woman.

"Okay," I heard myself say reluctantly. "Okay, I'll do it, but I can't promise you anything. I certainly cannot promise that we'll exit that hotel tomorrow morning and be joined at the hip."

"No, no. Of course not. I'll see you both later this afternoon."

I had a strong suspicion that a smile crossed my aunt's face as she hung up the phone.

* * *

"Wow!" Suellen said later that morning as I sat nursing a double latte at the coffee café. "I have to give your aunt credit. That woman sure knows how to get things done. So you and Chloe are driving into Gainesville together?"

"Yup," I said with no enthusiasm. "I'm picking her up at two o'clock. It ought to be a jolly good evening."

Suellen let out a chuckle. I gave her a nasty look, and she busied herself wiping down the counter.

"So," she said. "My boss said I could have a couple days off next week. Think you could cover for me?"

"Sure. Where're you going? Up to visit Ashley?"

"No. Down to visit Mitchell."

I felt my mood changing. Nothing like a bit of romance to make all right in the world. "Really? Oh, that's great. Going to spend a few days with him?"

"Yup. From the sounds of it, he has a gorgeous condo overlooking Tampa Bay, and he said there's some great restaurants down there he'd like to take me to. I think it'll be fun."

"Oh, I'm sure it will be, Suellen. I'm happy for you."

"I knew you'd cover for her," I heard Lucas say as he came up beside me and pulled me into an embrace. "Are you all packed for your overnight trip?"

"Yeah. I'm packed but certainly not looking forward to this."

"Give it a chance, Grace," he said. "That's all you have to do—give it a chance."

"Right, and that might be easier said than done."

Chloe was standing in front of her building, a small overnight bag at her feet, when I swung by at precisely two o'clock.

"Hi," she said, settling herself beside me.

"Hi," was all I said.

Neither of us spoke again until I reached US 19 and continued east on 24 toward Gainesville.

"Is Lucas on pet duty?" she asked. "Will he be taking care of Annie and Lafitte?"

"Yeah, he'll go this evening and feed Lafitte and then take

Annie for a walk when he walks Duncan and go back over in the morning."

"That's nice of him." When I remained silent, she said, "He's a really nice guy, Grace."

"I know that."

I guess she assumed conversation on my part was going to be limited and reached into her tote bag to remove her knitting. I glanced over and saw she was working on an incredibly gorgeous mint green cabled sweater with lots of intricate twists. I'd have bet anything the yarn was cashmere.

"Guess that's the Holiday Inn we're staying at," I said as we passed the sign.

"Right. Grace, thank you for agreeing to do this."

I just raised my eyebrows and focused on the traffic in front of me. *Did I really have a choice?* I thought.

By the time we found a parking spot at the hospital and got to our aunt's room it was close to three-thirty. We walked in to find her bed empty and looked at each other.

Without hesitating, I walked back out to the corridor over to the nurses' station. "Could you tell me where Maude Stone is? She had a pacemaker put in a couple of hours ago."

"Sure," the nurse said with a smile. "Let me call down there and see what's going on."

She punched some numbers into the phone while Chloe and I stood side by side waiting.

After explaining she was inquiring on Maude Stone, I heard her say, "Okay. Great. Thanks."

"She did very well. They just wanted to keep her in recovery to monitor her before bringing her to her room. She had a sedative and was a bit drowsy, but she should be back up here within twenty minutes or so. You can wait in her room."

"Thank you," my sister and I both said at the same time.

We went back to the room, each taking a chair, and as if on cue we both removed our knitting from our tote bags. There's no doubt that knitting has a calming effect—something all knitters know and probably the reason why so many of us take our knitting everywhere we go.

I had gotten through a few rows of my lace pattern when I looked up to see a gurney being wheeled into the room.

"There's my girls," I heard my aunt say, and I stood up at the same time that Chloe did.

I was pretty surprised to see the difference in my aunt's appearance from the day before. Color had returned to her cheeks. She looked less tired, and finally I felt a huge wave of relief wash over me.

She was easily transferred to her bed, and a nurse approached to take her blood pressure and heart rate. "Good job, Miss Maude. Your new ticker seems to be working perfectly. I'll be back in a little while to check on you again."

"Thank you," my aunt told her, a huge smile on her face. "Well, see, girls? I told you I'd be just fine."

"You do look much better," I told her. "You're sure you feel okay?"

"Right as rain. And you brought my clothes for discharge tomorrow?"

"I hung them up in your closet," Chloe said.

"Good. Very good. I'm anxious to get back on that island. I take it Lafitte is behaving himself?"

I smiled. "Yeah, he's trying, but I know he'll be glad to have you back. Poor guy, I'm sure he's confused and can't figure out where you are."

"I know. I'm his family, after all," she said, looking up to catch my glance. It was then she noticed our tote bags with the knitting. "Oh, show me what you girls are working on."

Chloe brought her sweater over, and I was right. It was cashmere and quite gorgeous. I produced my scarf done in a silk bamboo.

"You girls are master knitters. I'm proud of both of you. How's the yarn shop going, Chloe?"

"Wonderful. Dora and I are so pleased. I really love being a partner with her."

"I knew that would work out well. Now girls, I want you to run along. Go have yourselves a nice dinner, some nice wine, and a good evening. Oh, and by the way, the room is already paid for.

And in the morning, don't rush. Get breakfast someplace before you come to get me. I'm told I can't leave till about eleven anyway."

Leave it to my aunt, I thought. I might be a master knitter, but she was a master organizer.

We kissed her good-bye and walked out of the hospital together. Heading to the car I knew the moment of truth had arrived and wondered how it would all end.

❧ 41 ❧

Chloe and I removed our luggage from the trunk of my car, walked inside the hotel, registered, and got our keys.

Heading up in the elevator to our room, she said, "I was wondering if it would be okay if we call room service later for dinner. That way we can just relax and talk without going down to the restaurant."

"Sure," I said, stepping off the elevator on the third floor. "Fine with me."

While unpacking, Chloe produced a bottle of wine and held it up. "I thought maybe we'd have some," she said. "It's a Cabernet I think you'll like."

I nodded and went to sit on the sofa, allowing her to take the lead in what was to come.

She uncorked the bottle, poured some into two glasses, and passed one to me before curling up at the other end of the sofa.

"Here's to you and Lucas," she said, holding up her glass. "I know you're engaged, Grace, and I'm really happy for you. I'm wishing you both a lifetime of happiness."

"Thank you," I said before taking a sip.

She placed her glass on the table and leaned forward. "Can I see your ring?"

I dangled my hand in front of her.

"It's really gorgeous."

"Thanks. It belonged to Lucas's grandmother."

"And the wedding is set for October?"

I nodded.

"Despite what I've done in the past, Grace, with you and Beau—I really *am* very happy for you."

I remained silent and took another sip of wine.

She let out a deep sigh and did the same.

"I'm not sure where to begin," she then said. "And I'm not sure that whatever I say will make any difference at all with how you feel about me, but . . . I at least want to try and clear the air."

"Okay. I'm willing to listen."

"When I first came to Cedar Key we had the discussion about our parents, so I'm not going to rehash that. I just want to say that I know now that I was wrong in the way I perceived your years with them. I've come to see that Aunt Maude was right—they may not have loved me in the way I had hoped for, but I do feel they did their best. And what transpired between you and me was *my* problem. It wasn't caused by anything you said or did."

I nodded, waiting for her to go on.

She let out another deep sigh. "I wish I had a reason as to why I called Beau's wife," she said, fingering the stem on her wineglass. "But there is no valid reason for me to have done something so vicious."

"You're right. There was no reason whatsoever for you to be so cruel. What possessed you to do such a thing?" I clenched my hands as I could feel my anger building again.

Chloe shook her head from side to side. "I'm not sure," she said softly. "I did see you both leaving that hotel in Jacksonville late one afternoon. I had heard rumors that you were seeing Beau, and when I saw you I knew it was true. You were both laughing, holding hands, and . . . I was . . . jealous. My marriage to Parker had always been difficult and it was only getting worse. It's no excuse . . . I know that, Gracie. I know that. . . ."

"Your marriage was difficult? From what I observed you had a wealthy and handsome husband, two sons, a gorgeous home, you were well connected in the community—it seems to me that you got precisely what you'd always wanted."

Chloe nodded. "Right. A case of be careful what you wish for," she said, getting up to refill our wineglasses.

She returned to the sofa and took a slow sip of wine. "Things aren't always as they seem. I've come to believe that events occur in our lives that end up changing us—not always for the better."

I recalled how I'd always felt Chloe had changed during her college years and waited for her to explain, but she remained silent and I saw an expression of anguish cross her face.

"Wanna talk about it?" I asked.

She shook her head. "No, but I do want you to know how sincerely sorry I am for calling Beau's wife. No matter what was going on in my life, it was no excuse to ruin yours. I know you can probably never forgive me for what I did, but I want you to know how sorry I am. I also need you to know . . . that I've always admired you, Grace." She paused for a moment as if considering whether to continue. "You have strength—the strength I always lacked. I hope you won't be angry . . . but Aunt Maude recently told me about your miscarriage. Learning about that, and that it happened during the time I called Beau's wife, made me feel even worse. Your life hasn't been that easy either. I know that now, but I also know you're the kind of woman that goes forward, rather than wallowing in her past like I've done for so many years. I'm proud of you, Gracie. I really am."

She reached across the sofa to take my hand in hers.

"And Grace, I'm also sorry for telling Beau last year that you were on Cedar Key. I think in my warped mind I thought maybe what I'd destroyed years ago might be repaired. I honestly didn't know you were getting involved with Lucas."

I believed her. "Actually," I told her, "you probably did me a huge favor by telling Beau where I was."

A look of surprise crossed my sister's face. "Really?"

"Yeah, really. I've had my demons, too, Chloe, and despite what you might think, I haven't always been strong enough to face them. When Beau and I got together and talked, it provided closure for me. Without closure we get stuck. I think you've given me too much credit. Relocating to Cedar Key might seem like a bold move on my part, but I was also running away to avoid dealing with my pain and guilt. Finding a place to *retreat* can be a good thing because it enables us to be somewhere safe where we can heal, but if we're not willing to be honest, it can also be a sanctuary that prevents us from facing the truth."

Chloe nodded slowly and squeezed my hand. "Hmm, I see what you're saying. You're pretty smart. For a younger sister."

I smiled. "Must run in the family. In the past seven months, you've become pretty smart yourself. You're certainly not the same sister that showed up at Aunt Maude's last October."

"Oh, I still have a lot to deal with and improve on."

"Exactly," I said, getting up to refill our glasses. "We're all a work in progress. Chloe . . . I accept your apology . . . and I do forgive you."

She jumped up to pull me into an embrace. "You do? That's more than I hoped for. I just wanted you to know I never meant to betray you. Well . . . at the time, maybe I did. You were right. I was so miserable in my own life, I guess I just wanted to lash out. But I was so wrong and lost a damn good sister in the process."

I knew that all of the hurt and anger that Chloe had caused me was diminishing. I knew this because now what I had was understanding, and with understanding comes love.

"You didn't lose me," I told her. "We're family. For good or bad. Nothing can change that."

"Thank you, Gracie." My sister pulled out of our embrace to wipe her eyes.

I felt the moisture in my own eyes and jumped up to grab the wine bottle. "Well, sis, I think we killed this one. Should we call room service for dinner?"

"Brilliant idea."

I had to admit that later that evening, wearing our pajamas, curled up on each end of the sofa, a cup of herbal tea in our hands, it did feel like Chloe and I were having a pajama party.

"Can I ask you something?" I said.

"Sure."

"Did you love Parker when you married him?"

Chloe adjusted the pillow at her back. "At the time, I thought I did. Now I'm not so sure. Maybe I did, in the way one loves when we're young and inexperienced." She took a sip of tea. "I think Parker may have been a retreat of sorts for me. In the beginning he was very attentive and charming. His parents welcomed me into the family. Said I was the daughter they never had. I felt accepted— and I'm not sure I'd ever felt that before. So I worked hard to be the model wife and mother, and over time, I think Parker took advantage of my role. He became demanding and critical—and the ultimate slap in the face was when he left me for somebody not much older than our sons."

"Are the boys in touch with him?"

"From what I can gather, not very much. But then, I seldom hear from them either."

"How's it going with Cameron?" I asked.

Chloe shrugged. "Okay, I guess. He's a very nice man, but . . ."

"But?"

"When I married Parker, I felt like I needed to be protected. You know, taken care of. I've grown beyond that now because I've proved that I have no problem taking care of myself. I could be wrong, but I get the feeling that Cameron needs a woman to . . . take care of. That woman isn't me."

"Hmm, I see what you're saying."

"It's different with you and Lucas. I see that. You support each other, but you're equals. And besides, it's also easy to see . . . Lucas is that one great love of your life. I haven't met mine yet."

I smiled as I realized that I missed Lucas and I'd be happy to see him when I returned to the island.

"It's good that you're aware of this, Chloe. I think when a woman is willing to settle, she makes poor choices. Sounds to me like you're in a pretty good place. Take it slow with Cameron and see where it goes."

My sister laughed. "Well, I might end up being alone in my old age, but you know what? That's just fine with me. Because I think for the first time in my life, I'm truly happy. I've invested in some real estate, I'm a partner in a yarn shop . . . and I'm building a relationship with my sister and possibly a male companion. Yup, life is pretty damn good."

"I'll second that. There's something else I wanted to ask you. Any chance you'd like to be my other matron of honor? Suellen has already accepted, and I'd really like you to be part of my wedding."

Without hesitating, she said, "Oh, Gracie! I'd love that. Oh, but wait a sec, I'm not going to have to wear one of those glitzy Pepto Bismol pink gowns, am I?"

I let out a chuckle as a visual of that crossed my mind. "Ah, no. I can safely say I wouldn't subject you to that. As a matter of fact, I want you and Suellen to choose something you'd like and to give me some feedback on my gown. So the three of us can come into Gainesville next week. We'll go out for lunch and do some shopping."

"Sounds like a plan to me," Chloe said, raising her hand for a high five.

❧ 42 ❧

By the end of the week, Aunt's Maude's words proved to be correct—she was right as rain. Her energy had returned, the look of fatigue had disappeared, and I was very grateful to have my aunt back in good health.

On the day Chloe and I brought her home, well-wishers dropped by bringing casseroles, crock pot meals, homemade bread, and desserts. Another nice thing that I'd found to be true about a small town—everybody pitched in with kindness.

Before heading to the bookshop I stopped in to check on my aunt and found her comfortably seated on the sofa, her knitting in her lap and Lafitte curled up beside her.

"I'd say that's one happy cat," I said, scratching his head. "How're you doing this morning?"

"Feeling quite lazy just sitting here knitting. When's our next knitting retreat?"

"In about a month, and there's a huge difference between taking it easy and being lazy. So stop complaining and be a good patient."

My aunt laughed.

"Chloe called me last night," she said. "Seems Eli called her and they had a nice, long chat."

"Really? I'm sure she was happy about that. So what's going on with my nephew?"

"I'll let her give you all the details. She said she'd be dropping by the bookstore this morning."

"Okay." I leaned over to place a kiss on my aunt's cheek. "I'm heading down there now to open. Lucas is in Gainesville doing errands. Now, remember, if you need anything you call me, and I expect you to stay put and relax, right?"

"You're a tough caregiver, but yes . . . I'll behave."

Suellen and Chloe were waiting on the sidewalk when I arrived a few minutes before ten to open.

"Sorry, I would have been here a little sooner, but I popped in to check on Aunt Maude."

"How's she doing?" Suellen asked as we entered the bookshop.

"Raring to go. Trying to get her to relax and rest is an impossible feat."

Suellen laughed as she headed into the coffee café. "Want your usual double latte?"

"That would be great," I told her, and looked at Chloe. "Would you like one?"

She was gazing at a display of books on the front table and looked up. "What? Coffee? Yeah, thanks."

"Make that two," I hollered over to Suellen before asking my sister if she was okay. "Aunt Maude said Eli called you last night. How's he doing?"

Chloe plunked onto the sofa and let out a deep sigh. "Well . . . it appears my son is married."

"What?" No wonder my sister was looking down in the dumps this morning. "Did you know anything about this? God, who's the girl? You weren't invited to the wedding?" I might not have any children, but I was sure news like this had to be a disappointment to any parent.

She shook her head. "Thanks," she told Suellen, reaching for the coffee cup.

"I didn't mean to eavesdrop, but I heard you say your son got married?" Suellen said, passing me my latte.

"Yes, and apparently there was no wedding per se. They were married last week at city hall in Manhattan. Eli said that under the circumstances they felt it was easier to do it that way. A traditional wedding would have meant inviting his father . . . and new wife. So I guess I ought to be grateful that I was able to avoid that."

"Oh, I agree with you there. That would not have been pleasant. But how about the girl and her family? I've heard it's every mother's dream to plan her daughter's wedding someday. And what's her name? Do you know anything about her?" I felt the questions tumbling out of me.

"Her name is Treva Sanderson—well, now it's Radcliffe."

"What an unusual first name," Suellen said.

Chloe nodded. "And Eli explained it's pronounced *tree-vah*. He said it's Welsh and her mother was from Wales. She passed away when Treva was in her early teens. Her father works for the State Department in Washington and remarried a few years ago, but it seems Treva isn't close to her stepmother. So passing on a family wedding eliminated some problems there as well."

"Yeah, I guess that makes sense," I said. "Do they work together?"

"No, Treva's a senior at Columbia University and graduates at the end of the month from the nursing program. They were introduced a couple of years ago by mutual friends."

"Oh, so at least they've known each other for a while," Suellen said.

"Yeah, I knew he'd been dating a girl, but since I don't hear from him that much, I wasn't sure how serious it was."

The chimes tinkled on the coffee café door. Suellen leaned over to give Chloe a hug. "Well, congratulations, mother of the groom. Time for me to get to work."

Chloe forced a smile and mumbled, "Thanks."

"Guess you're not too happy about this, huh?" I said when we were alone.

"Well, it was pretty surprising news. It isn't that I'm not happy for Eli. . . . I guess I just feel disappointed. You know, it would have been nice to witness my son's marriage ceremony."

"That's certainly understandable, and making it more difficult is that you haven't even met your new daughter-in-law yet."

The sadness on my sister's face vanished and was replaced with a smile. "Oh, I wanted to talk to you about that. I told him that you were getting married in October . . . and he wanted to know if he and Treva might be invited."

"Oh, gosh, of course. That would be great, Chloe. I'd love to see my nephew again and meet his new wife. Absolutely. I'll be sure to mail off an invitation to them. Lucas and I are going into Gainesville next week to the printer."

The smile on her face increased. "I have to admit, I'm really looking forward to seeing Eli too. I haven't seen him in about a year, just before Parker and I separated. We'd gone to New York for a few days to catch a play on Broadway. Eli had just taken his new position at the accounting firm, so he was only able to get together with us once for dinner. Maybe now that he's married, he'll be in touch with me more."

"I think that happens a lot," I told her. "Especially with sons. Sometimes they drift away a bit during college and while getting their life organized, but once they settle down to begin their own family they find their way back home again."

Chloe nodded. "I hope you're right."

"So you think your sister's okay about not being present for her son's wedding?" Lucas asked later that evening.

I shifted my position on the sofa, snuggling into his arm. "Well, I'm sure she's not thrilled that she wasn't there. But I have to say, for somebody who used to be a control freak I think she handled it very well. So yeah, I think she's fine, and besides, she's really excited about them coming to our wedding."

"I'm sure you'll enjoy that too. With all the news about your nephew, I forgot to tell you that Jean-Paul called me today. His wife passed away yesterday."

I sat up straighter. "Oh, Lucas, I'm so sorry. Will you be going over for the funeral?"

"Yes, it's quite sad. They're having a very small service, so I won't be going. Jean-Paul said since she's been sick for the past few years, it truly was a blessing. I feel it also gave him time to prepare."

I nodded. "Our wedding is still five months away. I wonder if he'd consider coming over to be your best man."

"I think he might," Lucas said. "I'll wait about a month and then call to ask him."

"I really hope that works out. I know how much it would mean to you to have him here."

"Did you finish making out the list for invitations?"

"I did. It's over there on the desk."

Lucas got up to get the paper. "Are you getting good cards lately?" he asked, holding up my deck of tarot that had been lying next to the list.

I smiled. "Actually, I haven't done my cards in quite a while. Maybe your grandmother was right. We should just *live* life and take the days as they come—both good and bad."

Lucas returned to the sofa and pulled me into his arms, placing his lips on mine. I felt my desire climbing as his hands slid over my body.

"As long as I spend all of my days with you, I'll take the good *and* the bad," he whispered in my ear.

As he was about to resume the kiss, we were interrupted with a bark from Annie, which caused Duncan to jump up from where he'd been sleeping on the carpet.

I laughed. "This is a very inopportune moment, girl. Where's your sense of romance?"

Lucas joined my laughter. "I'm afraid when duty calls, romance disappears. Come on, why don't we walk the dogs now?"

I let out a groan. "Aww, do we have to?"

Lucas stood and grabbed my hand as that killer smile crossed his face. "*Oui, mademoiselle,* we have to. But when we return, we will continue where we left off."

I stood up and put my arms around his neck. "You promise?"

"I promise," he said, touching my lips with his.

43

"You've *got* to be kidding!" I said, doubled over with laughter as Suellen held up the most hideous wedding gown I'd ever seen. Rows of ruffles, frill, beads, and lace reminded me of a dressmaker's nightmare. Would a bride actually wear something like this?

"A tad too gaudy for your taste?" Suellen asked, trying to stifle her laughter.

"You think?" Chloe said, shaking her head. "Any bride who would wear that would deserve getting left at the altar."

Once we got our laughter under control, I said, "Okay," injecting some seriousness into my tone. "We've pretty much been to every damn place in Gainesville. I can't find anything I like. What am I going to do?"

"Well," Suellen said, "you still have four months. I guess we could exhaust the entire state of Florida."

"Very funny," I told her, although I wasn't finding my situation humorous. "Do you think I'm being too picky?"

When I got no response, I looked over to the faces of my best friend and sister, who both had noncommittal expressions.

"Well?" I demanded.

Chloe cleared her throat. "Well . . . I wouldn't say you're being too picky. I mean, you have to love the gown you decide on, but . . . honestly, Gracie, some of them were really stunning. But like I said . . ."

It didn't escape me that I saw her looking at Suellen for some backup.

"Right," my friend continued. "You do have to really love what you choose, and apparently so far . . . you just haven't found it."

"Thanks," I retorted. "So I *am* being too picky. This is supposed to be such a happy time, and the thing is, I won't ever be choosing another wedding gown in this lifetime, so . . ." I felt my crankiness ratcheting up and glanced at my watch. "You know what? I'm starved. I've had enough shopping for today. I can't help it if this is our second trip to Gainesville for a wedding gown. I'm done for now. Let's go eat lunch," I said, heading out of the department store without glancing behind me to see if they were following.

Two hours later with my tummy full and working on my second glass of Cabernet, I felt decidedly better.

"I'm sorry, guys," I said. "For being bitchy during the shopping."

"Hey," Suellen said, reaching across the table to squeeze my hand. "It's allowed. All brides get stressed and nervous."

"Absolutely," Chloe said. "You should have seen me before my wedding. It's a wonder anyone would come near me."

"Really? You were in St. Simons Island then, so I didn't see you much before you got married. I'm not stressed—I want to marry Lucas. I've never been happier."

"Yes, of course, you're happy," my sister said. "But the stress is just natural. You want your wedding day to be perfect. All of it— the flowers, the setting, the music, and your gown."

"Chloe's right, honey," Suellen confirmed. "Every bride wants her special day to be perfect, and yours *will* be. Including your gown."

"I hope you're right," I mumbled, then took another sip of wine.

"Hey, did Lucas hear from his cousin about being best man?" Chloe asked.

"He did, and it looks like you'll have a Frenchman as your partner to walk down the aisle. He called Lucas last night and said he thought it would be good for him to come here in October, and he was very pleased that Lucas asked him."

"Oh, that's great," Suellen said.

"Yeah." Chloe took a sip of her coffee. "What . . . ah . . . does this Jean-Paul look like? I mean, you know . . . I was just wondering."

Both Suellen and I burst out laughing. "Oh, right," I said. "It's always good to know something like that. Well, he's a few years older than you are, and from the photos I've seen of him, I don't think you'll be disappointed."

Chloe waved a hand in the air. "Aw, come on. The poor guy just lost his wife. I didn't mean to insinuate I was interested."

"Right," both Suellen and I said at the same time.

Later that afternoon the three of us were gathered in Aunt Maude's living room.

"No luck again, huh?" she said. "That's really a shame."

"I don't know what to say," I told her. "I'm not even sure exactly what kind of gown I'm looking for. I just know I haven't found it yet."

"Well . . . maybe I can help," she said, getting up and going into her bedroom.

Chloe, Suellen, and I exchanged a glance.

My aunt returned carrying a large, rectangular box held together with string. "Let's go into the dining room," she said, and placed the box on the table.

From the looks of the faded cardboard, the box was pretty old but in good shape. We watched my aunt carefully untie the string.

Before removing the cover, she looked at Chloe and me. "This was your mother's wedding gown," she told us. "And her mother's before that."

She lifted the cover, and my first glimpse of the gown literally took my breath away. I gripped the edge of the table and momentarily felt transported to another time, another place. I had seen this gown before. This was *it*—the gown I knew I wanted without understanding how I had known this. It was in that second, while my aunt removed the dress from the plastic where it had been ensconced, that I knew where I'd seen this dress before—it was the one that Bess Coachman or whoever she was had been wearing the last time she appeared to me. And I also knew I had been incorrect. It wasn't Bess Coachman who had visited me—it had been my *mother.*

I heard myself gasp as I reached out to touch the smooth ivory satin. Aunt Maude held the dress up in front of her. Sleek and elegant, a net yoke tipped in satin was above an I-shaped panel of cotton appliquéd bows. Making the gown even more stunning was the rich ruching to the center front bodice and side seams of the bust. When my aunt turned the gown around, I saw that the appliqués continued around the back bust and waist. This was the only adornment—no lace, no beads, just a simple, classic beauty. The sleeves were capped, and I noticed there was also no ostentatious train that many wedding gowns had.

When my left hand reached out to touch the gown, my right one had flown to my mouth where it still remained. I let out a breath and whispered, "This is it. *This* is the gown I was looking for."

"Oh, my God, Grace," I heard Suellen say as she also touched the gown. "This gown was meant for you. It's beyond stunning."

"It is," Chloe agreed. "It's so simple and yet . . . positively spectacular."

I felt her arms go around me as she pulled me into an embrace. "You're going to be the most gorgeous bride ever, Gracie."

I smiled as I felt myself returning to normal and watched as Aunt Maude carefully arranged the dress across the table.

"Why didn't you show me this right away?" I questioned. "I never even knew you had it."

"I wanted to give you the chance to choose your own gown, but when you seemed to be having so much difficulty I felt perhaps it was time to bring out this heirloom."

"Wow," Suellen said. "And so this originally belonged to Grace's grandmother?"

My aunt nodded. "Yes, and she passed it on to my sister when she married. The gown was handmade by a dressmaker in Paris in the twenties. My mother told me that she had a vision for the dress she wanted and found a dressmaker who agreed to do it."

Chloe laughed. "Sounds like you got a bit of our grandmother in your genes. You were so stubborn about the precise dress that you wanted."

"I know, and now I know there was a reason for that."

"Was there a veil with the dress?" Suellen asked.

"Oh, I don't want to wear a veil," I said, before my aunt could answer. "I want silk flowers in my hair."

My aunt smiled. "There was a veil, but I'm afraid it got damaged at your mother's wedding. It had been ripped by accident, so I imagine your mother just got rid of it."

"That's fine with me," I said, glancing at the gown again.

"So what do you think Chloe and I should wear? You'll probably want something similar in style?"

"Oh, I know," my sister said. "There's some vintage shops in Gainesville. Maybe we should look for something there?"

"Great idea. And maybe a color that's soft or muted. Nothing loud or flashy."

"Exactly," Chloe said, and I could hear the relief in her voice.

"Okay, so next week's excursion to Gainesville will be to find something for Chloe and me. I'm so thrilled you have exactly what you want, Gracie. I need to get going. Time to feed my Freud. I swear he has an internal clock."

"I need to leave too," Chloe said, giving me a hug and placing a kiss on Aunt Maude's cheek.

"Well," my aunt said after they left. "Sometimes what we want most is right in our own backyard. I'm glad you're so pleased with the gown. How about a cup of tea?"

"Sounds good. I'd like to talk to you about something."

"Okay. Let's go into the kitchen and after our tea I'll find a spot where we can hang the gown."

I waited till my aunt placed a mug in front of me before I said anything. "Remember when we first moved in here and I told you I thought I had a ghost appearing to me?"

My aunt nodded.

"And I was pretty certain that it was Bess Coachman, the original owner?"

My aunt nodded again.

"I don't think it was her at all. The last time she appeared to me, she was wearing a dress identical to that wedding gown." When my aunt remained silent I went on. "Her face had been misty, but I'd thought she looked vaguely familiar to me the first time I'd seen her." I waited a fraction of a second before I blurted out, "I think it was my mother."

I saw the raised eyebrows on Aunt Maude's face, but her expression showed no surprise.

"Really?" was all she said.

"Yeah, but it makes no sense. My mother never lived here. What the heck would her spirit be doing here?"

My aunt let out a sigh. "Love follows us, Gracie. Even in death. Spirits have no geographical boundaries. They go where they're needed."

I leaned forward across the table. "So you're saying those visions probably *were* my mother? But why? Why would she take those two sweaters I'd knitted for Monica's babies and then return them the last time she appeared?"

"I don't have any answers for that, but I think that sometimes spirits move items in order to get out attention. It's their way of communicating. As to why Yvette was here—you're her daughter, Grace. You always will be. You had a lot to sort out with Beau and also with Lucas. You needed to work through all of it—and maybe she wanted to be near you to make sure that you did."

I recalled the voice that I'd heard, either in my head or from the apparition. About listening and paying attention. A warm and loving feeling filled my senses.

"You could be right," I told my aunt. "You could be right."

44

By the second week of September all of the arrangements for the wedding seemed to be in place. Flowers had been ordered, confirmed invitations returned, music selected, the caterer chosen, and in six weeks I'd no longer be known as Grace Stone, but rather as Grace Trudeau. I liked the sound of that.

"So Jean-Paul's flight is all set?" I asked Lucas as we finished up dinner at his place.

"All set. We'll go to Tampa Airport the end of the month to pick him up."

"I'm glad he's arriving a few weeks before the wedding. It'll give me a chance to get to know him, and both of you will enjoy visiting."

"I'd say the only thing left is our vows. Have you given that any more thought, Grace? Do you want the traditional ones or will we be writing our own?"

I laughed. "Since when have I been traditional? We still have plenty of time. Let's write our own."

"I was hoping you'd say that," he said, getting up to stack the dishwasher. "The words from our heart mean the most."

I walked up behind him and kissed the back of his neck. "How lucky am I to have such a romantic man."

He turned around and pulled me to him as his lips found mine. "How about I skip the knitting group tonight?" I said.

Lucas laughed. "No, no. This is your evening with the women. You must go. I'll be here waiting for you when you get back."

"I think I'd much prefer to stay here," I said, nuzzling his neck with kisses. "But you're right, and I'm bringing Aunt Maude's carrot cake, so they'll never forgive me if I don't show up with that."

I walked along Second Street toward the yarn shop savoring the cooler air that had recently arrived on the island. With much less humidity, six weeks from now should be perfect for a garden wedding.

As I approached the yarn shop I thought it was odd that the lights were off and it looked closed. When I reached for the doorknob and stepped inside, lights flashed on and I heard loud voices hollering, "Surprise!"

It took me a second to understand what the heck was going on, and then my eyes spied the tables of food that had been set up, a chair decorated with white satin ribbon and bows flanked by beautifully wrapped gifts, and it hit me that this was my bridal shower.

"Oh, my gosh," I said, as my hand flew to my mouth.

Suellen and Chloe came running forward to give me a hug. "You didn't suspect?" my sister asked.

I started laughing. "No. Not at all." And I hadn't. I guess most women do have a bridal shower, but I hadn't thought about it.

"Well, come on, come on," Suellen said, leading me to the decorated chair. "You're the guest of honor, so have a seat."

I looked around and shook my head. I felt like most of Cedar Key had turned out for this event. Sitting on the chairs, sofas, and folding chairs were Aunt Maude, Monica, Sydney, Miss Dora, Polly, and so many others who frequented the bookshop and coffee café, and each and every one was special to me in their own way.

"Okay," Chloe said, taking charge. "We knew that between your house and Lucas's, you guys really had all the household stuff, so Suellen and I decided that your shower would be personal items."

"Right," Suellen said. "You know." She rolled her eyes. "Things that a new bride would use."

I joined the laughter of the crowd. "Oh, God," I said. "Maybe I don't want to open these gifts in public."

This brought forth more laughter.

"No, no," Chloe assured me. "They're in good taste. Well, at least I *think* they are. So let's get started." She passed me one of the gifts.

I opened the card to see Monica's name and removed an exquisite cream-colored peignoir set—what a bride traditionally wears on her wedding night and something I had never owned. I held it up so the women could see the delicate apparel with thin spaghetti straps and a long, flowing robe to match. Oohs and ah's filled the room.

"Thank you so much, Monica. It's beautiful and will be perfect for my honeymoon in Paris."

"Oh la la," Polly said, causing the women to laugh again.

The next gift was from Sydney, and I removed a breathtaking, black vintage nightgown from the box. With a long and full sweep of skirt, the lace chevron bodice added elegance and sensuality. "Oh, Sydney," I said, holding it up for a better look. "This is just stunning. I'd bet anything you got this in Paris when you were there this summer, didn't you?"

"I did, and as soon as I saw it, I thought of you."

The next card read, *For those practical evenings as a new bride. —Love, Eudora.* I removed a gorgeous pair of silk charmeuse pajamas in a pink pastel. I fingered the soft, light fabric and noticed how the satin finish caught the light. "These are beautiful, Dora. I know I'll enjoy wearing them. Thank you so much."

The box from Aunt Maude was quite large, so it was easier to kneel down on the floor to open it. Her card said, *May you and Lucas always be wrapped in your love ~ With all my love, Aunt Maude.* I removed one of the most gorgeous oatmeal-colored afghans I'd ever seen. Cables of various twists had been worked vertically. Spaced between the cables were bobbles and other intricate stitches. I could only imagine all of the hours and hours that went into this work of art. I jumped up to give my aunt a tight hug.

"Thank you so much, Aunt Maude. Lucas and I will treasure this forever."

"Open mine next," Polly yelled.

I opened her box to discover lingerie that bordered on the risqué and started laughing. Bras, tiny underpants, and garter belts in red and black filled the box, along with a few pairs of black mesh seamed stockings. I held up a few of the items and said, "Lucas thanks you very much, Polly."

She joined our laughter and said, "I figured he would. You know, when you're married to a sexy Frenchman, you want to make sure you keep his interest. Figured maybe one evening you might want to cook him dinner in one of those hot numbers."

"You're too funny, Polly, and thank you very much. I'll be sure to remember that."

When I unwrapped Suellen's gift I couldn't stop laughing.

"Come on, come on," everybody yelled. "Show us too."

I held in the air an upstairs maid costume complete with lace bra, G-string, matching apron, and gloves. I reached back into the box and pulled out a feather duster, and the room erupted in laughter.

"Hey," Suellen said. "Wouldn't want Lucas to get bored when you're doing your housecleaning."

When I finally got my laughter under control, she said, "That was the fun gift. There's another one there from me."

I opened that one to find a beautiful powder blue silky night-gown and an assortment of French bath products.

"Thank you," I told her. "I'll be sure to put that maid's outfit to good use."

When I opened my sister's gift, I laughed again. "Gosh, Chloe, you're no better than Suellen." I held up two peekaboo bras that were designed with a hole in the center to expose the nipples. Adding to the matched sets were two pairs of thong panties in silver and black.

These brought a round of applause and more laughter from the women.

"There's another one there from me too," Chloe said, still laughing.

I opened that box to find another gorgeous peignoir set, this one in black, along with a pair of beautiful black slippers with a one-inch heel and rhinestones across the front.

"Oh, I love it, Chloe. Thank you so much."

I continued opening boxes of nightgowns, bras, panties, scented candles, bath products, and even a couple bottles of wine. I was overwhelmed with the kindness that everybody had shown. Standing up to thank the women, I felt moisture in my eyes.

"You guys are simply the best," I said. "From the first day I arrived on Cedar Key, you welcomed me, and even more important, you accepted me. Each and every one of you women is an inspiration to all women in one way or another. I hope you know that. I love you all and thank you so much."

After more clapping, Chloe said, "Okay. Now it's time for some nosh. We have all kinds of desserts, coffee, tea, and wine, of course."

I got myself a glass of wine and went over to Chloe and Suellen. I had no doubt that it was the two of them who had gotten all of this together. After placing my wineglass on the table, I put an arm around each one. "Thanks," I told them. "Thanks for all of this, but thanks for being my sister and my best friend."

"It was our pleasure," Chloe said.

"Yeah, don't go getting all mushy on us or we'll all be boo-hooing."

"True," I said. "We have to save that for the day of the wedding."

"Oh, no. Not allowed. It'll ruin your makeup."

"Always thinking, Suellen."

We sat around and continued to talk and laugh until ten o'clock. I knew the evening I'd just spent was one I'd always remember.

Chloe drove me home with the backseat and trunk of the car loaded with gifts. When we pulled up, Lucas came out to help.

"You knew about this, didn't you?" I said, going into his arms for a hug.

"Of course I did. It was my job to get you out the door on time."

"Aha," I said, reaching for a stack of gifts from the trunk. "No wonder you scooted me out so fast and passed on lovemaking."

Chloe laughed. "When he sees some of these racy items I doubt he'll be passing on that."

"Really?" he said with interest. "Think I might get a sneak preview tonight?"

"Not on your life," I said, heading inside.

45

Driving to Tampa Airport with Lucas, I found myself feeling nervous about meeting his cousin. This would be my first time meeting any of Lucas's family, so I guess that was natural. But I shouldn't have been concerned. Jean-Paul was as sweet and friendly as Lucas was. And almost as handsome. The conversation driving back to Cedar Key was light and easy.

When we hit the Number Four bridge bringing us onto the island, Jean-Paul let out an exclamation of awe.

"This is so beautiful," he said, his head going from side to side looking out the windows.

Like Lucas, he had a wonderful French accent and his English was quite good.

After he got settled at Lucas's house, Jean-Paul joined us on the porch for a glass of wine. I saw a camera dangling from around his neck. Not one of the digital ones so common today but a bona fide 35mm Canon that actually required film. I was surprised anybody still used those.

He accepted the wineglass that Lucas passed him and held it aloft. "I propose a toast to both of you. Many years of happiness, and I'm happy to be here to share your special time."

"Thank you," I said before taking a sip. "So you like to take pictures?" I gestured toward the camera.

Both men laughed. "You could say that," Lucas told me. "Jean-Paul is a professional photographer. He had a gallery in Paris for many years before moving to the south of France."

"I didn't know this. Well, you'll certainly have an array of beautiful scenery to capture here on the island."

"Yes, I will enjoy that, but the main reason I brought my cameras and equipment was because I am to be your official photographer for the wedding."

I saw the smile on Lucas's face and now understood this had been a secret between the two of them.

"Oh, that's great. Gee, and here I thought we'd just have photos that the guests took. That's so kind of you, Jean-Paul. Thank you."

"It will be my pleasure to capture all of your memories for you."

After we finished our wine I gave Lucas a hug. "I have to meet Chloe at my place in about ten minutes, so I'd better get going."

"Oh, you will not stay for dinner with us?" Jean-Paul said.

"Not tonight. My sister needs to talk with me about something. I'm sure it has to do with the wedding. And tomorrow evening you and Lucas are coming to my place for dinner so you can meet my aunt and my sister."

"I very much look forward to it," he said, placing a kiss on both of my cheeks.

Chloe was sitting in the garden knitting when I arrived.

"Did Jean-Paul arrive okay?" she asked, placing a lilac-colored scarf in her bag.

"Right on time." I headed toward the stairs. "Come on up. He's very nice. I can see why Lucas is so fond of him. Oh, and Lucas never told me, but he's a professional photographer and will be taking all the photos for the wedding."

We walked into the kitchen, and I was greeted by Annie dancing in circles.

"Hey, sweetie." I bent down to give her a pat.

"That's really great. It'll be nice to have official wedding photos rather than just random shots from the people attending."

"I know. That's what I told them. Coffee, tea, wine? What would you like?" I went to the refrigerator and removed a tuna casserole, turned on the oven, and popped it in. "That'll be ready in about an hour. You're staying for supper, right?"

"Yeah, and a glass of wine would be nice."

I uncorked a bottle of Pinot Grigio, filled two glasses, and passed one to my sister.

"Let's go in the living room and get comfy."

I kicked off my sandals and curled up on the sofa. Chloe joined me at the other end.

"So what's going on? Questions about the wedding? You still love your dress, right?"

My sister laughed. "Yes, I still love my dress. No, it's not about the wedding, Grace." She took a sip of wine before placing it on the table. "It's something else I wanted to talk to you about."

I noticed that she'd clasped her hands together and seemed anxious.

"Remember when we were at the hotel back in May? I thought about telling you then, but I guess I wasn't ready."

I nodded and wondered what this was all about.

"Well, I think the time has come for me to finally confront some things from my past. I've given this a lot of thought, especially during the past year since I've come to Cedar Key." She picked up the wineglass and took another sip. "I guess things happen that should probably be confronted at the time, but I wasn't able to do that. Instead I managed to bury it, and I know now that was the wrong thing to do."

I thought back to Beau and my miscarriage. I thought I had faced my situation, but it wasn't until I saw Beau again and all of it came out into the open that I felt it was truly behind me. I had a feeling my sister was attempting to do the same thing.

"There was a party," she said. "A frat party at college. I went with a few other girls, and as usually happens, everyone was drinking. When I was ready to leave, the girls I'd gone with had hooked up with guys and wanted to stay. Another fellow overheard our conversation and offered to give me a ride back to the dorm."

She let out a deep breath, and for a second I wasn't sure she was going to continue with her story.

"What happened, Chloe?" I asked softly. I had a sick feeling in the pit of my stomach that I knew the ending.

"He gave me the ride but not to my dorm. Instead we drove to the woods on the outskirts of campus. He started kissing me, and when I kept telling him *no,* he got angry. And when I began screaming for help . . . he became violent. He dragged me out of the car . . . I felt myself being thrown to the ground and . . ."

Tears flowed down Chloe's face as I jumped up and pulled her into my arms. "It's okay, it's okay," I soothed.

But she pushed me away and swiped at her tears. "No, it's *not* okay. It's never been okay. I was raped that night. I had never been with a guy . . . and I was raped. And I've *never* told anybody until just now."

"Oh, my God," I said, pulling her back into my arms. This time Chloe accepted my embrace as she continued to sob.

She allowed me to comfort her, and after a few minutes she leaned back and reached for a tissue from the table.

"Twenty-eight years," she whispered. "Twenty-eight years I've carried that night in here." She punched her chest with her fist.

As if by osmosis, I felt my sister's pain along with her anger, humiliation, and guilt.

"You didn't report it, did you?"

She shook her head as a fresh flood of tears fell.

"Oh, Chloe. You did nothing wrong." I reached out to hold her hand.

"I know that now. *Finally* I know that. But I took the ride. . . . I didn't even know him, but I figured he was at the party and a fellow student. I never saw him again. I wonder now if he only crashed the party."

"You never told Mom and Dad or Aunt Maude either, did you?"

Again she shook her head.

"Parker?" I asked, but already knew the answer.

"That's how humiliated I felt—I never even told my husband when we were married." She blew her nose and then took a sip of wine. "I had some bruises on my face, so I lied to everyone and said I'd tripped and fallen on the walk home from the party. Nobody ever suspected anything different. But I was different—from that moment on, I was *different*. I felt dirty and used and . . . unworthy. Unworthy of anything or anyone. When I met Parker two years later, I felt like I was being given a second chance. A chance to redeem myself for what had happened. I threw myself into the role of the perfect wife and mother . . . but it was always there. That night was *always* there on the fringes of my soul. And over the years I allowed the anger and the helplessness to consume me—until it almost destroyed me."

"And you never went for any counseling either?"

"No. It wasn't until you and I reconciled and you told me about having closure after seeing Beau again that I began thinking about my own past. I felt maybe it was time for me to try and get that same closure. And then, ironically, I happened to see an article in the paper about RAINN. It's the rape, abuse, and incest national network and the nation's largest anti–sexual violence organization. So I called them, and I felt safe talking to somebody over the phone. They have a hotline with volunteers, and I've also been talking to them on their online site. I think eventually . . . I will see a counselor, but they felt it was important that I share this with somebody that I trusted. They said that in the sharing, the healing comes."

I pulled my sister into a tight embrace. "I'm so glad you chose to share it with me, Chloe. And the healing will come. I'm certain it will. I love you, sis."

"I love you, too—for always."

❧ 46 ❧

The next few weeks flew by. Chloe and I hadn't discussed her story again, and I had a feeling she had chosen not to share it with Aunt Maude. After learning what my sister had endured and then kept hidden inside for so many years, it made me realize even more that all human behavior can be explained. But sometimes we never know a person's story. This made me extra grateful that my sister had chosen to finally share hers.

My wedding was now only three days away. Eli and Treva were arriving that afternoon, and a family dinner was planned for the evening.

I rolled over in bed and noticed it was beginning to get light outside. No misty visions appeared. I'd never know for sure if what I thought I'd seen had been real, but I liked to think maybe it had been my mother. It gave me a warm feeling that perhaps she'd reached out to me from the beyond, but it made me wistful that she wouldn't be present to share my special day. My eyes strayed to the gown hanging from my closet door, and I smiled. Possibly she would be with me—in ways I couldn't understand.

Annie jumped up on the bed and began licking my face.

"Yeah, guess it's time to start our day," I told her.

After showering and getting dressed, I grabbed a cup of coffee and headed out to the garden with Annie at my heels. I found Aunt Maude cutting some of her flowers and placing them in a basket.

"I bet those are for the dinner table tonight."

"They are," she said, turning around with a smile.

"What can I do to help with the preparations?"

"I think everything's in order. But I was hoping you could check and see if we have any more inquiries for bookings for the knitting retreats."

"Sure. I'll do that this morning. You're not happy having them only once a month, are you?"

My aunt laughed. "Well, probably not, but you know me. I just like to be kept busy."

"Like you're not busy enough?"

"Oh, I don't mean the Garden Club or the Women's Club . . . I like to be involved with activities that make me feel . . . well, useful. The knitting retreats bring women together in a different way than community organizations do."

I nodded. "Yeah, I understand. Well, I wouldn't worry. Somehow you always end up finding something that accomplishes a feeling of satisfaction."

"Chloe called me last night. I guess there's been a delay in her new tenant coming here."

"Oh, right. Berkley was due to arrive this month. What happened?"

"She has some things to tend to up in Salem before she can leave permanently, so she told Chloe she'll be here before Christmas."

"I think that'll be good for Chloe. She has me and Suellen, but she needs a friend of her own. She and Berkley hit it off really well, so I think they have a friendship developing there."

"I agree. Has she mentioned anything about Cameron to you? Are they still seeing each other?"

"They are, but he's back out in California visiting his daughter. Apparently she's just gone through a pretty nasty divorce. And he's out there for about a month to support her and his granddaughter. Chloe isn't ready for a serious relationship right now anyway."

"I'm very grateful she realizes this, but it's nice she has a male companion in her life."

"From the way she's been gushing over Jean-Paul, she might end up with two male companions."

My aunt laughed. "Well good for her. He seems very nice."

I looked around the dining room table at the seven of us and smiled. Chloe was seated between Eli and Jean-Paul and was positively beaming. From the moment she'd walked into my aunt's kitchen with her son and daughter-in-law, I not only saw, but felt, the joy she radiated. It reminded me of Monica whenever I saw her with the triplets.

I glanced at my nephew and felt a sense of pride. Not only extremely handsome, he had a winning personality and made me instantly feel like I hadn't been absent from his life for so many years. His new wife sat beside him, and I smiled. I could tell that Chloe adored her, and it was easy to see why. Outgoing and friendly, she was a welcome addition to our family. Her looks had an almost exotic quality with her long dark hair and dark eyes. I had no doubt that Chloe had immediately considered Treva the daughter she'd never had.

Conversation buzzed around the table, and I felt Lucas's hand reach for mine. "Happy?" he whispered as he leaned over and placed a kiss on my cheek.

"Very much so," I told him.

"So what do you think of our little island so far?" I heard my aunt ask Eli.

"From what I've seen, I like it a lot. Very quiet and laid-back."

"I have to agree," Treva said. "Compared to Manhattan, this really is paradise. Do you ever have any crime here? It seems like such a safe place to live."

My aunt laughed. "Oh, it is. We have some typical small-town minor offenses. But nothing major."

"Yeah, not like the big city," Treva said. "Sometimes I feel like I'm always looking over my shoulder for the next mugger."

"Right." I buttered one of my aunt's biscuits. "I've never lived in a large city like New York, but I think I'd be pretty nervous. And after living here for over ten years, I guess I'm spoiled."

"It's all what we get used to," my aunt said. "I want to propose a toast." She held up her glass of wine. "I hope all of you know how delighted I am that we've all come together to celebrate Grace and Lucas's wedding. It's times like this that makes family even more important. So here's to family and here's to love."

We all clinked glasses, and I caught the wink and smile my aunt directed toward me. *And you've always been the glue holding us together,* I thought, as I returned her smile.

When I awoke on the morning of my wedding, I knew the wedding gods were shining down on me. It had poured rain for the past two days, and despite everybody trying to calm me down I had visions of my garden wedding being a washout. But I looked out my bedroom window to see a brilliant sun turning the garden into a golden glow. A white canvas cover suspended by four poles hung above the neatly arranged chairs. Huge ceramic pots of bright yellow hibiscus created a center aisle, and at the end was a white archway into which a purple passion vine had been woven. Off to the right, empty banquet tables sat waiting for the food that caterers would deliver. And on the left, tables and chairs were set up beneath a white silk billowy tent where the guests would dine. I let out a deep breath. Everything looked in order. The company that Aunt Maude had hired had been true to their word. They had arrived very early and like magic had turned the garden into a romantic setting.

I turned at a knock on my door to see Suellen enter with a mug of coffee in her hand.

"Good morning, bride to be. Since it's eight-thirty, I guess you slept well?"

"God, is it that time already? Yeah, I did. Once I fell asleep. I tossed and turned for hours. I was scared to death it wouldn't stop raining. Did you see the garden?" I asked, pointing out the window. "It's incredible."

Suellen passed me the mug and pulled aside the curtain. "It certainly is. I got up at seven and they were already out there setting up."

"I'm glad you spent the night here," I told her.

"Well, somebody had to keep you from going over the edge. I'm glad to see you're less stressed this morning. Now it's time to just relax and enjoy your special day."

"Oh, Annie. I have to take her out. Where is she?"

"Already done. I took her for a walk about an hour ago. I snuck in here and got her so you could sleep. She's in the other room."

"Thanks. Gee, I'm beginning to see that being a bride for the day has some perks. Well, besides the obvious."

"Oh, you have no idea. Wait till your sister gets here." Suellen looked at her watch. "Which should be within the hour."

"What are you guys up to?"

"You'll see," was all she said before heading out the door. "Come on, I'm making eggs, sausage, and grits for breakfast."

Chloe arrived an hour later accompanied by two women who looked vaguely familiar.

"Hey," she said, pulling me into a hug. "This is Tanya and Carol, from the day spa in Gainesville. They're part of my gift to you."

"What?" I said, and was sure I had a dumbfounded expression on my face.

Chloe laughed. "Every bride needs pampering on her special day, and you shall have yours. I'm not even sure what all they'll be doing to you—I just told them to give you the works."

My laughter joined Chloe's. "Are you serious?"

"Yup," Tanya said, heading toward the bathroom. "Follow me. Time for a nice long, relaxing soak."

Twenty minutes later I was submerged in my tub, a cup of coffee beside me, the scent of lavender filling the air. I had to admit—it *was* relaxing.

Feeling restored following the bath, I walked into my living room wrapped in a fluffy white robe to see a massage table set up.

"Okay," Tanya instructed. "Now up on the table to relax all those tight muscles from pre-wedding stress."

I laughed as I followed her instructions. "By the time I walk down that aisle, I'm going to be like Jell-O."

"Nah," Suellen said, as she closed the blinds. "You'll be all rejuvenated."

I saw Chloe lighting candles and heard strains of Enya softly filling the room as I gave myself over to the delight that awaited me.

By early afternoon, as Carol worked on my pedicure, I had to admit all the pampering was beginning to take effect. I not only felt wonderful, I *felt* like a bride—and very special, for Lucas.

I heard Aunt Maude holler, "Lunch is served, ladies."

Suellen and Chloe jumped up and headed to the kitchen. They returned with my aunt, carrying a tray of sandwiches and potato salad.

"Oh, my," Aunt Maude said. "You *are* getting the royal treatment. How nice."

I glanced down at my newly polished toenails in a soft shade of pink and smiled.

"I feel like Cinderella, minus the evil stepsister," I said, and everybody laughed.

"Here ya go." Suellen passed me a tray. "A bride has to keep her strength up."

After all of us finished lunch, I received a manicure, and then Carol said we'd tackle my hair.

"Oh, Lord. I've had no clue what I was going to do with this," I said, running my hand through my unruly curls.

"Just you wait and see," she assured me. "I can work magic."

And she was right. With a special shampoo, some wonderful conditioner, and God knows what else, my hair cascaded in natural curls framing my face, and instead of looking wild, they looked soft and sensuous.

I sat in front of my vanity mirror and smiled. "It looks great. Thank you so much."

She lifted the ivory silk flowers from the table and secured them to the side of my head. I was beginning to look like a bride.

"Your hair looks gorgeous," Chloe said, coming into the room with Aunt Maude and holding a champagne bottle. "We're right on schedule. It's four o'clock. One hour till showtime. I'd say it was a very successful day. Let's celebrate with some bubbly."

She expertly uncorked the bottle and filled six glasses. "Here's to you, my sister. May you be as happy the rest of your life as you are today."

I held up my glass as I looked at my sister, my aunt, my best friend, and two women who had transformed me into an honest-to-goodness bride, and I felt moisture stinging my eyes.

"Thank you. Thank you to all of you."

"Oh, no. None of that," Suellen said. "I think I see a bit of wetness in your eyes. That's not allowed. Carol spent too long doing your makeup."

We broke into laughter before taking a sip of the ice-cold champagne.

After we finished, Chloe collected the glasses while Tanya and Carol packed up their equipment. "Now is the hour. I'll be right back and then it's time to get you into that wedding gown. With all those buttons, I hope we're finished by five."

❦ 47 ❦

At 4:55, I swirled in front of my full-length mirror and couldn't believe my eyes. Aunt Maude, Chloe, and Suellen stood waiting for my reaction, which was a loud gasp.

"This is how I always envisioned I'd look on my wedding day," I said, staring at the ivory satin gown that fit my body perfectly. My hair was a soft cloud of auburn enhanced by the silk flowers.

"Your mother would be so proud," Aunt Maude said, coming to place a kiss on my cheek.

"You're absolutely stunning," my sister told me.

"You certainly are, and here's the finishing touch." Suellen handed me six white calla lilies tied with an ivory ribbon.

I turned around to look at the three most important women in my life. Aunt Maude looked elegant wearing a beautiful, ankle-length, ice blue dress. Suellen and Chloe wore similar-styled vintage dresses that each had a hem hanging in points midcalf, one in celery green and one in pale yellow. Sprigs of baby's breath had been placed in their hair, and each one carried a long-stemmed yellow rose encircled with a cream-colored ribbon.

"You all look gorgeous," I said.

Suellen and Chloe each kissed my cheek.

"Okay," my sister said. "This is it."

As we walked down the stairs to my aunt's apartment I could hear the music of Pachelbel's Canon coming from the garden. Since I had wanted specific music, we had hired a DJ for both the ceremony and dancing at the reception.

I stood on my aunt's deck and watched as Jean-Paul escorted her down the aisle to her seat. Next I saw Suellen link her arm with Mitchell's as they made their way down the aisle. Chloe had stood waiting at the back until Jean-Paul walked her down before returning to get me.

He gave me a huge smile and a nod of approval. "Ready?"

"I am," I told him, as the music changed to the haunting melody of Enya's voice singing "Only Time."

As I stood at the back of the crowd with Jean-Paul, I was only dimly aware of the guests rising to turn and face me. My eyes, along with my heart, were focused on the love of my life. Standing at the end of the aisle waiting, Lucas looked more handsome than I could ever remember. He wore a charcoal gray suit, white shirt, and pale gray tie. Sun glinted off his dark curls, and the smile, that killer smile, lighting up his face caused my heart to skip a beat. I walked slowly alongside Jean-Paul, my arm linked with his, wanting this moment to last forever, never taking my eyes from Lucas.

When we reached the archway, he took my hand and placed it in Lucas's before kissing both of my cheeks and taking his place beside Chloe.

"You are beyond beautiful," Lucas whispered.

My eyes continued to be locked on his handsome face, and I only vaguely heard the minister welcoming the guests before he explained that we had chosen to write our own vows.

Lucas and I faced each other, and he took my hands in his.

"I have loved you from the first moment I saw you, and I will love you all the days of my life. You have given me joy, compassion, kindness, and above all, love. I chose a quote from Napoleon to complete my vows: 'As for me, to love you alone, to make you happy, to do nothing which would contradict your wishes, this is my destiny and the meaning of my life.' *Je t'aime de tout mon coeur.* I love you with all my heart, Grace."

I struggled to hold back my tears and took a deep breath. "And

I have loved you from the first moment I saw you. You are my friend, my soul mate, and the man who has taught me the true meaning of love. My quote to complete my vows is from Elizabeth Barrett Browning: I love you not only for what you are, but for what I am when I am with you. I love you not only for what you have made of yourself, but for what you are making of me. I love you for the part of me that you bring out.' And I will love you into eternity, Lucas."

"Do we have the rings?" I heard the minister say.

Lucas turned to accept my ring from Jean-Paul as he placed it on the third finger of my left hand. "With this ring, we are now one. I love you, Grace."

I turned to Chloe as she passed me the gold band.

Sliding it onto Lucas's finger, I looked up into his dark eyes, which were filled with emotion. "I give you this ring because it is a symbol of my unending love for you, and I will always love you, Lucas."

He leaned forward to kiss me as I heard the sensuous voice of Édith Piaf fill the garden singing "La Vie en Rose."

"I now pronounce you husband and wife," the minister said, followed by the loud applause of the crowd.

As Lucas and I began to walk down the aisle, Aunt Maude reached out and squeezed my hand. *I love you,* I heard her whisper, and I nodded.

Lucas and I stood side by side accepting all of the well-wishes and hugs. It was only then that I saw Jean-Paul clicking away with his camera and realized he'd been busy throughout the ceremony in addition to acting as best man.

"Absolutely beautiful ceremony. One of the nicest I've ever attended. What a striking couple they make. Oh, to be loved like that," were some of the comments I heard as Lucas and I greeted our guests.

When the receiving line finished, my aunt announced that waiters were circulating with champagne so we could have a toast before Lucas and I briefly departed for a picture session near the water.

With crystal flutes held high, Jean-Paul gave the wedding toast.

"May all the days of your life be filled with love. And may this day always be a remembrance of the love you share."

Glasses clinked, and I turned to touch mine with Lucas's. "To us," he said. "To all our tomorrows."

"To all our tomorrows," I repeated.

I heard Aunt Maude instructing the guests to help themselves to hors d'oeuvres as Lucas and I walked to the curb, followed by Jean-Paul.

I saw the golf cart and burst out laughing. "Only on Cedar Key," I said. White ribbons and bows decorated the cart, and Lucas assisted me into the backseat. "Great idea," I told him.

"I thought you'd like it."

Jean-Paul headed down G Street over to First, where we parked and got out. When I realized what they had in mind, I started laughing again.

"Pictures in front of the Honeymoon Cottage?" I said.

"But of course," Lucas said, joining my laughter.

The Honeymoon Cottage was a structure that sat just off shore, balanced precariously on stilts. Once upon a time there had been a walkway across the water leading out to it, and it had been used as a guest house. But that was many years ago. In the years since then, it had stood there, tilting to one side, most of the wood rotted, home to pelicans and other birds. But stood it had. Throughout storms and hurricanes, the cottage managed to hold on, without toppling over into the Gulf.

I nodded my head and smiled. As I stood there near the rocks, with Lucas's arms around me, looking out to the water and cottage, I felt that perhaps it represented love. Love can be battered, sometimes attacked, but if it's true love, it will hold on. It will weather any storm. No matter what. And I knew that what I'd found with Lucas was exactly that. My path to find him hadn't always been easy, and neither was his to me. But we had found each other, and that's what counted.

I felt him pull me into his arms as his lips found mine, and I heard the clicking of Jean-Paul's camera. After a minute, Lucas stepped back, reached for my hand, and brought it to his lips.

"And now, Mrs. Trudeau, we can begin the rest of our life. To-gether."

I loved the sound of my new name, and I knew I'd be able to preserve this moment forever—because the camera was still click-ing away.

ACKNOWLEDGMENTS

As always, a huge thank-you to the community of Cedar Key for your support and encouragement with my Cedar Key series. You continue to inspire me with your love for family and friends and allowing me to see the really important things in life.

Thank you to Cedar Key Fire Chief Robert Robinson for answering all of my questions about the fire in my novel.

To Judy Duvall, I appreciate the history you shared with me about the Hale Building, which enabled me to take your place of residence and make it the fictional home for Chloe and Berkley.

Thank you to Arlene Myer, the winner of my Facebook Fan Page contest to name Aunt Maude's cat. Lafitte is perfect for the feisty Maine Coon cat.

For Bonnie Wenberg Thomas, you were a huge help with my crash course in understanding tarot cards, and I appreciate your time and information.

Thank you to all of my fans and readers on Facebook, Writerspace, and Fresh Fiction who have sent such wonderful feedback via e-mails and who have taken the time to come to my events and meet me. I fulfill my passion by writing the stories, but it's you, my loyal readers, who fulfill my sense of accomplishment.

I owe a tremendous debt of gratitude to four very special women in Quincy, Washington. What began as meeting a fan for coffee at Kona Joe's on Cedar Key evolved into some incredible promotion events at Big Bend Community College, Quincy High School, Wenatchee Public Library, Write On The River Conference, yarn shops, The Grainery, bookshops, and other venues—all of it due to the dynamic work of Candace Newkirk, Mary Bates, Corallee Morgan, and Pat Moore. You gals are the best, and I hope you know how much I appreciate all that you've done in the Spokane area in my behalf! And a huge thank-you to everyone who hosted and attended these events. I deeply appreciate your support and very much enjoyed meeting such a great group of people!

I'm also very grateful to my editor, Audrey LaFehr, for her professionalism and for giving a home to all of my Cedar Key characters. Thank you to Martin Biro for all of your assistance, to the Kensington Art Department for my beautiful covers, and to the entire Kensington team that I'm very proud to be a part of!

My personal assistant, Alice Jordan, is literally my right hand. While she's tending to booking my events, doing follow-ups, updating my fan page, keeping me straight, listening to me moan, giving me support and encouragement, and doing a multitude of other tasks, I'm able to take a deep breath and focus on my characters and plot. I hope you know how much I value all that you do for me!

Thank you to my husband, Ray, who continues to provide the support, the freedom, the space, and all the other necessary elements for me to create my stories.

And to all of my fans of the Cedar Key series ... thank you for granting me space on your bookshelf or inclusion on your eBook reader.

AUTHOR'S NOTE

I receive a fair amount of mail asking if Cedar Key is a real town or a figment of my imagination. It is indeed a real place—an island off the west coast of Florida, one hour west of Gainesville. It's a laid-back, funky, delightful little fishing village that many refer to as "Old Florida." And it happens to be where my husband and I chose to relocate six years ago.

Most of the places, structures, shops, or areas that I refer to in my Cedar Key series are also real. However, using one's imagination is part of the fun of being an author. Therefore, I don't always "see" a house or structure the way it actually is. I allow my creativity to take over, and in my mind I may see something a bit different.

For instance, in this novel there really is a Coachman House, and most of the history and information about it is correct. Bess Coachman and the ghost are of my own making. I described it fairly accurately, but I also allowed my imagination to embellish both the outside of the structure and the garden. There is no garden and there is no carriage house, where Aunt Maude has her knitting retreats. These were my creation, what I saw in my mind.

Although there is no coffee shop where I chose to put Coffee, Tea and Thee, there is a coffee shop at SR 24 and Sixth Street, which is Kona Joe's Island Café. The feeling of camaraderie and community that I tried to evoke with Grace's place was based on Kona Joe's.

We also do not have a combined coffee café / bookshop on the island. Lucas's attached coffee shop was entirely in my imagination.

The Hale Building, on the corner of Second Street and SR 24, is actually there. Downstairs it houses Tony's Restaurant, and upstairs there are two apartments and Accord Insurance. However, again I allowed my imagination to take over when I added another shop downstairs, which will be Berkley's chocolate shop in the fourth book.

And unfortunately, we do not have a yarn shop here on Cedar Key, but from the beginning with *Spinning Forward,* my imagination easily allowed me to see one—and who knows, someday it just might become a reality.

For more information on the real and the fictional, along with photos, please stop by the Cedar Key series website:

www.cedarkeyseries.net

SUNRISE ON CEDAR KEY

Terri DuLong

ABOUT THIS GUIDE

The following questions are intended to
enhance your group's reading of
SUNRISE ON CEDAR KEY

Discussion Questions

1. Grace relocated to Cedar Key ten years ago to heal and begin a new life for herself. Discuss if you think it's possible that a particular place or setting has the ability to provide this. Have you ever experienced a healing or renewal from a location?

2. Discuss the significance of the word "sunrise" that's used in the title.

3. In the beginning of the story Grace's sister, Chloe, is unhappy, jealous, and resentful, which resulted in a strained relationship between the sisters. Chloe finally admits to always wanting what Grace had. Do you feel this is a common feeling between sisters? If so, why or why not? Discuss if you have experienced a sister or girlfriend wanting what you have. Was the situation resolved? Did it change your feelings toward your sister or girlfriend? In a positive or negative way?

4. Chloe betrayed Grace ten years ago. When Grace learns about this, her initial emotions are anger and hurt. Do you think Grace was justified in her feelings? Discuss Chloe's betrayal in terms of whether you feel she was right in what she did.

5. Ultimately, Grace learns to forgive Chloe. What do you think accounted for this? Did you agree with her forgiveness of her sister? Discuss feelings of forgiveness—do you think some women are able to forgive more easily than others? Do you feel there is one particular character trait that allows forgiveness? Were there people in your own life that you did eventually end up forgiving?

6. Aunt Maude is a major balancing force between the two sisters. Discuss Aunt Maude's past during the nineteen sixties

and how it may have affected the older woman she became and the insight she displayed toward her two nieces. Discuss your feelings about Aunt Maude's character—did you feel sad for her? Did you feel she was justified in trying to bring Grace and Chloe together? Has there been somebody in your family similar to Aunt Maude who tried to resolve family issues?

7. Do you feel Grace was right when she left Brunswick with no contact with or explanations to Beau Hamilton? Why or why not? Discuss whether you feel Grace displayed strength or weakness by relocating to Cedar Key.

8. Both sisters were affected by childhood issues of abandonment. Discuss the difference in the ways Grace and Chloe each handled this in their adult years. What do you think accounts for people letting go of childhood issues and moving on with their lives?

9. Compare the similarities and differences between Beau Hamilton and Lucas Trudeau. Do you think if Grace had been honest with Beau ten years before that their relationship would have endured? Discuss your feelings on Beau's love for Grace—was she simply a fling in his life or do you feel he deeply loved her?

10. Why do you think Lucas held back on sharing his past with Grace? Discuss secrets in a romantic relationship. Are they always justified? By revealing secrets, do you think it results in bringing the couple closer as it did with Lucas and Grace?

11. Discuss Aunt Maude's knitting retreats. Do you feel that knitting (or similar activities such as sewing, crochet, etc.) has the ability to connect women on a deeper level? If so, what do you feel accounts for this? Do you think that activities like exercise or sports allow the same connection for women? Why or why not?

12. Berkley Whitmore enters the story toward the end of the novel. She will be the main character in the fourth book of the Cedar Key series. Discuss your reaction to Berkley, how she might fit in with Chloe and Cedar Key, and your thoughts about her relocating to the island.